For Barbara Y

My dear friend and fellow pursuer of creative insight.

HIGH ON A HILL

Lucy Daniels
November 4, 2001

HIGH ON A HILL

Lucy Daniels

AN AUTHORS GUILD BACKINPRINT.COM EDITION

To Tom

AN AUTHORS GUILD BACKINPRINT.COM EDITION
Published by iUniverse.com, Inc.

For information address:

iUniverse.com, Inc.

5220 S 16th, Ste. 200

Lincoln, NE 68512

www.iuniverse.com

Originally published by McGraw-Hill

ISBN: 0-595-20024-9

Printed in the United States of America

Contents

The Hill

THE RESIDENTS of the town of Perthville knew Holly Springs Hospital for Nervous and Mental Disorders simply as "The Hill." And they used that name often in a variety of jokes and threats.

"One more day like this," cab-driver Herb Shumann would groan, "just one more, and they'll have me on The Hill."

George Purdy, who ran Purdy's Select Grocery, would smile in response as he pushed Herb's pack of cigarettes across the counter to him. "I'll meet you there," he'd say. "That's where I'm going when I get rich."

Holly Springs was a private hospital rated among the top ten in the United States. It accommodated some five hundred patients—men and women—and required, all told, an almost equal number of employees. It boasted a nine-hole golf course and encompassed an area as large as Perthville itself. And because of the high cost of prolonged psychiatric treatment, many of the patients came from well-to-do families.

There was a constant parade of new patients at Holly Springs. Most of them gradually found at least a semblance of serenity and went home. For others, that search required years. And still others, too old and tired to try, never found peace at all, but settled down without it to live out their lives at Holly Springs.

Carson Gaitors had a joke about this. After three years in the hospital, she was at last on a privileged hall and making plans to work in the city; so the newer patients regarded her as an authority. "There's only two types ever leave here," she'd say, her heavy breasts shaking with amusement, "only two—alcoholics and the help."

When she told that to Dr. Holliday, the corpulent director of the hospital laughed, too. "Now, Mrs. Gaitors," he boomed in his friendly drawl. "I don't think that's fair. I fit in both categories, and here I am. Still here."

But for other people, it was not a joking matter. Pretty eighteen-year-old Evelyn Barrow, after six months on Hall 3, still insisted she'd been shanghaied. "It's my mother should be here," she said again and again. "She's the one; they let her trick them."

Jack Isaacs' dark eyes looked dead and far away when people talked about leaving the hospital. Sometimes his lips would tremble, and if he did not walk away quickly, his voice might cry out, "Lucie, Lucie!"

Nineteen-year-old Ben Womble did not allow himself to think about leaving Holly Springs. When other people spoke of it, he simply did not hear; and when, uninstigated, the frightening idea crept into his mind, the panic it aroused acted as an automatic switch-on device for the comforting void he had painstakingly developed.

For the world-celebrated surgeon, Jonathan Stoughton, Holly Springs was a tomb. When it rained or snowed and the nurses herded them to O.T. and gym through the musty black maze of underground tunnels, he felt as if he had been buried alive. All his life the old doctor had loved to walk in the rain, to smell the fresh earth, and feel the cool dampness on his face. Here in this grave he was not only denied that, but forced to walk past carts of garbage—of orange skins and oatmeal scrapings and rusty lettuce leaves, guarded by moldy little men who stood beside those carts and stared as if watching a circus parade.

But now it was April. Soon the rains would be over and the long, hot days of summer on their way. Though they were scarcely visible under her starched white coat, Martha McLeod, director of the hospital's women's division, had taken out her gingham dresses. And she spent all her free time—except that demanded by Tinker, her cat—spading earth for the tomato plants she planned to set out.

It was a busy place, Holly Springs Hospital, like a million other places. Yet it was a world unto itself, a world of no specified dimensions or description, representing something different for each person—a prison, a refuge, a job, a dedication, life, death, the beginning, and the end.

BOOK ONE

Someone to Be Kind

I

IT WAS already dark as they drove up the hill—the hushed damp darkness of evenings in early April. The muted black forms of the empty flag pole, the neatly trimmed bushes, the squat stone benches suggested loneliness. The lighted windows looking down from the forbidding brick buildings reflected no warmth.

Eileen O'Hara sat stiffly in the middle of the back seat of the black Cadillac and stared out the window. From the corners of her eyes she could see that Miss Martin, her supervisor of nurses at St. Timothy's Hospital, was decorously looking straight ahead. In front, beside the driver, Dan McCloskey, her mother's cousin, drummed his thick fingers against the back of the seat. No one spoke, and the silent tears dribbled down Eileen's face. Earlier, when she had broken down in the nursing office on Ward H, they had been hot, angry tears, aching floods. But now they were just slow, quiet streams with neither beginning nor end.

The car stopped before one of the dark Victorian buildings. They climbed out, stood on the curb for a moment, eyeing each other uneasily, and finally turned to climb the stone steps.

Afterward, when Eileen talked to Dr. Holliday about that night,

7

the act of going up those steps seemed the great changing point of her life, the entrance to a new world from which there could never be a complete return. But now, following the others in the darkness, it was only one step deeper into her depression.

Inside, a nurse with a solemn face directed them to a large, dimly lit sitting room. She murmured something to Miss Martin. Then she shut the door and left them alone. Still no one spoke. Miss Martin watched Eileen discreetly. After fidgeting for a moment in one of the green leather chairs, Cousin Dan began to pace the floor. Eileen looked at the lamp, at the design in the rug, out into the night. Always, the tears trickled down her cheeks, and when she tried to stop them, an unexpected sob caught in her throat.

"They think I'm crazy," she thought. "Out of my mind, depressed, suicidal. . . . If only they were right. If only I did have the courage to go against God and take my own life."

When the door opened again, Cousin Dan stopped his pacing and Miss Martin's eyes lifted to the white-coated figure who had entered. It was a dumpy little woman, elderly, with white hair and a wise, emotionless, pink-white face. Her blue eyes seemed cold and insensitive to Eileen; her precise voice was dead.

Later, when she came out of herself enough to think about things, Eileen wondered why it was not Dr. Holliday who admitted new patients. (What a difference his half-joking, half-sympathetic warmth would have made.) But now she was too frightened, too desperate to do anything but gape dumbly through her tears.

"Good evening," the woman said. "I'm Dr. McLeod. You're Miss O'Hara?"

"Y-Yes, I am." Eileen stood up.

"I suppose you've had this explained to you, Miss O'Hara, and since you're a nurse, you undoubtedly know what you're undertaking. But as a matter of form, I'd like you to read over the commitment paper and sign it."

Eileen took the sheet of printed white paper in one trembling hand and tried to read it. She wanted to understand the terms under which she was being committed to the hospital. But at last, when she realized time had elapsed and her mind would not take in the words, she took the pen which the dumpy woman held out to her and signed her name—Eileen M. O'Hara.

She realized then that she was sitting on the edge of her chair, writing on the edge of the table, and that the doctor was standing over her, looking down. She realized, too, that the tears were still trickling down her face.

"You are quite depressed, aren't you?" the bored voice asked.

"I ... I...."

"Have you been feeling this way very long?"

Only forever, Eileen thought. Only forever.

"Tell me, Miss O'Hara, have you ever thought of doing harm to yourself?"

"I ... I am Catholic."

"All right." The white coat turned to the solemn-faced nurse who had slid into the room unnoticed. "Miss Tucker will take you to your hall."

(2

After admitting the young nurse, Dr. McLeod returned to her office. As usual the people with the girl, especially the man, had wanted to talk to her. But they hadn't been as difficult as most families. They had been satisfied when she showed them the papers signed by Dr. Holliday and explained that St. Timothy's and Holly Springs were splitting the expense.

Most of the doctors' offices along the main corridor were already dark and locked, but in one a young man with glasses sat behind the desk on which a green-shaded lamp burned. Dr. McLeod went in.

"Dr. Pierson," she said with her usual cold detachment.

"Good evening, Dr. McLeod." The young man stood up.

"Dr. Pierson, I'm assigning you a new admission on Hall 3. A young nurse. Depressed. I'll write the order for constant observation. Here's the data so far." She handed him a sheet of paper and turned abruptly back to the corridor.

"Thank you, Doctor." He sat down again, studying the paper.

Dr. McLeod continued down the dim corridor into the supervisor's office. There she wrote the C.O. order for the new patient and then started across the hall to put her own desk in order for the night. On the way she collided with Hospital Director David Holliday.

"Lummox!" she thought. "As careless about where he walks as

how he talks." But her white face did not change, and by the time she had caught her breath, she was able to answer Holliday's apology with her usual toneless composure. "No matter. . . . It's hard to see in this light."

"Working late, aren't you, Martha? Something special come up?" His tone sounded concerned, but his drawl was as slow and easy as ever. And the familiar smile on his moon face faded only slightly.

"Always the cheerful gentleman," Martha fumed inside. But she smiled back at him—at least the pale simper that was her attempt to smile. "No, nothing much," she said. "Just that admission."

"Oh, yes. The young nurse Dr. Keller called about. Pretty much as he described her?"

"Yes. Considerably depressed. I've put her under constant observation."

The big doctor's round face darkened with a frown momentarily, but he did not speak.

"Also I took your suggestion and assigned her to Philip Pierson."

"Fine. Fine." Holliday smiled again and rattled the keys in his pocket. "That's fine. Well, I'd best be going. Came to check the mail for Mary Laine. She keeps looking for a letter from Lillian. Night, Martha."

"Good night."

He loped slowly down the corridor toward the post office, and Martha entered her office. She did not bother with papers, though, or even to turn on lights. For several moments she just stood there in the darkness and stared out the window, past the rolling lawns of the hospital grounds to the lights of the town below. How dark and alone up here, she thought, compared to all that down there. She was thinking not so much of herself as of the hospital, of broken young people like the nurse who had just come, and elderly ones like Dr. Stoughton whose lives had led them only to this futile, joyless existence of waiting for death.

Martha McLeod did not believe in yielding to such thoughts. That was one of the few points on which she and Dr. Holliday completely agreed and perhaps the most important factor in her attaining the directorship of the Holly Springs women's division. "The patient must be strengthened and educated to the point where he can fight his symptoms, not give way to them." That was the tenet she preached and practiced in her work. Yet at times, even she could not resist thoughts about the disparities of the world, memories of her lost childhood, pointless fears about death.

Almost impulsively now she shut the door on her office and hurried out through the dampness to the lonely slot where her blue Mercury was parked. It was colder than she had expected. She was glad she had not picked today to harden herself by walking up the hill from her little house. As she settled herself behind the wheel of the car, her thoughts returned to the massive bald-headed figure disappearing down the half-lit corridor. From the post office David Holliday would go home to a living room comfortable with untidiness, to a wife who loved him.

Martha frequently rebuked herself for thoughts like that. Ridiculous to resent the discrepancies between her lot and David Holliday's. She lived as she did—precisely, simply, alone with her cat—because she wanted to, because it reserved all her energy for the work to which she was dedicated. And any shortcomings this life might have were undoubtedly more than equaled by the trials to be faced by people like David Holliday.

No, despite its weaknesses, the life she had chosen was the right one. She straightened her shoulders now and smiled into the rearview mirror. "Tinker and I will have a banquet tonight," she told herself gaily.

❪ 3

Supper was over—a typical meal of noodles, salad, and canned fruit. Now they were in the smoker, nearly twenty women, trying to enjoy as many of their rationed cigarettes as possible in the half-hour time limit. A few sat in a group, talking freely of doctors, badminton scores, evenings at the Stork Club. Others sat in pairs, talking more quietly of their homes, their symptoms, another patient. Still others sat alone, staring into space or solemnly studying the material of their laps. Now and again someone crossed the room to the student nurse with the matches.

Whenever Jackie Harper spoke, the talkative group around her became silent. But she did not talk for them alone. Her voice was loud and authoritative, intended for anyone who would listen.

"You see, it's this way," she was saying now. "Maybe I was wrong. Maybe I did get started on the booze and not know when to stop." She laughed a horsy, masculine guffaw, infecting all around her. Even the student smiled in noncommittal friendliness. "So maybe I did. But if you ask me, that's a hell of a lot better than being a prude without sense enough to take a drink." They all laughed again. Even Mrs. Peters, who never stopped tittering to herself anyway, seemed to understand that this was a real joke. But then suddenly a hush fell over the group. All the eyes fixed on Jackie and followed her gaze down the long corridor to the day room.

"Hey," she reported softly, enticingly to the others, "here comes another prisoner. Looks young, too. Twenty or so. Tucker's up there with Joslin. They're taking her belt and wrist watch. Poor kid."

Jackie was silent then, and no one else spoke. Even the student nurse forgot her professional disinterest and stared as the solemn-faced supervisor and the evening charge nurse escorted a small, thin, dark girl into one of the rooms off the corridor. In a matter of minutes they came out again, this time without the girl. At the door they paused. The supervisor rolled up the girl's brown leather belt and took the wrist watch from the nurse.

Apparently oblivious to the group of curious patients, she said, "Keep an eye on her. The order hasn't been written yet, but I'm sure she'll be on C.O." Then she went out and locked the door behind her.

After she had gone, the nurse, Margaret Joslin, stood there for a moment, scanning the report on her newest patient. "Eileen O'Hara, Miss," it read. "24. Irish. Registered nurse. Specialty: surgery. Extreme depression. Mention of broken love affair."

Slowly she folded the report in half and started back up the corridor to the nursing office. Disgust and anger crossed her smug face.

"Broken love affair!" she thought. Nothing irritated her more than these little sissies who kissed a young man twice and decided they could not go on living when he went away or kissed somebody else. She, Margaret Joslin, could have told them what it was to have a "broken love affair." To give your life, your heart, your body to a man; to build a dream life of love for forever and then to wake suddenly, brutally when that dream blew up in your face.

Just short of the day room she stopped and called back to the student supervising smoking, "Hasn't it been thirty minutes, Miss Llewelyn? Empty the ash trays. I need you to give an admission bath."

Then she turned and went back to the new patient's dark, doorless room. Glancing in at the crumpled figure on the bed, she flicked on the overhead light. Startled, the girl turned away quickly, holding her hand to her eyes.

"Miss O'Hara, we like to keep the lights on till ten. Why don't you come into the living room with the others for a few minutes? Then Miss Llewelyn is going to give you a bath."

"I'd rather stay here." Tears still streaked Eileen's thin, white face. "I'm tired. I'd like to be alone." She turned toward the wall again and buried her face in the crook of her arm.

"Miss O'Hara, it won't help at all to lie here feeling sorry for yourself."

Eileen did not answer. Anger crowded her throat, and the tears flowed relentlessly. She prayed the woman would go away; she prayed she herself would not lose control again. But Margaret Joslin put a strong hand on the girl's shoulder and turned her over.

"Miss O'Hara," she ordered, "I want you to get up."

Though her tears did not stop, Eileen's face was quiet for a moment, her gray-green eyes stretched wide. She realized the nurse was just doing her duty, just trying to "draw the patient out." She even remembered that under other circumstances she might have been that nurse, and she braced her voice for the proper clipped accent she reserved for orders and cutting retorts. But the words exploded loud and furious. "Leave me alone. Leave me alone." She turned over, face down in the pillow, and felt the bed shake with her sobs.

Mrs. Joslin walked out into the hall again. "Miss Llewelyn," she called to the student emptying ash trays. "Never mind those or the admission bath. Just come sit outside this door."

(4

Dr. Pierson looked straight ahead as he crossed the courtyard beside Miss Tucker. His lame leg dragged awkwardly—almost comically, he thought sometimes. But he was not conscious of that now. It was dark, and there was no one to see. Besides he was concentrating on the supervisor's rundown of things to be done on the next ward—Hall 3.

It was always a relief to Philip Pierson to come to this comparatively quiet hall after rounds on the disturbed and semidisturbed ones below it. Should be just the opposite, he thought. If he really possessed the "remarkable perception and sensitivity" the doctors at Bellevue had praised him for, if he in any way deserved his place as Dr. Holliday's protégé, he would have felt increased interest in those desperate, sometimes animalistic patients on the more violent halls. But Pierson never had any sense of power or importance there. Those wild, broken women pleading for relief, for salvation from their private terrors only made him feel tired, inadequate, bitter, sometimes even afraid.

"Of course there's the new patient," Miss Tucker added as he unlocked the door of the indoor passageway.

"Yes. She's assigned to me."

The supervisor nodded and continued her recital of tasks to be attended to. "Then the tube feeding."

"Oh yes, Maggie Evans. She's been here a long time, hasn't she?"

"Over two years. Sixteen when she came. Weighed only fifty-four pounds."

The doctor opened the Hall 3 door then, and Mrs. Joslin, the charge nurse, met them. "Good evening, Doctor," she said with her cosmetic smile. "Most of the patients are in the living room. Except Miss Evans; she's in pack and the feeding's ready. I've got a student with Miss O'Hara. She won't come out of her room."

Dr. Pierson looked intently into the cold face of the nurse. And an unpleasant shudder passed through him—a vague mingling of loathing and fear. He was almost glad to hear his name called.

"Dr. Pierson," the excited voice shrieked. "Dr. Pierson, wait a minute. I've got something to talk to you about."

He stopped, but with one foot poised, as Evelyn Barrow came flitting down the hall. He hated situations like this. They made him feel so awkward. "Good evening, Miss Barrow." His voice was carefully aloof. He looked at her coolly, analytically.

A pretty girl, in spite of, or perhaps enhanced by, the restrictions of the hospital. Her shiny brown hair hung loose and waving, unconfined by the forbidden metal bobby pins or even by the plastic ones permitted. A smear of bright lipstick was her only make-up, and her fingernails, though colorless, were filed long and talonlike.

"Dr. Pierson, did you mail my letter to Rod? He's dying to hear. He wants to come see me."

"I'm sending that letter back to you, Miss Barrow. I think when you see it again, you'll want to rewrite it."

"Oh, Dr. Pierson!" she stamped one tennis shoe angrily but then looked up at him with feigned candor, sudden sweetness shining in her eyes. "When am I moving to Hall 4?" she asked. "I've been here nearly two months now. And it's ridiculous. I was fine the day I came in." The anger crept slowly back. "You know that, Dr. Pierson, don't you? You know I was fine! It was just my mother. She can't bear for me to have a good time when she's getting old. When will I get out of this hell hole?"

He turned away in silence.

"When!" she demanded, stamping her foot again. "When!"

He moved slowly, gently away and down the hall with the two nurses. "We'll discuss that next time I see you, Miss Barrow," he said quietly; then to Miss Tucker: "Where's the new admission? She's to be my patient."

Eileen did not see the doctor when he came on rounds. She heard the voices in the hall outside her room. She even heard them say her name, and that she was depressed, and something else. But she lay flat and still on the bed and carefully kept her face turned toward the wall until she heard them go away.

Immediately afterward, a student nurse came in to ask her to undress. She was carrying a heavy muslin hospital gown, and she flicked on the horrible glaring overhead light as she entered. "Miss O'Hara, we'd like you to undress and put on this gown. Your doctor is coming to examine you."

Slowly, numbly Eileen obeyed. Then in white-faced silence she followed the student to the examining room.

It was small—just large enough for an examining table, instrument cabinet, writing desk, and two straight chairs. A very ordinary room, similar to many Eileen had worked in. Yet, suddenly, as they entered, the bitter futility and despair surged over her. Once more her trickling tears gave way to wrenching sob-choked torrents. The student helped her climb onto the table, then took the muslin gown and covered her with a sheet. She was gentle and offered Eileen a Kleenex, but otherwise showed no awareness of her tears. "Please lie still here a moment, Miss O'Hara," she said, going out. "I'll tell Dr. Pierson we're ready."

When the door opened again, heavy, uneven, footsteps followed the student's efficient rubber-soled ones. Then there was a white coat beside the table, and despite her fear, Eileen looked up at the face above it.

"Good evening, Miss O'Hara," he said quietly. "My name is Dr. Pierson. I guess Dr. McLeod told you I'm to be your doctor."

Eileen did not answer; the tears still came. The doctor made no attempt to shake hands. "I understand you're a nurse," he continued. "So undoubtedly you're aware that this examination is simply routine." He smiled uncomfortably. "A kind of deference we pay to the red tape involved in running a hospital."

To her own surprise, Eileen realized her eyes were glued to his face as he talked. It was a kind face—dark, intellectual perhaps, and somewhat homely, with a troubled look about the bespectacled eyes. His voice was deep and simple; not at all sympathetic, but discreetly considerate. All in all, a sharp and relieving contrast to Dr. McLeod.

"When we finish with this," he continued in that painstaking tone, "we can talk a little." He pulled the sheet back gently, probed her neck glands and manipulated her breasts. Then, even before the end of Eileen's embarrassed quiver, he was examining her abdomen. As he replaced the sheet, he went on as if there had been no break in the conversation. "We need not talk at great length. I know you're very tired. . . . But perhaps just a few minutes would make you feel less strange here."

He pulled the sheet up from the bottom, examined her pubic area and her legs. Then he replaced the sheet and made the pencil test on the soles of her feet. Lastly he asked her to sit up with her legs over the side of the table and tapped her knees with his rubber hammer.

But the interview was not that simple. Huddled tensely on the edge of her stiff chair, Eileen felt far more naked than she had on the examining table. She clutched the rough, oversized gown around her simply because there was nothing else to clutch. Her tears had stopped, leaving stiff, damp streaks down each cheek. Her throat was tight and aching.

Dr. Pierson sat at the desk and studied his notes in silence. Then abruptly he placed the notes inside his brown notebook and turned to face Eileen. Thick dark lashes shielded her downcast eyes, and her small tight fists quivered in her lap.

"I understand," he said slowly, "that you've been feeling... well... unhappy for some time now.... I wonder. Would you want to tell me a little about it?"

Eileen's dark lashes flickered. But she did not answer. What could she tell this stranger—considerate or not—about the despair inside her?

After a brief silence, he continued, "Certainly, Miss O'Hara, it's your privilege not to discuss anything you consider private. I would like to help you, though. Perhaps you could tell me whether you feel anything besides depression? Resentment? Fear?"

Eileen still did not look up. But she spoke clearly. "No. Just sadness... just depression." Then the tears began again.

"Have you felt this way very long, Miss O'Hara?"

She did not answer. The tears flowed unchecked. Though she could not see his face, she imagined the doctor's eyes must be peering down at her. She thought she heard his pen writing in the notebook.

At last he asked more matter of factly, "Probably you can tell me this, though, Miss O'Hara. How do you feel about being here? In a hospital, I mean?"

For another moment Eileen's silence prevailed. But then suddenly she raised her head. "I won't argue," she began in a voice still tear choked but now almost defiant. "I won't argue, because I know it's pointless. You doctors have decided I'm sick; so, for all practical purposes, I am." A runaway sob stopped her, but the doctor waited, and soon she continued more calmly. "But I don't feel I'm sick. I feel alone and empty and useless. But I don't think these are delusions. Anyone in my position would feel the same way. And no hospital can cure that. It's just a matter of...." Eileen's tears overtook her.

Pierson fingered his black pen solemnly. When the girl seemed calmer, he said, "I'm sure you're justified in some of these feelings,

Miss O'Hara, but.... Perhaps, if you're willing, we can discuss them at greater length tomorrow or the next day. In the meantime...." He hesitated deliberately, waiting for her to look up at him again. "In the meantime, you'll have a big adjustment to make.... I suppose Dr. McLeod told you you'll be under constant observation?"

"No."

"Well, I'm sorry, but you will. 'C.O.' we call it. I'll leave an order for something to help you sleep. And...." He paused again. Perhaps now at the last she would respond. But her eyes still looked down, her fingers remained locked.

"But," he went on, "if at any time you feel I could do anything else to help, you need only have the nurse call me. Is there something you'd like to ask?"

"No."

Slowly he gathered up his pen and notebook. Then he stood up. "Let's stop there then, for now."

II

"AND THIS IS where we work," Dr. Holliday said, turning his key in the heavy door of the brick building. "This is our occupational therapy building." His Southern accent resounded in the cool silence of the stone room. It always did; even when he tried to suppress it. The young couple with him looked around in awed, almost frightened silence.

He knew they were wondering how a great lumbering idiot like himself could be director of a hospital as highly regarded as Holly Springs. He knew they were thinking that, because people always did. Sometimes, after he had shown visitors around, they would ask to see the director of the hospital.

Ever since he was a little boy in Millboro, Alabama, David Holliday had hidden his thoughts, his anger, his sadness, even sometimes his gentleness behind a good-natured bluff of obtuseness. That bluff was no longer a front; it had become a part of him now, and in his twenty-five years of psychiatry he had found it increasingly useful.

People expected a psychiatrist to be thin and bearded and long haired. Confronted by this, minds froze, defenses tensed. But those same people were not afraid of a potbellied, bald-headed, loud-talking bumpkin. David Holliday took advantage of that. People talked to him as to a real estate agent or a country minister or a fellow passenger on a bus. He never wrote down what they said or even asked questions. He just let them talk and listened with sleepy friendliness.

No one spoke now as he led the young couple back across the lawn to the main building. But at the entrance the husband said, "Thank you very much, Dr. Holliday. You have a fine hospital. . . . It's hard to think of Dad in a place like this. But if that has to be, I'm thankful there is a Holly Springs."

Holliday was silent momentarily; he had never worked out the perfect answer for that. Then genially, with an understanding nod, he said, "I'm glad you're pleased, Mr. Stoughton. I think your brothers have been, too. But if any time you want to see me again . . . have questions . . . new problems, I'm always here." Then, turning to the woman, he added, "It was a pleasure, Mrs. Stoughton."

He stood on the steps in the chilly afternoon haze, watching as they drove off. They would be back, he knew, many, many times. And tragically, they would never go away any happier than they were today. For, the road led only downward to increased irascibility, severe withdrawal, and hallucinations. Eventually, perhaps, to physical collapse and complete vegetation with no more communication than the gibberish of a two-year-old. Unless, of course, the one salvation—death—intervened.

Dr. Jonathan Stoughton, one of the world's most gifted surgeons, had been a paragon among men, blessed with much more than brains and talented fingers. He was a man who had known and fully appreciated the extremes of human joy and sorrow; who had loved deeply and yet had, apparently, survived the death of his wife ten years earlier with iron strength.

The old man's three successful sons regarded their mother's death as the cause of their father's incredible deterioration. They had been told, but probably had no conception of the extent to which the disease would go. Senile psychosis was little more than a name to them—a meaningless title for something they did not really care to understand. And undoubtedly his wife's death had precipitated Stoughton's decline.

David Holliday wondered now if anything like that might happen to him at Mary Laine's death. The immediate answer was simple enough: "Certainly not. I'm too plodding, too easy-going." Still, the anxiety lingered. He was excessively preoccupied with death—had been all his life—ever since he had listened to his grandfather talk of his grandmother, who had died in a diphtheria epidemic when she was only twenty-seven. Holliday no longer really dreaded death, but he wondered about it more, he fancied, than most men, because his work confronted him with it every day.

With some effort, Holliday could reassure himself about losing Mary Laine. He knew that he would feel useless and lonely without her, but he knew, too, that his life would probably go on much the same. He would smoke and play golf and continue his study of Abraham Lincoln. He would have his drink before dinner and send Lillian's allowance to her at school. And as always, he would have his work and Holly Springs.

But Mary Laine was different. If he should die, she would never be able to go on as before. She was too dependent, her life too deeply enmeshed with his. She might easily become an "incurable" senile simply because she was too scared and too tired to do anything else.

This thought saddened Holliday, yet not nearly so much as the realization that separation from Mary Laine no longer held great pain for him. Once, his whole world had revolved about Mary Laine. He could not have imagined life without her. But in the last five years all that had changed. Perhaps it's just Lillian's being away at school, Holliday had reasoned with himself, or the climacteric difficulty of all women. Still, going home to Mary Laine had become an obligation instead of a reward, and David Holliday found duty a bitter replacement for love. He longed for a remedy. And often, as now, he wondered if final, physical separation could really be worse than this.

But at that moment the Stoughtons' car started down the hill.

Expertly, the doctor relegated both Mary Laine and the visitors to their separate compartments in his mind. There was still life to consider—life and the young—far more vital statistics.

A young male patient had written him a note requesting a conference. Dr. Holliday did not have many letters like that; mostly his letters were from patients on disturbed wards, scribbled in pencil or typed on drawing paper at occupational therapy. Usually they were long, wandering demands for release which his secretary, Mrs. Weaver, redirected to the patient's doctor.

But the Womble boy—he was only nineteen—was not really disturbed. He was on a convalescent ward, Hall 4, and had been for two years. His letter was neither long nor wandering, nor did it mention leaving the hospital. It was written neatly in blue ink on white stationery. It said simply: "Dear Dr. Holliday, I would like very much to speak to you at your convenience. Sincerely, Benjamin Womble."

Holliday felt almost happy about that letter. He did not know what it meant. The boy had never been decisively diagnosed. At best, his trouble was a severe and complicated psycho-neurosis. But more and more of late his behavior had indicated schizophrenic tendencies, so that much of the staff, including Holliday, had begun to think Ben's case might be another hopeless one. Still, they had made errors before. As he entered the main corridor, Holliday reminded himself not to jump to conclusions. But the letter *did* suggest change. And change, he had learned long before, was evidence of life and hope.

⟨ 2

Carson Gaitors put down her knitting when she saw the men patients come out of the gym with their golf bags. There was a high, chain-link fence between the walkway to the golf course and the lawn bench where Carson sat. But she was close enough to distinguish those she knew, by carriage if not by appearance.

Most people still thought the weather too chilly for sitting outdoors. But this afternoon the sun was warm, and Carson felt almost content there, alone on her bench. She hated Holly Springs. At best, it was tedious, more often, exasperating and depressing as well. But somehow just a little freedom like this, just the few extra privileges of being on Atkins, an open hall, made that boredom more bearable.

As the men trooped past, she watched them openly with the usual confident smile on her wide, dark face. She waved and called to the gym instructors she knew. "Hey, Mack. What's new, Winslow?"

"Afternoon, Mrs. Gaitors."

And that bothersome eager-beaver Jim Reilly called, "Hi, Carson. See you at square dancing tomorrow."

"Hi, Jim." But mostly Carson watched the Isaacs fellow. She did not know him. She had spoken to him a couple of times, and danced with him once at a hospital party, yet she had decided she liked him more than any of the other men, staff or patients, she had known in her three years at Holly Springs. For, Carson's appreciation of the opposite sex had no dependence on friendship or even acquaintance. She found men simply indispensable.

Now that she was on open hall, she came here often, as well as to various other spots on the grounds from which she knew their goings and comings to be visible. That was probably the privilege she valued most. She often wondered how she had survived the last three years without it. But at the same time she was painfully aware that this new visual contact seemed to increase rather than alleviate her need. A bad sign, she had admonished herself repeatedly. You're no better than before. Still, she had skipped O.T. to come here this afternoon, and tomorrow, undoubtedly, she would skip something else. The excuse was easy and logical enough. What normal woman wouldn't need a man after being cooped up with a bunch of loony females for three years? . . . There was Jesse, of course. She couldn't discount him completely. But, really, how much of a man was Jesse? Old and blue-blooded, virtuous and dull. Probably that was the key to the whole miserable mess she'd made of her life. One older man after another. Lords and fathers, but never lovers.

Jack Isaacs was young, though—perhaps younger than she was. He did not look up as he walked past now. He was smoking a cigarette and speaking occasionally to the thin, stoop-shouldered boy beside him, but mostly he just plodded along with dark head bowed and eyes on the ground. Carson's heavy breasts throbbed, and goose pimples prickled her arms. It took deliberate effort to return to her knitting.

He was married, of course. And even if he hadn't been, nothing could have developed between them here. Besides, he seemed a quiet, brooding person who would shy away from a married woman with four wrecked marriages behind her. Still, there was the longing.

"Well, Mrs. Gaitors, what are you doing here?" The voice took Carson by surprise, and though its heartiness was familiar, she looked up slowly, squinting against the sunlight. Anita Falkenburg, charge nurse on Hall 1 Women, had a six-foot frame that even her dark skirt and sweater could not disguise.

"Well, I'll tell you Falkenburg," Carson replied, laughing softly, "I'm supposed to be at O.T., but I just decided after three years of weaving baskets I deserve a day off."

Falkenburg laughed, too, but uncertainly and with restraint. Then her deep voice went stern, "Mrs. Gaitors, you know better than that. O.T. may seem pointless, but you're too near the end to risk trouble over a little thing like that."

"No, they're getting tired of me. I've run out of jokes."

"Now, I can't believe that, Mrs. Gaitors." A smile flitted across the nurse's hard-set jaw and momentarily softened even the alert discipline in her blue eyes. "Really, how are you these days? Going home soon?"

"Doesn't look that way." Carson looked up from her knitting and shook her head in disgust. "I have McLeod, and you know how fast she moves."

Falkenburg smiled and straightened up self-consciously.

"Still just weekends," Carson added. "But they may let me start commuting to work in the city soon."

"Good. Most people like that. An opportunity to earn some money and get away from the routine here at the same time."

"Yeah."

Falkenburg loomed backward in the direction of the nurses' residence. "Well, I certainly hope everything works out, Mrs. Gaitors. Good luck, in case I don't see you again."

Carson continued knitting, but she was sad, watching the tall figure disappear down the path. She always had liked Falkenburg, even back on Hall 1 when she herself had sometimes rebelled against that brute strength. She sensed a kind of frustrated gentleness behind the nurse's masculine exterior, something akin to the restless longing she herself had never been able to master.

Suddenly, though, it came to her what her mother would have said about Falkenburg. "Common, my dear . . . so pitifully gross and charmless." Carson's mother had been dead fifteen years. Though her judgment meant nothing now, once it had been the final word in her daughter's life. This had been true as far back as Carson could remember. A proper, shy little girl with corkscrew curls and organdy pinafores, she had thought her mother the most beautiful, elegant, wonderful woman in the whole world. She had wanted to grow up to be just like her.

That wish seemed incredible now. There was a vast difference between what she had wanted at five and what she not only wanted but had at thirty-five. Carson still admired her mother as she remembered her, but she despised her cool composure. Instead, she longed to be and was a warm, vibrant woman; she longed to live life to the hilt and did, at the expense of virtue.

The change had been gradual. At seventeen, though a little too buxom and a little less demure than her family would have wished, she *had* made her debut. And at eighteen, though "properly you should wait at least another year," she had married Gerald Moore, a successful lawyer ten years older than herself, but highly acceptable to her parents. And that had only been the beginning— the first of five marriages, of which four had ended in divorce and the fifth was on the brink of it.

The sun was covered by gray clouds now; a wind was blowing up. Shivering, Carson looked down to check the time—4:45. The men should have returned to the gym by now. That was really what she'd been waiting for—another glimpse of Jack Isaacs. She wanted, she *needed* to see the tall sensuous body, the dark face. They could have made everything less dreary: the windy darkness coming on; the drab hall she must go back to; the damn women. But it was too late now. They'd obviously gone the other way. At last Carson stood up and pushed her knitting down into the basket. She would have to hurry to get back before they locked the hall doors.

❲ 3

Ben Womble was just teeing off when the student nurse spoke. He was standing feet apart, driver raised, eyes peering hard at the white speck hurtling over the green.

"Mr. Womble . . . Mr. Womble, you're wanted on the hall."

"What for?" His thin, muscular body twisted around to look at her.

"Doctor's appointment, I think."

He knew it couldn't be. He had just seen Dr. Richards that morning. But he didn't object. Nor did the tired smile on his pale face change. He dropped his club to the ground and, without speaking to the young men with whom he was playing, walked off toward the hospital beside the student.

They walked slowly, he with his eyes on the ground, his thin shoulders stooped, his arms folded across his chest. He wondered only vaguely about the significance of two conferences in one day. But when they had climbed the steps to Hall 4, when the student had locked the door behind them, there was no Dr. Richards. Ben sat down on the couch in the hallway and counted the squares in the carpet. It was not until the door unlocked at the other end of the corridor and Dr. Holliday's obese, bald-pated figure entered that he remembered the note that he had written two days before, after his father's visit.

The memory of that note came back to Ben with cold sinking horror. He really had not expected any answer to it. His father had said they were planning to give him electric shock again. That had frightened him and made him angry, and he had written, asking Dr. Holliday to come so that he could say, "Go to hell."

But he knew now—actually he had known when he wrote the note—that that would be futile, even dangerous. Momentarily he panicked for a way out, then remembered his faithful one—silence.

As the sound of the loping strides came closer down the hall, Ben pulled at his fingers and stared at their hard white knuckles. Suppose Holliday demanded a reason for the note? Ben pretended not to see and hoped that in turn the doctor would not see him. But Holliday spoke even before he reached the couch. "Afternoon, Womble. Could I see you, please?"

Ben nodded and followed him down the hall. In the conference room he sat down quickly, arms still folded across his chest, eyes fixed on the knees of his brown trousers.

Holliday waited a long time to open the conversation. He settled himself in the swivel chair behind the desk, lit a cigarette, and glanced up at a print on the wall. Probably it was too much to hope that the boy would talk of his own volition. "Well, Ben," he said at last, carefully looking at the picture instead of the boy, "I got your note. What was it you wanted to talk to me about?"

The boy did not answer. Not a muscle flickered in his face.

Holliday waited, then cautiously tried again. At nineteen, he too, had been afraid of people, but he had always protected himself by the same superficial exuberance. "I gathered from your note, Ben," he said gently, "that there was something you thought I might help you with."

The boy's face did not alter; he still looked down. But clearly and precisely he said, "No."

"Then why the note?" Holliday asked. He was looking at the boy closely now, staring at the stooped shoulders, hoping to force the blue eyes upward. "You did write to me, Ben."

The same flat, "No."

So once again the doctor waited. Another approach. "Your father dropped in to see me the other day, Ben. I guess he told you. We had a nice visit."

For a moment the boy remained as inert and silent as ever. Then suddenly he *did* look up, screwed his face into a hideous grinning, sneering grimace, and again, just as abruptly, returned to his position of silent inertia.

"Your father's a busy man, isn't he, Ben?" Holliday persisted with determined coolness. "I gather he doesn't get to see you often."

"No."

Still the statuelike remoteness, but at least an answer.

"Does he write you often?"

Silence.

"Ben, do you ever write him?"

Though his face remained expressionless, Ben twinged with fear at that question. He had worried about it often. How could Holliday know about his letters to his father—five, sometimes six a day. He tore them up so carefully, into such tiny, tiny pieces before he flushed them down the toilet. How could he know if they did not spy on you, if the night lights were not really cameras recording your every action, if there was not a vast radio system set up in the light fixtures.

Still, he did not speak. His thin fingers gripped his elbows more tightly. His face was, perhaps, more intent in its lack of expression. But he did not stir. And above all, he did not give the doctor a chance to look into his eyes.

Holliday leaned back and turned to face the picture again. "How close are you and your father, Ben? You reckon you know him very well?"

As expected, no answer.

"I don't think I ever really knew my father well. He was always very busy—like yours. But there were other reasons, too. I loved him; but sometimes I thought I hated him more than anybody else in the world. You ever have feelings like that, Ben?"

The boy still did not move or look up. But he droned clearly, "No. My father is good. He helps me."

"Does he? That's very fine. How does he help you, Ben?"

Without hesitation, in the same flat voice, "My father helps me."

"You think he could help you more if you were home? If you could see him every day?"

Ben did not answer. But from the corners of his eyes, Holliday could see the thin fingers grip the elbows more tightly. Slowly the doctor swiveled around again to face the boy. "You had a good talk with your father Saturday, didn't you, Ben?"

No answer.

"Did he, by any chance, tell you what he had discussed with me?"

Still silence.

"What are your feelings about more electric shock therapy?"

For a moment there was continued silence, then, abruptly, a repetition of the earlier hideous grimace and a cackle of sarcastic laughter. Immediately afterward the flat-faced silence returned.

"Don't you think the treatments might help you?"

No answer. No change of expression.

"We want to help you, Ben."

"My father helps me."

Holliday leaned forward on his elbows, trying to force his way into the boy's blue eyes. "Since you're here, Ben; since you really have very little say about whether you stay or not—how do you feel about Holly Springs? What do you think of us?"

The boy still did not look up, but a faint smile crossed his lips. "Humpty Dumpty," he said clearly, flatly.

Then there was silence.

❪ 4

When they came in from golf, the gym instructors made them stand together in the smoker for a count check. The list of patients didn't gibe with the number counted in. There was one face too few.

Big Mack chewed a pencil and frowned at the list. Winslow counted over and over. A student came to help. But it took a roll call to discover that Ben Womble had not been crossed off as coming in early. By then everybody was grumbling.

"How come Ben came back early?" Jim Reilly asked a student nurse. His round coarse face was flushed.

"He's seeing the doctor."

"But he saw him this morning. I know, because we both have Dr. Richards, and I saw him, too." Reilly's forehead puckered; his eyes darkened with unrest.

He walked down the hall with the others, and as he passed the conference room, he glanced in. Only a glimpse, but he could see that the occupant of the doctor's chair was Dr. Holliday and not the small, almost wizened figure belonging to Dr. Richards.

"Hey." He pulled on the sweater of the young man in front of him. "Hey, Isaacs," he said in a loud whisper. "Ben's talking to Holliday."

"Yeah. That's nice." Jack Isaacs was a tall dark Jew. He was twenty-nine, married, and the father of two children. He was friendly, had a good sense of humor, and had run an exclusive woman's clothing shop on Madison Avenue. People regarded him as the "up and coming" young man in fashion design. Few could understand why he had been at Holly Springs for two years. Now he continued down the hall in silence, barely listening to Jim

Reilly's conversation, only giving an automatic, noncommittal answer where it was necessary.

"Wonder why Holliday's talkin' to Ben?" Reilly prodded. "Did you ever see him?"

"Yeah."

"I haven't. Wonder why he never came to see me?"

"If you want to see him, write and tell him so." Jack's voice sounded irritated. He could not stand people like Reilly—people for whom Holly Springs was a country club with the added prestige of being "emotionally upset." He quickened his pace to get away.

In the room he shared with Ben Womble, Jack pulled off his hand-knit gray sweater and folded it neatly in the drawer. Then after brushing his curly black hair, he grabbed up the two cardboard folders on the bureau and lay down on the bed.

At just that moment, Ben sauntered in, his reedlike body slumping from the shoulders. There was a half-amused expression on his adolescent face, but his vacant, blue eyes were sad.

"Hi, Ben," Jack said. "Missed you at golf. How was Holliday?"

But, naturally, there was no answer—not even a smile or a grunt. The youth lay down on his bed and stared into space. Jack found some music on the radio and went back to his pictures.

The first—the one of Lucie—always made his throat choke up and little beads of perspiration pop out on his forehead. Even in the photograph you could see the fragility and the toughness that were such important parts of her—the frightened little girl and the strong woman. Jack shut his eyes and tried to make her sad, blue eyes and brown hair appear before him. He tried to console himself, too, by remembering that tomorrow was visiting day and Lucie would be there. But with his eyes shut, even with the music on the radio, the relentless fear overwhelmed him. He opened his eyes quickly and glanced over at the inert figure on the other bed. Why that should comfort him he did not know, but somehow it did. It brought him back to the reality of the hospital, of the people all around, of the safety of the building and the bars. It enabled him to reason with himself and, to some degree, to subdue his terror. But, still uneasy, he called out to the next person who passed the doorway—a student nurse. "Hey, Miss Sokolov. What's for supper?"

She stopped in the doorway, smiling. "Well, aren't you two the ones?" she quipped. "Lying there like kings. . . . It's not bad tonight. Liver and bacon, baked potatoes, brownies for dessert, and some kind of canned fruit."

"Probably peaches," Jack laughed. "They're on a binge of peaches. Must have cornered the market."

"Must have." She grinned and turned to go. "I've got to help in the kitchen."

Just a kid, he thought—younger than his baby sister. Yet he felt quieter inside. He placed Lucie's picture carefully on the bedside table and began to study the one of the children. A futile endeavor. They had been chubby conversational babies when he left home two years before: Lucie, four and Peter, one. Now in this picture, which was already six months old, they had become rabbit-thin, sensitive-faced individuals. Jack did not know them. Their large eyes mirrored depths, experiences completely foreign to him. Still, he could know them, he should know them. When Lucie came tomorrow, he should go home with her, or at least go for a ride with her where he could see the children. If Lucie could be so strong, so brave—even gay and at the same time gentle—how could he be such a coward? He ought to go home with her tomorrow and back to the shop.

Ben laughed, and Jack looked over at the other bed. But, as usual, the laughter was over nothing, or at least, over nothing visible. The boy was just staring at the wall and giggling. Jack looked away again. Poor kid, he thought guiltily. Now somebody like that needs to be here. But me—just a lazy coward. Tomorrow when Lucie comes I'll make myself go with her.

But he knew he would not. He remembered the tension he experienced many times each day when he had to walk with the group outside from one activity to another. And this memory brought back the horror of how it had been before. The long frightening night he had spent at the shop when Lucie and the children were visiting her father—all alone there with the ghostly manikins and the endless racks of clothes, just because he was afraid to go down alone in the self-service elevator and then across town to their empty apartment; the night he had made Lucie sit up and play gin rummy because he couldn't sleep and couldn't bear the suffocating caving-in vacuum of the sleeping world around him; the humiliation of the day he had passed out from fright among the bustling people on Fifth Avenue.

Jack put down the pictures and turned over on his side to look at Ben. "How good to be like him," he thought. "What a relief to be completely out of it and not give a damn."

(5

Ben lay on his bed and stared through the doorway to the hall beyond. The thing with Holliday had gone all right after all. The doctor's questions had been crazy—especially the ones about his father and what he thought of the hospital. But the only really bad one had been the one about the letters. How could Holliday know? Ben glanced over by the bureau where the smooth block of glass enclosed the night light, then up at the brass light fixture on the ceiling. No. If there *was* a camera-radio network, Holliday would have known and said much more. If he *did* know about the letters, it was probably from some nosey nurse.

Probably the worst thing about the conference was what the fat old doctor had said about shock treatments. Still, the boy refused to let himself get upset by that. He'd meant to fight, but what was the point? He'd had the treatments before, and he could take them again. And smart as these doctors thought they were, there'd probably be no difference.

Jack turned on the radio, and the music was pleasant. Ben didn't recognize it as he should have, or as his father would have expected him to. No, in his three years at Holly Springs Ben had taught himself not to recognize music any more. He had come here because his parents were worried about him, because he lay on his bed all the time at home and would not do anything except take long walks alone when it rained, because he had given up talking and, indeed, any form of communication, because his mother had heard him laughing out loud at nothing at all. His parents had become pale and thin-lipped with anxiety. He was their one and only, their hope, their life, their pride and joy. His mother, who had lost two other children at birth, regarded him as a miracle. His father, whose own musical talent had found its lucrative but unsatisfying success in Broadway hits, had always said, "Benjy, some day you will be a great man—the composer I have not become, a talented artist. You must never forget that, Benjy. You must work toward it."

Ben never had forgotten. He looked across the room now at Jack with the picture of his wife, and he laughed. Not because Jack looked funny or because his own thoughts of his father and mother were amusing, but because the meaningless laugh was a part of his act.

He wished in that moment—at least he let his mind touch on it vaguely, more than he usually let his mind touch on any part of reality—that he were Jack Isaacs. That he had a wife and children waiting for him, a job he knew he could do, some safe, definite niche in which he belonged. But, though only nineteen, Ben had known for years that this type of security could never be his. At first he had met his father's challenge and worked for artistic success. But at sixteen he had become weary and deeply conscious of his own inadequacy. The impossibility of his becoming a great musician had loomed before him terrible and frightening. And he had decided—he could no longer remember the moment of his decision, nor the reason for it—but he had decided it was easier to give up and let people pity him than to work for the impossible and have them say, "Womble just didn't have it."

A student nurse came in to speak to Jack. She smiled and talked about supper. They looked at Ben from time to time, trying to include him in the conversation. But he was careful not to show he saw. They're sorry for me, he thought. They think it's sad that I'm so young and won't ever get well. The certainty of that made him feel safe. He relaxed again into the happy world where he was a little boy for ever and ever.

❪ 6

It was nearly dark outside as David Holliday left the main building and cut across the parking lot toward the staff residence. It was dark and damp, chilly, as it had been that afternoon. Holliday remembered the Stoughton couple, and then, Mary Laine. She had said something about her bridge club meeting today. He hoped there would be no lingerers, but also that they had stayed long enough to leave her in good spirits, that their conversation had not made her even more dissatisfied with Holly Springs.

Then his thoughts returned to the precise, rasping voice of the supervisor on the telephone a few minutes before. She had wanted him to order restraints and constant observation for a depressed young writer on Hall 3 Men. She had not said so, of course, but her sadistically efficient explanation of the young man's "disturbed state" and the "disturbance it is causing on the hall" had implied as much.

Holliday had not humored her. He had simply ordered 30 milligrams phenobarbitol T.I.D. for twenty-four hours. Yet now, as he walked homeward, he could not forget the irony of that situation and others like it: that people—even those as well trained as Holly Springs nurses—should be so alarmed by an outward show of emotion. Whereas those who most desperately needed help were lost, frightened individuals like the Womble boy, whom he had tried to talk to that afternoon, or the young Isaacs fellow, whose wife had come to see him a week or so before. Quiet, still-faced mutes, who knew all the pain, all the fear, all the loneliness, but found no outlet for it, no escape except into the confused numbness of themselves.

Just ahead now, moving slowly, laboriously in the same direction, was a shortish, slender figure. By the limp, Holliday recognized young Philip Pierson.

"Hey there, Pierson," he called. "Let me catch up."

The younger doctor turned slightly, almost suspiciously, and stopped. In three long strides Holliday was beside him.

"Good evening, sir. I didn't hear you behind me."

Pierson struggled to speed his pace to match that of the big man beside him and then realized suddenly that Dr. Holliday had slowed down himself.

"You off t'night?" Holliday asked.

"Yes, sir."

"Why not come home to supper with me then?"

"Thank you, sir. I would, but there's some reading I should do."

"All right, I'll buy that. But you better come next time. Else I'll tell Dr. McLeod you're antisocial." They both laughed feebly at the familiar joke. "Tell me, Pierson," Holliday said. "You got anything specially interesting now?"

A pondering silence. "Well, there's this Irish girl. Came in last night. Miss O'Hara."

"Oh?"

"Not interesting, I guess, psychologically speaking. But a fine person—the kind you'd like to know, sick or not."

"Depressed, isn't she? On C.O.?"

"Yes, but different from most. Still has a trace of humor, though a little bitter. Personally I don't know why she's on C.O. She'd never hurt anybody—even herself. She's Catholic. And probably what depresses her most is that her conscience doesn't permit suicide."

"Mmm."

"She's a nurse, trained in London. I guess I'll be learning about English hospitals."

"You been able to have a real interview yet?"

"Yes. Last night and again today." Phil Pierson had a feeling it was more than her illness that interested him. He wondered if that had made him neglect someone else—someone like Miss Barrow.

"That's fine, way it should always be with new patients." Holliday clapped a friendly hand on the young man's shoulder. "I'll see her myself soon—this week sometime, I hope."

They were in front of the doctors' residence now, and Pierson turned in abruptly. "Good night, sir," he said. "Enjoyed the walk."

"Night, son." Dr. Holliday frowned in the darkness, embarrassed by the affectionate term. Perhaps he did think of Pierson as a son, or even more, as a better edition of himself, with the opportunity as well as the ability to realize his own wasted dreams. He had felt that way for some time, probably as long as four years before when he read the boy's application for residency accompanied by the recommendations of the doctors under whom Pierson had worked: "intuitive understanding . . . brilliant coordination of discipline and sympathy . . . eager to learn." In the past four years, Holliday had observed those qualities in operation—fumbling sometimes, but always growing.

He gazed after young Pierson now until the door of the residency had slammed behind him. Then, still lost in his thoughts, he again moved homeward.

III

"I KNOW. I know them all by heart—all your reasons for not going." Mary Laine Holliday's voice was as plaintive as a sick child's. "But none of them make sense. After all, you *are* director of the hospital. You should be able to go and come as you like— at least take a week's vacation in Florida without feeling guilty."

Her graying blond hair was still disheveled from sleep, her round face, pale and sagging. Her large brown eyes blinked nervously over the coffee cup.

David Holliday finished tying his huge black shoes and crossed to the bureau to put on his tie. "I wish I could make you see, darling," he said evenly, careful not to let his eyes stray again to the figure on the bed. "Darling, you ought to understand by now that my position makes it even more necessary that I take no special privileges."

"I know. You've told me. But I know, too, that you like being hard on yourself, pretending you're one of the boys, dedicating yourself to science." Her voice faltered in its attempt at sarcasm and caught in a sob. But despite the tears that sprang to her eyes, she hesitated only a moment. "Don't you ever think of me any more, David? Does it ever occur to you that I might like to have some friends besides nurses and old-maid doctors?"

"Now, Mary Laine. . . ." Irritated, Holliday concentrated determinedly on his own reflection in the mirror.

Even now, at the height of her self-pity, Mary Laine recognized her childishness. Tears trickling down her cheeks, she reminded herself that she had known long before their marriage, that life with David Holliday could never possess the bustling though luxurious comfort of her father's great stone house on the Hudson.

"Yes, I know you like it," she continued now, dabbing at the tears and straining to cover her sadness with anger. "Otherwise you'd have left Holly Springs years ago. We'd have a house in New York and Lillian would be making her debut."

Holliday buttoned his vest in silence, then fumbled around on the dresser for his billfold and the scribbled telephone message about George Purdy's wife. But before he left the room, he stopped by the bed.

"You're right, darling," he said gently, jogging her coffee as he sat down. "I do like it. The work is more interesting here and more challenging. I like feeling useful. But we aren't poor. Lillian goes to the best girls' school in...."

"No, not poor," Mary Laine cut in. Her anger was in earnest now. "But we have to live as if we were. In a charmless outdated two-story house, heated with coal. Because 'A hospital director *must* live on the grounds.' No, 'Not poor.' But with no place to entertain. And worse, no opportunity to meet people we even *want* to entertain."

"Yes, Mary Laine, I know. And I know, too, that I made you a promise a long time ago—a promise I mean to keep. When I retire, we will go to the city. I'll open a practice there, and you'll have your house. Mary Laine, we will."

"But think how old we'll be when you retire. Old, if not sick and dying."

"Really, darling. I'm fifty-two now. Sixty's not old. It will be just a beginning."

The tears had dried on Mary Laine's cheeks, and she spoke with more composure. "Oh, David, I'm not asking you to leave Holly Springs now. I have faith in you and in the promise you made me. I can wait eight years. But I wish you would remember me sometimes. If you did.... Well, David, the Florida trip with Jack and Edith Beckwith...."

"I can't go, darling.... But you could go without me."

"You know I wouldn't do that."

"I'm sorry, my dear. I've got to go. I'm late."

"Please come home for lunch."

"All right. Bye."

(2

David Holliday kept remembering the discussion all day long. No matter what happened, who came in, who called him on the telephone, it reminded him of Mary Laine's sad face and pink bedjacket. And his only defense against his guilt was the "eleventh commandment," which he so often quoted to patients: "Be happy. That's a man's first duty in life."

In the beginning, back some twenty years, Holliday had mis-trusted his reasons for quoting that maxim. It sounded radical, and he wondered if it wasn't desire for recognition rather than devotion to truth that motivated him. With the years, those doubts had faded. His faith rarely failed him. But when George Purdy came in that morning, the happiness code was no help at all.

George was a small, gray, shriveled man, probably ten or fifteen years older than the doctor. He had already been turning gray when the Hollidays first set up housekeeping. They had started buying groceries at his store because Mary Laine liked the way he cut the meat. And over the years he had proved to be one of the finest men the doctor knew.

He stood beside the desk for a long time after he entered, rolling a moldy brown hat between his yellowed fingers. "You see, Doctor, I'm not a bright man. I can cut steaks and measure sugar. But I can't understand things like this." He said that over and over. "I'm just not bright."

Later, after sitting down in the leather chair, he tried to describe what had happened. "I shoulda known. Probably I shoulda done something much sooner. I saw she was acting peculiar. Praying all the time. Going to mass whenever they had one. Kneeling every-where, even in the street. But, you know, Doctor, I never thought anything like this could happen to us. I thought we were too poor, too dumb."

"Nobody ever knows." Holliday reflected that Mary Laine's pampered selfishness was a much more logical prey, and he won-dered if he would look as frightened as George. Probably more so, because he was aware of the obstacles to recovery in women her age. He reassured the little man about the expense, explaining that the hospital took its quota of charity patients and that there was no one he would rather help.

"But she'll get over it, won't she, Doctor? I mean, you got things you can give to make her snap back, don't you? She won't be like those folks has to be locked up the rest of their lives?"

The doctor's face grew dark momentarily but his voice was con-fident. "Oh, certainly, George. These things take time. But we'll help her. You just be patient."

"Thank you, Doctor. I don' know how I'd manage 'thout her.

Can't cook or sew or even work that cash register in the store very well.... Think now of all the things I could've done for her and didn't. I feel downright guilty."

"Don't," Holliday said automatically. But the man's words again touched off his own anxiety. "Look, George," he said, leaning across the glass top of his desk. "We don't live but once. And so we got just one obligation: We got to be happy."

"Thank you, Doctor. Thank you kindly." The little gray man rolled his moldy hat and edged backward toward the door.

When Purdy left, Mrs. Weaver came in to say there was a distraught woman waiting to see him, a Mrs. Milliken. She was a tall woman, blond and coldly, stylishly attractive. She wore a mink cape over her olive tweed suit, and her nervous gloved hand gripped an alligator handbag. "It's good of you to see me, Dr. Holliday," she said, taking out a cigarette. "I'm sure you've heard of my husband—Thomas Milliken, the decorator?"

"Oh, yes ma'am."

"Doctor, I'm frantic about my daughter, Millie. Dr. McLeod —isn't that her name—wouldn't let me see her."

"How old is she? Fifteen?"

"Yes. And neither Tom nor I can understand this. She has everything, Doctor, everything a child could want. Why should she try to hurt herself? And us? ... I was terrified. Millie will be all right, won't she?"

Dr. Holliday felt the old anger inside which he so often felt when confronted by relatives. "Yes, Mrs. Milliken," he soothed. "She's young. She'll be all right.... But these things aren't easy," he added as complacently as possible. But the anger was increasing inside him—just the woman's impeccable appearance. "These things can take a long time, Mrs. Milliken," he said at last. "Sometimes a terribly long time." Then he pushed the button under his desk for Mrs. Weaver to take her away.

❴ 3

"I don't like this. I've been in that room before, and I don't want to go in again." The young woman's face was red and twisted; tears streamed down her cheeks, and she struggled frantically against the restraint sheets.

"They're horrible in there. They plug you in and blow your brains out! No! NO! Untie me."

"Sh-h-h." A student nurse smoothed the patient's forehead and tried to take a temple pulse. "It'll be over quick; you won't even know. And it's going to help you get well, Mrs. Hill, and go home to your children. You know how much you want to go home."

"No! No! I might hurt them! I might.... Please untie me! Please!"

But inside the EST room that morning everything moved smoothly. In fact, to Philip Pierson, the methodical serenity seemed almost eerie. He was grateful for every sound that preserved reality.

Most of the early patients were screaming restraint cases or less violent ones who still required coaxing or physical force. "Like to get them over with," Mrs. Bigelow, the big gray-haired room supervisor explained to the student nurses. "We'll be tired later."

The students meekly, silently did as she told them: handed him the electrode jelly, the gauze mouth gags; watched tensely, wide-eyed as he pushed the button on his black box and the patient advanced through the various stages of the seizure; wheeled the unconscious patients away to the recovery cubicles.

So far, there had been no complications—no *petit mal*, no coma reactions severe enough for Mrs. Bigelow's attention, not even exceptional resistance. There was only one mild touch of apnea, and even then breathing had returned with the first efforts at artificial respiration.

"This finishes Hall 1 Women," Mrs. Bigelow announced to her helpers. "When we start with the men, you girls get around the bed." Her gruff voice was vaguely impatient, almost threatening. "You been watching nearly an hour. No excuse for mistakes."

The students nodded mutely and exchanged frightened glances. Their fingers fidgeted around the bibs of their starched aprons. One girl rattled her keys. Watching them, Phil Pierson recalled that once this room had had the same effect on him—only, his anxiety had chiefly concerned Mrs. Bigelow. Just another nurse, he had tried to reassure himself. And nurses were supposed to help the doctor, anticipate his needs, obey his orders. But he had never been able to think of Mrs. Bigelow as that. The words ELECTRIC SHOCK THERAPY SUPERVISOR seemed to dance in bold fiery letters over her head. He knew of nothing more formidable than her hard, wholesome face, except the authority of her deep voice. For months he had lived in dread of his mornings at EST. His mouth had felt dry when he entered the room, his throat knotted, his face paralyzed, and his lame leg had seemed to drag him back more than ever. He'd lost confidence in his ability to carry out even the perfunctory motions of the treatment, had felt compelled to check the voltage meter again and again. One day Mrs. Bigelow had said, "Could you speed it up, Doctor? We're an hour late already." For some reason, instead of the biting retort he usually mustered, he had only murmured, "Yes, ma'am." And after that he had hated her. He had thought of her as a frustrated tyrant who comforted herself by throwing her weight around in the treatment room. Then gradually his hatred had faded to quiet dislike at first, then acceptance, then begrudging approval. Until now, he realized, looking at the frightened students, he felt a deep respect for the big woman.

The next person was a tall, thin boy from Hall 4 Men, Benjamin Womble. The lank hair falling across his forehead was fawn colored, and his expressionless face with downcast eyes seemed equally colorless. He tittered as he entered the room, but after that was mute, apparently oblivious to all around him. He walked stoop-shouldered with his arms folded across his chest and offered no resistance as the students took his bathrobe and helped him onto the treatment table.

Pierson noted from the chart that this was not the boy's first experience with shock, that, indeed, he had had two complete series before. Still, Ben was afraid. The doctor saw it in his wide, blue eyes and in the quick swallowing movements of his throat. When he touched his arm to help him lie down, it tensed.

For the other patients—the screaming, struggling ones—Pierson had a simple unchanging line of reassurance: "Don't be afraid. We aren't going to hurt you. It'll be over quickly, and you'll be better." Those words did not really help, just soothed a little. Nothing could reach a patient in that disturbed state.

But for a quiet, remote boy like this one, visibly straining to hide his fear, even from himself, there ought to be something that *would* penetrate. Mrs. Bigelow.... If he were as good at his job as.... But there seemed no way.

The students adjusted the pillow under the patient's knees and fidgeted in readiness to hold his legs. Mrs. Bigelow smeared the saline solution and the electrode jelly on his temples, then she adjusted the electrodes. Now it was the doctor's turn. Pierson took the mouth gag from the student. "Don't be afraid, Ben," he said. "You've had this before; so you know it doesn't hurt. And I promise, it can't harm you in any way. . . . Just bite on this."

The boy obeyed, and Pierson showed the student how to hold the roll of gauze in place. Then he stepped back and pushed the button on his box. And again they saw the familiar pattern of the convulsion—the momentary flexion, the whole body drawn rigid, the first fast jerky movements. Pierson noticed that the hand of the student holding the mouthpiece was trembling. With the next phase—the slower, more violent spasms—the knuckles of that same hand froze white.

Then it was over. The body lay still and limp. The reedlike boy was the same as when he first lay back on the bed, except that his eyes were closed now, his muscles relaxed in the serenity of coma. Quickly the students shifted him to his side, but there was no aspiration, only the usual momentary breathlessness.

A sigh of relief went round the bed. The aids came to wheel it away, and Mrs. Bigelow went for the next patient.

(4

It was quiet, quiet—death quiet. The room Gladys Purdy was in was small with nothing in it but the bed on which she lay. The walls and the ceiling were bright white with little holes everywhere, like a cribbage board. Panic came when she opened her eyes. She did not know this place; she had never been here before, and she could not remember coming or where she had come from. Where was George—her man George? She sat up to look around the room, but a sickening dizziness made her lie flat again.

Then she noticed the window at the foot of the bed. It was small and high up so that she could not really see out. But lying there, staring upward, she could see that the sky outside was dazzling blue, divided into strips by black bars. Bars? Bars? Her benumbed mind struggled hazily to understand. Bars! Then she knew. This was prison, and they were going to crucify her! They were going to crucify her for being a Christian. Gladys stared at the bars, terrified, and sat up again, defying the dizziness this time, to look at the door beside the bed.

Bracing her short, heavy body between the doorknob and the bed, she tried to look through the tiny window in the door. The dizziness was overwhelming at first, and she thought she was going to fall. But she held on and gradually her eyes cleared a little. She tried the doorknob, but it wouldn't turn, so she just looked out into the hall. It was wide and dark compared with the brightness of the room. "They take you down that hall to the cross," one of the spirits told her.

She shuddered and pulled her disheveled gray hair down over her eyes so that the guard in the hall, who was disguised as a nurse, could not see her. Then, because of the dizziness and because she was so very tired, she lay down on the floor.

Right away the door opened, and someone was standing over her. It was the guard. "Are you all right, Mrs. Purdy?"

"Go away." She sat up and tried to slide backwards on the linoleum floor. Finally she pulled herself up and sat on the edge of the bed.

"Would you like to go to the toilet, dear?"

"Go away!"

"Come, let's go to the toilet."

The guard tried to pull her to her feet, but Gladys did not yield. It was all a plot to get her to the cross. The spirits had warned her. In her fear, she kicked her bare feet wildly to hold the guard off or trip her up. At last the nurse scooted out the door and locked it behind her.

Gladys sat still for a minute on the edge of the bed and stared suspiciously at the pane of glass in the door. Then hastily, still watching the window, she took off the white wrapper tied around her and stuffed it under the mattress. She was ashamed standing there with nothing to cover her fat, sagging body. But she felt proud too. She had fooled them. She had taken off the robe of crucifixion; now they would not know whether she was to be killed or not.

A holy cross of light was shining in the corner by the door. Gladys knelt before it and said the Seventieth Psalm, her special prayer for evil times. "Make haste, O God, to deliver me. . . ."

When the psalm was finished, when she had opened her eyes and unfolded her hands, the light was still there. "God is watching over me," she thought. "As long as I stay with Him, I'm safe." So she lay down on the cold floor and basked in the light. "I should've listened to George," she reflected sadly. "I shouldn't have knelt down in the street that time when he told me not to. Then I wouldn't be here. Then they wouldn't be trying to crucify me."

For a moment she thought of George. He was probably at the store, weighing apples and cucumbers, cutting up chickens. Maybe he didn't even know they had gotten her, didn't even know she was gone. He was probably smiling as always, wiping his hands on his striped apron and talking friendly to the customers. Or maybe he'd gone in back for a can of cold beer.

But the light moved then, and she had to follow it to the window. It was time to pray again. She had to ask God to kill the people outside, to help her escape so they couldn't crucify her. "Unto thee, O Lord, do I lift up my soul. . . ."

But suddenly, in the middle of the prayer, she felt very sick. She vomited in the corner. And then, because the dizziness had come back and she could no longer see the holy cross, she lay down on the floor and went to sleep.

(5

Millie was awake, but she did not want to open her eyes. She wanted to sink back into the kind, gray, stale-tasting world of sleep. When her eyes opened a crack, the light hurt them, and she closed them again quickly.

But just that glimpse frightened her. She had the impression of being in a strange place, a tiny room she did not know with walls caving in all around. Someone else was in the room, too, sitting at the foot of the bed, and that scared Millie even more. She opened her eyes all the way and looked again.

It was a nurse, only in a blue dress instead of white. She was young. Her eyes watched the bed, but she did not speak. In the silence, Millie gazed around the room, at the white walls marked off into squares filled with tiny holes, at the small, high window with its diagonal grillwork, down at the strange white nightshirt she was wearing.

She could not understand any of it. Where was she? Who was this watching her? Why wasn't she in her own room with the pink flowered wallpaper and the dotted-swiss curtains? Why was she in this ugly, narrow little bed instead of her own lovely wide one with the ruffle around the top? In her confusion she wanted Rex, and involuntarily she called his name over and over.

The nurse came and stooped beside the bed. She put her hand on Millie's forehead. "What's the matter, honey?" she asked. "Don't be afraid. You're going to be all right."

That surprised Millie. In all her fifteen years she could not remember anyone speaking to her so gently. The tears welled up in her eyes, and she was silent. She could not look into the face of the nurse. Instead, she looked down at the rough nightshirt.

Suddenly she realized that something was missing. Rex's ring that she wore on the chain around her neck. Then, with a crushing jolt, it all came back to her. Rex was going steady with a new girl —a senior instead of a sophomore like herself. The ring was the other girl's now; she probably wore it on a chain around her neck. Millie shut her eyes again, longing for sleep to smooth away the pain of her memory.

Gradually, she became hazily aware of where she must be and how she had come to be there. She turned over on her stomach, away from the eyes of the nurse, and buried her face in the pillow. For a moment she thought with a shudder of relief that at least she was alive. But in the next moment that same knowledge brought despair. What, after all, was there to be alive for? Who, in the whole world, really cared whether she was living or dead? Her father didn't. He was way out in California; she never even heard from him except for a five-dollar bill at Christmas. Her mother and Tom Milliken certainly didn't. They gave her everything she wanted—pretty clothes, a record player, her own beautiful room— but they were too caught up in themselves, in making love, in talking about their baby son. Even Gwen and Harriet, the eight-year-old twins who were probably as left out as she, didn't care; they had each other. Rex had been the only one who cared. She thought of his strong hands, of his tall athletic body, of the way his forehead puckered when he did algebra. He had cared, and that was why the world had ended when he no longer did.

Millie had put up with the other things—her parents' divorce, the

locked-out feeling with her mother and Tom, the restless time between the two. But she could not bear to think of Rex's ring hanging around that other girl's neck. That was why she had taken the
sleeping pills. She remembered vaguely how she had sneaked into
Tom's bathroom after he left for the office and emptied the contents of the green bottle into her hand.

As she took the pills, forcing them down one by one with gulps
of water, she had halfway wanted to die and halfway hoped Rex
would find out and be sorry and come back before she did. But
later when the great waves of sleepiness came sweeping over her,
she was terrified. She wanted to run and tell somebody so they
could save her. But then she could think of no one to tell—it
seemed just as well to die.

But somebody had saved her after all. She turned on her side
and stared at the white hole-punctured wall. Probably Cleo, the
maid. In desolation she sought sleep again, but the nurse wouldn't
let her.

"No," she kept saying. "No, Miss Pratt. Don't go to sleep. It's
time for supper. Don't go to sleep."

But why? Millie thought. What's the point? Tomorrow I'll go
home, and it'll be just the same. Tom will bring me a bottle of
perfume, and Mama will give me a new dress, but then they'll go
out to the theater. And at school there'll be that big girl with
Rex's ring.

After that she ignored the nurse's voice and the tugging at her
arm. After that she just shut her eyes and tried to sleep.

I V

AFTER NEARLY three weeks, Eileen O'Hara decided
the hospital wasn't half as bad as she had expected. There were
many things she did not like about it—the sadistic, unreasoning
self-importance of some of the nurses; the way they collected the
eyeglasses every night; living for three days in her one woolen

dress without its belt while they marked her other clothes; and worst of all, never having a moment in the whole day to be peacefully alone. C.O. meant anxious, questioning eyes watching her all the time, even in bed at night or in the bathroom, walking back and forth to the water fountain, or wherever the other C.O. patients happened to go. From time to time, she felt caged in, under lock and key, at the mercy of these solemn, often cold doctors and nurses.

Still, there was the washed-out weakness of relief. No longer did she have to strain to maintain a front, to keep an iron grip on herself, lest she give way completely, lest other people—the doctors or nurses with whom she worked, or even the patients under her care—see the despair beneath her lacquer of efficiency. She no longer had anything to hide. Only the bleak, undeniable memories remained now, grim justification for the grief locked in her heart. And if her strength should run out, if she should feel compelled to do something as weak and sinful as committing suicide, it was almost comforting to know there were those eyes on her and people all around to keep her from doing it.

Eileen thought sometimes of her small sterile room back at St. Timothy's—the bookcase, the scratched brown bureau, the narrow closet. But mostly she remembered the hard, low bed where she had lain for so many hours, her forehead pressed against the lumpy mattress, trying to forget Kenneth, yet wondering where he was and why he had gone away.

Always when she remembered those sleepless hours, she was glad it was over. But there were still the splinters of anxiety forcing their way in to torment her. The crumpled notes Kenneth had written when he was going to be late or couldn't come or just wanted her to think of him after he'd gone home were still under the mattress. She'd kept them all, and in the first days after he left she'd read them over and over. Now, undoubtedly, some other nurse lived in that room. Perhaps the letters were still there, but more likely, the sloppy little maid had thrown them away when she turned the mattress. She might even have read them.

At first, Holly Springs seemed even lonelier than St. Timothy's. The people all around her here—patients as well as staff—were friends and talked together constantly. Eileen felt herself an outsider. Yet, she neither tried nor really cared to change this. It was easier to relax and give herself up to the painless inanities of the daily routine, to speak only when spoken to, to ask for nothing.

At St. Timothy's she had had to struggle to keep up with all the rituals she felt compelled to carry out: saying her rosary over and over; remeasuring medicine dosages two and three times; checking the supply closet first once, then twice, later four times before she went off duty; always polishing, polishing, polishing those dreadful white shoes. She was convinced that it had been these compulsions rather than Kenneth that had broken her. Coming to Holly Springs, if nothing else, should have relieved her of them.

And so it had, but only to make room for the relentless thoughts of Kenneth which her useless activities had formerly crowded out. His face, his voice, the sound of his feet on the stairs filled her memory. Why had he gone? His letters under the mattress. How weak she was and evil, pampering herself like this, living on self-pity. Eileen knew she should fight these thoughts. But as the initial shock of being in a hospital wore off, she only gave into them more. Finally, convinced it was a sin to be so self-centered, she determinedly set about another pastime for the dragging days. She tried to recall her own psychiatric training and to understand not only the problems of the other patients, but also the methods the hospital used in coping with them. Gradually, she came to know people as lost and unhappy, sometimes even as shy and introverted as herself.

Gaunt, martyr-faced little Maggie Evans somehow had convinced herself it was a sin to eat—perhaps because she feels guilty about something, Eileen thought, or maybe just because she thinks it'll make people worry and love her more. The pretty vivacious girl they called Evie was obviously manic. Jackie Harper, had made no secret of being an alcoholic but undoubtedly hid immeasurable pain beneath her easy humor. Mrs. Peters, her middle-aged C.O. partner and roommate, was more openly disturbed; she was having electric shock and giggled to herself all the time—so was another little woman Eileen saw at O.T.—a funny looking shaggy-haired one who knelt down everywhere and kept saying Hail Marys. But others looked sick and well at intervals. Alice Morrisson, for instance, was a fat girl with a ready sense of humor, but when she was not laughing, she was likely to be sitting alone staring blindly at television or chewing her fingernails till they bled.

And there were many more whose illnesses were scarcely distinguishable. One, a big, vivacious, dark woman on open hall, had been hospitalized for over three years; yet she talked with more clarity and self assurance than most of the people Eileen had known on the outside. Also, one little girl on Hall 1 appeared a typical gawky adolescent, except, perhaps, for the solemn hungry look in her gray eyes.

Eileen could understand all the others, yet she could not consider herself sick. She tried to make herself believe it, because then she could have hoped to get well. But she knew that her sadness, her loneliness, her losses—first of Kevin, then of Kenneth —were real, not imaginary things a doctor could change.

She had had no alternative when the authorities at St. Timothy's said they wanted her to come to Holly Springs. She had had to do as they suggested or give up her career as a nurse and probably end up in Bellevue besides. Even in her confusion that fatal afternoon she had realized that. And at Holly Springs she knew better than to try to convince them they were wrong.

She had mistrusted doctors after her session with the psychologist at St. Timothy's, and she had been infuriated by Dr. McLeod's impersonal coldness. But when Dr. Pierson came, she had felt sorry for him because of his lame leg and his badly concealed shyness, because he was young and doing the dirt for somebody like Dr. McLeod. She had wanted to tell him right then that he was wasting his time, that, in the first place, she was not sick, and in the second place, she did not intend to talk to anyone about what she had found or failed to find in life. But she had not dared to say it. And after a few uneventful sessions, she began to like him, to feel, indeed, as if they had a kind of partnership against Dr. McLeod. He could not help her, but it was nice having someone to talk to. His questions seemed genuinely interested, not just clinically curious. His brown eyes, though they studied her, though they sometimes forced her to look away in embarrassment, were never probing like those of the C.O. nurses. He always carried a notebook, but after the first day when he asked the questions about her family, he never wrote in it.

It was because of Dr. Pierson that she was not surprised the morning Dr. Holliday came to see her. He had told her the older man was a wonderful person, a fine human being as well as a brilliant doctor. She could not believe that, because she had seen the lumbering dolt and heard the hearty crassness of his Southern drawl. Holliday reminded her of nothing so much as her mother's brothers, who were farmers back in the County Cork, and there was certainly no brilliance in men like that.

Still, she was curious as she watched the big man lope briskly up the corridor. And when his oversized hand touched her shoulder, she could think of no escape. She was caught—pinioned between the vigilant eyes of the attendant on C.O. and the quiet brown ones of the tall doctor.

"Morning, Miss O'Hara," his friendly voice drawled. "I'm Dr. Holliday. Like to talk to you if it's all right."

She stood up slowly and followed his gallumphing footsteps to the conference room.

(2

She was too thin to be really pretty. Her freckled face had cheekbones so high there were hollows beneath them. Still, Eileen O'Hara was charming. Dr. Holliday pondered her wavy dark hair, the flecks of light in her gray-green eyes, the subtle grace of her slim body. The real attraction lay inside, though. She was polite—more than that, she was kind—even when she made it clear she remembered her psychiatric training and meant to use it against him. She was sensitive—even of him, the gross, easy-talking dolt whom no one thought had feelings. She had a gentle humor, that sometimes lit her whole face.

Young Pierson spoke of her intelligence, of her interesting conversation. But Holliday wondered if it wasn't really these other things that attracted him—the humor and sensitivity and, maybe even more, the quiet strength behind the wistful smile. Also, of course, her name could not fail to appeal to someone with Pierson's sense of the poetic.

She was still talking about the nuns in the Surrey hospital, how serene, even cold, they appeared on the surface, yet so human underneath. "Of course, you are not of the Catholic faith," she said. "Probably you hold the common concept that sisters are remote, martyrlike beings, but. . . ."

"But they were kind to you? You needed someone to be kind."
He didn't want her to talk any more about Surrey. As Pierson had
said, it was interesting. But he saw now that she was deliberately
using it to avoid talking of herself. Somehow he must outwit her.

"Oh, yes, they were very kind to me, very kind. But then, they
were kind to many. There was one; Sister Angela was. . . ."

"But weren't you a nurse? A registered nurse, I mean? Why
should they be especially kind to you?"

"Yes, I was a nurse there." She swallowed hard and her eyes
blinked tensely. "That was my first duty, but . . . Anyway there was
Sister Angela. She was quite old. . . ."

"I suppose Surrey was hard for you. Most first jobs are. Were
you very unhappy?"

"Well, uh . . . No, uh . . . uh . . . I had a great deal to do; I worked
very hard."

"You must have been very homesick and lonely off by yourself
for the first time. It's a wonder you didn't fall in love or even get
in trouble. Many young girls do at a time like that."

"Well, uh . . . uh . . ." Her eyes dropped to the floor. Her face
became thin-lipped and hollow-cheeked. Her fingers tightened into
a knot. She had lost. All this time, despite the peering eyes and the
insistent questions, she had maintained her privacy. And now suddenly, this blundering, good-natured old man had swept it from
her. She groped frantically for an escape, then realized the best she
could hope for was compromise. And that raised another vital
question: How big must the compromise be? How much could
she hide from those friendly but unfaltering eyes?

Perhaps if she told him a little about Kevin, he wouldn't get to
Kenneth. She could try skimming the surface, giving him a vague
sketch—but not the true picture, not her picture. She could waste
a lot of time describing the advanced hopelessness of Kevin's illness
even from the first, when she knew him only as one more number
in a great ward of tuberculars. Or she could sidetrack by discussing
her own disgust at the insidious nastiness of the disease coupled
with the whining complaints of the patients.

But glancing at him furtively, she realized that Dr. Holliday
would not be satisfied. She would have to tell him how she had
come to like Kevin, even to care a great deal for him, because of
his stubborn lopsided smile, because they had both come away

from Ireland, because of their common liking for Yeats and Dylan Thomas.

Or maybe she wouldn't tell him about the poetry; she would like to keep that just for herself. Maybe she would leave out the poetry altogether, because if she didn't, she might have to mention the long hours she sat reading to him, hours when she wasn't even on duty, when the sisters would tiptoe past and smile or shake their heads sadly without speaking. And if she got that far, she would probably be unable to stop before she told of Sister Angela's warning and her own deafness to it, or even of the last hollow, echoing morning when she came up the stairs behind two frightened students gibbering about "the frightful, gushing blood" and went in to find the orderlies from the morgue in Kevin's cubicle.

"Why didn't you marry him?" the slow voice persisted. "Was it the church? The nuns?" The doctor's face was quiet, as if unaware of her discomfort. "You know, at that age—you were twenty-one? —convents can seem very appealing. An escape that looks big and noble. It's frightening to be suddenly on your own."

"Oh, no," she answered quickly. "Oh, no, it wasn't the church. I ... I guess I was in love. Though maybe not. Maybe I just thought I was, because I wanted to be and he would've satisfied everybody—even my mother. He was from the County Cork, too, you see—a town only sixty miles from my father's farm. Probably that's what interested me. ... B-but he was just a patient, a-a tubercular. Mostly we were good friends. Maybe eventually— maybe we'd have married. But he was quite ill, and we never talked about it. ... Then he died."

There was a long silence during which the omniscient eyes wandered to the floor, then back to her face. "That must've been difficult for you. ... Death seems so strange and remote to young people."

"But in medicine—you know that—in medicine it is an every-day occurrence. Ke-Kevin was just another patient."

"Yes, but ... your father died, didn't he? When you were a child?"

"Yes." She returned his steady gaze. Relief crept through her. She did not like to remember her father's death, but it was good here. Far enough away to be sad but not painful, and she had gotten over Kevin with much less trouble than she'd expected. Now she could talk about Ireland—about the farm, the fields of barley and the sheep, about Christmas Eve and the county fairs, about the cold wet winters, and the long days in summer. Perhaps if she did it well, if she made it sound happy, he would have her taken off C.O. or even let Dr. Pierson handle her case alone.

But he didn't give her a chance. He came right back with another attack: "That must've made you feel especially lost when the boy died too, like everything that mattered to you would always be taken away." He watched her carefully as he spoke. He was touching on something vital here. He knew that by the flat composure of her face, by the quick, too-sensible tone she used in speaking of the boy's death. He saw the colorless lips tighten, the eyelids flicker as if to keep back tears. "Some of that lost feeling must've hung on," he continued softly. "I think it would with me. Probably I'd feel very alone. But at the same time, determined to keep that loneliness, afraid to let myself care about anything, afraid of getting hurt again."

There was no answer. The white lips were still pressed together, the eyelids had closed. The thin face was lined with a shiny wet path down each cheek. In her lap the tight fists had collapsed into two trembling hands, ten fumbling fingers.

❬ 3

When Evelyn Barrow came out of the Hall 3 dormitory that morning, the other three patients were still asleep. It wasn't light yet, but she had already lain awake for a long time listening to their breathing, watching the nurses' flashlights on the ceiling, listening to the opening and locking of the nursing office door.

So Evie was angry when she got up because she could not sleep, because of the diagonal bars on the windows, because of nothing and everything, just because of the wild, white fury burning inside her. She had heard the clanging of the bedpans in the bathroom, and so she was not surprised when the attendant asked her for a specimen. Still, she was angry. She wanted to hurt someone, and the woman's frightened subservience irritated her more. "No, I won't give you a specimen," she blurted. "I will not!"

The timid little woman patted Evie's shoulder and spoke gently in her broken English. "Now, now," she soothed. "Be a good girl. Just come with me. Then you go right back to bed."

"No! Shut up!" Evie jerked away and started up the hall toward the water fountain. On the way, she grabbed up a pottery vase full of daffodils and dashed it to the floor. She knew it was an insane thing to do. It accomplished nothing. Hurt no one. Broke no iron bars. Did not even release the anger twisting inside her. It could mean C.O. or even a transfer to Hall 1. Still, she had to do it; her hands moved with a will of their own.

The attendant touched her again, gently, but infuriatingly, and took her arm. She said something, too, but Evie didn't hear. "God damn you, bitch!" she screamed. "Leave me alone. Don't touch me, or I'll kill you. I'll kill you! I'll kill the whole lot of you!" Then she struck the woman hard across her surprised white face and ran, kicking her slippers behind her, to the end of the hall.

Now she was free, fighting anyone, everyone, the world. And she did not care about Hall 1. They would come after her, she knew, the great strong bullies. They would drag her off to Hall 1 and tie her into one of those canvas-covered bathtubs and keep her there for hours. But she did not care.

She did not care about anything now—not her pious mother or being a dancer or "making out" with men; nothing except fighting off the nurses when they came, nothing except letting loose with all the fury she possessed. She grabbed up the chair beside the bathroom door and ran with it against the window at the end of the hall. There was a splintering of glass and wood. In the silence that followed, Evie glimpsed the attendant running toward her first and then in the opposite direction. She screamed after the little woman, but she did not know what she said. Gone to get the others, Evie told herself. She flung the lamp on the table beside her to the floor and ran back up the hall to where she had left her slippers. She picked them up and began beating against the door to the outside passageway.

Then they were there—the starched blue and white uniforms, the grim iron faces, the metallic rattle of keys. Some came at her silently. Others spoke softly, kindly: "Come on, honey." "Be a good girl." "Miss Barrow, won't do you any good to struggle."

Still she fought them. She kicked their shins and scratched their faces. She struck at their glasses and bit their hands.

Then, suddenly, her taut white face crumpled like a burst balloon. Her arms and legs stopped swatting and kicking. Convulsive sobs shook her plump body. It took only two nurses to hold her in the wheel chair as they pushed her along the corridor to Hall 1.

(4

Gladys Purdy had been in the tub for hours—since before the day shift went off the afternoon before. She had had her supper spooned to her by a "student nurse" (Gladys knew she was an assistant torturer). She had seen McLeod come on rounds in her starched white executioner's coat. And later McLeod had come back with the head guard to give Gladys an injection they said would make her sleep.

Gladys hadn't believed them, of course, and had fought them all the way. It was really poison. So she had screamed and cursed them and called on the Lord. She had kicked to splash water over the canvas cover tied around her neck, and she had struggled to get her head through the hole down into the tub, so that they would think she had drowned and would take her out to put someone else in. When she ripped the heavy canvas, they only put a stronger one on. When she begged to go to the toilet, they told her to do it in the tub.

She must have gone to sleep for a little while, though, because the next thing she knew there was a different torture assistant with her hands on her temples, "taking your pulse, Mrs. Purdy."

Gladys realized then that her throat hurt and her eyes were fuzzy. (The poison, no doubt.) Her muscles ached, and her knuckles were raw from rubbing against the canvas. She prayed to the Lord and said Hail Marys over and over, but she could not see the holy light. She was so sleepy . . . so sleepy. She had to kick and bite her lips to fight it.

It was really a relief when they brought old lady Larson in. She didn't seem particularly upset—at least not unhappily so. She didn't fight, and it took only Falkenburg and one extra assistant to put her in pack. She sang and danced around the treatment room while they unrolled the wet sheets. Her wispy white hair stuck out all over, and her blue eyes had a wild unfocused stare.

"It's Independence Day," she said, playfully removing one of the torturers' organdy caps. "Where are the fireworks?"

"You've got your dates mixed," Falkenburg answered, deftly regaining the cap. "Take your clothes off, Mrs. Larson."

"Not yet. De da de dum . . . I'm Jewish, and Jews only do what they want."

"I'm sorry but your pack's ready."

"Who's the Jewish doctor here?"

"Mrs. Larson. . . ."

"There has to be one or Governor Dewey'll close the place up."

"Here, I'll help you." The student nurse began to unbutton her dress.

"Don't touch me."

"Miss Hudson, come help us, please," Falkenburg called to the student in the tub room.

"Only Dr. Holliday can touch me."

"Well, take off your shoes."

"Oh . . . oh, no. My doctor told me never to take off my shoes."

"Come on, now. No more foolishness." The three nurses went to work then, and in minutes had Mrs. Larson mummified in the cold wet sheets. "Quiet down now," Falkenburg said, "and get some rest."

"Dr. Holliday is going to be very disappointed with you," Mrs. Larson retorted. But the nurses had gone.

Gladys must have slept again then, because the night seemed much shorter than she had expected. When she woke, she didn't fight any more and just let the guard do what she wanted. Once she even drank some of the water the guard kept bringing.

It was nearly morning when the big commotion came. The poor girl in the next tub had awakened and was crying for breakfast. And the guard kept saying it wouldn't be long, but that meantime she could have crackers and milk if she wanted.

Then suddenly there was screaming outside and a loud banging. Voices—harsh guards' voices—shouted orders. A key turned in the lock, and the supervisor—the quiet, suspicious looking one who'd been coming around all night—stepped in and said, "Get another tub ready, Miss Fletcher. We've got a girl here from Hall 3."

That brought Gladys to. She sat up in the tub as straight as she could and watched.

They brought the girl in in a wheel chair. She wasn't fighting, but there were lots of guards holding her as if she had been. Instead, she was sobbing—loud, wrenching, choking sobs—as if her heart was breaking. And in between the sobs, she was screaming, "Not fair, not fair! . . . Damn you! . . . My mother, my mother, not me! . . . Oh-h-h."

She seemed a pretty girl, despite the fact that her face was red and swollen. Her hair was a rich brown color and long and wavy. When they ripped her clothes from her, Gladys thought she must be as beautiful as any young girl anywhere.

She kicked and cursed them as they lifted her bodily into the tub and fastened the canvas cover on. When they finally went away, Gladys tried to talk to her. She had heard the guards call her Evie, and so she did too. She thought that between them they might be able to find the holy light. But the girl was screaming and sobbing so loud she couldn't hear. Every fifteen minutes when the student took their pulses, Evie screamed even louder and tried to bite the girl's hand. At last Gladys just gave up and ate the scrambled eggs the student wanted to feed her.

V

THE PINK LIGHT of the May morning sifted past the ornate grillwork on the window into the corners of the room. Dr. Jonathan Stoughton pulled the sheet up under his bony, sagging chin and breathed deeply of the cool air. In that moment the fury, so often raging inside him, was almost still. A kind of peace—more than that of a good night's sleep—flowed over him.

The blue eyes were bright in his wrinkled, white face. His thin lips, so often pressed into a hard line, were slightly parted, revealing the vacant pinkness of his gums. His long delicate fingers, knotted and veined, lay open and relaxed atop the gray blanket. His mind was wandering in a pleasant nimbus of nothingness.

In the midst of that peace, though, he felt someone touch his shoulder, and when he turned to look, he found it was the nurse. The old one, the frizzy-headed biddy he did not like. He couldn't remember her name. He saw that she was trying to tell him something, but he could not hear. "What?" he asked. "I don't have my hearing aid."

"It's time to get up," she repeated after she had fumbled around on the dresser and handed him his hearing aid.

"What?"

"I say, it's almost time for breakfast. You'd better get a move on."

"A movie? Well, I don't care to see it. I don't enjoy movies— can't hear."

"No, no, no. GET UP!"

"Up? What time is it?"

"Seven twenty-five."

"Seven twenty-five!" he exploded. "Good Lord! Get out of here and stop tormenting me!"

She scurried off in her usual busybody way to wake the other patients. He lay still under the covers and tried vainly to remember what he had found so pleasant before she came. Her voice and scowling face had swept the glow from the morning. He only knew now that it was outrageous to be awakened at 7:25 on a morning when he didn't have to operate.

He raised one hand, looked at it closely and could not understand why it was so thin and wrinkled. For a moment, it made him painfully conscious of the reality of the present. Sometimes—as when he had first awakened this morning—it seemed to him that he was still a young man, one of New York's leading surgeons, that Nancy was still living, and that the boys were still small, well-scrubbed children in knickers.

More often, he was too caught up in his fury to be aware of the tragic bleakness his life had come to. He fumed about the inconveniences of a mental hospital, the injustices, the disgrace—being forced to get up at daybreak and weave foolish baskets or paint pictures; playing croquet or bridge with old men too stupid to lead out trumps; eating food cooked to disintegration and slopped with gravy.

He pushed back the covers now and stood up. Lying in bed had lost its pleasure. He took his teeth from the plastic cup on the dresser and glanced at the leather-framed photographs there. They were pictures of each of the three boys and one of all of them together with their wives and children. When Dr. Holliday came, he liked to look at those pictures. He always said he wished he had three sons. Now Dr. Stoughton angrily folded them one by one and jammed them into the bottom drawer of the dresser.

"Ungrateful wretches!" he snarled loud enough for even his deaf ears to hear. "Think they know everything!... 'Sick,' they say. Mean, 'Crazy.' 'Need somebody to take care of you!' Mean, 'We're tired of having you around.' "

He yanked a clean shirt and a pair of shorts out of the middle drawer, then he let his pajamas fall to the floor and began to dress. "Well, if they're that way," he growled, "there's nothing I can do. But I won't have their oranges and cigarettes. No! Not their new shirts either, or their sweaters. God damn it! Or their shoes!" And he kicked the pile of shoe boxes in the closet before he stooped to put on the scuffed, black pair he always wore.

Joe Marx was already at work on his crossword puzzles when Dr. Stoughton shuffled up the hall to his couch that morning. A shriveled, little man with round, pink face and oversized hands, Marx peered arrogantly over silver-rimmed spectacles at Dr. Stoughton, but said nothing. Puckering his wide forehead and biting the end of his pencil with crooked, yellow teeth, he went on with his work.

Even when the doctor sat down beside him, he only sighed loudly and bent more determinedly over his puzzle. When Stoughton strained to look over his shoulder, he snapped, "Look, Doctor, would you please kindly not to breathe down my neck? I'm trying to work."

Stoughton did not hear. He kept his scrawny neck stretched over the puzzle book until finally he sat back and made the statement he eventually made to everybody: "Isn't it outrageous? What right have they to lock up a lot of people just because they're old? No music, no brandy, public bathroom. Criminal!"

Marx looked up. His face—eyelids drooping, thick lips turned down at the corners—wore a pained, haughty expression. "Ja," he said, sighing with affected tragicness. "Ja, there are things I miss too: glass beer before supper, Mama's pot roast, the store. I run a very fine store, Dr. Stoughton, very fine store. Good merchandise, brand names. Very fine store. I got three sons, taller than you, Doctor, and two lovely daughters. All married. All want Papa to live with them. But I can't. It's better I stay here. Too sick, too feeble. And Mama not there to take care me." Mr. Marx looked down at the puzzle again, shaking his head sadly. "Makes me very nervous."

But Dr. Stoughton had not heard a word. His blue eyes stared straight ahead; his thin lips muttered unintelligibly.

Then a quick, sly smile crossed Marx's puffy lips. "Listen, Doctor," he said, tapping the other man's shoulder with his pencil, then glancing around suspiciously before he began to speak more loudly. "Doctor, I got something to tell you. It's not so nice. But you my friend, and I think you want to know."

"Yes . . . Yes." The doctor listened intently, nodding his head up and down. He reached into his pocket to turn up his hearing aid.

"You know Corry? How he always ask you to play cards and chess? He say to me, 'Marx, please play with me.'

"I say, 'No, Corry. I'm busy. Get the doctor.'

" 'Okay,' he say. 'But I rather play with you. The doctor cheats. Besides, he is snob. And he talks too loud. His voice hurts my ears.' "

"He said that? When did he say that?"

"Yesterday, after supper. . . . I say, 'The doctor very nice.' He say, 'The doctor crazy and deaf.' Then he walk away."

"So I cheat! So I'm crazy!" The veins in the doctor's neck stood out like cords. "Well, he can rot before I play with him again. Outrageous to be locked up with people like that. No wonder his wife keeps him here." Dr. Stoughton stood up and stamped off to his room.

Joseph Marx smiled after him and went back to his puzzle. But a little later when Edward Corry himself sauntered down the corridor, the old man called out to him. "Come here, Corry," he said. "I got something to tell you."

Corry had been up a long time already, pacing the floor, staring gloomily out the barred windows. There were dark shadows under his eyes. His face was gray with self-pity. "Can't right now, Marx," he answered. "Want to get the doctor for chess."

"That's what I got to tell you." Joseph Marx's dark eyes were shining. "You better listen," he said. "You'll be sorry if you don't. . . . It's what the doctor said about you. I was just talking to him."

"What did he say?" Corry's overstuffed figure turned clumsily back to the couch. He was frowning. "What did he say?"

"Well, could be he didn't mean it be passed on. But seems to me you ought to know."

"What did he say?"

"Said, 'You know, Corry's an awful pest. Always gotta play something—chess or cards or something. He must've run a gambling joint.' "

"He said that?" Corry's face reddened.

"Yeah. He did. And he said more."

"What? What did he say?"

"He said, 'Thing that bothers me isn't being pestered all the time, I'm used to that. But he cheats. Marx,' he says. 'He's an awful cheater.' "

"That's a lie!" Corry's face was scarlet to the top of his bald head.

"Yeah." Marx winked confidentially. "But I thought you'd want to know."

"Thanks." Corry rubbed a dimpled hand across his mouth and stood up. His eyes were mournful, his shoulders sagged as he walked wearily back to watch the clock.

([2

By 9:30 Jonathan Stoughton had worked himself into a fever. He was so angry at breakfast that he made the fuss-budget nurse move his place clear across the dining room from Corry. And after that, though Corry did not try to talk to him, he constantly expected it and kept his anger primed. "Bastard!" he growled as he trudged to O.T. with the others. "Sniveling bastard!" And instead of going to weave pot holders in the small crafts room as usual, he headed for the metal shop.

Months before he had started a pewter tray there, for what he did not know, except that it was more interesting than basket weaving. Today the instructor seemed glad to see him and asked where he had been so long. He gave him a place at a table with a thin dark Jewish boy, Isaac something. A nice-seeming boy with anxious eyes and a tightness about the mouth that seemed half sadness and half fear. He looked familiar to Stoughton. One of his patients perhaps. No, too young, too long ago for that. Probably just here in this room, maybe at this same table. The old man looked down at his tray then, at the beginnings of the design he had done earlier. Yes, obviously his hands were getting stiff and clumsy.

Jack Isaacs was working on a set of pewter ash trays. Lucie didn't wear jewelry. But there was something hard and real about metal that made him like working with it. When old Dr. Stoughton sat down with him, Mr. Craig, the instructor introduced them, though they had worked together months before. The old man smiled and nodded, but it was obvious he neither heard nor remembered. So Jack tried to act the same way.

Painstakingly he daubed the black acid-proof paint on his circle of metal. He had chosen an ivy design because Lucie liked ivy. . . . There was to be a hospital dance tonight, and he would have to go. At least if he didn't, they would nag the living daylight out of him and give him a lousy report at the next staff meeting. It wouldn't be fair to Lucie to hear he was worse simply because he didn't go to a dance.

It was hard to keep his eyes off *the* Dr. Stoughton. The old man was bent intently over his tray. The work he had done earlier looked fine and delicate—plainly the art of skilled hands. But the design he painted in now was not the same. It would be effective—perhaps as attractive as Jack's own—but it appeared gross and clumsy beside the other. Yes, Stoughton had changed a great deal since the last time they worked here together. At that time he had seemed in a fog, but he had broken through occasionally to talk, and he had called Jack by name. Now it seemed more than fog that surrounded him, something like thick cotton. He still did not remember Jack, and the only talk he indulged in was an indistinguishable muttering to himself.

"Are you going to the dance tonight, Doctor?" Jack asked loudly. He remembered the old man was deaf.

There was no answer; so Jack leaned forward, making his question even louder. Foolish really. Probably the old man didn't even know there was a dance. It would only remind him of his wife, who, he had told Jack before, was dead.

Jack looked down at his own discs of metal, and suddenly they seemed as frail and gaudy as paper doilies. What would there be for him without Lucie? How long would it take him to become as lost and helpless as this one-time genius?

He must not think of that. Indeed, he must not think of Lucie at all—not the brown hair or the serious, animated face or the small strong fingers or.... He felt the hungry scream crowding his throat, and he looked down quickly at the work before him. Craig had said all discs painted this period could go in the acid this afternoon. That meant working hard and fast.

As he tried to do that, Jack realized his own hands were young and strong-looking compared to the knobby, veined ones of the old doctor. Stoughton had grown more feeble in other ways, too. He was thinner, and his hands shook visibly. His fine hair, partially gray only months ago, was snow white now. This hair and the narrow distinguished nose, which Stoughton's gauntness emphasized, were the only things Jack envied in him. He knew that nothing, even age, could add dignity to his own hooked nose and coarse, black hair. "Are you making that for one of your sons?" he shouted across the table to the old man.

But again, no answer. Just the growling mutter.

"And this," Jack thought, again applying himself to his ash trays, "could happen to anyone—to Ben or me or anyone." Probably it had already happened to Ben. A shiver set the hair of his arms on end. It must not happen to him. He set his lips tight together and began painting at a furious rate. He did not look at Dr. Stoughton again till the end of the period.

❰ 3

As usual they had to wait a long time in the lobby of the O.T. building while the tools were counted and recounted. And as usual, many patients griped.

But Ben Womble was pleased by the delay. The longer they stayed here, the less time they'd have at gym. And he had no desire to bowl or play badminton. He could not win; in fact, he would not even let himself try. So what was the point in playing? He mostly just sat in the pool room with the old men where the gym guys couldn't find him as easily.

As they waited, Ben leaned against the huge heavy table in the center of the main hall. His arms, as usual, were folded stoop-shouldered across his chest, and his blue eyes stared blindly straight ahead. He wondered how many of these people would go to that stupid dance tonight. He would simply because that was the easiest thing to do. If he stayed on the hall, doctors and nurses would nag him for days, but if he went, he could get a chair against the wall and not dance or speak to anyone and even get some ice cream when it came around.

He was musing about that, half imagining the music and the disgust on his father's face if he heard it, when the old man came over to him. Ben did not notice him at first. His eyes and thoughts were focused too far away.

But then, startlingly, the old man put his hand on Ben's shoulder and said, "I miss you, Don. Why don't you ever talk to me any more?"

Ben was frightened at first. He did not know the old man. He'd only seen him around and heard Jack say he'd once been a very famous surgeon. So the bony fingers on his shoulder were scary. But Ben did not let this show. He kept his eyes fixed glassily straight ahead, and though his arms tightened their grip on each other, he did not shift his position.

"I worry about you, Don," the old man continued. "They keep me locked up here, but I think of you a lot. You were always closer to me than the other boys."

Ben looked at him then; he could no longer resist that pathetic, imperative voice. But he lurched away from the grip of the skeleton fingers.

At that a sadness crept into the glaze of the blue eyes, and the old man's tall, thin body quivered, as if from pain. But he went on talking: "You look thin, Don. Have you been sick? How are you doing in school?"

For a moment more Ben just stared in silence at his intruder. Then he said with the foolish giggle he regularly used to reassure himself, "You're crazy. You aren't my father, and my name isn't Don."

Suddenly the old man's face was no longer gray and pathetic. It turned scarlet with fury and his lips tightened into a hard straight line. A vein in his forehead swelled thick and blue. "Impudent rascal!" he shouted. "How dare you call your father crazy? Spit on the hand that's fed you?"

Ben shrugged and walked away. Crazy old man! He decided to go over and wait with Jack.

As they walked slowly through the cool May morning to the gym, most of the men smoked the cigarettes forbidden inside. Ben ambled along as listlessly as ever, but made an anxious effort to stay close to Jack Isaacs.

"You know, Jack," he said after a while, "a crazy old man in there tried to tell me he's my father."

"Oh ..." Jack wanted to say more but couldn't think of anything. Ben was talking more since he'd started shock, but sometimes, like now, Jack wasn't sure he was talking sense.

"That white-haired old man you said was a doctor. He kept calling me 'Don' and asking me about school. I think he was trying to make me go crazy." Ben still walked listlessly, but his face was twisted with fear and anger.

"Oh, that was Dr. Stoughton," Jack could comfort him now. "Don't worry about him, Ben. He was a doctor, a brilliant doctor once. But he's old now, and his brain is decaying. Probably he *did* think you were his son."

Ben still frowned. "He's crazy."

"Yeah, but don't let it get you." Jack was surprised to hear the confidence of his own voice. It felt good to think he could soothe somebody else even when he couldn't do the same for himself. For once he did not feel afraid in the vast open area through which they had to walk to gym.

Ben was still frowning, but he said nothing.

"Are you going to the dance tonight?" Jack asked.

Ben shrugged.

"I think I'll go." Jack tried to sound confident, but the thought of the great room crowded with people made his voice quaver.

"I'll probably go too," Ben mumbled. "Probably they'll make me." But he wasn't much concerned about the dance right then or even about the crazy old man.

He liked the cool breeze on his face. He liked the fresh, growing greenness and the sense of vast, but restricted and carefully protected freedom. They made him feel as if he were a little boy again, walking in the park with his mother, holding her hand and knowing that as long as he did he would be safe.

He walked with the group now, obediently at their pace, but he had forgotten about Jack and the others. Across the lawn a woman was seated in one of the brightly painted benches. She looked happy there, relaxed and content, and yet as if at any moment she might get up and walk away to something else she wanted more. For a moment he envied her. It would have been very nice to sit alone like that in the morning sun. But then suddenly he was glad to feel Jack's sleeve brush his arm. The bench did look pretty but not very safe.

V I

"IT DOESN'T seem fair," Mary Laine complained as she helped herself to mint jelly. "David, I just can't see why you have to go to this dance. It's Lloyd Wilson's turn. We went to that card party."

"I know, darling, I know. I get bored at these affairs, too. But I can't just go down to the hospital and say 'Appendix or no appendix, Lloyd, you get up and go to that dance.' And one of us has to be there. Means so much to the patients. Like seeing the governor at a state fair."

"Yes, dear, I know. And I *am* selfish about it."

"No, no. Probably I'd be the same if there was any way out." He concentrated on his plate as he scooped up a large forkful of mashed potatoes and gravy.

"Well, what do I have to do?"

"About what?"

"I mean, it seems ridiculous for me to go and sit through it. You have too many women and too few men as it is."

"Oh, no. There's no need for you to do that. Just so you're there to pour punch or whatever it is they have."

"I think the younger doctors and their wives would be much better at this."

"Yes, my dear, but they all have children. Besides," his large hand reached out to pat her soft white one. "Besides, none of them could take your place."

She smiled at him gently, unwillingly, and was silent.

And aware that he had won his battle, for a few minutes Holliday didn't speak either. It seemed to him he had spent his whole day urging people to come to this dance—old Dr. Stoughton, the young Irish girl, Jack Isaacs. Urging them, not so much because he wanted them to come as because it was his duty. Even Phil Pierson had been annoyed when he asked him to be there. He had not said so, of course, but he had been.

That's the worst of being a resident, Holliday mused now. You not only have to do what you're told, but you have to act as if you enjoy it. He remembered how once when he was new at Holly Springs, old Dr. Horace had asked him to take rounds on Mary Laine's birthday. Somehow that wouldn't bother him now, but it had then. It had infuriated him, and despite his quiet, friendly acceptance of the order, he had promised himself that some day he would say all the things to old Horace he wanted to say then. Of course, he had never done it. Old Horace was long since dead, and he, himself, had come to realize that it did not matter who you were—resident or patient or hospital director—you still had to be pleasant about a lot of things you hated.

"Lillian isn't coming home till Tuesday."

"What? Oh. I thought she got out Friday."

"The school does close then, but she's going on a house party. . . . I wish we had gone on that trip with the Beckwiths."

"Yes, I wish we could've."

"You know, David, I still don't understand that. Why you couldn't just cut a week out of your vacation later and go to Florida now."

"Mary Laine, we've discussed that a thousand times."

"I know, but David, Jack Beckwith works hard too. He has quite a practice."

"Yes, darling, he does. But it's different. . . . Mary Laine, talk like this doesn't get us anywhere."

"All right, we won't talk about it. But I think I'll have them to dinner next time Jack comes out for a board of governors meeting."

"Fine. Fine. Look, my dear, please excuse me. I'm about to be

late. Will you come later? I'll come back for you around nine."
"All right, David."

❨ 2

"All right, ladies, let's get together now. Everybody for the
dance, down to the office. Time to start. All right, ladies. . . ."
Eileen felt angry as she watched the aides and students go up
and down the hall, herding together the brood for the dance. Most
of the patients were like herself and did not want to go. But
many—also like her—had been persuaded or trapped into it one
way or another.

Little Maggie Evans, for instance, had said that she wouldn't
go. But her doctor, Collins, had left an order that she must. Then
she'd canceled Maggie's tube feeding for that evening as a bribe.
So the poor thing had no alternative.

"All right, ladies, let's get together. . . ." Eileen was already sitting
beside the door. Being on C.O., she had to wait where a nurse
could watch her. Little by little the others assembled. Poor fat
Alice Morrisson had decked herself out in a blue taffeta cocktail
dress with rhinestone trim. And Mrs. DuPree, of Boston, was
perched haughtily, white gloves in hand on the edge of a chair.
She was wearing a tweed dress and brown skin shoes.

Unfortunately, there were others who wanted to go and could
not. Molly Fleming, the new C.O. patient, had assumed everyone would go to the dance. All morning in between her restless
corridor pacing she had pestered Eileen about the "appropriate
apparel for these affairs." Eileen had told her that new patients
usually stayed on the hall. But, refusing to believe that, she had
spent the afternoon begging the nurse to call and ask her husband
to bring her chiffon cocktail dress. Even now she was pacing
anxiously around the door. Eileen wondered if she would cause a
scuffle when the others went out.

Pitiful Mrs. Peters, Eileen's roommate and C.O. partner, also
seemed to be planning to go. She was wandering around tittering
in her usual confused way, but for a change she was wearing both
lipstick and high heels. Seeing her irritated Eileen even more
than the other women. She, herself, had made up her mind days
before that she wouldn't be going. Ordinarily C.O. patients weren't

permitted to attend entertainments, and it had pleased her to think there might be at least one advantage to constant observation. But tonight Joslin had fixed that. She had come over just before supper to say, with that taunting smile on her face, "Miss O'Hara, you'll be going to the dance with the others. We have extra help tonight; so I got Dr. Pierson to write the order."

Eileen had wanted to scream out at the woman. "Nurse, you call yourself! A fine nurse! Plaguing sick people to see how long it will take them to give way completely." But instead she just nodded indifferently—the way she'd been training herself to do— and replied in her most composed voice, "Yes, Mrs. Joslin. Thank you."

Since supper, however, Eileen had decided this dance business might be partly her own fault. Holliday had stomped through the hall that afternoon and stopped in the living room to speak to her, probably just to be friendly, just because he happened to see her, but maybe to remind her that he had her trapped and would return one day to take advantage of it.

"Hello, Eileen, how are you?"

"All right."

"Going to the dance tonight?"

"I guess not. I'm on C.O., you know."

"Oh yeah. I forgot that.... How long you been here, Eileen?"

"Six weeks."

"Would you like to go to the dance?"

"No."

"Well, I'll be seeing you."

So he'd ambled away, apparently dismissing the dance. But probably he'd gone straight to the nursing office and changed the order. Joslin had just been trying to sound important when she said *she* had had Pierson do it.

"All right, ladies, let's try to be quick about this," Joslin was saying now. "Go out the door as I call your name, and wait with the nurses there until we have everybody checked." Cautiously, still standing half in front of it, she unlocked the corridor door. "Miss O'Hara, you go first with Miss Moore."

❨ 3

On one wall there was a gaudy mural of a Paris street scene. Along the other three, strings of crepe-paper flowers were draped around the tops of the yellow pillars with streamers of green and yellow crepe paper hanging down. The six-man band was installed under one half of the mural, and under the other half were four stiff cane-bottomed chairs. One of these was occupied by the mammoth, forbidding personage of Miss Ethel Bell, director of women's physiotherapy. Her wholesome, ill-tempered face scowled dutifully at the men and women crowded against the walls of the room.

The dance floor was still empty. The musicians sat idle in their chairs, fingering the white carnations in the lapels of their shiny jackets and peering curiously across the room at the Holly Springs inmates.

Dr. McLeod stood beside the door leading to the women's wing of the hospital. Dr. Pierson and Miss Tucker stood with her. But Dr. Ellen Collins, who was also on duty, had not yet arrived. Charlotte Darrell (Charlie), assistant head of women's gym, was in front of them, greeting the women as they entered.

Across the room, beside the door to the men's wing stood Dr. Holliday, surveying the crowd like a real estate broker evaluating a lot. He was almost glad now that Lloyd Wilson, administrative director of Holly Springs, was sick. Only at times like this did he have a chance to judge the full scope of his work. Beside him stood Dr. Richards and Dr. Steinman.

Jim Reilly, seated in the front row at the opposite end of the room, strained to see the sexy girl with wavy brown hair. She was talking excitedly to the fat girl beside her and shrugging her shoulders beneath her tight, black dress. Reilly kept tightening his tie and wiping his florid face with a white handkerchief. He knew that some guys—Isaacs, for instance—thought married men shouldn't have to come to these dances. But Reilly told himself it was therapy and good for him to get as much pleasure as possible out of things like that sexy doll. When the music started, he glanced at the doctors only once before walking over to her.

Eileen O'Hara sat against the side wall with two rows of women in front of her. She had decided the dance wasn't so bad after all. The C.O. nurse was still there, but otherwise, it seemed to Eileen, she had more privacy than usual. The room was jammed with people, but none of them knew her, few even saw her.

Beside her Maggie Evans sat stiffly, almost defiantly in her straight chair. She had brushed her red hair, but, as usual, wore no lipstick, and she had refused to change her socks and loafers for high heels. She was listening to Evie Barrow tell Alice Morrisson about all the men she'd "made out" with. Maggie didn't know much about Evie except that she talked a lot and loud and usually about herself. Maggie didn't care to know more than that, because she had decided Evie wasn't a nice girl—very sick, of course, to be carried off to Hall 1 like that—but Maggie couldn't even feel sorry for her, only surprised to see her at the dance, because usually Hall 1 patients weren't allowed.

Gazing out over the dance floor, she wished that someone would ask her to dance, but at the same time she knew she would refuse if they did. Way across the room in a hiding place comparable to her own she saw a boy with light brown hair falling across his forehead. He looked down most of the time. And Maggie wondered if he was as afraid to ask someone to dance as she was of being asked.

Once the music got under way, the conversation in front of her stopped. Poor fat dressed-up Alice Morrisson was also a wallflower, but Evie danced every time.

Sometimes she danced close, pressing her cheek against her partner's and encouraging him to hold her tight. Other times she just talked gaily about all the things she had done or almost done. Either way, she knew with blissful confidence that the fellow was captivated.

Jack Isaacs had not meant to spend much time with Evie. He'd only asked her out of curiosity, because of all the things he'd heard. He had even figured after one dance he might be able to put her off on Ben. Ben *had* come to the party, and though he was just sitting there, looking at the floor, it might be that with someone who could take the initiative. . . .

But before they finished one dance, the music stopped and refreshments were served. He couldn't just say good-by and leave her to stand in line for her own ice cream. But the thought of devoting the rest of the evening to her pained and angered him.

He listened curiously to what she had to say at first, wondering a little how she had managed to be a dancer and a model and an airline hostess all at once. For a moment he even imagined her plump curvaceous figure in leotards. But then guilt swept through him. He thought of Lucie at home, alone with the kids, worrying about the money and about the business and, above all, about whether he would ever get well. The afternoon before, he'd been afraid even to go for a ride in the car with her. The memory sickened him; he felt the terrifying dizziness sink over him. And still the little flirt talked, shaking her wavy brown hair, emphasizing every curve under her black dress, until the young doctor came. Jack knew him only as the crippled one on the women's side. He was not headed in their direction, and Jack would have expected little help from him anyway. The doctors rarely interrupted when two patients were conversing. But suddenly Evie called out to him. "Dr. Pierson! Dr. Pierson, I haven't talked to you all night!"

The doctor turned, startled, and stood there stiffly while she jabbered on. Jack picked up his ice cream dish and walked away. Philip Pierson watched him go and felt the same despair he had felt other times when he thought a girl was taking advantage of him. And the simple fact that he, as a doctor, had the upper hand was no reassurance at all.

"Dr. Pierson, I wish you'd dance with me."

His face turned red. His eyes dilated behind his horn-rimmed glasses. It seemed to him that his crippled leg had taken on new and gigantic proportions, that it was huge and hideous, the center of interest for all eyes in the assembly room. "I'm sorry, Miss Barrow," he said with determined coolness. "I'm sorry, but I never dance. Why don't you ask Miss Evans? I'm sure she'd like to, and a girl as shy as she probably doesn't get asked often."

Evie stood very still for a moment, her brown eyes swallowing him up, her fine pointed nostrils opening and closing. "Thank you very much, Dr. Pierson," she said. "But don't feel bad. I'm really not that hard up. I only asked you because I was sorry for you." She turned to stalk back to the table she had been sitting at with Jack Isaacs.

But, as the music started again, Dr. Holliday tapped her shoulder. "May I have this dance, Miss Barrow?"

He had actually wanted to go over and talk to young Pierson. Since he couldn't do that, this seemed the next best thing. The girl turned toward him eagerly, proud, he knew, for the other patients to see her dancing with the head of the hospital. He wondered what stories her confused and giddy mind would invent.

Jack Isaacs had made a fast retreat when he saw Dr. Holliday come to his rescue. The nausea and dizziness which accompanied his guilt still menaced him, and blindly he groped for a place to sit down. He held his face in his hands to ease the dizziness so that he wouldn't pass out. Gradually he came to himself again, and because covering his face seemed to help, he did not hurry to straighten up.

Suddenly he felt a timid hand on his shoulder, and a solemn, whispering voice asked, "Excuse me, but are you all right? Would you like me to get a nurse?"

Quickly then he sat up and looked about him. He was sitting on the side of the room where the women mostly sat. Beside him was a red-headed skeleton girl about Ben's age. But the voice that had spoken to him, the hand that had rested on his shoulder belonged to a small, dark girl sitting directly behind him.

"No. No, I'm all right," he said at last. "I just get dizzy spells."

"Yes. Well, I didn't know. I'm sorry if I bothered you." Her voice was low and serious, with a peculiar sort of British accent. Her thin face looked very, very tired, as if possibly she might be in pain. For a moment Jack thought of talking to her longer. He thought he would like to, that perhaps, even with his own weakness, he might have something that could help her.

But that was as far as it went. Apparently, as far as she was concerned, the conversation was ended. And at the same moment, Jack heard his name called from the opposite direction. It was Mickey Ellis, the young divorcee he'd danced part of the first dance with.

"Jack...." He had to stand up and walk past two rows of seats to meet her. "Jack, I hope I didn't interrupt you, but ... well, you know I'm leaving soon and I wanted to be sure you met a friend of mine." She stepped aside slightly to reveal a dark, buxom young woman with a pleasant smile, a woman Jack felt sure he had met before. "Jack, this is Carson Gaitors ... Carson, Jack Isaacs ...

Somehow I've always thought you two might have a lot in common."

Jack realized he must ask the woman to dance, but he wanted to wait for slower music. He wouldn't really mind dancing with her. She seemed a comfortable person, and Mickey had said she was already married. So there should be no problem similar to the one with the Evie girl. Still, he felt exhausted and hoped the next number would be slow and she would do all the talking.

Then, surprisingly, he was saved even from that. The next tune was "Good Night, Ladies."

"Heck," Jack said. "Carson, I was going to ask you to dance."

"Don't worry," she quipped. "I'll probably be around till the turn of the century. Unless you take off, I'll see you at the next one."

"Okay. That's a date . . . Good night."

As the band went into variations of its tune, the crowd slowly drifted to the doors at either side of the room. At last the music ended, and nurses and aides counted the patients as they filed out. The kitchen help began to gather up crumpled napkins and dirty ice cream dishes. The men in the band folded their instruments and took the carnations out of their lapels.

❨ 4

Carson Gaitors hurried back to the hall after the dance. She was disappointed about not having danced with Jack Isaacs. But at least they'd been formally introduced, and that was a beginning. She strode deliberately through the crowd of other patients now, and her broad, dark face still wore the self-assured smile that had been on it from the beginning of the evening.

All the women patients had to pass through the smoker of Atkins Hall on the way back to their various wards. Carson liked to sit there and talk to them as they went by. She liked them to see her light her own cigarettes. Since she had been on every ward in the hospital in the course of her three-year stay, she knew all the nurses. She talked to them through the crowd about their homes and their hobbies and their friends in the same familiar friendly way she talked to everyone. She could see the other patients were impressed, and she liked that. Tonight she had brought a paper napkin full of cakes back from the dance. She sat down in the big chair beside the couch and, instead of smoking, opened the napkin and began to eat. Besides the nurses, she called to various patients asking how they were, if they had had a good time, commenting on how pretty they looked or how much they had danced.

Actually, Carson knew few of the women well and only cared about them in terms of their liking her. Behind her easy, unaffected smile that was all important. And no matter how confident she was of their approval, there was always a longing for it inside her.

When they had all gone, she still sat there, finishing her cakes. And soon a few of the others came for a last cigarette before bed.

"Some diet they've got you on, Carson." Heath Webster laughed. "How much cake is prescribed for bedtime?"

At another time or, perhaps, said by someone else, that might have angered Carson, but Heath's gentle smile appeased her. Besides, it was obvious Heath was slipping again. She had not said how or why, but she had gained permission to stay home from the dance. Every day, it seemed to Carson, you could see the gray, numbing depression creep over the poor thing more and more.

Anyway, Carson did not really care about her weight. Eating was like everything else with her—like love, sex, money—something to be enjoyed to the hilt while life lasted. And her robustness had never been a detriment. Regardless of the results, she had caught herself five men. So she grinned now as she answered, "Please, Heath, stop picking on me. I'm very sensitive."

They laughed. Then the conversation turned to the dance. "I'd like to shake Maggie Evans," Mickey Ellis said. "She could be so pretty with her red hair and blue eyes. Yet if they get her to one of these things, she comes in the same old skirt, without a trace of lipstick."

"I don't think Maggie's too well lately," Bette Palin said. Bette was finishing her six-month term for alcoholism and would be going for good in another week. "Who was that girl sitting beside her?" she continued. "The little dark one?"

"Oh, she's new, I think. Somebody said she's on C.O. She sure looked down, didn't she?"

"What'd you expect? Hall 3 isn't my idea of heaven."

"Well, that Evie What's-Her-Name sure doesn't let it bother her," Carson broke in. "She. . . ."

"And she's on Hall 1 now. The one who put the chair through the window."

"Is that her? Well, she was having a ball. Danced every dance."

"If you ask me," Mickey said, looking up for a moment from the cigarette she was trying to light. "If you ask me, she's got the hots. Her partners'll probably need extra doses of saltpeter tonight."

Carson crumpled the paper napkin between her hands. "I think the kid's all right," she said, standing up. "Anybody who can have a good time or give a guy a charge with McLeod breathing down her neck deserves the distinguished service medal."

They all laughed hard.

"Ah, ah, Carson," Mickey said. "Mustn't talk that way. Think of how hurt McLeod would be. And her your doctor, too."

"Hell with McLeod. I'm going to bed. Soon Sullivan'll be down here to give you all hell for smoking after ten."

In her room, Carson unzipped her blue taffeta dress and threw it over the back of the chair. Then she ripped the spread back on the bed and pulled her red and white nightshirt from its hook in the closet. She stood still for a moment in her black lace slip and stocking feet, scowling at the annoying garment. Even now, after three years of Holly Springs purity, it bothered Carson not to sleep nude.

That reminded her of the conversation about the dance, about the girl with the "hots." It amused her a little to think of how little they knew and how much they talked, of what they would have said if they knew her story.

All of them knew she had been married and divorced and married. But none of them—not even Mickey—knew how many times or at what brief intervals. Possibly if she told them, they would simply give her the cold shoulder of disapproval. But more likely they wouldn't believe her. They would think she was either kidding or hallucinating. And accordingly they would either laugh or be unbearably kind. Because, after all, it did sound pretty incredible.

Her first marriage had lasted less than two years, and a year later she had married actor Larry Linden. Because of her mother's death two months earlier, the wedding had been a small home ceremony. But her father had liked Larry and had been generally pleased about the whole business.

In fact, he had been quite upset when she insisted upon suing for divorce three years later. So upset, indeed, that he had almost disinherited her. But, of course, he couldn't because her mother was dead and she was their only child. Poor Father. He never had had much will of his own as far as women were concerned. Besides, he had been getting old then and was hindered by painful arthritis and doctors who talked of "coronary complications." He had not hesitated to give his blessing eight months later, when, at the age of twenty-six, she decided to marry opera singer Joel Hansen.

Probably that had been the worst of all her mistakes. But unfortunately, Father, too, had been dead when, twenty-six months later, Joel divorced her on grounds of disloyalty. She had not contended the charges or even tried to get alimony in that case. Because, in truth, she *had* been and was *proud* of being disloyal to Joel. He had proved to be cold and calculating and selfish. He had wanted her when he wanted her and at no other time. He had sprayed his throat religiously six times daily, and that had been more important than anything else in his life. So Carson *had* gone elsewhere to find what she needed—to some places and people she remembered with shame now. But also, fortunately, even blissfully, she had found warm, fine Fred Weil, whom she had married as soon as her divorce from Joel came through.

A wine merchant, Fred had been big and lustful, apparently the answer to everything she had searched for and never found. He had made her feel a woman again. But he, too, had had his shortcomings. His lust had known neither satiety nor loyalty, so that in the end, Carson had gone right back to the people and the things she had married him to escape.

And it was then, when she was lost, lonely, sick, and afraid, that Jesse Gaitors had appeared on the scene. What he had seen in her, Carson still could not figure. But love or not, she had been in no position to turn down the security offered by a wealthy pencil manufacturer.

Bracing her elbows on the top of the bureau, Carson leaned over to study Jesse's cardboard-framed picture. He *was* very distinguished-looking with a thin, serious face and graying hair. She had to admit to herself that even after four years, she still felt a fondness for that face.

Whenever Jesse came to visit her, the other women gaped in solemn awe. And when he left, they said, "Carson how fortunate you are! How wonderful to have a husband who is so devoted. Such a fine face."

She liked that. It made her feel important and loved. Sometimes it even made her wonder why she wanted to end her life with Jesse, why she had asked him for the divorce. Still, she had. A new life separate from Jesse seemed absolutely imperative to her now. "A clean slate, a fresh beginning," she called it in talking to Dr. McLeod or even in reasoning with herself. Yet she knew inside that for a woman with her background that was anything but a fresh start.

Jesse was everything they said—good, devoted, understanding. He had certainly put up with more than any husband had to: Harris, Ira, Ken, Joe; the nights, the days, even the weeks when she had not gone home; the "reefers" she'd stupidly dropped on the floor of his car. And he had never been anything but kind and gentle, a little stern, perhaps, but always forgiving.

Still, all that must end. As in her other marriages, it seemed to Carson now that there was an important part of life she was missing, a certain thrill which the restrictions of marriage made impossible. Therefore, "fresh start," "a clean sweep." She folded the photograph and jammed it in the top bureau drawer.

"Mrs. Gaitors, it's eleven o'clock. Please turn your light out and go to bed. Supervisor'll be here soon."

That was Sullivan making her final rounds with the night nurse. Carson turned out the light. "Okay, okay," she barked. Then she threw the nightshirt over the taffeta dress on the chair and slipped into bed, black lace slip and all.

VII

"OH, DR. PIERSON, how wonderful to see you! Even after the dance last week I knew you couldn't let this terrible injustice go on forever." Evelyn Barrow lounged in the doorway of the Hall 1 day room and looked up at him suggestively. Her wavy, brown hair seemed much longer than the last time he had seen her, her heart-shaped face plumper. And, despite the regulation socks and sneakers, the fingernails bitten to the quick, she looked more seductive than ever. Her blouse fit snugly over her breasts, and the top button was missing so that a trace of black lace showed at the neck.

Philip Pierson swallowed hard before he spoke. In spite of his reason, this girl with her dark, ogling eyes had set the panic loose in him again. "Good morning, Miss Barrow," he said coolly, taking great care not to look at her. "Suppose we go down to the conference room? I think it's empty." He nodded to the student sitting beside the door. "I'm taking Miss Barrow." She smiled and nodded.

In the conference room it was worse. She realized she had his undivided attention and tried to take advantage of the situation. But there, at least, there was only her to see if he made a fool of himself. And no one, certainly no one of any importance, believed the things she said.

He lit her cigarette, and she sat back on the leather chair. Then pulling her skirt up slightly, she crossed her shapely legs. He opened his notebook and took out his pen, reminding himself again that there was no reason to be apprehensive.

She began immediately, talking fast and brightly, shaking her wavy mane back over her shoulders, pausing only to take deep dramatic drags on her cigarette. "Of course, Dr. Pierson.... You know, I hate to call you that. It seems so stiff, cold—especially when we know each other so well. Wouldn't you like it better if I called you Phil? Philip's your first name, isn't it? Somebody told me it was."

Pierson could feel his cheeks burning; he concentrated on the notebook. "It's customary, Miss Barrow," he said, "for a doctor to use his surname, no matter how well he knows a patient."

She took another drag on her cigarette. "Certainly you realize by now that this is all a hoax, that my mother brought me here because she's jealous. . . . You know she hasn't come in over a month. They even send my clothes to this horrible hospital laundry."

"I've talked to your mother several times, Miss Barrow, seen her twice. She's very concerned about you. I haven't let her visit because I thought it might upset you."

"I don't want to see her. But you needn't think she's so sweet and concerned; she's just pulling the wool over your eyes." She put out her cigarette, took another from the pack he had left on the desk, and leaned forward for him to light it.

"You know, another thing gets me about this place," she continued. "These damn C.O. nurses. Can't even get away from them in the john—you know, there's no doors on the booths down here—they stare at you like you might try to hang yourself with toilet paper. . . . I can't see why I'm on C.O. anyway. I never tried to kill myself. I'm not that stupid. I'd never make an ass of myself either by trying to run away like that girl the other day. Lois Greer. She's a dope anyway, a real nut. She belongs here as much as that crazy Purdy and that weird girl—I forget her name—who keeps screaming about her kids. Even if you are taken in by my mother, you should have sense enough to see I'm not like them."

"I'm afraid I don't have much to say about that, Miss Barrow. Dr. McLeod writes the orders for C.O. and hall transfers. She feels you need to stay here on C.O. for a while."

"She's a crazy prude, looks like a bag of flour, and has just about as much sense. I bet she hasn't done half the things in her life I've done in mine.

"I was an airline hostess, you know—piloted a plane to a crash landing once. Then I modeled and did nightclub work. But I gave that up to do ballet on Broadway. I'd be in Hollywood now if my mother hadn't gotten jealous over Rod. . . . Why don't you mail my letters to Rod? He's probably frantic by now."

"You study the ones I've sent back to you," Pierson said gently. He looked at her. Even someone with all this outward veneer had feelings underneath. He thought of Eileen O'Hara, of the humor with which she tried to hide the sadness in her eyes. He searched the brown eyes before him for a similar glint, but saw only rich velvet, bristling with excitement. "I think you'll understand if you read those letters," he added.

"Really, Dr. Pierson, I hope you haven't gotten the wrong idea," she said huskily, thick black lashes lowered to half-mast. "Rod's just a friend. Really. Nice, but not like you. None of your intellect or sensitivity. I know, you see. I'm not blind."

He tore his eyes away in alarm and concentrated on his notebook again.

"I think you're wonderful, Dr. Pierson. And I respect you for making me use your last name. I can see you hate the formality, too, but must be ethical. I understand, and I think you're even more wonderful for doing it."

He could feel his face redden again and he began gathering up cigarettes, matches, and pen with unsteady hands. "Thank you, Miss Barrow," he said shortly. "I appreciate your perceptiveness. Sorry, but I have another appointment." He stood up and moved deliberately toward the door.

"I understand," she said softly, standing up also and stepping close to him. "And I want you to know something, Dr. Pierson. You mean a great deal to me. In fact, I love you." She reached out to touch his hand, but he pulled it back quickly.

"M-Miss Barrow . . ." he began.

But she cut him short. "I love you. That's the real reason I'd never try to escape, even from this hell hole. I love you, and I want to be near you. I. . . ."

"Miss Barrow, I'm sure you'll think about this later and see your lack of judgment even more sharply than I." Somehow he had managed to get the door opened and was standing in the hall now looking at her through the doorway. "I'm sorry, I really must go now," he added. "Here comes Miss Falkenburg; she'll take you back to the day room."

(2

The business part of the staff conference was over—permissions granted and the order book for each hall approved. They had agreed on what patients could be moved forward, which ones needed closer supervision, and where a change of therapy might help.

Most of this was routine. But David Holliday was pleased and deeply interested in the report that Ben Womble seemed to have come out considerably as a result of his five electric shock treatments. Fred Richards, the boy's doctor, said he thought three more would be sufficient for the present. Martha McLeod agreed.

Ellen Collins suggested that it might be a good time to try insulin therapy on Maggie Evans again. "I think not, Ellen," Martha McLeod said. "I'm sure you haven't forgotten all the delayed coma reactions she had last time. And the results, limited as they were, didn't last. . . . No, I think we should stay with the tube-feeding approach. It relieves her of the anxiety produced by eating and it shows her that whether she eats or not, she will be nourished."

Then the younger doctors brought forward their problems. Dr. Pierson wanted to know if there wasn't something more you could do for a person like Miss Barrow before she lost all control as she had several weeks before. Dr. Barrett thought it a terrible waste, taking time to talk to senility cases, time which could be devoted to young people like Ben Womble and Mr. Farrell. Dr. Greenwood took up the eternal question of when it was time to take the struggle out of the patient's hands by giving him a boost with shock or insulin or one of the new drugs.

Each matter was bunted around and finally answered by Dr. McLeod. Her white face was quiet, expressionless, but there was impatience in her flat voice, irritation in her blue eyes. She explained painstakingly that it was sometimes better for a patient to go off the "deep end," always better for him to find his own solution if he could. But then she felt obliged to quote again her own rule: "Common sense is psychiatry's most important requirement. Remember that always—common sense and experience. There is nothing without them."

They listened and they nodded their heads. Dr. Holliday wondered how many of them were really taking this in; how many just trying to appear competent. Martha was right, of course. Her common-sense theory was the same as his. It had been largely responsible for putting them both where they were. Still, it ir-

ritated him to hear her droning voice set forth the principle. She
removed all life from the idea and made it, like everything else,
narrow and old-maidish. "Common sense" to her meant using
one's own judgment to apply the most useful rule at the right time.
She left no freedom in which to modify those rules or even, perhaps, to break them. Granted, if rigidity was her code, she must
uphold it, but why couldn't she smile as she talked?

Finally someone interrupted to ask how long Dr. McLeod
thought it would be before Holly Springs began trying such new
drugs as Serpasil and Thorazine.

"Some time," she replied. "I'm sure you realize by now that
Holly Springs is noted for its use of only tried and effective therapy.
To employ either of those drugs in the near future would be ex-
perimenting. And we do not experiment on patients at Holly
Springs."

David Holliday knew differently—that his request for both drugs
would probably be met in less than four months. But he did not
mention this, any more than he would have brought up the point
on which he and Phil Pierson agreed—that Eileen O'Hara should
be taken off C.O. An argument with Martha McLeod never got
you anywhere, and one before the whole staff could be demoraliz-
ing as well.

David Holliday liked Martha McLeod, admired and pitied her.
But it worried him to see how she wearied these young men.

It had been so different when they were young. They had both
come to Holly Springs the same year—she as a resident, he as an
intern. Because of that, perhaps, they had become close friends.
They had shared everything with each other first—good news, bad
news, discoveries, feelings, gripes about the hospital. Off duty
they had taken long walks in the woods. She had let her honey-
colored hair flow free and her solemn voice had often risen with
earnestness or even enthusiasm, punctuated by gay, though subdued, laughter.

Yes, Martha had meant a great deal to him then. She was probably the closest friend he had ever had. At one point Holliday
had even thought he was falling in love with her. He never kissed
her, but he considered it many times. It was with great relief that
he had finally convinced himself he could not ask her to marry
him. She was married already—to her work.

Still, their friendship had not flagged. Rather, it had grown, aided by their joint feelings of rebellion toward old Dr. Horace. And when David decided to marry Mary Laine, Martha had been the first one he told.

He had hoped then—and for some time afterward—that the friendship could continue after their marriage. Even, perhaps, that she and Mary Laine might find things in common that would draw them still closer. But Mary Laine's shy dignity had faded to a kind of introverted resentment, and Martha's natural tendencies toward lonely, inflexible propriety had made of her this prim pasty-faced tyrant.

Ellen Collins leaned over then to whisper something about a patient she felt he should see. "Millie Pratt . . . fifteen-year-old suicide . . . Hall 1."

"Yes, I've been meaning to . . . this week, I hope. . . . Saw her mother." He looked at Ellen's frizzled gray-black hair, then at the warm smile on her freckled face. Why couldn't she have a little of Martha's confidence?

As the conference dragged hopelessly on, his boredom gave way to exasperation. Finally he scribbled an excuse to Martha about an important phone call, then puffed stealthily across creaking floorboards to the doorway.

(3

From the conference room Holliday went directly to Hall 5 Men. He made it a point to see Dr. Jonathan Stoughton regularly. But for various reasons, nearly two weeks had elapsed since their last meeting. And consequently, Dr. Barrett's talk this morning of "waste" and senility had touched off a sense of guilt inside him.

Dr. Stoughton was one case to which the word "waste" could never apply. Holliday not only pitied the old man, but liked him, even found him stimulating. A little confused at times, perhaps even irrational. But always, a fascinating—if tragic—example of a brilliant mind crumbled to ruin.

As he walked down the corridor, he nodded at the sagging white faces peering from the chairs and doorways, at the same time remembering that there was no assurance that he himself would not come to this same end. Nothing ever troubled David

Holliday more than the image of himself, like Jonathan Stoughton, sitting here day after day, staring at the same crack in the wall. Because the lock on the conference room was broken, they sat in the smoker. During the first cigarette, Stoughton sat stiffly in a corner of the couch and watched the smoke spiral slowly upward with an absent expression on his sagging face. He nodded conversationally now and again. But never at the right time, never in response to any of Dr. Holliday's remarks about his children or the weather.

Then, suddenly, when Holliday asked him about his chess, he reached into the pocket of his starched white shirt and turned up his hearing aid. "Chess?" he asked. "Did you say chess, sir?"

"Yes, I did. How's your game coming?"

"Chess! I tell you, sir, I don't play chess any more. You couldn't pay me to play chess!" The old man's gray face turned scarlet, and a vein swelled thick and blue in his forehead.

"That so? I'm surprised. Thought you and Mr. Corry had a regular tournament going."

"Mr. Corry! I have nothing to do with Mr. Corry. He's a despicable person. If I weren't here in this prison, I'd sue him for slander! Called me a cheater, Dr. Holliday, a cheater and a snob. I will not even eat my food at the table with him any more."

"Certainly if he said that I don't blame you. I'm surprised at Mr. Corry. . . . Tell me, Doctor, any of your children come lately?"

"My children?" The old man's pale eyes became cloudy; his sad voice trembled with bewilderment. "Yes, I have three sons," he said softly. "Jonathan . . . Donald . . . Hinton." Slowly it came to him what they looked like. Three little blue-eyed, blond-haired boys in knickers. When he came home from the hospital, they rushed at him like wild Indians, tripping each other up, shouting about the day's accomplishments and injustices, sweaty and smudged from head to toe with soot or glue or flour. But suddenly the picture was shattered, and he remembered that it wasn't that way any more. His face went red again, the vein grew large.

"My children!" he exploded. "My children! I tell you, Dr. Holliday, I hope you have no children. They are selfish, hard, ungrateful. They are cruel! They have homes, all of them. Children and nice homes. But do they take me to their homes? No. They lock me in this prison. They come once a month and bring me oranges and cigarettes and new clothes. They call me 'Dear Dad.' But they don't care. They leave me here in this crazy house where I must eat slop and not have wine or music, where I can't even take a walk in the park without an officious attendant telling me to slow down."

Dr. Holliday waited for the storm to wear itself out. He looked deep into the lightning-white eyes, and watched with relief as the twisted face faded from purple to red to pale pink. Stoughton's use to the world was over. The brilliant surgeon was past. Yet when a man was isolated like this—cut off by his own mind, with nothing to look forward to except the death which even confused men must fear—was it really wasteful to try to help him?

Dr. Stoughton puffed on his cigarette and berated himself inwardly for his outburst. Not that he was ashamed for the doctor to see his temper. He liked Dr. Holliday. He couldn't agree with those who called him a "genius." The man was too young, too inexperienced. But Jonathan Stoughton liked him, respected him, trusted him as he trusted no one else now.

It was a relief to have poured out all these injustices. But Dr. Holliday was a busy man. Perhaps he did not like to linger in unpleasantness. Soon he would hurry off to another appointment, and it would be a long time before they could talk again of theories and other doctors and the things they had both seen accomplished in medicine. Stoughton struggled vaguely, urgently to bring forward some idea like that now.

But Dr. Holliday was already pushing his cigarettes into his pocket. "Well, nice talking to you, Dr. Stoughton, sir. Very nice. Sorry to draw it short, but my wife's expecting me for dinner." He laughed and stood up. "You must know how wives can be about that."

Dr. Stoughton smiled too. The quiet, professional smile that still came to him unconsciously when his mind eluded the crippling iron web of bitter loss, of hopelessness and injustice. For a moment his shriveled, thick-veined hand gripped Dr. Holliday's strong, smooth one. "Enjoyed it, Doctor," he said. "Please come again." Then slowly, as he watched his visitor lope off down the corridor, the old man's face lapsed back into its sagging grayness. He reached into his pocket to turn down his hearing aid and then wandered forlornly back to his room.

(4

Ben Womble was tired of everything that morning—tired of
the way Jack stood before the dresser fixing his tie, tired of boiled
eggs and hard rolls for breakfast, tired of seeing the doctor on
rounds. By the time they lined up for O.T., he felt ready to
explode.

"This is stupid," he said to Jack. "Aren't you sick of it?"

Jack looked at him hard before he spoke. And for some reason
his dark face seemed kind, which irritated Ben all the more. "Why
don't you come do some metal work with me?" Jack said. "I guess
that clay business would get on my nerves, too."

"No," Ben answered scowling. "That old man does metal work."

"Oh, he won't bother you. May not even be there. And if he is,
he'll have forgotten about the other day."

"He thinks he's my father. He thinks he can tell me what to
do! . . . My father is a big music man. He writes Broadway hits."

When they got to O.T., Jack suggested again that he come down
to the metal room. But Ben refused. He'd made up his mind he
wasn't going to do anything—not weave a basket or a pot holder
or piddle in clay or anything. And if anybody bothered him about
it, he'd let them have it.

He'd decided, too, that if that crazy old man came around
calling him "son" again, he'd swat him one right across his thin,
white face. That ought to show him. He had no right. Probably
doing it on purpose, because he knew this boy was mixed up already from the shock treatments.

Jack had told Ben if he didn't want any more treatments he
ought to ask his doctor to stop them. But Ben couldn't remember
who his doctor was. Jack had said it was Dr. Richards, but that
didn't help, because Ben couldn't remember which one Dr.
Richards was.

Ben stood around the center room for a few minutes and finally
sat down in one of the corner seats. He could see the student
nurses watching him as if he were a panther about to leap. And
that made him laugh out loud, because that was just how he felt.

At last one of them came over and asked him if he wouldn't
like to make something. But he didn't get mad at her as he had

planned. Instead, he giggled and said, "You're pretty. You know you'd be very pretty without that dress on."

Her face went white, and she straightened up very tall and stiff. "Mr. Womble," she said, "why don't you come down to the crafts room? I'd be glad to help you start a clay ash tray."

That made Ben angry again for a moment. "I'm sick of clay," he said. Then he smiled and added, "Why don't you take off your dress and we could go for a walk?"

Her face turned even paler, and she almost ran away.

Old Kemp came after that. Not quickly or directly, not as if the student had sent him, though obviously she had. Kemp just wandered around the main room for a few minutes, looking interested as the director ought to. Then he sat down beside Ben.

At first he didn't say anything except, "Hello, Ben." Yes, even Old Kemp knew better than to tell Ben to work at something. He just sat there for a while, saying nothing, and then slowly, sleepily began to tell his pointless stories.

Ben didn't listen. The stories reminded him of a friend of his father. And that, in turn, made him think of his father himself.

Ben thought about the opening night of that show. He couldn't remember the name of it any more, but it had been a great hit. At the big party afterward his father had been proud of him. He had taken him around to many, many people, saying, "This is my son, Ben.... Now this is a boy really knows music.... Not like me. Not these two-bit flash-in-the-pan spectaculars.... You ought to hear him play." Even now, sitting in O.T., Ben grimaced at that memory.

And with still more embarrassment and shame, he remembered the gruesome evening two days later when some fifty of those people actually *had* turned up to hear him play. He had gone through with it somehow—enough to please his father, but he didn't know how.

Father had not come to see him lately. Jack said it was because of the shock treatments, that they didn't like you to have many visitors when you were having shock. "But if he does come," Ben thought—and he could feel the anger surging inside him— "if he does come, I'll sing him those rock 'n roll songs Jack plays on the radio." Then he laughed out loud at the cruelty of the idea.

"What did you say?" Old Kemp asked stupidly.

"Nothing." Like everybody else, Kemp thought he was strange and pitied him. Maybe he was a little afraid of him, too. Ben hoped so. That gave him a sense of power, of uniqueness, and security.

Now he looked over at the large metal lamp beside the work table in the middle of the room. A fascinating lamp with shaded bulbs branching off at different angles. A group of patients was seated around the table, each with a large pad and a piece of charcoal. One of the instructors was helping them sketch the casement windows. She did it every day with different pupils, a slight change in subject matter. But always her, and always the big pads and the pieces of charcoal. The sight angered Ben. He stood up and started toward the lamp. He wanted to pick it up and beat the top of it—shade, light bulbs, and all—against the stone floor.

He knew that Kemp would be right on top of him, that they would have the orderlies cart him back to the hall and tie him down with wet sheets. But he didn't care—not until his hand touched the thick, cold stem of the lamp. He gripped it hard, and the muscles in his upper arm hardened to swing it. Then, out of nowhere, came the memory of his father. The intent, sensitive face, the kind but earnest voice: "Benjy, some day you will be a great man—the composer I have not become, a talented artist. You have a great gift, Benjy, and you must never forget that. You must use it."

Once more Ben felt that half-forgotten shiver of pride. His fingers fell reluctantly from the lamp.

But in the next instant his fear returned, warning him that he was being fooled, that such daydreaming was meaningless, even dangerous. And then, quickly, before he could weaken again, he swung the lamp up over his head and down, full force against the smooth, flat stones in the floor.

VIII

IT WAS early in the morning—8:30 or so. You never really knew the exact time out here in the Hall 1 courtyard—no clock like the one inside built into the wall of the day room. You could always ask a nurse. But then, what difference did it make? There was nothing to hurry to or even to wait for. Just the day's routine the same as yesterday's, the same as tomorrow's.

Millie Pratt knew it was early. Breakfast was over. The special showers for insulin patients were over. They were all washed and dressed and out here in the courtyard. But still it was early. Millie knew because they hadn't been to O.T. yet or even gym. She stretched her leg out, so that her tennis shoe reached one of the spots where the grass had been made to grow. It was wet with dew. At least, she thought it was dew, though it seemed strange there should be dew here, in this small, dead area walled in by brick buildings. The more she looked around, the more it reminded her of the prison in that poem they had had to read for English, the one about, "Each man kills the one he loves."

That was wrong, though. She had not killed Rex. She had tried to kill herself. Was it really herself she loved? Sometimes Millie thought that might be true. Like the time they had let her mother come. She ought to love her mother. All girls loved their mothers. Besides, Mother and Tom had given her everything. But that day Millie had been afraid, afraid her mother might take her home—back to New York, back to school, back to the big girl with Rex's ring on the chain around her neck.

Dr. Collins had told her her mother was coming "for a short visit." Millie knew now that she could have told Dr. Collins she didn't want to see her mother, but she didn't know it then. She worried all night, and then the next morning she tried to run away. If they didn't catch her, she'd figured, she would be free of her mother as well as the hospital. If they did catch her, they would take her back to the hall and tie her in a tub and tell her mother she was too sick to have visitors.

They caught her without the least trouble. She had forgotten about the C.O. nurse. And before she thought she had even stepped out of line, three students were clutching her.

Because of that Millie was still on C.O. Evie said she had been a fool to run when they were watching her. Evie was on C.O., too, because of something she had done somewhere else in the hospital, before they brought her to Hall 1. Evie hated C.O., and Millie always pretended to, too, when she was with her. Really, though, she almost liked the attention and knowing they cared enough about her to be specially careful. She was the youngest patient in the whole hospital, somebody said. And that made her feel important, precocious, like the baby boy at home. Most of the people here liked her, and all of them were sorry for her because she was so young, because of C.O., because of the insulin needles, and the way she had fainted a couple of times when the sugary orange juice didn't come soon enough.

The nurses got almost angry when that happened; they said she ought to tell somebody when she felt dizzy. She never did, though, because she hated to ask people for things—even the thick, sweet orange juice that cleared away her trembling dizziness. Besides, she actually liked the "insulin reactions." Not the fainting; it frightened her to feel her arms and legs go numb and tingly, to be sealed inside the silent vacuum, to see the world drop blearily away. But it was nice waking up to hear the anxious jabbering voices, to feel the gentle hands fingering her wrists, smoothing her temples, even to feel the needle in her arm vein and the handsome doctor saying, "You're going to be all right. Don't be afraid, Millie. It's going to be all right." She was almost happy, she thought, at times like that—relieved and safe and not alone, all open to the world.

That was sort of how it had been when she took the sleeping pills. She hadn't really meant to die then. Everybody thought she had—her mother and Dr. Collins and the nurses here; that was why she was on C.O. But every day she knew more clearly that she had really meant for somebody to find her and save her and be sorry. But she couldn't tell anybody else that, because she was ashamed. Besides, this way they would go on being sorry.

She looked across the grass-patched courtyard at Grace Hill grimly pacing her eternal trek from corner to corner. She wondered what Grace thought of her. Though she knew almost resentfully, that Grace thought of no one but herself, or the things she feared, or sometimes the silent world into which she escaped.

Mrs. Purdy was walking behind Grace now, preaching in her soft, martyr drone. She'll get it in a minute, Millie thought. Grace put up with something for just so long and then blew up. Just yesterday when the funny old lady was kneeling in front of the television, Grace had told her to "get the hell up. You'll make us feel like we're really crazy."

"Grace's in a nerval." Evie Barrow sat down on the steps beside Millie and puffed at the butt of her cigarette. "Told her to come sit with us. That way Purdy wouldn't bother her. But she wouldn't listen. Said she didn't like to be watched by the C.O. nurse. I think that's silly, don't you?"

"Yes."

"Still, I hate C.O. Don't you?"

"Yes."

"Pierson said they'd take me off soon. Did you ask Collins?"

"Yes."

"What'd she say?"

"I forget."

"Well, she doesn't think you're crazy, does she?"

"No."

"Hey, lookit, Millie. Here come the gym girls. Maybe they'll let you play badminton today."

(2

For Grace Hill the morning had already been interminable. She knew it was early yet, because the gym girls had just come, but it seemed to her she had been pacing the brick-walled court-yard for days. Evie Barrow had asked her to come sit with her and Millie. But Evie was a crazy kid, and it made Grace angry to hear her talk. Raising all that hell about how it was really her mother who was crazy and had tricked the doctors. Always laughing and telling dirty jokes that weren't even funny and bragging about how Dr. Pierson tried to seduce her in her conferences. Dr. Pierson who couldn't even look at you when he made rounds!

Besides, if she sat with them, it would be right under the C.O.'s nose, and she'd rather have anything than that—even crazy old Purdy with her kneeling and her Hail Marys and the rosary she had made of dried clover. Grace didn't think she could take that much longer, though, and as the nurses called the roll for gym, as they lined up before the door leading to the open hospital grounds, she became more determined to carry out her plan of the night before. Of course, she'd never get away, even though there weren't many nurses today, and they might be afraid to leave the C.O.'s. Only Falkenburg could match her running. But if they did catch her, it would still be all right. They'd stick her in the tubs for a while and put her back on C.O. But even that would be better than one more day as eventless as all the others.

The door was unlocked, and they filed out slowly, forlornly onto the vast, tree-happy lawn of the hospital. "When you get to Hall 3," Evie told Millie, "you have gym out here. See the shuffleboard and the croquet?"

"Yes . . . Yes." But Millie scarcely looked up. She did not like this beautiful place. The air smelled different here than in the courtyard—fresher, sweeter, freer—and that frightened Millie. It seemed wrong, threatening to see the world stretch out so wide in all directions without iron bars or even a fence to stop it.

Gladys Purdy dallied at the end of the line. She did not want to reach their destination; it terrified her to think what it might be. They seemed to walk here nearly every day. It was lovelier than any place she had been in years, since she was a little girl and she and Brother played hookey together in Central Park. No one told her why they walked here now, but she knew.

Every day so far they had taken her to the building that looked like a church, the dark building with the high arched roof where they made her play ping-pong. But one day—they thought they were fooling her, but she knew—they would go around a different bend in the path and end up at the cross where they meant to crucify her. That was why she walked so slowly and looked carefully all around and kept moving her fingers along her clover chain rosary. She did not intend to be crucified; she meant to fight with all her strength. But if, after all, they did nail her to the cross, she would at least have said her prayers.

"Come now, Mrs. Purdy. Walk a little faster. You're holding up the whole group." The giant guard or nurse or whatever she was took hold of her elbow and tried to pull her along. Mrs. Purdy did not struggle, but moved as slowly as possible.

Then suddenly the hand no longer gripped her elbow. In fact, the guard was not even beside her any more. She could not understand. It scared her. She looked up to see if the sky had turned dark; she knelt down to ask the Blessed Mary's protection. Then, with a flood of relief, she realized that the big guard was running, running, running with three others, way off in front of the line. Down, down the hill they ran, around in a half circle to the front of the hospital and the long gravel drive up from the main gate.

Anita Falkenburg had never seen a patient move so quickly and still avoid the tall fence concealed by the shrubbery. There was a stabbing pain in her side, and her head throbbed with weariness. She should have foreseen this. She should have kept a closer watch on the girl. Anita motioned to one of the students to go inside for help.

The student, Alice Rothgeb, was terrified. You were supposed to expect this working on a disturbed ward. Tucker had stressed that point in their Practical Training classes. "Be alert. Never take anything for granted. Maintain your self-confidence." But it was very different—knowing all that and doing it. Alice's legs ached, and she was out of breath. Her cap had blown off somewhere.

Suppose they caught the girl? What would they do? Falkenburg was there, but what could she do? "Even in cases of violence, remember you are dealing with a sick person; be careful not to injure her." But Mrs. Hill was bigger than any of them. How could they stop her without a struggle without hurting themselves as well as her? Falkenburg was gesturing wildly now; something about the main building. Alice realized with relief that she wanted her to get the supervisor.

When she had almost reached the building, she looked back and saw one of the students fall down. But the other one was still running after Falkenburg who had caught up with Hill and was struggling with her. Alice dashed up the steps, but was pushed aside at the doorway by Tucker and two attendants coming out. She was confused and out of breath. She stepped into the supervisor's office and collapsed in a chair.

Dr. Holliday was in there. He was standing calmly in front of the window with his back to the door. Probably this was nothing to him. Probably he'd seen it so many times that it no longer mattered—not the struggle or the nurses or even the patient.

❰ 3

Holliday's face was stone serious as he watched the struggle taking place outside. What could he do? Ethics said, "Nothing. Hands off." And any reputable doctor had to observe ethics. Still, standing there at his window he felt useless, weak, trapped, just as he had when he was a boy back home and many times since. Trapped? Perhaps that wasn't the right word. Never—not back in Millboro or in college or med school or even here at Holly Springs —had he been in a situation where there was no out. Sometimes it had been hard to find; sometimes he'd had to close his eyes and run through it blind. Maybe it was that that made him feel weak; the squeezed eyes, the running.

The straining blue and white knot reached the bottom of the hill. Squinting at it, he was reminded—as if seeing something he had already seen in a dream—of the first time he had ever experienced this sensation of helplessness. He had been just a little boy then. A plump first-grader with light brown hair and freckles. He had had to wear glasses and a clean ironed shirt every day, instead of a striped jersey like the other boys. He always had an apple to eat at recess; never a cold sweet potato or fried corn bread and buttermilk.

The first week he was lonesome at school. But then he made a friend. A blond boy, tall for his age, pale and skinny, with faded jeans and frayed tennis shoes. He said "ain't" and "I be" instead of "I am." David took him home one afternoon to see his father's big glass aquarium of tropical fish. They sat there for a long time peering through the glass at the darting bright colors and whispering to each other. And when he left, they agreed he must come back the next morning to see the fishes fed.

That evening, though, before David went to bed, his mother spoke to him with sternness in her gentle voice. "David," she said, "that little boy you had here this afternoon may be very nice, but he is not the type of friend I want you to have. He must not come to this house again." And next morning when the doorbell rang, that same voice said, "I'm sorry, but David can't play today." From his perch at the top of the stairs, David had seen the faded blue pants tremble, and on Monday when he did not ask the boy to go home with him, he saw the hurt, questioning silence on the thin face.

The nurses had caught up with her now. Holliday could see from the contortions of the blue and white uniforms that they were struggling to subdue their victim. He wondered who the poor thing was. A youngster, no doubt. Even fear couldn't drive an older woman that fast. He wondered, too, what the girl's reason for running was. Fear? Rebellion? Something more complex than either of those?

People who knew him regarded him as a rock, steady and firm, unmoved by things like fear and anger. But David Holliday could have told them that running away was good in a sense, because it outsped stagnation. But also, that no matter how fast you ran or how far, you could never get away completely.

They seemed to have mastered the girl now. He still couldn't see her, but the movements of the nurses had become strong and deliberate, no longer frantic.

Yes, he had run away to prep school, to college, to med school, and finally to Holly Springs. He had quietly left them all behind— his mother, his father, and the all the rest of Millboro. The shrieking perfumed ladies in big hats. The dead-faced men who had called him "the spittin' image of your father." Even the dark-haired girl named Betsy who had looked at him so shyly, so sadly at church. He'd been supposed to fall in love with her.

But he'd run away instead to the great sophisticated North—to New York where they drank martinis instead of mint juleps and went to the theater instead of to church. But here, also, there were the ladies who cooed at children and the affable, insensitive men. Here, too, were authoritarian fathers like his own—perhaps the Womble boy's was one of them, soft-spoken and easy as he seemed. And here, too, were gentle, unyielding women. What else, for instance, was Martha McLeod? Was he standing here now motionless, irresolute because of Martha? Of course not. Martha was his subordinate. He could invalidate any order she ever wrote.

Yet, now as he watched the nurses move slowly up the hill with the subdued patient, Holliday thought again of that helpless feeling he had had long ago.

(4

Eileen O'Hara was at hydrotherapy when the runaway girl streaked past. She was standing beside an open window, and the girl's tennis shoes crunched in the gravel outside. Eileen glanced out just in time to glimpse her brown hair flying as she turned down the hill with the nurses straining in pursuit. A startling sight —even if you could grasp the situation. Any speed was startling at Holly Springs where everything moved so slowly, cautiously, with such fatiguing control.

It was pleasant beside the window. The morning air was fresh against her face, cool after the steaming shower and massage rooms. Eileen sat down there to wait for the others. As usual, they'd taken the C.O. patients first. Her eyes followed the fleeing girl and her pursuers, but they went over the hill, beyond her range of vision. Eileen wondered how long the girl would be able to hold them off. Then she felt sorry for the nurses. The students, eager, frightened colts, would have fun telling about this in the dorm, but the charge, poor thing, must already be condemning herself, recalling all the minor precautions she had not taken. Eileen smiled. She need not worry about those things now.

The other women straggled in one by one from the dressing room, and the nurse checked her list. A few talked softly together. But mostly they relaxed in the soft chairs and leafed through the ragged magazines. Their faces were flushed and scrubbed looking, their motions slow and easy, like vacationers' at a seaside resort.

Eileen had to admit now that there was some sense in all this. She had never quite been able to think of hydrotherapy as anything but a kind of voodoo. How could showers and backrubs restore the mind? During her first days at Holly Springs it had embarrassed her to stand nude before the other women wrapped in sheets, waiting to have the hoses play water over their bodies.

But now such disbelief seemed stupid. Even if the warm, tingling easiness was only temporary, perhaps that brief respite was just what some people needed to renew their fighting strength. Strange, the complacent routine in a place where everyone was struggling. Aside from the chase outside this morning, the only violence Eileen had witnessed at Holly Springs was the time the Barrow girl went on the rampage.

She stood up again and leaned closer to the window. The straining cluster of nurses had moved back into view. She shouldn't look like this. Still, there was so little to see here. She would not speak of it, just save it to think on later. But that in itself was despicable. She stepped back quickly, head bowed, right hand furtively tracing the outline of a cross. "Holy Mary, have mercy on me in my transgression," she murmured. "Help me to earn forgiveness." Wretched to stare like that at the poor girl! Curious as an old gossip. She, for whom personal privacy was almost sacred, had she lost all respect for others?

That's one thing about the Irish, she thought. They respect the individual. She could still hear her father's brothers, for instance—big clumsy dairy farmers—poking fun at John O'Flynn, the tight-fisted owner of the general store. But when John's boy killed one of his drinking cronies, they all turned up with the same quiet kindness they themselves would have wanted.

They had laughed at her father, too, for being a foolish dreamer. But they had never, as far as she knew, questioned him about those dreams. No more than anyone—even her two sisters or her domineering mother—had ever demanded her reasons for leaving Cork, for training in England, and then coming to the United States.

It was a long time since all that—since, holding her father's hand, she had looked up at the gray hills; since she had wondered at the contentment of the dead-faced sheep; since she had first felt cramped in their white-washed cottage. It seemed good and sweet and wholesome, looking back. She had to think deliberately of her mother, of her father's tired face, of the ugly little privy to remember the bitterness. She might go back one day, just for a visit. She ought to; she owed it to her mother.

Outside, the struggle had ended. The starched blue and white figures were laboring toward the main building and out of sight again. Poor girl. Eileen could not tear her eyes away. She could not forget the willowy brown-haired creature running past. She wondered what was wrong with the girl.

"Let's stand by the door, Miss O'Hara. We're almost ready."

"All right." But Eileen didn't move. She stared after the last white apron on the lawn and then at the stark blue sky divided into diamonds by the window's grillwork.

"Please, Miss O'Hara. You're holding up the group."

She turned abruptly, but her mind would not relinquish the pittances of sky. Poor girl, you'll see now there's no escape, least of all from yourself.

"Miss O'Hara! Please...."

❰ 5

On Atkins Hall, Carson Gaitors saw it all from the window of her room. She had jumped up when Mickey Ellis yelled about a "big commotion out front," because something like that was always a relief. You could gossip about it the rest of the day. Carson wondered momentarily who the girl was they were chasing. But then she recognized Falkenburg's towering figure and realized it was someone from Hall 1. Probably a new patient she didn't even know.

She remembered the day—it seemed years ago now—she had tried to escape. She had been much smarter about it than this girl. She'd been on Hall 4, so that she wasn't being watched. Besides, she'd thought about it for days, planned it carefully. But not quite carefully enough, because they caught her anyway. It had been in the spring like this, warm enough to sit outside. She saw they were shorthanded that afternoon. So when they went out, she carried her knitting bag with a pair of pumps inside and the change she'd been saving from her visits with Jesse in town. And when they all seemed settled and unconcerned, she simply walked away.

They didn't catch up with her until she was already off the hospital grounds. And when they did, she didn't have sense enough to go back with them quietly. She staged a riot there on the main street of Perthville and ended doing a four-month stint back on Hall 1. It had taken two years to work back up to her present status. But it seemed worth it now. Otherwise she would never have talked to Dr. Holliday, never have learned the truth in his words: "Live for yourself. Life's main purpose is happiness."

Of course, she and Holliday disagreed. He thought four divorces was enough for any woman and that she should go back to Jesse whether she loved him or not, if for no better reason than that Jesse loved her and wanted to help. Holliday said it was obvious she'd been seeking something in her numerous marriages, something she had not found and probably never would find. "You might as well face that," he told her again nearly every time they talked. "Sometimes it's necessary to compromise to have any happiness at all.... You might learn to love Jesse."

But she could not do that. She liked Holliday. He was a human being with human weaknesses he didn't try to cover up, with humor and common sense; no dried up, theory-packed psychiatrist like McLeod. She valued his opinion and got a kick out of his jokes. But she could not think of him as a master mind who knew all the answers.

For Carson, life was vital, precious. It had no room for compromise. She knew, of course, that that was why they kept her at Holly Springs with only weekend passes or occasionally four days, and always under Jesse's jurisdiction. They thought that one day she would see the light or at least accept compromise as the prerequisite of freedom. They did not understand her loathing for anything so uninteresting as marriage without desire.

When the floundering group out front disappeared, she went back to her magazine on the bed. Dragging the poor devil back to the tubs, she thought, back to the tubs and C.O. The hall was quiet again. Mickey had gone back to her crossword puzzle; most of the others were at O.T.

She really should be at O.T., too. But she wanted to be on the hall to grab Holliday, or even McLeod, in case one of them walked through. She wanted to know if Jesse had called. When he brought her back Sunday night, he had promised he would. Now it was Tuesday, and she wanted to know.

Over the weekend she had asked Jesse if he could get her a job in New York, say as receptionist for his stepbrother's talent agency. The doctors might let her do that, commuting from the hospital daily. Jesse thought it was a great idea. He had squeezed her hand and smiled, running his hand fondly over her ring finger. "That sounds wonderful, darling," he had said with just a trace of the usual caution in his voice. "Makes me so happy to see you working things out."

Jesse knew she wanted a divorce, but because of what the doctors told him, he thought it was just a phase that would pass with time and treatment. So, he had been all enthusiasm with only one reservation: that they wait until he talked to Dr. Holliday. "Just

to be sure. This has been too long a fight to take chances now."
Carson tried to go on with her reading, but she couldn't concentrate. She had to listen for footsteps in the hall. It seemed so
important for them to agree to her plan. Perhaps she was simply
seeking something new. She had been confident for some time that
she didn't want to go back to Jesse or accept any life which involved that. Still, there had to be something else better, vital, exciting. She might find it in New York.

She heard footsteps in the hall then, and impulsively she jumped
to her feet. She tried to judge who it was through the crack in the
door. But she couldn't. She had to go out, pretending to look at the
hall clock, to see. But it was only Pierson. He said good morning,
and they exchanged some innocuous remarks about the commotion
on the lawn. And she ended up back on the bed, annoyed at herself
for not recognizing Pierson's limp.

❪ 6

Philip Pierson wondered how she would be this morning—
antagonistic or seductive. He would cope with her, of course; he
always did. But he never knew whether he would go away feeling
master of the situation, or whether he would have to stand up
abruptly and sneak out, like a little boy caught with wet pants.
He must keep cool, efficient. "Miss Barrow, how have you been?
Is there anything particular you want to discuss today?" And then
if all else failed, if he found himself incapable of deterring her
lewd innuendoes, of shifting the conversation to less dangerous
areas, he could always tell her he had another appointment. But
he must do it authoritatively.

He had to pass through Atkins Hall on his way to Hall 1. Halfway down it he saw Mrs. Gaitors come out of a room to look at
the big clock. She seemed to stop there deliberately, peering at
him, and so he slowed down, trying to adapt his pace more to his
dragging leg instead of the good one. Ridiculous, though. Probably
she wasn't even looking in his direction. He must stop yielding to
such irrational anxieties. After all, he liked Mrs. Gaitors. Despite
what he knew of her history, she was one of a very few women
who did not oppress him with a combination of hatred and fear.
There seemed such a wholesomeness about her hearty humor and

her gruff, candid easiness. A conversation with her might even be helpful. He quickened his pace again and resolved to speak. Just a fleeting friendly remark. But he would speak first.

"Good morning, Mrs. Gaitors."

"Good morning. Glad to see someone's still calm and collected."

"Oh?" He blushed. He didn't know what she was talking about, but he feared the worst.

"Yes. When I looked out my window a little while ago, looked like the whole damn staff was trying to retrieve one poor girl."

"Oh. I didn't see it." He kept his face blank, but inside he wondered in panic if it had been Evie Barrow. That would be the final blow to his confidence.

"Student nurse told me it was somebody named Hill, some young girl who's taking shock."

"Oh yes. Too bad." Relief flooded through him. "Well, good morning, Mrs. Gaitors."

On his way down the other corridor he noticed that the fat, red-headed attendant, Sullivan, was in the nursing office. She reminded him of the woman who had stayed with him the year his mother and dad were in Europe. She'd had black hair instead of red and wore neat gingham dresses instead of white. But there'd been the same laughter in her eyes, the same comforting, motherly look about her bulging figure, her blunt sepia-blotched hands—a sharp contrast to his own aristocratic mother. "Mrs. O'Shea, the housekeeper," his parents spoke of her to guests. But while they were away, she had taught him to call her "Nannie," and he had kept it up until he was twelve and she left to "go back to the old country."

It gave him a start on his way out to come upon Mrs. Ellis in the smoker. "Good morning, Dr. Pierson," she said. Her voice was sweet and cool, crisp but unconcerned. She was doing a crossword puzzle.

"Good morning, Mrs. Ellis," he said, jamming his key into the lock so hastily that it stuck crooked. "How's the puzzle?" He struggled with the key.

She was like Miss Barrow in a way—though more sophisticated. He could feel her flinty eyes probing him. "Would you like me to get Mrs. Sullivan?"

Yes, sorry for him; a kind deed. Pierson straightened up abruptly.

"What? Oh, no. No thanks. Think I've just about got it." And miraculously the key turned free. "Well, good-by," he said, smiling. He pulled the door quickly behind him. But outside he paused to straighten his tie and mop his forehead.

IX

BEN WOMBLE FELT exhausted—he had for two days —ever since they'd brought him back from Hall 1 and his eighteen-hour stint in the prolonged bath there. Maybe it was the water, or all the energy he'd exerted, or possibly something they were putting in his food. Anyway, he felt he could hardly move. He just lay there on his bed, as he had so many times before, and stared out through the doorway to the hall and the couch beyond. And just one thing surprised him. The fact that after all that had happened, after all he'd done and been through, nothing had changed. Not the hall, or the couch, or the doorway—not even the room, or Jack, or the radio. All were exactly the same as before.

Just one thing would be different, and that was good. His doctor—Dr. Richards, he said his name was—had come to see him and said he wouldn't have to have any more shock treatments. Ben felt relieved about that, but surprised, too, because that hadn't been his purpose in smashing the lamp.

Actually, Ben didn't know why he'd done what he did. In the last two days he'd tried and tried to think it out, but couldn't. Still, he did know one thing. After his day on Hall 1, he knew he was damn lucky they hadn't kept him there. He hadn't minded the canvas-covered tub so much—after all, he mostly just lay around anyway. But the other patients screaming in the tubs beside his, or shouting from the pack room, or just silent and weird-looking in the big day room, frightened him. Of course, many were just putting on an act as he was. But some of them really were that way. And they made Ben afraid that in time he, too, might really go "crazy."

Jack came in then to   mething from his bureau. "Hi, Ben," he said as he entered. But it was not just an ordinary, automatic greeting. It sounded as if it took great effort, as if Jack were a politician or trying to cover up something. He took a candy bar from a drawer and came over to Ben's bed with it. "Split it with me, Ben?"

Jack had been very kind ever since the lamp scene. He never interfered, but he was always suggesting that Ben might want to do this or that, and offering him things like this candy. Ben had decided he really liked Jack. If he could ever talk to anyone, he thought it would be him. Still, his only response to the candy offer now was a silent shaking of his head. That didn't seem to bother Jack, though. "Okay," he said. "I'm going down to the smoker, but if you'd like to play the radio, you're welcome to." Then, with the same sort of deliberate, carefree stride, he turned and went out the door again.

Ben watched him go with wide expressionless eyes. He'd been wondering about Jack lately. He seemed so normal, as well as any relative who came here to visit. Yet, he stayed here and did not protest as others did. In fact, he didn't even go off the grounds on visiting day, as Ben remembered he himself had sometimes done before shock. Jack had a pretty wife, and on the bureau was a picture of their two children. She came every visiting day and she was always smiling. But there was something sad about her, too— her eyes or the way she walked or something. Still, she was pretty, and she always kissed Jack as if she loved him very much.

Ben's father had told him Jack was an extremely successful fashion designer. Jack never talked about that, as if he were ashamed of it, or maybe he was just being modest. And that made him even harder to understand. Because Ben thought that if he had a wife and kids and something he could do successfully, he'd leave Holly Springs as quick as he could. Still Jack stayed. Maybe, pretty as she was, Jack didn't love his wife.... But no, he did. You could tell that by the way his face grew sad every time he looked at her picture.

Perhaps Jack had made his success dishonestly. In that case, he would be both ashamed and afraid of getting caught. Dishonest success did not seem so despicable to Ben, because he figured that if he himself ever made good at anything, it would have to be that way. Still, that might explain the shifty look in Jack's eyes and his act of exaggerated normalcy. That would explain, too, why the hospital didn't let him go. . . . Probably they knew all the things Jack didn't want anybody to know, and were observing his every action, his every word for proof.

Ben looked over at the glass-block night light and then up at the brass light fixture in the ceiling. His thoughts of Jack made it seem almost certain that there was a hospital-wide radio and camera system. He began to feel uneasy lying there—awkward and naked. Perhaps there was an x-ray machine, too, that looked into your head and recorded your thoughts. If so, they would know he was acting and that he hated his father.

Tired as he was, Ben felt an almost panicky necessity to get away from the watchers. Slowly, as casually as he could, he got up and went over to his bureau, where he took his box of writing paper and blue ballpoint pen out of the top drawer. Then he went down the hall to the bathroom.

There were sentries all along the way, of course—on the ceilings of both the corridor and the washroom. But inside the toilet booth Ben felt safe at last. He sat down and took out a sheet of paper. Then he poised his pen to write the same letter he had been writing over and over for months. . . . Because, whether he admitted it or not, to himself or to that Dr. Richards, he had made that scene with the lamp to hurt his father.

Quickly, but neatly, he began to write: "Dear Father, I miss you, and I am sorry I am not living up to what you expect of me. I am sorry about the lamp especially. I know you are good and have worked hard for me, and I am sorry. I will try to do better. I am sorry. Affectionately, Ben."

After that he addressed an envelope to "Benjamin J. Womble, Esq." and read the letter again. Then he crossed out the sentence about the lamp and added a postscript: "Father, I really do love you very much." And that made him feel better. Quickly, as always, he folded the letter and placed it inside the envelope. Only, this time Ben did not tear it up. Immediately, before he had a chance to lose his nerve, he pushed open the toilet booth door and carried his letter to the basket for outgoing mail.

❨ 2

Jack Isaacs looked determinedly into the big man's pleasant face. He always did that with doctors; he didn't want them to think he was afraid or had something to hide. And he was especially careful to do it with this doctor. He had talked to Holliday before and was well aware that the friendly smile, the genial easiness were merely a guise to take you off your guard.

After all, Jack knew psychiatrists and all their tricks. He knew all the different types: little Jews with shiny, black eyes and goatees who spoke in mysterious foreign accents of deep analysis and Freud and the subconscious; shy, cautious ones, fresh out of medical school, weighted down with the world's troubles; scholars who took notes the whole time and sent you away anxiously with a prescription for mild sleeping pills; the hearty businessman type, all confidence, who took over completely, stressing the importance of "horse sense" and telling you to "buck up, boy. Nothing serious. Just a matter of how you look at it."

Yes, he knew psychiatrists, had been studying them for nearly seven years, ever since he'd first decided the anxiety was too much to go alone, ever since he'd first hoped—vainly, he realized now—someone could help. And after all this time, here was still another—a fat, jovial Rotarian, who Lucie thought was "so fine, so brilliant."

This would, of course, be just one more futile venture, but Jack couldn't quite abandon the stubborn hope which persisted inside him. Not since he had seen Lucie's face, heard the promise in her voice, and even less now with Dr. Holliday actually sitting before him.

The man had many of the qualities of other doctors Jack had known. Indeed, he almost seemed a combination of them all. He had a cautious, unobtrusive sympathy, but also an unctuous confidence, a kind of unwillingness, almost a fear, to take things at face value. He had common sense, but even more, a suggestion of the quiet analytical sifting for answers common sense could not find.

Slowly, painlessly they worked through the preliminaries of the fashion business, O.T. and gym, Jack's three brothers and sisters, and how he had grown up in Brooklyn. Holliday seemed genuinely intrigued by a story so different from his own, "as he must, of course," Jack kept telling himself, "to draw me out." And he kept his arms braced casually against the sides of the chair; his legs ached with the tension.

Holliday shifted his weight from one elbow to the other, uncrossed and recrossed his gangling legs. "Saw your wife the other day, Isaacs," he said, coolly smoothing away the silence. "Sweet girl, lovely girl. Seems to love you very much." As he said that, the doctor was surprised by his own words. Because they were true, because there was no need to be gentle here, no need to make reality less painful. In fact, as he looked into the trapped, shadowy eyes, he could not help thinking how lucky this boy was, how much he had that he himself could never have.

He thought of the girl that day in his office—fragile looking, but with so much personality in her face, so much strength. Vibrant hands that gestured as she spoke. Mary Laine had never possessed such vitality. Even when she was young, she had been too much the pawn of her own fears, her own selfishness.

"She seemed to think you were discouraged, felt we weren't helping you. That right, Isaacs?"

"Yes, sir, I guess." He wanted desperately to look down at the floor then. Instead he interlaced his fingers more tightly, "Doctor, I've been to a lot of psychiatrists. I've had nearly every treatment there is, including deep analysis."

"And you don't think there's anything left to try? Here at Holly Springs, I mean?"

"Well, sir, I wonder."

Dr. Holliday studied the tense guarded face. He chose his words carefully. "Isaacs," he asked, "did you ever wonder if maybe this thing you're looking for, this 'help,' wouldn't have to come from you?"

There was no answer. His dark eyes seemed to wince.

"Did you ever think it might mean a compromise, a very difficult one that only you could make, where all the rest of us—your wife and me and Dr. Richards—could only encourage you?"

"Doctor, I've tried everything I know." His voice was hard, offended.

"But you're afraid. . . . What're you afraid of, Isaacs?"

That was infuriating. The slow friendliness had annoyed Jack from the start because it seemed a scheming way for the doctor to perform the essentials of his job and yet remain disentangled, offering no help. But these questions were too much! What did the slob think he'd come here for? Insinuating he wasn't trying! "What are you afraid of?" A question he'd answered a million times. He sat up straight and tightened the knot of his fingers. When he spoke, his words were measured steel.

"I think, sir, that if you were at all familiar with my case you would not have to ask that question."

"Perhaps not, Isaacs." The doctor's voice was unruffled; his expressionless eyes did not shift. "Perhaps not, but I'd like to hear again in your own words what you're afraid of."

"Well, leaving here, mostly. But, of course, that's only now. It's always been crowds, but also of being alone; claustrophobia in a little room like this, or something else out in the wide open street. More than those, there's this something vague. I can't put my finger on it, but it's always there. Like an atom bomb about to be dropped or the sky falling or knowing you're going to be squashed by a bus."

"But what is it really?" the easy voice persisted.

"I told you; I can't put my finger on it."

"I don't mean that. I mean the thing underneath, the thing you're really afraid of . . . in your heart."

Jack did not answer. His face went white, and in spite of himself, his eyes shifted to the floor.

"You know, Jack, there's nothing wrong with being a Jew. Even a Jew who doesn't go to the synagogue or eat kosher, even a Jew who's married a Gentile."

The white face shot up.

"People talk, of course; but people always talk. And you *are* different. Like I am, being a Southerner in the North. But I use that. I make a business of that.

"Besides, it doesn't matter what folks say or what they think . . . except, of course, the ones we love. . . . And, Jack, I don't think your wife . . . What's her name?"

"Lucie."

"Yeah. I don't think Lucie cares whether you're Jewish or not. I don't think it even enters her head."

The young man's eyes were cold stones again, focused determinedly on the doctor's face.

"What do you think, Isaacs?" Holliday asked.

"I think you're wasting your time. I don't think this has anything to do with what bothers me."

"Could be you're right." The doctor stood up and pushed his chair against the wall. "But we'll keep trying," he said. "I'll be back, and we'll try again." He followed Isaacs from the conference room and locked the door behind them. "Perhaps, though," he called after the rigid, retreating figure, "perhaps you'll think about what we discussed."

❨ 3

He was strangely quiet that morning. "Brooding," Carson Gaitors told herself. "Must have had a fight with that plump, pink wife of his." Anyway, he wasn't at all the Dr. Holliday she knew. His eyes were dull; his round face sagged. His hearty laughter, when it came, faded quickly. He even disregarded her tight sweater and either forgot or discarded his usual joke about how she'd be a national security hazard if she didn't lose weight or buy some new clothes before she left Holly Springs.

She knew, of course, why he had come and was glad he didn't waste time getting to the point. Still, the conference seemed a little strange, a little empty without their usual friendly bickering. Carson had come to look forward to that. It was such a relief to talk to a man instead of some giddy or dried-up woman. And not just a man, but a man who was not a threat, who provided companionship without desire.

So, as the session began, Carson felt disappointed. Perhaps she'd been wrong all along about there being a pleasurable as well as a professional basis for their relationship. Then it struck her suddenly that she might have underestimated the gravity of her New York project. Maybe they weren't going to let her do it.

She wants this very much, he thought, and she's afraid she won't get it. He studied the tracings of tension on her mature, well-painted face, and he wondered exactly what lay beneath them. Just anxiety, perhaps, but he had a feeling it was something more, something closer to trapped despair.

Not like the Isaacs boy's face, he mused, not just a smooth sheath. This face was more complicated. Probably that was one thing that attracted him to her. The fact that there, exposed unconsciously, were so many of all the same forces he knew to be struggling inside himself. The sadness and the longing and the hungry frustration were always there in the shadows of her dark eyes, even when she smiled or laughed her genuine, hearty laugh.

"Your husband called me the other day," he began. "Guess you already knew."

"Yes. But that doesn't mean much. He wouldn't brush his teeth if you didn't say it was all right."

"I gather you discussed this New York idea with him at some length. He seemed very enthusiastic."

"He was Sunday. But then McLeod hadn't got at him with her 'experience proves' and 'this is the most crucial phase.'"

Holliday laughed softly. "Might surprise you to hear that Dr. McLeod thinks it a very sound idea."

Carson laughed too. "That's one for the books! I thought Dr. McLeod was as good a scapegoat for you as that farmer drawl."

That struck him dumb for a moment. He knew she was joking, of course. Besides, he had never known anyone—not even Mary Laine—who seemed so much his perfect counterpart as Carson Gaitors. Her words should not have surprised him; rather, he should have expected them. Still, it was always jarring to realize parts of him were transparent, too. Made him wonder about other things—things he was more reluctant to have seen. "You think I drawl?" he asked smiling.

"No. But it's obvious you aren't from Maine like Dr. McLeod."

They both laughed.

"Well, as I was saying, you might like to know both Dr. Mc-Leod and I think it's a good plan, staying here and working in New York. A very realistic plan. We think you should try it."

Her face lit up—even the haunted eyes. She wanted to jump up and wave her arms, shout, and even kiss this ridiculous man. But instead, she joked. "I hope you sent a release to *The New York Times* so's people can get more flags for the national holiday."

He laughed halfheartedly, because he was suddenly aware again of the contrast between this young woman's audible eagerness and the silent terror the same news would have painted on the Isaacs boy's white face. "Dr. McLeod'll discuss the details with you," he said. "That's her realm. . . . But I wanted to talk a little about the whole idea . . . about some things you may not've considered."

"What?" She was still smiling, but there was impatience and distrust in her voice.

"Everybody knows why you want this . . . partly, anyhow—because you feel bored and trapped, maybe even desperate, like you won't ever get out."

"Well? Is that so strange? After three years behind bars?"

"No. I'm sure I'd feel the same. . . . Only maybe you have another reason too. Maybe you're going to look around, maybe you want to see something new. And that's not strange either . . . excepting you ought to be careful."

"Oh, cut it!" She laughed bawdily. "Don't you mean 'prudent' or 'chaste'? You should know me well enough to know I can take it straight. I don't have to be coddled like a damned virgin!"

He smiled again, but absently, as if he were trying to placate a child. He admired her frankness and her ability to speak openly when it must cause her a great deal of pain. "Yeah, I know," he said at last. "Only that isn't what I'm talking about. . . . I figure we know each other too well not to accept each other's opinions even if we can't agree. Still, this is a big step. Even if I wasn't a doctor, I'd feel obligated as . . . uh . . . uh . . . a friend."

"Thanks." Her face was serious again.

"I know one reason you want to do this is to look for something different, something better than what you've got. You'll see a lot in New York. A million worlds—some of them mighty tempting, especially from a distance and after such a long time. I only want to remind you again that Park Avenue's a pretty good world—even if you're bored—pretty easy and safe. And your husband's a pretty good man. Maybe you'll remember that, maybe you'll weigh it against the alternative when you think of making a change."

Later, when he had gone and she was back in the smoker, Carson could not forget the abruptness with which he ended the conference—puffing quickly to his feet, fumbling in his pocket for his keys, laughing too loudly. Nor could she forget his warning. She knew he had said the same thing many times before, but somehow now she felt uneasy, confused, dubious of her own intentions. Suppose she couldn't find what she wanted? Even worse, suppose she found what she thought was it and it wasn't? She didn't have much time now for another disappointment.

(4

Martha McLeod was annoyed when the aide told her Mrs. Gaitors was in with Dr. Holliday. "Thank you." She nodded and started abruptly down the corridor again.

Next time she saw him, she told herself, she'd simply ask David Holliday coolly, cuttingly, why he didn't take over the Gaitors case completely. She knew that was childish. He had every right to talk to Mrs. Gaitors, and he did have to make his patient interviews fit the rest of his busy schedule. Still, he might have told her. He might consider that she had obligations too. He might remember —with all his economy talk—that time was the most expensive commodity in psychiatry, that everybody couldn't go shuffling around spreading Southern charm.

At one time years ago, Martha could have told all that to David Holliday simply and quietly, without any fear of tension or hurt feelings. Probably they would even have discussed it at length, looking a little into themselves and coming up with an overly earnest, but practical solution. Not now, though. Too much had happened in the intervening years. Half-formulated theories had become inflexible doctrines. And the distance between Martha McLeod and David Holliday had both widened and deepened.

Among other things, Martha felt there were times when Southern charm didn't fit, when it was even dangerous. Now, for instance. She'd intended to tell Mrs. Gaitors about their decision herself— slowly, solemnly, to impress her properly with the gravity of this step. Instead, David Holliday was in there right now, undoing all her work, making it sound like a lark. Joking, laughing, letting her think she was completely free to make life the bawdy spree it had been before.

He was a brilliant man, David Holliday. Martha had seen it when he first came to the hospital, when he was still an intern with thin, brown hair and a stride close to a trot. She had seen it then and admired it so much that with a little more encouragement she might even have considered sacrificing her own ambition for his. And truthfully—though David Holliday's wisdom had become her competitor rather than her companion—Martha had to admit that his brilliance was even more apparent now than in the beginning. In fact, sometimes she was still amazed by the simplicity with which he solved the impossible, by observations he expressed with a wisdom verging on omniscience.

At the same time, Holliday was infuriating. He refused to get excited or observe regulations. He lacked reverence for the word, "experience." "Rules are made to be broken," he'd say. He received all the credit for things which he accomplished with such haphazard ease it seemed almost as if it were just luck, as if he just happened to be there at the right time. He abandoned theories for his own intuition. Most times he was right, but Martha could not help feeling it was wrong to take risks like that—especially with young doctors looking on.

She had intended returning to her office to transcribe some notes. But at the end of the corridor she went out the side door to the front lawn instead. It was a cool day for June. Almost like home, she thought. She tried to let the fresh, piney memory of the Maine woods clear her anger. But the best she could do was remember another morning like this one, only colder, with her father, on the weathered gray pier behind their house.

Her two brothers and her cousins were going off that day on a camping trip across the lake. But because she was a girl and only five years old, they had left her home. That was very unfair, because she could catch fish and make a fire and tie knots as well as any of them. It wasn't fair, and it made her furious. Her face was red, and she howled long bellowing sobs as loud as she could. She kicked the warped gray boards and shook her fist wildly after the disappearing rowboats. "Stop that, Martha! You're too big a girl to carry on so. You must learn to control your anger." The quiet sternness of her father's voice and the patience of his lined face came to her as clearly as from yesterday. She had obeyed that order.

She had mastered her anger as well as all other passion. Too well, perhaps, she reflected sadly now. Perhaps that was the reason for the dead boredom of her summers in the old house in Maine; for the spotless gingerbread stagnancy of her house here; for the emptiness which neither Tinker nor her hospital work could fill.

《 5

"A bakery worker," Jackie Harper thought, looking across the conference room desk at Dr. McLeod. "With an apron instead of that white coat, she'd make a perfect Danish pastry cook." Jackie couldn't help smiling at the thought. Especially when she imagined what the dumpy, poker-faced little woman must look like at home, huddled in a rocking chair with her gray cat and some knitting and maybe big, felt bedroom slippers.

That made Jackie laugh at herself too. She, the inveterate boozer, the hardened woman of the world who'd sworn to a thousand different men in just as many lurid little bars that when her time came she meant to die with a drink in her hand. She, Jackie Harper —I.W. to her old cronies—sitting here, sober as a judge, talking purity and temperance with a virtuous spinster psychiatrist.

She knew what was going on behind those still blue eyes. But she didn't care. Undoubtedly the woman thought her a stinking degenerate, whom she only talked to because it was her duty as a doctor and a Christian. Or perhaps, for the pasty face was gentle as well as pure, she pitied her as a poor, lost sheep she must help find the way. In fact, being a doctor, she might even consider this an interesting challenge.

To Jackie it didn't much matter—any more than moving up here to Hall 4 had mattered. The other patients thought that was great. They thought it heaven on earth to be allowed belts and jewelry, to have twenty cigarettes a day instead of ten, to run your own bath and take it in private without a nurse breathing down your neck. But to Jackie all those things were incidental. How she'd ever gotten into this mess she didn't know. She couldn't remember, but they must have shanghaied her some way. It seemed unbelievable she would have signed the six-months commitment paper of her own volition. Still, it was there—McLeod had showed her— her signature in hasty blue script, like on a check or a charge slip. It was there, and she couldn't get out of it. So she might as well settle down and make the most of an unpleasant situation. At best it could be only one more experience, an interlude of dull, wholesome living with no D.T.'s. At worst, it could be no more than six months of insatiable longing. Then, if she wanted, she could go right back to where she'd left off. In the meantime it seemed immaterial whether she had earrings or belts or even clothes.

"Tell me, Miss Harper, how do you like it up here on Hall 4? Have you noticed any change in the way you feel?"

"Oh, it's okay. Sure, I like it fine."

"I wonder about the other patients, if you've made any friends."

"Friends? Sure, I got friends." And that was true. She always found friends wherever she went—in delicatessens or bookstores, museums or bars. There were always people who laughed at her jokes and poured out their troubles to her, who seemed to like her and to want to sit and talk for a while. But that was all. It never went any further. She couldn't get close to them or let them close to her.

So it was here. Sure, she had friends, even people who looked up to her because of her external confidence. People like little Maggie Evans and Evie Barrow, like Alice Morrisson and Eileen O'Hara. Of them all, she had a feeling she could almost be friends with Eileen, perhaps because she, too, seemed apart from the rest.

But Eileen would never condescend to be her friend. Eileen guarded her solitude. She kept her distance. Besides, Eileen was delicate and fine. She read poetry and went to Mass. She might be polite and kind, but she would not be friends with a dirty drunk.

"Have you heard from any of your friends in New York?"

"No." How in hell could she? Even if you did call them friends, they were all probably too far gone to hold a pencil.

"What about your agent? Your publisher?"

"Oh, my agent sold a couple of my stories."

"Well, now, isn't that fine." There was a simpering smile on the white face. Looking at the young woman across from her, Martha McLeod considered the different solutions people sought for very similar problems. She, herself, at the age of thirty-four had probably been just as lonely as Miss Harper here. Yet she had dedicated herself passionately to her career, whereas this girl had just as passionately given herself up to alcohol. Because of her own success, Martha found it hard to pity or even understand such weakness. But at the same time, she hoped and would have felt it a great accomplishment to convey some of her own strength to a person like this. "Yes, that sounds very fine to me," she said again, now. "Doesn't it make you feel good?"

"Sure. Fine." Why did they have to make such a fuss about her writing? They were crappy stories; even her agent called them "pot boilers." But here people thought if you wrote anything you were Shakespeare's reincarnation. She wouldn't argue though; she'd go right along with them. She smiled when McLeod got up to leave, and made the old lady really beam by saying she'd heard a lot about her cat.

Then, when the doctor went away, she walked back to the smoker. Sure, she could take this. She knew now that she'd never find the things she always looked for—the friendship, the sense of belonging—not here or anywhere else. But she could manage till her time was up here, and then she could go back to living without them or numbing the clawing emptiness with the same anesthesia she had used before.

([6

"Sure, I saw him," Jack was saying. "He came, as you said. . . . Sure, he's all right. Remember, I saw him before. Like any other doctor. . . . And who knows? He might even help."

Lucie Isaacs watched her husband anxiously. His face looked tired and perplexed. She was acutely aware of the tic in his left cheek and of the way his eyes shifted restlessly under lowered lids. She would have liked to ask, "Darling, what troubles you so?" But she would not; she knew better.

She looked around vacantly at the other patients on the lawn with their visitors just enough to make Jack think she did not care, to keep him from seeing that his pain hurt her, too. It occurred to her in those few minutes that this lovely place might be a park or some kind of picnic area. Most of the people looked well enough and even happy. There were few faces as dejected as Jack's.

"I didn't see Dr. Holliday today," she said. "There was too long a line outside his office. When was it you talked to him?"

"This morning."

"Oh! . . . Did he say anything special? Now, please, Jack, I don't mean to interfere. If I ask questions I shouldn't ask, just tell me to shut up. Or, if you'd rather, lie; but don't feel guilty about it. What goes on between you and the doctors is strictly your business . . .

unless you want to t-talk, or ... or think I could help." She pressed one of his thin, limp hands.

"Oh, no, Lucie. That's okay." His lips tried to smile, but his eyes remained shielded. "I don't want secrets from you. It's just that we didn't discuss anything much today ... nothing you don't already know. There's always a lot of dead wood the first time with a doctor." He wondered if she could hear the caution in his voice. He wondered, too, how much his hooked nose and curly, black hair shamed her. Then, smiling determinedly, he forced himself to look into her eyes. "Maybe we'll get somewhere next time."

"I hope so, darling." Lucie wanted so much then to kiss him hard on the mouth, to pour out even a little of her aching, stored-up love. Yet, she must not. Above all else she must not do that. Because how could she tell? The doctors never mentioned it. And Jack, if he really did have any understanding of his trouble, kept it locked carefully inside. But it could be. Much as she loved him, much as he appeared to love her; it could be she was his problem. Certainly there had been no signs of this illness before their marriage. Maybe he didn't really love her. Yet, if that were even partially true, the doctors would have known and told her. She forced his eyes to look at her. "I know you'll get somewhere soon, Jack," she said. "I believe it and you must too. I love you and miss you so much."

"I try, Lucie, because I love you too. And I do have faith in Holliday." He was lying, of course. That was obvious—from the way he suddenly perked up and smiled, from the uncertainty of his veiled eyes. But then, anything she could see, Dr. Holliday must see more clearly. Perhaps he even knew what lay beneath the lies, behind the shifting eyes.... She couldn't see him today. She couldn't leave early without making Jack suspicious, but she'd call tomorrow.

How she dreaded going home to supper and baths and bedtime stories and the endless questions. And after that, after the children were asleep, she would be alone with the silence—the lonely, longing, doubting silence.... Yes, she'd have to see Holliday.

"Did you see Dr. Richards today?"

"No. Really, darling, I've never seen the main corridor so crowded."

"Oh, that's okay. He must've told me the truth after all. Kept

asking how I felt with shock. So I told him flatly I had no intention
of taking it again. Of course, he practically rolled on the floor telling me nobody was even considering it. But I didn't know; some
of these fellows lie through their teeth."

"But shock didn't help you."

"No."

There was a long silence. They were both remembering that
many other things besides shock had not helped. Lucie's face was
sad as she gazed out over the lawn again. A short distance away
some feeble old man was blasting his visitors. "I don't need you;
I don't want you! You or your gifts. Go away and stay away!" She
felt sorry for the young couple on the bench. But still worse, she
could not suppress the fear that some day she and Jack might come
to that. Her throat was so tight she could not have spoken if she
wanted to.

Jack glanced furtively at her wistful, vacant face and searched
for some harmless remark to draw her back. "How are things at
the store?" he asked. "Sales good last month?" But then he hated
himself more than ever. He was always telling himself he didn't
care about money. But if he didn't, why did the question come
to him?

He was a Jew all right—a kike. Even Papa, if he were still alive,
would have told him that.

"No, Papa, no," Mama would have scolded. "He is good boy.
He just lives in a different way from us."

"Because he marries a Gentile does not change him. He is still a
Jew. He should remember that."

"Yes, but he is good boy, Papa. Smartest of them all. Because
he lives different does not mean he is different inside. . . ." Yes,
Mama had defended him. But probably even her big heart would
find it hard to forgive the crassness that was so much a part of him
now. He had abandoned it all—the Talmud, the kosher, the synagogue. In the beginning he'd convinced himself he was doing it for
Lucie. But he realized now that was only an excuse, a lie to soothe
his own guilt. He was a greedy, conniving, money-loving kike.

"Oh, the store's fine." Lucie's eyes came back to him, and she
smiled her old I-love-you smile. "Really, darling, you mustn't
worry about that. You must just rest and get well." She reached
out again to touch his hand.

He was looking away—at the couple on the bench with old Dr. Stoughton—but her fingers sent a little ripple up his arm. That reminded him of the nights not really so long ago, when they had lain close together under the sheet with a breeze skimming across the room from the open window. He remembered the firm, warm nipples of her breasts pressed against his body, her eyes half closed when he looked at them in the darkness, her quick hushed breathing, and the sweet, almost wild desire that had swept over him, too big for one body to contain.

He wanted all that again so very much. Now. Today. Yet the very idea sickened him—greedy, blaspheming animal taking her warm, brown sweetness. Holliday's words came back: "... There's nothing wrong with being a Jew ... even a Jew who's married a Gentile."

But that only made him angry. How easy it was for that self-satisfied lummox to talk! He didn't know what it was to be Jewish. He had no memories of a home steeped in the Orthodox rituals of centuries. Probably his mother had been a Southern lady. Certainly not a dumpy little woman who spoke broken English.

Lucie talked about Peter then, and the funny little things he was beginning to say. But Jack couldn't listen. Suddenly the panic was upon him. He wanted to run; he wanted to dig a hole into the earth. He must escape, even if it meant into death, beneath the wheels of a train or with a rope around his neck. He put out a trembling hand to grip Lucie's arm. "Let's go in. I can't stay out here any longer."

❡ 7

So here they were. Young Pierson and Mary Laine and himself, all sitting around the living room, sipping from after-dinner coffee cups and trying to talk. David Holliday wondered now why he had ever thought it would be such a good idea or even hoped they could help the boy.

The evening was warm. A soft breeze puffed the curtains at the open windows, and there was an elusive scent of something like honeysuckle. Mamie's fried chicken and chocolate cake should have reminded the boy of home, should have made it easy for them to compare Kentucky and Alabama and, for a little while at least, to forget about this North foreign to them both.

But it was all wrong, and had been from the moment Mary Laine met them at the door in her blue lace dress. Instantly when he saw her, he remembered he had promised to drive into New York tonight to see Jack and Edith Beckwith. He had forgotten completely, and he realized guiltily, probably on purpose, because he had not wanted to go. She had looked forward to this evening all week. Besides, poor thing, it was true she rarely had a night with people she really enjoyed. Also, he had not forewarned her about bringing Pierson home, had thought it better to be spontaneous. So she had every right to be irritated. Still, even when he saw the lace dress, Holliday had hoped Mary Laine might exert her charm to master the situation.

But she had sat silent most of the evening, puckering her lips and taking tiny, impatient stabs at her needle point. When she did speak, it was in a tone that would have disconcerted the Queen of England.

With each attempt at conversation Holliday's annoyance grew. From uneasiness to irritation to exasperation to fury. What husband would put up with such behavior? More than that, how many wives would dare to be so blatantly unpleasant? He thought of his mother, a fine lady, but certainly no more cultured than Mary Laine. And the Isaacs girl. Despite her husband's fears, she felt no shame because of his Jewishness. She would have been kind to the "kikiest" of his friends just because she loved him. There was no excuse for Mary Laine's behavior.

Pierson smoked cigarettes and sipped coffee, but he sat on the edge of his chair and occasionally glanced from his hostess to Holliday as if about to depart. The older doctor wished that Lillian had not already returned to school.

They struggled on. "Is that cross-stitch, Mrs. Holliday?" Pierson asked pleasantly. He tried not to admit to himself that her open displeasure as much as the sewing reminded him of his mother. He wondered momentarily if she was equally as domineering or if this was just a defense.

"No," she replied haughtily. "This is needle point. Much more intricate than cross-stitch." Mary Laine realized she was being childish. Yet she could find no incentive to be otherwise.

"Oh, forgive me. I'm terribly ignorant about such things. I just recall my mother doing something on that order; she called it cross-stitch." Pierson smiled broadly, hopefully. But she held her eyes on her work and continued to pucker her lips silently in and out.

Pierson felt thoroughly stomped on. And yet, because Holliday, himself, seemed so determinedly content, he began to think about his hostess rather than his own hurt feelings. Surely all this could not be simply because of him. Yet, if she was like this a great deal, why had Holliday married her? Perhaps this was new—something that had developed long after their marriage. Still, Pierson thought, it could have a lot to do with Holliday's success as a doctor. Maybe he worked long and hard because he didn't want to come home to her. Or perhaps the reverse. Maybe Holliday, in his zeal for his work, had hurt her, so that she was simply lonely and bitter and not at all the domineering woman Pierson knew his own mother to be.

"So your mother did cross-stitch? She must've been a fine lady. My mother didn't have time for such. She mostly darned socks."

"She is a fine lady, sir."

"She's still living?"

Still working, Mary Laine watched her husband from the corners of her eyes. He was enjoying this so, this talk with a boy young enough to be his son. They had never had a son. So much trouble with Lillian. And then when they lost the second baby, the doctor had decided that was enough. David had always said it didn't matter. Yet, probably it did. Probably he had wanted a son all along.

"Yes, sir."

"In Kentucky?"

"Yes, sir. In the house my father built, where I grew up."

"Doesn't she get lonely?"

"Yes, sir, I guess. But she knows the people there, and she has the farm."

"Oh, your father was a farmer too? I was raised on a farm, you know."

"I guess you'd call him that. Only he mostly bred horses. That's what Mother does now." The more they talked, the more Pierson realized he would never have the opportunity, let alone the nerve to bring up the matter he wanted to discuss.

"Should think she'd miss you, her only boy. Should think she'd want you near."

"Yes, sir, she does." The young voice sounded hollow.

"Will you go back?"

"No, sir. Not to Kentucky." Pierson kept his eyes on the rug. His words came out bitten hard.

At that moment Mary Laine glanced at the mantel clock and began folding her work. Holliday's eyes bored into her with urgent orders not to go. She saw, but did not heed those orders. She was already furious, and this simpering talk of the "good old South" did not help. Besides, what good was she here? Probably they'd be glad to have her gone.

So she stood up silently and extended a plump, white hand to Pierson. "I hope you'll forgive me, Doctor," she said, "but I think I'll retire. I have a little headache, and I'm not accustomed to late hours."

Pierson stumbled quickly to his feet. "Oh, not at all, Mrs. Holliday. I was just noticing it was nearly nine and time for me to go."

"Nonsense," Holliday cut in. "We've just begun to talk. . . . Go on to bed though, if you have a headache, my dear."

Neither of them spoke for a few minutes after she left. Pierson saw clearly the meaning of her sudden departure. But he realized also that this might be his one chance to talk to Holliday.

The older doctor strained to hide his anger. This might be the opportunity he had longed for to help the boy. "Well, what'll you do if you don't go back home?" he asked at last. "Seems funny we haven't talked about that before. I never went home again either."

"Well, I'm not quite sure what I'll do. I prefer hospital work, I think, but where there is plenty of contact with the patients. Not where the paper work leaves only a minimum of time for psychotherapy. . . . Then, too, I've never tried private practice. Not that the money difference really matters to me, but there'd be more chance to set your own rules." He was silent for a moment, then looked down at his hands and cleared his throat. "Also, I sometimes wonder. . . ." He stopped to clear his throat once more.

"I have certain inhibitions, Dr. Holliday. Well, like everybody does," he laughed self-consciously. "But I sometimes wonder if my patients might not sense this. If, in short, I might not do better at another type of work."

Dr. Holliday studied the young man's carefully controlled face. For a moment he thought of the son he had wanted and never had. Then, instead, he saw himself thirty years earlier. He had never been able to speak to his father as Phil Pierson was speaking to him now. His father had been a tyrant of the first order, a man so convinced of his own rightness that he could listen for hours to differing opinions without even hearing them. He had mildly berated David for "running off to the North," but after all, it had not bothered him much. He had four other sons, a wife, and a daughter as convinced as he that theirs was the only life.

Probably, since he was dead, Pierson's father had never talked to him either. Holliday felt a comforting new sense of usefulness. "You've finished your analysis, Phil, haven't you?" he asked.

"Yes, sir."

"I thought so. Then you must understand these inhibitions much better than I do. Are they scattered or centered in one area?"

"Mostly centered."

"Well, I have anxieties, you know. Not as bad as I used to, but I have them."

"Yes, sir."

"I think it's like anything, Phil—a matter of living with them. Makes no difference what your work is, so long's you keep it bigger than your worries. All I know is what I try to do every day: be happy as I can, useful as I can, and ignore the things that get in my way."

"Yes, sir . . . You don't think . . . Well, uh. . . ." He laughed again foolishly, self-consciously, without looking up. "You know, sometimes I think I just can't face some of my patients. Miss Barrow, for instance. Just can't face her!" His downcast face was flushed and scowling.

But Holliday surprised him by laughing. Not just politely, but loudly, heartily, as if he could not stop. "I tell you, Phil," he finally replied red-faced. "You may call that 'inhibition,' but I call it natural. . . . Lord knows I do everything I can to keep out of that girl's clutches."

Pierson laughed also, softly, with restraint. Relief flooded through him.

X

IT WAS hot in the conference room that afternoon. Just breathing was an effort. Dr. Pierson got up three times to readjust the small floor fan. The room throbbed with a breathless stillness which reminded Eileen once more of her own sterile little room back at St. Timothy's. That memory was almost comforting now because that room, as well as so many other things, was past.

Suddenly, though, she realized that the doctor was not only settled in his chair again, but watching her deliberately, trying, of course, to get her to start the conversation. But she would not. She had nothing to say, and she could certainly stand silence as long as he could.

"Miss O'Hara, you've been feeling a little better lately, haven't you?" he began at last.

"Yes, I guess so. Time is a good healer." She still looked at her lap when they talked, and yet she was beginning to feel it might not be so painful to face his eyes after all.

"I remember the first time we talked," Pierson continued, "you said you didn't think you were sick. Have your feelings about that changed any?"

"No." Yes, his voice *was* kind. Eileen remembered that his face was, too, and she wondered for a moment if *he* had been hurt in some way. Probably just his foot.

"Then you still think your feelings have always been perfectly normal?" He studied her downcast face carefully in hopes of glimpsing some kind of signal there. But instead, he realized with a start that he had lost himself in fascination with her dark hair and small, heart-shaped face.

"Yes. . . . Of course, I've been depressed. When I came in, I guess I was even desperate. But after all we've talked, don't you think I had reason to feel that way?" To her own surprise, Eileen looked up with that question.... His face *was* kind, his dark eyes understanding, not at all probing.

"Well, we think you're better, too," he said smiling. "Dr. McLeod plans to take you off C.O. soon."

"Good." Eileen smiled too. Then she looked down again quickly. "But, of course, you must realize we still consider you disturbed."

"Yes."

"Probably with your training you can understand why we don't just let you go."

"Yes." Her small face was stone still, but, the thick lashes flickered.

Pierson felt for a moment as if something inside him was trembling in sympathy. The same old thing, he told himself—the inhibitions he had confessed to Holliday. "What do you think our purpose is in keeping you longer?" he asked.

"I ... Well ... I suppose you want to strengthen me emotionally."

Her face remained passive, but Pierson saw her hands clenched together in her lap. "Yes," he said, "you might call it that. But perhaps it would be more realistic to say we want to weaken you. ... We've talked a great deal about this, Miss O'Hara. I wonder —of course, I want you to tell me if I'm wrong—but do you think you are afraid to love again? Perhaps even determined not to?"

Eileen was silent for a moment. But then she looked up at him again and spoke clearly, precisely, almost indignantly. "Of course, I'm afraid to fall in love. Who wouldn't be? After what I've told you ... about Kevin ... about Kenneth, don't you think I'm justified? Put it this way: I've learned my lesson. I've been hurt twice, and I will not be hurt again."

Pierson was startled by her voice and surprised that she was able to suppress the tears that misted her eyes when she mentioned Kenneth. Immediately after speaking, she looked down again, and he asked, "But, Miss O'Hara, do you think that's right? Can you really call that 'normal'?"

"No, I guess not. But I can live with myself that way." His question angered her. She wanted to say, "You live with your foot, don't you?"

A bitter smile crossed her lips, something Pierson had never observed before. "In the past, Miss O'Hara," he began again, "at least from what you've told me, I gather you've committed yourself —your heart, I mean, your emotions—completely. Is that right?"

"Yes, I suppose. I guess I'm like that about everything, just that kind of person."

"But consider this. Couldn't you teach yourself to be moderate? Enjoy a good time, a friendship for its immediate pleasure, just for, shall we say, the joy of living? In that way, love might creep up on you some time, take you by surprise, and—this is *very* important —*not* hurt you."

A long silence followed his words. And when Eileen did speak, it was almost inaudibly. "I am not a moderate person."

Silence again. Her face became even whiter and more tense. The hands in her lap tightened their grip on each other. Then suddenly, her voice, no longer soft and controlled, began pouring out words at a frantic rate. "You see, I want very much to love, to be loved. I—I long for it. I've experienced it, and I know how beautiful it is. So I'm greedy for it. If I don't keep a grip on myself, I give way very easily."

Philip Pierson had never realized the passion inside this girl's trim, almost fragile being. Something in him, more than professional kindness, went out to her. Admiration for someone who could not only experience but express such feelings. But also, compassion, tenderness, even a kind of affection. "But if you force yourself to practice moderation," he continued carefully, "don't you think your hunger might eventually fade?"

"No. Because basically, I'm not moderate. . . . That's what helps most here. There's no threat."

"You know, of course, that there is always the possibility of transference therapy?" That was very difficult for him to say, aware as he was of his own new weakness. He hoped she could not sense the uncertainty in his voice.

"Yes, I know," she said with her old composure. "But you aren't using it."

"You aren't afraid that I might?"

She was silent for a moment. She felt her whole body tremble. Then, just as calmly as before, she said, "No."

"Why, Miss O'Hara?"

But there was no answer.

"How can you feel so secure in that?"

She could not speak. If she did, she would lose control again; her tongue would go wagging off like before. And then he would know. She would be at his mercy.

"You're very perceptive, Miss O'Hara," he said at last. "I hope you'll think over these things we've discussed. Perhaps that will help you to see things in a different light. Perhaps you can help yourself more than I can help you."

❲ 2

Martha McLeod was tired that afternoon. She had worked late the night before. Then this morning the state examiners had shown up, and, automatic as that always was, the endless inspection and interview ordeal had left her aching. There were no admissions scheduled for that afternoon. So she called Beth Tucker to cancel her interviews and leave word she'd be at home if anything came up.

It would be a fine afternoon for tying up tomato plants and gathering the roses already out on her bushes. Perhaps she would bathe Tinker, and then give her an extra big piece of fish for supper to make up. The sun was terribly hot, and as she started down the walk toward the residences, she thought of what a relief it would be to take off her starched coat. She thought, too, how sensible she was to wear her hair in wrap-around braids.

Approaching the moss-covered stone house that was the Hollidays, she saw Mary Laine puttering in the garden. At first the plump, pink-gray figure was kneeling in one corner—probably pulling weeds. Then she stood up and went over to the little stone bird bath. She walked slowly, cautiously, as if she had a pain somewhere or was afraid of falling.

"Makes you realize how time's passed," Martha thought, "how much older we all are." She had become almost accustomed to her own age. There were so many daily reminders—the thin, white hair to be braided, her corset, the fact that she could not drive her car much less write an order without her glasses. Sometimes when she fed Tinker, she remembered he was her third cat.

Somehow, though, she usually forgot that the rest of the world had changed, too. Now she recalled the first time she had seen that figure in this garden. Very slender, with blond hair that glistened in the sunlight. She'd been transplanting a little pine tree, singing a song loud enough to be heard up the path, until suddenly she had caught sight of Martha and whoever had been walking with her.

They'd called to her: "Good morning, Mrs. Holliday." She'd turned and walked toward them. Her voice was gay and soft, friendly, a little too cultured, but with laughter in it. Martha and the other person had gone off saying she seemed very sweet and that David Holliday had been as smart in this as in his work. She'd be a "great asset" and probably an "entertaining addition" to the Holly Springs social world. Not at all the superiority you would have expected of a New York debutante.

Things certainly had changed. Besides the heavy, settled look the lithe young figure had taken on, there was the aloofness which Mary Laine increasingly maintained toward the staff. Also, there was the loneliness in her eyes and the weary, almost sad way David Holliday trudged homeward.

"Hello, Martha. How are you?" Mary Laine called. She put down her watering can and came over to the wall. Her soft, white face was lined, and there were little, blue half-moons beneath her eyes. She reached out and touched Martha's shoulder. "It's been so long since I saw you. Do come in for a while. . . . Yes, please have a cup of tea with me."

Martha didn't want to, but the pleading loneliness in the blue eyes was imperative. "All right," she said, smiling her automatic simper. "I should go home and tie up my poor tomato plants. But I never can resist a cup of tea."

As they entered the house and a few minutes later as she was taking out the tea cups, Mary Laine kept contemplating her guest's appearance—the white face as stiff as the white coat, the heavy, bow-legged way she walked, the grandmother braids. It seemed miraculous she had ever felt even a twinge of jealousy toward such a lifeless blob.

The tea was very nice. Mary Laine rarely had anyone for tea any more. They talked about the weather at first, about Lillian, about the advantages of sucaryl for dieters. Martha spoke of her vacations in Maine. Then, to the doctor's surprise, Mary Laine launched impulsively into her own longing to be somewhere else.

"You know, Martha," she said. "I seem to get much lonelier than I used to. I have nothing in common with anyone here. I try to be content, because I know I might as well be. David is so devoted to his work at Holly Springs. But I can't stop resenting it."

There was a long pause before Martha answered. She had known when she came in that a conversation with Mary Laine might be as trying as a patient interview. But she hadn't anticipated this and had no answer. How could she console David Holliday's wife? "Well, I don't know," she said half mournfully at last. "I guess we're all lonely.... At least lonelier than we ought to be."

Then she did the same thing she often did with a patient when she found an interview unproductive. She waited a moment in silence. Then, with the same sweet simper, she said, "I'm terribly sorry, Mary Laine, but I really must go now. I've had poor little Tinker locked up in that house since early morning." She stood up almost immediately and placed her empty cup on the little walnut table. "I hate to rush off. It's been so nice. But I know you understand."

"Certainly."

Mary Laine followed her to the gate and watched as she walked off down the path. And at that moment she almost hated Martha McLeod. Martha might have tried to help her. If she was as smart as David had always said, at least she could have said something kind. But, no. Too caught up in emotional crises to help anybody with an everyday unhappiness.

Back inside, Mary Laine put away the gardening shears and rinsed the tea dishes. After that she sat down with her needle point. But all the while a restless resentment simmered inside her. It wasn't fair she should sit here day after day at David Holliday's beck and call. It wasn't fair she must live in isolation except when he felt like making it different. At last, when the needle pricked her finger she threw the work down impatiently. "Why? Why do we have to fix everybody's life but our own?"

❰ 3

It seemed impossible to David Holliday that this solemn-faced, flat-chested child was only three years younger than his Lillian.

He'd heard Ellen Collins talk about how "brutal" it seemed to "shut a baby like that up" on Hall 1. But it had never entered his head that "Mildred Pratt, 15, attempted suicide" could be as much a baby as this.

He ought to have sat there a long time, trying to search out the story behind the placid, almost determinedly sad face. But he plunged in immediately. Actually the girl bored him. But also, if the silence lasted too long, she might become too frightened to talk at all.

"I've heard a lot about you, Millie," he began. "From various doctors and nurses. Also, your mother came to see me."

"Oh, yes, mmmhhh." The child's murmur seemed exaggeratedly composed. She nodded her head quickly several times. Holliday wondered if she were ashamed of her mother.

"Yeah. And I've been wondering, Millie. 'Course, when you don't know somebody, you can wonder about a lot of things. But you're young; only fifteen. I've been wondering why a girl as young as you would want to die."

There was no answer. He had not expected one; certainly not an honest one. Still he persisted: "Of course you don't have to tell me. You don't have to say anything you don't want to say. But if you don't mind, I would like to know why you took those sleeping pills?"

"I—I don't know. . . . I just didn't feel like living."

"I wonder why?"

"I wasn't happy."

"I'm sure of that. But was there anything special made you unhappy?"

"Just everything, I guess. Mother and Daddy's divorce. Then living with her and Tom. I hate Tom. He doesn't like me because I'm Daddy's little girl. Of course, Harriet and Gwen—they're my twin sisters—are too, but they were still little when he married Mother. Tom's persuaded Mother that I'm bad. So I can't have anything or do anything and must just stay in my room—dark, ugly room—and study all the time by myself." She stopped suddenly and made fists of her hands.

Dr. Holliday remembered the blond woman in the mink stole, her soft voice and the delicate, if selfish, expression on her face. He had realized then that the child probably felt unloved. Still, it had not occurred to him she might invent lies to emphasize that rejection. "Weren't you afraid of dying?" he asked. "Most people are. I am."

"No, I wasn't afraid." She kept her face turned tensely to the floor. "I wanted to die."

"At the very end, though, after you'd taken the pills, didn't you hope somebody'd save you then?"

"No, I wanted to die."

"You feel the same now? You still want to?"

"I don't know. I guess, but there's no chance here. I would if I was back home with Tom."

Holliday studied her face in silence. "What about this boy?" he asked then, "this boy named Rex?" It had interested him in reading her chart that he had been the one person she called for in the coma.

"Rex?" Her lips closed quickly on the word, and for a moment her flickering eyelids were still. Then she continued with a guarded self-conscious indifference. "Rex? Oh, he was just a boy at school. We went steady for a while. He gave me his class ring. But I got tired of him. I gave it back."

"When you did, though, didn't you hope he'd ask you to take it back?"

"No. I was tired of him."

The contrast between those words and her puckered forehead was obvious. He wondered how far she had gone with the boy. "How close were you to Rex?"

She kept her eyes on the floor. "I told you. We went steady. He gave me his ring."

"Did he ever do more than kiss you?"

Her face went dead white. "Oh, no. . . . He did kiss me twice."

"All right," Holliday continued more sympathetically. "So it was mostly home? Home and your stepfather?"

"Yes." Her forehead smoothed over.

Of course, he knew that in the main it really was her home; it usually was. But a strange twist. This child was guarding her privacy as skillfully as a woman twice her age. Yet, here it was the insignificant details she wanted to cover up, not the real sore spot. Perhaps she doesn't know what hurts, he thought; probably doesn't even realize she's afraid of being a sophisticated strumpet like her mother. Maybe she even feels guilty because she thinks of her mother as she is. "And you think if you went home again, you'd want to die?"

"Yes, I guess."

Ever since medical school he had been somewhat repelled by suicide cases, especially those, like this child, who so obviously did it for attention. Now, however, he wondered if torn by similar loneliness and guilt, he might not have tried the same thing. Because he *had* run away from Alabama. For him, that had not been suicide, but the beginning of a new life. Still, with the same reasoning behind it. He remembered faintly his fear and homesickness that first year away at school. When Millie glanced up, he caught a similar fear in her gray eyes.

So, as he pushed back his chair, he was conscious of a begrudging sense of kinship. "Well, Millie, I've enjoyed it," he said. He reached out his huge hand and wrung the small limp one she put into it.

(4

"Well? Tell me quick; is he going to let you go?"

Millie was barely inside the Hall 1 day room when Evie pounced on her. She was bewildered, and for a moment just stood there in the middle of the floor, frowning at the older girl. Then, suddenly, she understood. "We didn't mention that," she replied solemnly, her tone implying much more serious matters. "I guess I'll be here for a while."

"Gee, that's too bad." Evie's voice was sympathetic. But immediately afterward she giggled. "Anyway, we'll be here together—at least as long's McLeod's in charge. Just saw Phil, and she's got him eating out of her hand. I've decided he's a drip."

Millie sat down on the floor beside Mrs. Purdy and pretended to watch television. She didn't feel like talking to Evie, especially if she was mad and wanted to gripe. She kept thinking of the big man with the drawling voice and the half-wise, half-laughing face. She felt like covering her face with her hands now when she remembered the times during the interview when those all-seeing eyes had caught her own off guard. But she had to think about that. She had to think it all out.

There were many questions. All of them important and yet so confusing, so unanswerable. Why had he come? What did he think of her? Did he know she was lying about Rex? What had her mother told him? Had he seen what her mother was really like? Did he think she was really sick or not?

Evie pulled at her elbow. "Well, what'd he come for then, if he's not going to let you go home? . . . Are you getting off C.O.?"

Millie squinted at the television.

"Hey. . . ." Evie grabbed her arm again. "'Hey, is he taking you off C.O.?"

"I don't know," Millie whispered back, still looking ahead. "He didn't say. . . . Why don't you watch this show?"

The C.O. question made her wonder all the more what Dr. Holliday had thought of her. One minute she recalled the glimmer of a smile on his smooth, round face, and she was afraid. Undoubtedly he had seen there was nothing wrong with her. When her mother came again, he'd suggest she take her home. But on top of that came the memory of his wide forehead puckered with worry. He must think she was very sick. That was why he had come. They were going to give her electric shock. She'd be all lost and queer like Grace Hill and Mrs. Purdy. She felt trapped. Grace said shock was like being electrocuted.

Millie shivered and tried to shut that thought out. His drawling voice came to her again—and the quiet understanding in his eyes. She had known for some time that he was important and supposed to be smart. But she had made up her mind he wasn't really smart at all, that he was just fooling people. And she would not be fooled. Now, however, she liked the big man in spite of herself. He was not dumb. The question now was how smart was he?

They brought the supper out then on trays with the same ugly plastic dishes and the one spoon to eat everything with. She took hers and went over to a corner by herself. But Evie came after her. "Millie," she said, "did you know people die here? That crazy old lady told me in O.T. this morning—you know, that one who weaves baskets all the time—she said. . . ."

"Please go away, Evie. I don't feel like talking."

"Well, I certainly will! I was just trying to be nice; you don't have to be so nasty about it." She picked up her tray and flounced away.

Millie felt sorry about that, but soon she was thinking about Dr. Holliday again. Why should it matter what he thought? He was a big man here, but if things got bad enough she could always persuade her mother to take her home and save the money. (Evie said it cost two hundred dollars a week.) Looking around her now at all these women, she realized how foolish she had always been to place confidence in grownups. Even when she was sad and alone, even though she remembered that inside Mother wasn't really the pure, fine lady she appeared, Millie had always felt she could ask her advice about things like clothes or money or spelling words. But here, all these ladies were as helpless as herself. And who was Dr. Holliday? A man. Maybe a big man. But only a grownup after all.

"Miss Pratt, the others want to go to the bathroom." That meant "come." She stood up and followed the student's flapping white apron across the day room to the corridor.

Walking quickly like that so that she could see only the limp, slumping forms and not the faces, Millie felt lost in a limbo of zombies. "People die here," Evie had said. "When they give you shock, it's like being electrocuted." "You better pray, honey; you better say your Hail Marys. They're going to crucify us all."

"I'll come back soon," Dr. Holliday had said. Millie hoped he wouldn't forget.

BOOK TWO

The Big Gamble

I

IT WAS a long, hot summer. It dragged tediously for everyone at Holly Springs, staff and patients alike. Most saw only one real advantage in the warm weather—more freedom. Open hall patients were allowed out on the hospital grounds until 8 P.M. Patients on closed halls were escorted outside after supper to sit, smoke, play croquet, etc. But to some, even this apparent freedom seemed more a bane than a blessing. There was still no choice. It was outside when the nurses said "out" and in when the nurses said "in." Some—especially among the women—preferred indoor stuffiness to mosquito bites and upholstered couches to hard wooden benches. And many on the disturbed wards, which had been air conditioned, agreed with Evie Barrow: "Who in hell wants to bake in a cramped, brick-walled courtyard when they can sit inside with air conditioning and TV?"

The hospital routine, though as rigid as ever, always underwent a complete change with the arrival of warm weather. Gym for all but the disturbed halls was moved outdoors. Tennis, baseball, croquet, shuffleboard, and golf instead of bowling, ping-pong, pool, and badminton. Gardening was added to occupational therapy. Because of poor ventilation, hospital entertainments and church were discontinued.... All this brought a welcome newness at first. But before long it seemed even more stale and wearisome than what it had replaced.

One by one the doctors took their vacations, except for a few like Pierson and Neville, who had gone in the winter. So for one month nearly every patient had a substitute. Some liked this, seeing in it perhaps another possibility for help. But others felt frightened and angry, deserted at a time when they felt they most needed not to be.

There were many visible changes too. Most nurses changed to short-sleeved uniforms, and even Martha McLeod was occasionally seen without her white coat. The front driveway was resurfaced. With much inconvenience the main corridor received a fresh coat of pale green paint. And the familiar silence was replaced by an almost constant roar of electric lawn mowers. But the biggest changes—especially to doctors returning from vacation—were in the people. Every day, every week there were new patients. And at the same time there were others leaving. Jackie Harper went back to her Greenwich Village apartment and her typewriter. Bette Palin went out to Colorado to settle her husband's estate.

In July, Martha McLeod and Tinker went to Maine. Martha still had a few friends there who were glad to see her. Also, she had Beth Tucker, the nursing supervisor, up for a week. But mostly she spent her time crocheting, sorting out books and papers, and fixing up the old house for another empty winter. She was glad to get back to Holly Springs, and she found some amazing changes. A whole group of patients recently promoted from Hall 1 Women to Hall 2 had made remarkable progress. Mrs. Purdy, Evelyn Barrow, little Millie Pratt, and Grace Hill all appeared ready for Hall 3. Mrs. Gaitors seemed to have worked out very reasonable arrangements for commuting to work in the city. And Martha Mc-Leod waited only a week to let her start.

Some other things, of course, seemed not so happy. Heath Webster had given way to another cycle of depression and had been sent back to Hall 3 and constant observation. Also, the Womble boy, whom Holliday suggested she keep an eye on in his absence, seemed to have lost much of the ground he had gained with the shock treatments. Indeed, he appeared more withdrawn than ever.

Jack Isaacs, feeling trapped and stagnating in his own fear, made a determined effort to help Ben. He asked him to play cards and tennis; he offered the use of his radio. But always there was no more than a head-shake refusal. That depressed Jack. Somehow everything was worse in the oppressive heat. Old Dr. Stoughton seemed to grow more feeble, less in touch every day. When Lucie came, her face looked sad and tired. Jack began to have doubts that there could be any end for him better than that overtaking Stoughton.

But at a garden party in July he talked to a young female patient who gave him a little more hope. Her name was Eileen O'Hara, and as it turned out, she had been the one who tried to help him at the spring dance. She was a nurse, she said, still on Hall 3 but in hopes of moving along soon. She told him it was ridiculous to compare himself to a man like Dr. Stoughton. The old man's trouble was physical, she said, whereas Jack need only search out the truth he feared, face it, and find his own solution. Jack did not tell her he knew what he must face and could not do it. But he admired the fact that she could concern herself with him when her own gray-green eyes reflected so much pain.

Mary Laine Holliday wilted through June and July with iced tea and indecisive preparations for their vacation. When eighteen-year-old Lillian was home between house parties, Mary Laine brightened up and went on shopping trips, but the rest of the time she was besieged by migraines.

David Holliday, of course, was busier than ever, and he thrived on it. He felt so vital after such menial tasks as making rounds and giving tube feedings that he had enthusiasm left over to encourage Mary Laine. It was probably only because of this that they finally did take off for Vermont early in August.

For those who could not go away, however, there remained six more weeks of summer. They did pass, each day with the slowness of a fading rose petal. But when they were gone, when the last flower had bloomed and the grass dried to its final brownness, what was there?

Autumn. The same waiting dressed in a different costume.

❲ 2

It was strange, walking up the hill to the hospital that first morning after vacation. Almost as if I'd been sick, David Holliday thought, and were still weak, or as in a dream, walking some place you've been before but can't remember, seeing it like a picture from a distance.

That out-of-place sensation had bothered him once. As a young doctor, he'd worried about losing his touch. But not any more. He expected it now as much as the changing seasons. And this year, this bright September morning, the illusion of inadequacy merely flashed across his mind and was forgotten. He could not worry. Everything was going too well. The day was too beautiful, the sky too blue, the air too sweet with early coolness.

They'd had a fine time in Vermont at the inn on Lake Champlain that Jack and Edith Beckwith had recommended. Just the kind of place the Beckwiths would choose—full of successful New York doctors and lawyers. He'd swum and fished and played golf. Lillian had gotten brown as an Indian and caught three new beaux. Even Mary Laine had enjoyed it. She'd found other women—some of them "very prominent socially"—to play bridge and knit with under the trees. She'd taken cruises and nature walks; she'd puttered around the craft shops and bought some "priceless bargains."

The gray dissatisfaction had faded from her face, and her lips had smiled again. She'd slept nights and almost scarcely seemed to notice when he went off somewhere without her. Even this morning he'd been able to just kiss her and leave her, a sleepy-eyed bundle under the sheet.

It was good to be back at work. There was a freshly typed patient list on his desk, and when he sat down to compare it with the old one, he found many differences—a number of unfamiliar names and some old ones no longer listed. The others began coming in then—Dr. Neville and Dr. Richards headed toward the men's division. Next, footsteps in the opposite direction, and after that Martha McLeod came in. Her plump, pasty face was beaming. "Well, it's certainly nice to have you back," she said. "And you at least look as if you had a good time. You're brown as a berry."

Even conference was enjoyable that morning. Holliday remembered other such sessions when he'd felt bored and sleepy and annoyed with Martha McLeod's primness. But it wasn't at all like that this time. Everybody seemed so glad to see him. Especially Phil Pierson, who, despite his old careful stoicism, came up to shake Holliday's hand. There seemed a new confidence about the boy, though clearly an artificial, convention-type front.

Holliday concentrated hard on the discussion, even scribbled a few notes on the back of a folded envelope. When Martha McLeod went into an explanation of Holly Springs' commitment policy, he leaned over to ask Ellen Collins about some of the names on his old patient list which did not appear on the new one. Mr. Corry was out, she told him; so were Mrs. Ellis and Mrs. Palin, though she was afraid Mrs. Palin had gone back to drinking.

Remembering Pierson's warm welcome, Holliday thought of the O'Hara girl and scanned the type for her name. Finally he found it under Hall 4. He must congratulate the boy. . . . Four months, maybe five, and already Phil had her moving ahead. In spite of what Martha McLeod had said in the beginning about the girl's suffering from "complicated and deep-rooted neuroses to which she clings tenaciously." Martha had even admonished him briefly then for taking on too many "long-term charity cases."

"Interesting," Pierson had said. "Nice person." And that was the key, the gift Dr. Keller and Dr. Williams at Bellevue had been referring to when they spoke of the boy's "brilliant insight and sensitivity. The promise of a genius," they had said somewhat sadly, ". . . if he could only subdue his own resentment."

At last Martha closed the conference, and Holliday hurried off to look over the changes recorded in type.

(3

Jonathan Stoughton was in O.T. that morning when Dr. Holliday walked through. He was surprised to see the hulking pot-bellied figure; they'd said he was on vacation.

The old man had wanted to talk to his friend for some time, the one person who seemed to remember who he was. He wanted to cross the room now and shake the doctor's hand and tell him he hoped to see him soon. But he didn't. He just bent more dutifully over the red and blue bands he was weaving into a potholder. After all, it was up to this younger man to speak to him.

He was hurt and angry when Holliday passed his table without speaking. "Very ill bred," he muttered. "Like all the young men nowadays."

"Yes, he is," he answered himself. "Even looks like them, 'specially since he got so brown. Very ill bred."

Stoughton had finished his potholder by then and began slowly, methodically to take it apart. He always did that now. Every day at O.T.—made a potholder and took it apart. He had done other things for a while. But then he'd heard you paid for everything you completed and took back to the hall. His eyes gazed out the window as his fingers performed their familiar task. Summer was nearly over. The grass was mostly straw brown now, and when they went for walks around the grounds, there were asters and daisies instead of roses. The trees hadn't turned yet, but they looked tired.

So, another summer was gone. They passed so quickly now, so relentlessly, like sand in an hour glass. There was scarcely time to smell the honeysuckle or feel the hot sun on your shoulders. And he was getting old; you had to admit that at eighty-three. Some day the summer would come and he would not be here. And in the meantime, he would just sit in this prison making potholders and taking them apart, waiting for the death which he dreaded and yet must accept as his only chance for freedom.

"While those ungrateful wretches sit home on their fat tails!" he muttered angrily, ripping out the last strip of cloth. "Sit there, and come here once a month to soothe their consciences with a carton of cigarettes." He wondered if one of them would come this next visiting day. They'd been coming more this summer, especially Hinton. They said the roads were better but he thought it was because he looked older and they felt guilty. He rather liked them to come, though. It gave him something different to be angry at.

He thought of the hall, of its musty smell, of Marx peering at his crossword puzzles. He hardly ever played chess any more. Corry had gone home. Corry was lucky. He missed Corry. Even though they had had a fight, even though he had called him a cheater, Corry had come and shaken his hand before he left....

A student nurse tapped him on the shoulder then and said it was time to put his things away. He nodded and began to pile the strips of cloth back into the box. They'd go back to the hall now and wait there.

(4

"Hey, did you know Holliday was back?" Jim Reilly called as he approached the tennis court, carrying his racket, a sweater, and a can of balls.

"Yeah," Jack Isaacs answered without concern. "Saw him at O.T." He noticed the anxiety on Reilly's face and felt cruelly pleased. Reilly was jealous; he didn't like Holliday to have conferences with anyone. Reilly was on Open Hall now but he still played tennis with them during gym. Played a good game, too. It was fun if you could make him play and not talk.

The others, Fred Grimes and Peter Winslow, stood up as Reilly put down his sweater and his balls. Ben Womble just sat there resting his chin on the handle of his racket and gazing far away with a smirk on his face.

"Want to play, Ben?" Jack asked.

The boy shook his head. Every day the gym guys sent him out with a racket and balls and the order to "Get in there and play." And every day Ben just slumped here, smiling his secret smile.

Jack stood up, too, then, but his mind wasn't on the game. He was thinking what a crazy threesome they were—he and Reilly and Ben. Reilly who was getting well and didn't want to, who could be free and instead wanted to be sick and locked up. He, himself, who longed for that freedom and didn't know the way. And poor Ben, who seemed to have no feelings one way or the other, or even any choice.

"Hey, come on, Jack. We don't have all day." Reilly stood on the service line, impatiently slamming balls into the net.

"Okay, okay." Jack took the receiving position on the opposite side of the net. He returned the first serve successfully, but then couldn't concentrate on the game. When it was his service, he even forgot to keep score.

Reilly got mad. "Christ, Isaacs!" he said. "What's wrong with you? If you're gonna play, play!"

144 HIGH ON A HILL

Jack didn't answer. He finished out the set, then let the gym guy take his place.

Sitting there on the grass, he wondered if he looked like Ben, if people felt sorry for him and thought of his case as hopeless. That was frightening, because it seemed so plausible. A little shiver ran down his back. He reached for his old gray sweater.

Summer's over, he thought, pulling it over his head. If you looked hard, there were glimmers of yellow in the trees—and a couple of weeks ago he would have given anything for a breeze to blow on his hot body. Another month, pretty soon another half year. They'd have gym indoors instead of out. Then there'd be the compulsory movies and parties, and church, though he never went to church. Lucie would start coming on the train instead of driving over icy roads, and she'd have to leave early to catch the train back.

Jack felt his cheeks grow warm, his eyes burning and damp. It was just too big, too much to fight. But he couldn't let them see him cry. They'd say he was depressed. They'd send him back a hall and put him on C.O. And that would be the finish. He'd never have the strength to work up from that.

Next time Holliday came to see him, he must make himself look into the brown eyes—not defiantly or elusively, but honestly. He must look into them and say, "Yes, Doctor, you're right. I am ashamed of being a Jew. Not a Jew; a kike, who's cut himself off from everything good and honorable about his ancestry."

Holliday's brown eyes would open wide at that. But he wouldn't interrupt because he wouldn't know what to say. Another shiver ran down Jack's back, despite his sweater. Yes, he must do that. And the very next time he saw Holliday, he *would*, unless he could think of an easier way out before then.

(5

Carson Gaitors felt bitchy that morning. Bad enough having to stay at the hospital over the weekend. But it was infuriating to be stuck there on a weekday besides and to be expected to *go* along with the stupid routine of O.T. and gym.

It was quite natural for her brother-in-law Olin to have closed up the talent agency today because of his father's death. Some people might even consider it Jesse's duty as a brother to accompany Olin and his wife, Barbara, to Baltimore for the funeral. But it was absolutely insane of McLeod not to let her go, too. What could she possibly do at a funeral? What could be more upsetting, after three weeks of comparative freedom, of commuting to the city? What could be more depressing than sweating out three whole days in this virtuous bughouse?

McLeod hadn't even had the decency to come tell her herself. She had just called Sullivan and told her to cancel Mrs. Gaitors' weekend permission and Monday work pass. Well, if McLeod could be nasty, she could too. She'd decided when she got up that morning that she'd be damned if she did one thing she didn't want to. She had a book to read and some socks she was knitting, and no amount of nagging would get her to O.T. or gym.

By midmorning she'd simmered down again to a point of acceptance, even persuaded herself this might be for the best, what with the confusion she'd been feeling of late about Francie Francoli. But as the minutes passed so did her complacency. The hall was deadly quiet; from the smoker Carson could hear Sullivan in the nursing office turning the pages of her magazine. Her anxiety over Francie quickly grew to a ferment. If she allowed herself to think about him in detail, she was revolted by the memory of his slick black hair, his olive skin, his eyes forcing their way into hers. Still, she felt she could not endure one more day without him.

If someone disgusted her, why should she want him? "Might as well face it," she sneered. "They've got you booked as a nympho, and that's what you are. Shitty but true." She forced herself to laugh out loud. But it wasn't just a joke. It was quite true. She had asked Dr. McLeod:

"Well, if I'm so sick, what's the diagnosis? Nymphomaniac?"

"Mental illness isn't as simple as that, Mrs. Gaitors. Each case is an individual."

"But that's what you'd say, isn't it? If you had to answer in one word? Nymphomaniac."

"I suppose that's the closest word to it. But I couldn't answer in one word." As wobbly a hedge as you could get from a psychiatrist. No laughter could cover that.

It was easy enough to tell herself that Jesse was the best choice.

If she stayed with him, she might make a life of their relationship. In contrast, Francie was just a flash of excitement, doomed to become only one more mistake. Yet how could she ever find life complete or even safe as long as she was dazzled by forbidden excitement?

So it was a relief when Dr. Holliday came loping down the corridor. "Well, well, Mrs. Gaitors," he boomed. "Thought you'd be at work."

"Oh, hello, Dr. Holliday," she said, dropping her knitting. "I thought you were off in Vermont."

"First day back."

"Hope you had a good time. . . . I would be working today, only Jesse's stepfather died and they all went to the funeral. Of course, McLeod didn't think I could 'quite cope with a funeral yet.' " She emphasized the last with a snort, and they exchanged their old looks of exasperated amusement.

The doctor pulled a pack of cigarettes from his pocket and sat down heavily in the chair beside her. "Maybe you couldn't," he said with another smile.

"Oh, Lord! You know me better than that. Might do me good to get depressed."

He lit a cigarette and drew on it in silence. "How's it going?" he asked her. " . . . the work, I mean. Like it?"

She laughed. "Anything's better than this."

"That all?"

"No, I really like it. Fascinating people. And I hardly ever see my brother-in-law who runs the place, you know. I'm on my own in the front office. People come in and I take down whatever they have to offer and make an appointment for them to see whichever of our people I think would suit them best. There are five in the firm . . . Then, of course, we have some regular clients who don't have to have appointments." She cut herself off there.

But Holliday was interested. "Any specially well-known clients?" he asked.

"Oh, a few. Rima Gandy, the singer; the Jazz-boes Quartet; Willie Winters, the trombonist." She picked up her knitting again and pretended to examine it. Perhaps this visit wasn't haphazard after all. Perhaps he had heard something and was here to pick her brain. . . . Could be McLeod was communicating with people in the New York office.

"You get a chance to really know any of them?" Holliday continued.

"A few, I guess." Her hands trembled so that she dropped three stitches. But she was glad, because she had to concentrate on picking them up. Ridiculous getting shaken like this. Holliday would be suspicious now even if he hadn't been before. "I go out to lunch with them sometimes," she said with determined calm. "We close the office between one and two-thirty. If one of the regulars comes in around then and his agent is busy, why quite often he asks me to lunch."

She tried hard to fix her thoughts on the situation at hand, but she could not. Even his pudgy hand shaking out the match reminded her of Francie.

Still, why not tell him? He'd find out sooner or later in that mysterious way he always did. Besides, who could she trust more? Who would understand better? He might even have a suggestion.

"Met anybody really interests you?"

"Well, yes, I guess you'd say I have." Then she was off—quickly, boldly, with the joking frankness she used to speak of serious matters. "An orchestra leader . . . very talented . . . a little flashy, I guess . . . the calypso type. He's Italian." She laughed affectedly.

But Holliday did not join in this time. An expression of something like pain twitched at the corners of his mouth. He studied her face in solemn silence.

"I know what you're thinking," she defended herself. "That I'm as foolish as when I came. But I'm not. I know I shouldn't fall for a Wop. But I did. And how can I help that? How can I help that?"

"Well, at least you recognize your weakness. . . . Why did you start seeing the fellow if you feel like that?"

"Maybe I like to see him. Maybe there's nothing I can do that I like better."

"What about your husband?"

"Sure, I know—'kind, substantial, understanding.' Besides, he's the fifth. I should stick with him; he's a safe bet. But maybe I want more than security. Maybe I'd like a little excitement, a little thrill."

"I wasn't going to say that, but I guess I don't disagree. You aren't unhappy with your husband, are you? I mean, that's a pretty comfortable situation?"

"Oh, yes. He's very comfortable." She laughed softly.

"You think you'd be happier with this orchestra leader?"

"Maybe. For a while anyway."

"But you see the doubt?"

"Sure. But how can anyone be a hundred per cent sure about anything?"

"I guess you can't. But there's a margin in most cases, a limit you can count on. You're pretty happy with Jesse. Why change for something you don't know about, something might even be worse?"

His words echoed her own thoughts, but she couldn't accept that yet. "It might be better though."

"Yes, there's always that chance. But you've tried four times and it hasn't been. That happens a lot, I guess. Looks like change'll fix everything ... new dress, different job, another neighborhood. But usually it doesn't. Old problems still there, just under a different cover."

Carson did not answer. She knew he was right; yet the part of her that did not want to believe him would not let her speak. "Well, what are you going to do?" she challenged him at last.

"About what?"

"About me. About what I've told you."

"I see nothing to do ... unless there's more you haven't told me."

"I bet you beat it to McLeod the minute you leave here."

"No, you needn't worry about that. As far as I'm concerned, what we've discussed is confidential. You know, of course, that we're keeping a careful check. But there'll be no change in your privileges, unless you do something rash to warrant it. You've got to learn to control these situations yourself."

Carson did not speak again. She looked up hopefully into the doctor's brooding eyes. But his round face was not reassuring. He did not smile before he stood up and turned down the corridor again.

(6

Evie Barrow made an ugly face as she picked up Millie Pratt's three cards. "I hope someday I get to pass cards to you," she said

with mock bitterness. "I'll give you a taste of your own medicine."
Millie smiled sheepishly. She liked to be kidded like that. It
made her feel like she was a pretty smart girl, like these people
enjoyed her even if she was very young.

"Now don't you talk mean about Millie," Mrs. Purdy said
absently, still examining her hand. "She's my baby."

Millie liked that, too. Because Mrs. Purdy was an old lady, and
she liked to please old ladies. Not so much because she wanted to
be petted, as just to know they approved of her and told people
she was a "sweet child." Besides, Mrs. Purdy was a very nice old
lady. She was fun as well as kind. She was the one who had
started them playing hearts.

It was funny when you thought about it, the way they had
all been together way back on Hall 1 in packs and P.B.'s, having
shock and insulin, throwing cups of cocoa at each other. So close
together, and yet they'd had almost nothing to do with each other,
until they got here on Hall 3 with other people they might have
made friends with.

It was almost incredible about Mrs. Purdy. To think how weird
she'd been back on Hall 1—parading around with her toilet paper
halo and her dried clover rosary, standing up in bed in the dark
of night, saying Hail Marys loud enough to wake the whole dorm,
telling you over and over that you'd better pray before they
crucified you. Everybody had been horrified by that; they'd spent
half their time laughing or griping about her. And now she was
just a nice old lady with a sense of humor, who liked little girls
and knitting and playing hearts. Sometimes she said she'd be glad
when fall came and they started church or when she moved to a
better hall where she could have her rosary and a prayer book. But
that was all she ever said about praying now, and Grace Hill
had told Millie Catholics were supposed to be a little that way
anyhow.

Grace wasn't a Catholic, but her husband was, and they were
raising their kids in the church. Millie had never realized before
there were so many Catholics. The nice Irish girl with the "Gone
With the Wind" name, Eileen O'Hara, was Catholic, too. Evie
had pointed that out to her one Friday when Eileen wanted to
know what kind of soup it was and if there was meat in it. But
Evie said everybody from Ireland was Catholic anyway.

Eileen had been very nice to them, nicer than anybody else. She'd told them all the Hall 3 rules—which were easier than either of the other halls Millie had been on—and she'd offered to lend them her ballpoint pen if they wanted one before their families came again. Millie liked Eileen. She loved to sit nearby and listen to the way she talked. But Eileen was upstairs now on Hall 4, the best hall in the hospital except Open.

Millie didn't see her too often now, but whenever she did, Eileen always asked her how she was feeling and said she hoped Millie would be moved to Hall 4 soon. In a way Millie hoped so, too, but mostly she dreaded that. It frightened her to think of getting that near the outside again, that near New York and home and Mother and Tom.

"Hey, Millie, wake up and play." Evie tapped her fingers on the table edge. "You look like you used to with insulin."

They all laughed.

"And try to take it if you can. Grace is trying to shoot the moon."

She played a high heart, but Grace took the trick anyway. After that she didn't have to think about it any more, because all she had was low clubs. She looked around the room at the other patients also dressed in nightgowns and bathrobes, sitting through one more dull evening. Most of them were older, except for Maggie Evans, the thin girl, and Alice Morrisson, the fat one. Evie said that when she was on Hall 3 before, they had fed Maggie with a rubber tube through her nose. Evie didn't know what was wrong with Alice. Millie thought they were nice girls. But they weren't too friendly, and it was easier for her to hang around with Grace and Evie and Mrs. Purdy.

After that hand they put away the cards. It was nearly ten, and Millie went down the corridor to brush her teeth. She hurried, because she wanted to get in the dorm before Mrs. Purdy started saying her prayers. There was nothing wrong with the way Mrs. Purdy said her prayers now, but Millie always worried the nurses might misinterpret it and give the old lady a bad report. And Mrs. Purdy had become very important to Millie. She was ugly and had bad breath and spoke what Millie had always been taught was bad English. But she was a good person. Not because she prayed; just because there was goodness inside her that showed in everything she did. Millie had been talking to Mrs. Purdy more and more lately. She'd even told her she was afraid to go home. Mrs. Purdy had hugged Millie when she told her that. "Don't you worry, baby," she said, "I'm sure your mamma loves you. But even if she don't, these people here'll be looking out for you. Even after you're home, they'll be looking out." Then she'd laughed her queer cackle and said, "Besides, there's always Grandma Purdy. You're my baby now, too, you know."

(7

"And how're you?" Eileen O'Hara's cousin, Dan McCloskey, fidgeted on the hard leather couch and drummed his thick fingers on the arm rest. Ever since he came in the door, he'd been gripping his cigar as if it were his only hope in a shipwreck, and looking around furtively with each puff, as if the smell didn't reveal it to everyone. Now, at last, he crushed it in the ash tray.

Eileen smiled at him, pitied his discomfort and wished he had not come. "Oh, I'm fine," she said pleasantly, her thin face going hollow as she drew in on her cigarette.

"That's what the doctor said. I stopped to speak before I came up. Just a young fellow, ain't he? But he said you were doing much better, that it was good you were on this hall. More freedom or something. But I saw they locked the door when I come in; they still locked the door."

"Yes, Cousin Dan, they lock the doors everywhere here."

"Well, I don't like that. It's unnatural. I like to know I can get up and go when I want. . . . And there's one thing I don't understand. If you're so well, if you're so fine, why do you stay here and let them take your money?"

"I can't leave till they say, Cousin Dan, till they think I'm really well." That was a new twist—patient soothing relative. "Anyway, St. Timothy's is paying the bill."

Eileen had reminded herself of that often in recent months. It had been a comfort in the beginning when she was feeling trapped, a helpless victim of injustice. "At least it's not costing me," she had pacified her resentment. But with time that same thought had become more a torment than a solace. What right had she to the luxury of any psychiatric treatment, let alone the superior type offered at Holly Springs? The world must be full of unhappy lovers, and for the most part, they nursed their broken hearts in silence. While she pampered herself with the sinful selfishness of open despair.

"Well, I wrote your mother you were better," Cousin Dan said. "And, like you said, I didn't tell her what kind of a hospital it was. Though I don't see that matters. I think you were just worn out and needed a rest. They'd been working you too hard at that other place."

Eileen smiled. She didn't mind Cousin Dan—not even his open-neck sport shirt or his smelly cigar or the way he got all excited over something he didn't understand. If she could just keep him off Mother and the County Cork and the old days when she was a little girl and her father still alive.

Those memories in themselves weren't so painful any more. Except that they started the chain reaction of remorse, guilt, and anxiety for which there seemed no check. County Cork. Her father, Kevin, the smell of ether and blood. Kenneth.

Kenneth? Where was he? He had loved her. He had said it, and his face, his hands had shown it. And Eileen had believed him then and later. "If only I had realized," she had told herself a thousand times since.

But Kenneth's principles, though perhaps less noble, had been as strong as Eileen's own. He could go to great extremes—make infinite sacrifices, love to the limits of his being, hate just as ferociously. But he would not marry a Catholic. "Besides, that isn't necessary.... Not for tonight.... That will work out in time."

She had insisted just as obstinately that it *was* necessary. Partly through sanctity, she admitted now, but mostly through fear. Yet he hadn't been angry. He'd been as kind as ever for weeks, for months. As if, when he could not have his ultimate, he would make himself happy with the next best thing. Until that night when he did not come.

Why, though? Was it her fault? How had he really felt about her? If he had died, there would have been no questions. She had been a fool.

But Cousin Dan had fully launched his reminiscing now. "You know, Eileen," he said, "I wonder sometimes why you don't go back to be with your mother now she's getting old. It's a good country, Ireland. I see it better since I've been away."

"Yes, it is."

"I can see it now ... you a wee girl on your father's knee. You were the apple of his eye, Eileen ... more than either of the other girls."

"Yes, I guess I was."

"Do you remember the year he died, Eileen?"

"Oh, yes. I was a big girl then—twelve or so." Her cheeks drew in a little as they had before when she was smoking. Her mind searched numbly for something to change the subject.

" 'Twas the next year we left. I guess that depressed me ... seeing a poor man work hisself to death and nobody care. A young man, too; he was young, Eileen. But he wasn't strong, and he had to work too hard because of the poor soil. He worked hisself to death and there was no help for it."

His talk of her father reminded Eileen of Dr. Holliday. She'd thought of him a great deal since her move to Hall 4. She liked the new freedom here, being a person again instead of just another caged animal, and the idea that she was closer to the outside and work again. But at the same time the uneasiness inside her was growing.

She had told Dr. Pierson about it, stressing her doubts of ever becoming a competent nurse again. He had seemed sympathetic and very interested and had been seeing her nearly every day, discussing the obsessive anxiety and depression in as much detail as she would let him. It appeared a real project with him, but in no way a gloomy one. He'd even mentioned some new drugs, one of which had brought remarkable results with cases like hers.

Only, Eileen could not tell him about what bothered her most. She must depend on herself now; the doctors expected her to control her emotions. Yet every time she had a conference, every time Dr. Pierson even walked through the hall, a curious quivering tightness squeezed her chest and prickling warmth rose in her cheeks. At first she had tried to ignore it. Later she had considered mentioning it to Pierson. When she could not, she had thought of Holliday. Now she had even decided on the exact words with which to tell him.

It had reached the point that she considered her feelings morbid. She not only feared them, but was ashamed of them, and wondered if she might be one of those women people spoke of as having "hot pants." Ridiculous to fall in love with your psychiatrist—especially when he wasn't using those tactics and you were well enough trained to know he wasn't. If she weren't careful, this would just be Kevin and Kenneth all over again.

Cousin Dan was fingering his floppy gray hat now. She was glad he would leave soon. She would go back and read some more from Yeats or maybe write a letter to Holliday so it would be there when he came back from vacation.

"Well, child, I must be going," he said, standing up stiffly and kissing her cheek. "It takes a while on the train, you know, and Mary's there alone. She'd come—she wants to—but she has the arthritis so bad she can't move from her chair."

"Give her my love, Cousin Dan."

"Yes, I'll do that, and you keep getting strong."

II

"I DON'T KNOW why I always let myself get talked into it," Mary Laine Holliday complained. "Every year I swear I won't, and every year David comes to me with his sad talk about these poor boys going out into the hard world. So that I give in in spite of myself." She sighed and sat down, resting her elbows wearily on the improvised banquet table.

"Yes, and it's such a waste of time and energy," Elizabeth Wilson, wife of the administrative director of Holly Springs, replied. "Going into such a frenzy, I mean, when we both know those boys would much rather drink beer and cook steaks outside somewhere." She settled her plump figure in the chair beside Mary Laine and gazed down the extent of the table.

"Oh, but my dear, you know that's impossible," Mary Laine

mimicked with a sarcastic giggle. "This is the social occasion of
the year. The Board of Governors may eat fish, but nothing less
than *filet mignon* for the retiring residents!" She was, of course,
poking fun at her husband, but it was a futile attempt, because
they both knew she was lying.

They'd been setting up these good-by parties together for nine
years now, and they'd disagreed from the very first.

Elizabeth Wilson was an easygoing woman, not very vital or
even interesting, but pleasant and friendly and easy to talk to. She
liked things to be cozy, and the first year she had helped with
the party she had been very enthusiastic about buying a couple of
kegs of beer and broiling hamburgers outside. But Mary Laine
had been horrified. So they still used the banquet table with
flowers and some of the kitchen help to serve. And every year
they had parsley potatoes and roast beef with lime sherbet for
dessert. Elizabeth didn't really dislike Mary Laine, but she thought
her terribly dull and hoity-toity. Sometimes at home she and Lloyd
joked about her; they felt a little sorry for poor Dave.

The worst part of the whole ordeal for Mary Laine was having
to work with "that frumpish little fool." Though really, Elizabeth's
shortcomings were no more irritating than those of most of the
other women Mary Laine knew at Holly Springs. And despite the
fact that much of what she did and said was unrefined, even in
bad taste, she was the only woman in the whole hospital com-
munity with whom Mary Laine felt any social rapport.

"Perhaps it's just Vermont that makes her so much harder to
take today," Mary Laine tried to soothe herself. Their vacation
had been wonderful this year. Not only had David enjoyed his golf
and fishing, but for once she had been able to do more than sun
herself and read. So many interesting, intelligent people. Women
who could discuss music and books, whose faces did not go blank
when you mentioned places in Paris and Vienna, who preferred
bridge or backgammon to canasta. Women she ought to be as-
sociating with.

Naturally Elizabeth Wilson was a hard letdown. But so was
the rest of Holly Springs. Mary Laine wished—oh, how deeply she
had wished in the last few weeks—that David would give up now
and go into practice with Jack Beckwith or someone else in New
York. Yet, David had promised. And she could and must have

faith in him. More than that, in the meantime she must live up to her end of the agreement.

Still, Elizabeth Wilson was one of the things that made patience most difficult. "I don't think there's too much left to do," Mary Laine said now, "except put the place cards around. The flowers won't come till late this afternoon."

"You know, I just love these boys," Elizabeth ventured. "More each year. It always makes me sad to see them go."

"But they don't all go," Mary Laine stood up and began putting the place cards around. "I think hardly a year goes by that one doesn't stay on.... Like Philip Pierson; he's been here three years and Jack Richards five."

"I know, but most of them go. And it always makes me sad."

"But why? I think it's fine. Especially when they get right into private practice. I wish David had done that."

"Do you really? Even when he's director of Holly Springs? No psychiatrist can be big cheese like that in private practice."

"I don't consider it so wonderful being 'big cheese' at Holly Springs. Especially not when you have to work yourself to death and be so grossly underpaid to boot."

"You know, I'm just the opposite," Elizabeth chattered. "I'm happy just the way we are. I don't even care about Lloyd moving up. Administrative director sounds plenty good to me. Prestige is nice, but I don't think it takes the place of fun at home."

Mary Laine nodded obligingly as the pleasant voice went on to remind her how fortunate she was, how much Dave Holliday was respected, and how happy she should be to have been able to help him in his great contribution to medical science. But finally she pushed her chair back and stood up. "I really must go," she said. "If I don't rest now, I'll be absolutely useless at the party tonight."

⟨ 2

The page before him was still alarmingly blank, with the single name, Eileen O'Hara, written in blue ink at the top and underlined three times. "If you keep your mind on the problem, there won't be room for the anxiety," Philip Pierson always told himself. But there were times like this when it didn't work at all.

"At least she's not aware of it," he comforted himself. "Too preoccupied with herself." He scanned the girl again—small brown leather loafers, tense fingers clinging to each other, downcast eyes lost in a study of the floorboards. He tried hard to remember the questions he meant to ask. But they had deserted him. All he could think of was her hair, the reddish lights with which the sun varied its darkness, the shadow the lampshade made across the upper half of her face. A deep, gentle, quiet kind of beauty, he thought. He sketched a salt-box house on the stark page.

It must be wonderful to see that face asleep. The anxiety that showed sometimes between her eyes would be gone then, and the soft breathing would set a subtle rhythm for the whole innocent body. The small, sweet breasts would move to that rhythm, up and down, so gently that you could hardly see. The body would be warm and willing, and if you held it close that warmth would flow into you.

That startled him back into the present. He could feel the blood rushing to his face. And as he stared at the doodle-dotted notebook paper, in an effort to control himself, he was once more grateful for her preoccupation. "Damn good thing Holliday is back," he thought. "I won't wait as I planned. I'll speak to him today, tomorrow at the latest." He strained again to ask her some innocuous questions: "What are you making at O.T.?" "Who are your friends here?" "How are you sleeping?"

She answered them all calmly and politely, but he felt all the time that she knew he was just trying to fill the silence. He could not concentrate on her voice. . . . If he had stayed in Kentucky as his mother had begged, and lived in the big house with her and spent his father's money, he would never have had to worry about things like this. If he'd wanted, he could even have gotten himself a wife, a fragile debutante, who would love him despite his club foot—because he was rich and because his grandfather had been Keith Vinson. That name reminded him of the subject he'd meant, in fact, needed to pursue with her. "Tell me," he ventured, "have you thought any more about our discussion of last week?"

"Well, yes, I suppose. We've a lot of time for thinking."

"Did you . . . I mean, were you able . . . Rather, do you agree, or do you still think I was wrong about the parallel I drew between the two young men—Kevin and Kenneth?" He tried to look at her coldly and analytically, but he could feel his insides washing away like sand. He had said the names kindly, softly, as one speaks of the dead, but they echoed loudly inside him, vibrated with a restlessness close to jealousy.

"Yes, I see your point." She looked down at her hands. "But I see mine, too. I guess I see it all clearer now. And I think we're both of us right—right and wrong."

"Right and wrong?"

"Yes. I'm right one way, and you're right the other, and we're both wrong because we're extremes."

He ought to end this feeble attempt at conversation, ought to simply tell her about the thorazine and leave. Unpardonable of him to go on like this—not only loving her, but wanting her to love him. Foolish for himself, because he could not have her and, therefore, could only be unhappy, but downright cruel for her. She had been hurt too much already. She wasn't strong enough yet to take it again. And this would surely hurt her. . . . It was one thing to come away and declare your independence of a sweet-voiced, selfish little woman in Kentucky, and quite another to rebel against the whole world. He was not big enough for that.

"Yes, we both believe in an extreme," she continued. "You underestimate the importance of these men because you never knew them. I overestimate their importance because I did know them and they are gone. We're both right and wrong."

"I suppose you could look at it that way," Pierson replied. He cleared his throat and fixed his eyes obliquely on her face. "Miss O'Hara, there's one thing I particularly wanted to speak about today."

"Yes?" She seemed to sense the subject was a safe one. Her eyes rose slowly, calmly to meet his.

"The staff has decided to try you on thorazine."

"Thorazine?" The word was a question, but there was guarded alarm in her voice.

"Yes. You remember, we talked about it before. It's brought marked improvement with some anxiety depressions. May make it easier for you to discuss these painful matters."

"We used to give that to surgery patients. For nausea, you know. . . . I suppose this dosage will be quite a bit larger though."

"Yes. We'll start at around fifty milligrams a day and increase it gradually."

"Are there . . . Well, I recall we had to be on the alert for adverse reactions. Jaundice. Once a woman developed agranulocytosis. What. . . ."

"Very little danger of that. We'll keep a careful check on your white count and your blood pressure. Some people have no side effects. At worst, they're usually no more than inconveniences—drowsiness, nasal congestion, faintness, low blood pressure. Occasionally a rash or slight tremors."

"Yes. Well, of course, that wouldn't matter. I wonder, though. . . ." She looked at him with surprising sharpness. The British precision coated her voice. "Would I have the choice of stopping the drug if . . . I want help, but I don't want to lose control. I think I have a right to that choice."

Still afraid, holding the world at a distance. But was it really the world or just him? "I wouldn't like to promise anything, Miss O'Hara," he said. "Dr. McLeod makes these decisions."

No answer.

He sketched another house on his pad. Of course, if he was willing to risk it, he could still marry her. They couldn't stay at Holly Springs; maybe he wouldn't even be able to practice around here. But they could go somewhere. If nowhere else, back to Kentucky. And even if it ended that way, even if he did have to admit he was a parasite, he'd still be happier than if he'd married a debutante.

She wasn't talking any more. Angered—or perhaps just frustrated—by his incombatable reference to McLeod. Her gray-green eyes stared at him defiantly. Pierson only saw this with a side glance, because he knew that looking closer would cause them to flutter and turn away. He was a fool to call himself a doctor. More than that, a damn bastard. He stood up a little too quickly and opened the door. "Thank you, Miss O'Hara," he said. "They'll probably start that medication this week. I'll see you soon."

❡ 3

The old man seemed different that afternoon—haughty, almost angry. At first David Holliday thought he might not have his hearing aid turned up; then he decided it was just himself still a little out of step after his vacation.

"Well, how've you been, Dr. Stoughton?" he asked cheerily as they settled down in the smoker. He held out his pack of cigarettes, but Stoughton shook his head irritably.

"How's the summer treated you?" he tried again.

"Well, I'm still here, am I not?"

"Yes, I guess you are." Holliday smiled, trying to seem sympathetic and at the same time to make a joke of it. But the old man continued to scowl.

"I've been on vacation, you know. We went to Vermont this year, and it was beautiful. Slept under blankets nearly every night. Dr. Stoughton, you ever been to Vermont?"

"Yes."

"Beautiful, isn't it? Where'd you go?"

"Yes."

"Where'd you go?"

"We had a cottage. Used to go every summer." The sullen scowl faded gradually. "In the beginning Nancy and I went to Lake Ossipee. Had a cabin. I liked to read and walk in the woods. She used to sit by the fire and knit." When he spoke of it, he could almost smell the crisp, woody smell of that cabin, though it must be thirty, forty, almost fifty years now. He could see Nancy in her faded gingham dress and red woolen jacket puttering around with the iron frying pan or sitting on the hearth writing letters for their next trip to the post office. "But later when the boys came," he added, "we went to Lake Winnepesaukee."

"We were on Lake Champlain," Dr. Holliday put in. "Marvelous. Very civilized. Didn't have to lift a finger if you didn't feel like it."

"We did that, too, later when we were alone again, the last four summers before Nancy died." The old doctor was talking freely now, apparently oblivious to his original grudge. "But with three boys it was really easier and pleasanter to have that cottage on Lake ... Lake ..."

"Winnepesaukee?"

"Yes, Winnepesaukee. We had a couple—a cook and a gardener, Nicole and uh ... I can't remember his name. They were French. Anyway, we took them both." And, if possible, that was an even nicer memory. The boys scrambling in with scratched legs and berry-stained fingers, talking of birds and buried treasure and sailing winds.

David Holliday looked at the shriveled smiling face and wondered if some day he would be able to recall memories as pleasing as that. He could not now, and he could see nothing in the present that even time might transmute into a sweet dream. Thinking back forty years, there were some nice things: the smell of the big cedar tree at Christmas; fried chicken and wine jelly with whipped cream; his mother's lips on his cheek at bedtime. But even then everything had not been perfect. There were his mother's reprimands for playing with "common" children. There was his father's bitter harangue about how any decent-minded Alabamian would stay at home and take up his father's business instead of gallivanting off to the North.

"I have three sons," the old man interrupted his thoughts. "Did I tell you I have three sons? All grown now. One's a doctor."

"Yes, I know," the doctor nodded affably. "They been to see you lately?"

The scowl came back then, and the vein swelled thick in Stoughton's red forehead. "Sons, bah! Ungrateful rascals!" he exploded. "Feed 'em, dress 'em, send 'em to college. And all they do is lock you up!"

"They don't come to see you?"

The wrinkled face was almost purple now. "Oh, they come, they come! But I wish they didn't."

"Why?"

"I'm no idiot! I know they put me here."

"You don't like it here?"

"No."

"What about chess? And O.T. and pool and the movies?"

"Don't play chess."

"You used to."

"Don't any more."

"What do you do?"

"Nothing. Except read sometimes. Nothing." There were tears in the old man's eyes.

"That's too bad," Holliday replied. "You must be very lonely." He wondered for a moment if in the same position he would be lonely. But he didn't think so. In fact, he thought he might even enjoy it. He'd feel lost without Mary Laine, of course, and he'd miss his bourbon and sleeping late on Sundays and going places like Vermont. But he'd have all his books brought in and just read and read and read. "What would you like to do?" he asked the old man.

There was no answer.

"Would you like to leave the hospital? Would you like to live with one of your sons?"

"They don't want me."

"But you couldn't manage alone, do you think?"

"No." The face was pink instead of purple now; the vein small again.

"Suppose they did want you? Would you go?" Holliday thought of his mother again. Of her tall regal posture, of her vicious devotion to propriety. Then he remembered the wizened, spider-like creature clutching the sides of the nursing-home bed. His round face grew sad. "Would you go home with them if they asked you?" he asked.

"Of course," the old man snapped. "I'm only here 'cause they put me here."

❪ 4

Their voices rang like glass, clear and sharp in the cool evening air. Young voices vibrating with laughter. A little like college, Phil Pierson thought.

But he did not join in. Because it was all just jabber—a confusion of sounds too remote for him to grasp. He was remembering this same party last October and the October before that. Perhaps he should have gone then or should be going now. Maybe he'd been wrong to listen to Holliday: "a big challenge . . . an opportunity for much deeper experience, much nobler sacrifice . . . always learning and giving of your own growth." Or had it been his own heart he listened to, his own weakness, the need for security, the dread of failure?

Pierson struggled determinedly to keep his crippled foot from dragging him behind the group. Anyway, if I had gone, he thought, there wouldn't be this problem now—loving her and knowing it's wrong, impossible, risking hurting her even more than myself. I should speak to Holliday, he told himself for the thousandth time. I will. I'll do it tonight. Soon as he's had a drink.

"This kind of gets on your nerves after a while, doesn't it, Phil?" Fred Richards had slowed up and was walking beside him. "Reminds you of giving oranges to the poor at Christmas."

"Umm . . . Yeah."

The others had reached the door of the main building and were waiting for them. "Hey, Phil," Charlie Nichols called. "Isn't roast pig always the main dish at these affairs? Steinman won't believe me."

"Sure," he called back gaily, laboring hard to hurry. "Sure. A whole roast pig with an apple in his mouth. The apple's for dessert. They divide it up."

Everybody laughed.

It was much easier after the second drink. David Holliday smiled benevolently into his glass. Martha McLeod was still sober as a judge and probably shooting pious, incriminating looks in his direction. But he didn't mean to be intimidated tonight by Martha or anybody else. He meant to have a good time, and, if he couldn't do that, to at least make it as painless as possible.

He knew that none of them had really wanted to come—not to something like this anyway. Just as the liquor which soothed him made Martha McLeod indignant; so these young men must find it difficult to spend an evening with people like him and Mary Laine and the Wilsons. They were probably like him, preferring either to get roaring drunk, sing songs and laugh at obscene stories, or to spend the evening at home with a book.

He looked across the room at Mary Laine talking to Ellen Collins. This was Mary Laine's party. In the beginning it had been his idea, but she had taken it over and made a tradition of it. Every year she got in a tizzy over the work involved, but she loved it all the same. Of course, the others might enjoy it, too, later, though not in the way she intended. They would enjoy it because of the bourbon which was already beginning to work a little. Ellen Collins was talking more, not just to Mary Laine or softly, stiffly to Martha McLeod, but easily, almost heartily now with a half-smile on her flushed face to Phil Pierson and the Steinman boy. He'd seen her at the bar a few minutes before when he went to refill his glass, and they'd exchanged smiles. They would be the last ones here tonight—they and Charlie Nichols and possibly Steinman. Ellen could be fun when she let herself.

They were talking about other fields of medicine now, ones in which there was money without the drain on your time. . . . "Yes, they're loosening up," Holliday comforted himself. The young ones; the ones that would. All except Pierson. You could never tell about Pierson. Right now he was standing there scowling at his glass, forcing down deep gulps at regular intervals. But any minute he might laugh or say something clearly to signify he had broken through and meant to belong. Or he might stay like that all evening.

"Well, what about OB–GYN?" Neville asked. "Birth rate's going up every year, and it's getting more and more complicated. Diet, psychology. Getting ready, getting back into shape. It's limitless."

"Yeah, and when they're too old to be pregnant," Steinman put in, "you can treat them for tumors."

A few titters went around the room. Holliday looked at Martha McLeod, saw that she was scowling primly and wanted to guffaw just to spite her. Mary Laine was standing beside her, and he was surprised at the difference in their expressions. Mary Laine looked neither shocked nor embarrassed; she was listening intently.

"You know, Steinman, you may think that's funny," Fred Richards cut in, "but I was reading somewhere the other day about what a tremendous increase there's been in uterine and mammary cancers. Fabulous field for research."

"Well, you know," Phil Pierson said, draining his glass with one last determined gulp, "this isn't the most realistic conversation for people who've just slaved away eight years of their lives to be psychiatrists. Could be we're maladjusted."

"Come now, Phil, be fair," Neville laughed. "You can't expect us all to be as altruistic as you and Dr. Holliday. Sacrifice is noble; so is psychiatry. But some of us like to eat!"

Even Mary Laine smiled indulgently.

"So, it's off into the cold, hard world," Charlie Nichols added. "Eat hearty, Dickie Boy. Everything costs ten cents at the Automat now."

David Holliday laughed, too, but inside he felt sad, defeated, shut out. If only I could tell them, he thought. If only I could get close enough to talk to them like an equal, to share the things Martha McLeod never talks about, the things you can't help but learn in time. But he couldn't get close to them—not even to Pierson. It suddenly occurred to him that the whole world was like that. Too timid, too afraid of being hurt to make even the smallest sacrifice toward easing its loneliness, until they got to be like old Dr. Stoughton—tired and finished and like a baby. Then it was too late. The risk was gone, but so was your world. But I can't tell them that, he thought. He saw Ellen Collins at the bar again then and decided he'd try that too.

(5

The creaking of the floorboards again and the glare of the flashlight. Eileen O'Hara closed her eyes and lay motionless. The night nurse would know by her breathing that she wasn't asleep, but at least she'd go on down the hall without trying to make conversation. It must be very late now—1:30 or 2:00. Strange that the supervisor hadn't made rounds. Perhaps there was trouble somewhere.

When the nurse moved away again, Eileen turned over to look at the luminous dial of her little clock. Ten of two, and she hadn't slept yet. She'd be tired tomorrow, and if they started the thorazine. . . . It probably wouldn't matter, but she'd rather be alert to start with. Maybe if she tried that relaxing system, one muscle at a time.

Toes first. Toes . . . toes. Then legs. Let them go limp. Relax. Legs . . . legs. She closed her eyes to aid the process. But it didn't help. Probably the other idea was better—fixing your mind on a single uninteresting thought. Like the floorboards; the way they creaked and why. Or the big clock in the hall; its dead, even ticking.

Kenneth had not liked clocks. He'd claimed they were depraved, insidious contraptions gloating as they ticked men's lives away. He'd worn a wrist watch, though; a "professional necessity." He'd laughed when she said it was so big it might as well be a clock. He was never late, at least not without calling, except that one night. She'd waited and waited for the phone, for the reassuring rumble of his voice . . . It must have been her, her foolish stubborn propriety. But why hadn't he said so? Or had he really, many times with his eyes? And she had not dared.

Eileen opened her eyes, but there was no comfort in the walls of the shadowy room. It was time she stopped pampering herself with these useless self-pitying obsessions. She ought to be over Kenneth by now. And even if she weren't, she could no longer run away from the realization that he had not loved her enough after all.

Perhaps the thorazine would help. Somehow she couldn't have the faith in it she should. But then, she never could when she herself was concerned. She couldn't believe she was "mentally ill" or that anything other than self discipline could help her.

Still, the doctors ought to know. Night and morning for four days now they'd taken her pulse, blood pressure, temperature. And the blood work. Probably the medication would start tomorrow. Eileen squinted against the darkness trying to remember: was thorazine the little orange pill?

Warm bitter coffee fragrance floated in from the hall. Lucky night nurse. It seemed deliberate torture with morning so far away and then the two-cup limit.

Eileen knew that the people who were jealous of any attention received by others would envy her for the thorazine. And those who felt they were not receiving the treatment they should, who could not understand the therapeutic value of rest, exercise, wholesome food, and human contact would be jealous, too. Until they saw the consequences. Drowsiness, he had said, faintness, low blood pressure, "slight" tremors. But there was no way of knowing just how severe those reactions might be. Or whether she might be one of the rare people to develop jaundice or even agranulocytosis.

Agranulocytosis. The technical word set Eileen's whole body prickling with cold beads of perspiration. She could feel her heart thumping its fear against the mattress. Agranulocytosis. She'd nursed only one case of it, but she would never forget.

Jaundice could be cured. But agranulocytosis? "Provided it's caught in time," they said; but how often was that? That dying woman's face loomed out at Eileen from the gray walls. They'd filled her with drugs, and still her body wouldn't fight. Still the soaring fever, the throat so sore she wouldn't speak to anyone except her husband. And nearly three weeks to the end.

"Little danger of that," he'd said. A possibility though. Enough to terrify anybody with any knowledge. Still Eileen knew it wasn't really that that frightened her. It was Dr. Pierson—the pained intensity of his eyes behind the horn-rimmed glasses; the determined, almost stubborn firmness of his gentle mouth; his voice straining after authority; his square fingers; and, of course, his poor, lame, wagging foot.

She'd been foolish about him already, let her mind daydream too freely. Suppose, weakened further by the drug, she allowed that foolishness to show? Still worse, suppose she lost control to the point that her tongue wagged openly. To Eileen that seemed almost more ghastly than the possibility of death.

There was a commotion in the hall. The supervisor. The night nurse shuffled and creaked to meet her. Then the usual whispering. Only, three voices instead of two. Eileen strained to identify the doctor. It might be him. He seemed to get a lot of the less desirable chores. But it was McLeod. She could tell by the hushed, dead-toned voice, and by the way the stupid nurse kept saying "Yes ma'am" instead of "Yes, Doctor."

When she heard them heading toward her room, Eileen turned over on her stomach and pretended to be asleep. Perhaps it would be good if McLeod were her doctor. She seemed cold, insensitive, uninteresting. But she must have some strong points. Maybe when you got to know her, she could be kind. Certainly, she seemed strong and sensible. Anyway, she was a woman.

The other day in their conference—had he seen? What had he noted on his pad or, even worse, in his mind? When he was doodling or staring into space, wasn't he really scanning her face, her trembling hands for proof of what he already suspected? That might even be one reason for the thorazine. Could be they were trying to break her, to expose her emotions and deal with them in the open. They'd call it "therapeutic transference." They'd never know how much it hurt, how much it mattered to her.

The door locked at the end of the corridor, and the creaking footsteps, the shifting flashlight came up the hall past her door again. Eileen blinked at the darkness, listened to the ticking of the clock and the droning, sleeping silence. It seemed to her she had never been so trapped.

III

DAVID HOLLIDAY hadn't meant to have a conference with anyone that morning. He was tired and his head throbbed from the party the night before. He didn't feel like solving anybody's problems—even his own. So when he'd finished his mail, he went over to Hall 3 Women to see some of the new patients. Martha McLeod had been nagging him about it for weeks. That would be easy. No straining to keep his intuition and his probings subtle. Just the pleasant, automatic part of him would have to work, the grin and the warm handshake.

But when Mrs. Joslin wasn't in the nursing office, he walked down the hall to find her. On the way he smiled and nodded to the women he knew. George Purdy's wife, knitting; Mrs. Webster; a sweet-faced woman who smiled as if she knew him but whose name he couldn't recall; and in the living room, little Millie Pratt bent over a jig-saw puzzle.

"Hello, Millie," he grinned. "How's it coming?"

"Hello, Dr. Holliday," she said, and even as he turned he could feel her hand on his coat sleeve. "Excuse me, sir." Her voice trembled, and when he looked at her face again, he saw her eyes were open wide, her lips thin as if she were holding her breath and gulping the words out. "But I . . . If you have time, I'd like to talk to you."

He didn't want to stop. He wanted to say, "I'm sorry; as a matter of fact, I don't have time." But the tremble in her voice compelled him. "All right," he said. "I have a few minutes."

And as it turned out, it wasn't what he'd expected at all. She began the minute they were inside the conference room, pouring the words out frenziedly, breathlessly, as if afraid she might not finish. She was afraid, she told him. She wanted to get well, at least to be treated like a well person, but she didn't want to go home. She'd been wanting to talk to him for a long time, ever since they'd moved her to Hall 2 and then up here to Hall 3. She liked it here. She liked the people and not taking insulin and not being watched so much. But everybody kept telling her how well she was doing, and Mother kept talking about when she would go home. And she was afraid. She hoped they wouldn't make her go home. She couldn't bear to go home.

"Why is that?" Holliday asked wearily. The drawn whiteness of her face reminded him of Mary Laine's that morning. And that was irritating. Partly because he thought Mary Laine's anxiety was feigned; partly because he feared it wasn't. "Why don't you want to go home?"

"Well, because they hate me, I guess. Because they're so mean. Tom mostly, but Mother, too, a little."

"Now, I doubt that. I can't believe that. Don't you think it could be partly you? That you're a little greedy? Want . . . or even need . . . more than your share?"

She did not answer. He recalled how Ellen Collins had wanted to try thorazine (She was sometimes more eager than the youngsters about these new drugs.) and how he had opposed her on the grounds that what they wanted to achieve here was long-range stability, not immediate appeasement. He wondered with more concern now if this might not be another of the cases where the two had to be accomplished simultaneously. "Where would you go?" he asked gently. "What would you do if you didn't go home?"

Still no answer.

"You needn't worry, though," he added. "We wouldn't make you go home or even leave the hospital until you wanted to. We wouldn't *let* you go; you'd still be sick."

"You wouldn't? No matter what Mother said?"

"Of course not. You're the one who works with Dr. Collins; not your mother."

"Oh. Yes."

She seemed greatly relieved. "There's one thing, Millie," he continued cautiously. "There's one thing you've got to make up your mind to. We want to help you, and we will. But we can't do more than that. Home—your mother, your stepfather, the boy at school —they all exist. We can't change them. It's you must change. It's you must compromise. Take what you can and forget about the rest."

"But how can I change?" Her voice was distraught and surprisingly loud. "I don't love them. I hate them."

He didn't try to reason with her or even to soothe her obvious distress. He just listened solemnly, a little remotely. Because suddenly he didn't know what to say. Perhaps I've been mistaken all along, he worried. Maybe pliancy isn't the big thing; maybe it's obstinacy, putting your teeth into something and holding on till the bitter end—till you either have your wish or are no longer alive to want it. "You should be glad," he said at last. "You should be glad the thing you have to accept is only temporary." He realized as he spoke that she could not see that and that he should conceal the annoyance in his voice. But his head ached and he didn't care. He almost wanted to hurt her.

"You won't always be a little girl," he added more kindly. "You won't always have to live with your mother and your stepfather. You're growing up to where you can choose where you live and who you want to love and make love you." He looked deep into her small worried face. The impatient anger gnawed at him again. "There are many people can't say that," he finished curtly.

After that he left. Out into the cool fall mist. His head was still throbbing, and he thought of going home for a nap. But he knew he wouldn't be able to sleep, and he couldn't bear the prospect of Mary Laine's pale, dissatisfied face.

What he really would have liked to do was talk to someone like Mrs. Gaitors. Someone aggressive and cheerful. Someone who took what she wanted out of life without feeling sorry for herself or waiting for it to be handed to her. But she was working in the city now.

Then he thought of the Womble boy. There was a patient who could make anybody's head ache. Yet, maybe the challenge of an interview like that was what he really needed to feel better. Impulsively he took the turn in the corridor which led to the men's wing.

In the conference room on Hall 4 Men, Holliday made no effort to hurry. Obviously any conversation must come from him, but also, Ben Womble was not one to be frightened by silence.

A sad spectacle. Holliday had not talked to Ben since that afternoon in the spring prior to the boy's electric shock series. But there had been so many good reports immediately following the treatments that Holliday had almost refused to believe the more recent ones describing Ben's present withdrawal as worse than ever before, until now, seated opposite the boy. Seeing for himself the grim inertia so inadequately recorded by the typed words, he realized the diagnosis of dementia praecox could no longer be denied.

Physically the boy had changed little. He was just as tall and thin, just as pale and stoop-shouldered. Only now, instead of the earlier tension, fear, and apparent feelings of inadequacy, his most obvious symptoms seemed remoteness and perhaps, judging from the suspicious way he glanced about the room, hallucinations.

It sickened Holliday to look at him. To realize that talent and intelligence, sensitivity and emotion could be so crippled before it even looked toward its potentials. To think that a brilliant boy, the hope and pride of a gifted musician, seemed doomed to gradual disintegration.

"Well, Ben," the doctor asked at last, "how was your summer? ... I've been away, you know."

But there was no answer. Not so much as a shift of the glassy blue eyes; not a twitch in the pale, expressionless face.

"Have your parents been able to come more often with the good weather? Or did they take a vacation?"

Still no answer. But underneath Ben was worried—worried and, consequently, irritated—because Holliday had come to see him. He knew why. The doctor had read that letter he once wrote his father, and he wanted to pick his brain about it. He must have heard it on the radio and seen it in the pictures and on the x-ray plates.

"Tell me, Ben," Holliday continued after a brief silence, "have your feelings about your parents changed any lately? How would you feel now about going home?"

Ben was openly angry then. He shifted his eyes to Holliday's face and stuck out his tongue with a hideous grimace. "Why don't you listen to the radio?"

For a moment Holliday was silent—surprised, then trying to understand the significance of what the boy had said. At last he asked, "Radio? What radio?"

"You know. I know you know everything. What I think, what I say, what I do. You watch and you hear and you know. And then you come to pester me, to try to drive me crazy." Ben made another ugly face; then he glanced about the room to see how many cameras, x-rays, and radios there were.

Holliday did not wait to answer this time. He realized that what he was dealing with here was not only beyond his comprehension but probably also beyond anything he could do if he did understand. "I don't know what you're talking about, Ben," he said confidently. "I came to see you because I had some free time and thought you might want to talk. It's as simple as that. And I don't know what in the world this other garble of yours is for."

Ben stared glassy-eyed at the floor.

Holliday resolved to make one more attempt. And he eased back slowly, creakily in his chair before he spoke. "How you and Jack Isaacs getting on?" he asked then. "Jack a pretty good roommate?"

But again no answer.

After a moment Holliday stood up and unlocked the door. "Well, Ben," he said, "if you ever *do* want to talk again, just drop me a note."

It was still too early to go home. Yet, after that interview Holliday could not face another patient. Instead, he went outside again, and deliberately headed away from the hospital buildings and carefully tended grounds. Slowly but freely, he walked out through the tall, dry grasses of the unkempt back fields, through the potato patches, past the barren, age-twisted apple trees, which would come down one day, he hoped, to make room for an out-patient clinic. His oversized feet rustled through the dead leaves. He picked a straw and stuck it between his teeth. For a little while he could forget about it all—about his headache and Mary Laine and the complexities of right and wrong. For a little while nothing was very vital. Everything was temporary.

(2

From noon on Mary Laine sat in the front window looking out at the drab October day. David had said he wouldn't be home till twelve-thirty. But perhaps since it was visitors day he'd come a little early. All morning she'd worried and made trips to the bedroom to examine herself and searched through medical journals for some kind of information.

But nothing was any good. The material in the journals was either too general or not what she wanted to believe. And as soon as one self examination helped her decide her trouble was imaginary, she had to check just one more time and ended up convinced of her worst fears. So, at last she had decided she must tell David.

THE BIG GAMBLE 173

No matter what he said, or how foolish it might seem, she wouldn't feel free or safe again until she did.

It had been weeks now since she first noticed the lumps in her breast and almost as long that she'd had the pain. "Quite common in women of 45 and over," one of the books had said, "but often benign, especially when a number appear together.... Usually there is no pain with malignant growths until the condition is fairly well advanced." So if it were cancer ... though, of course, she couldn't be sure—the pain was so slight. It might be she didn't really have any at all; might be she just imagined it because of the lumps. And they themselves weren't terribly conspicuous. Probably she wouldn't even have discovered them if she wasn't so vain, if she didn't have that foolish way of drying herself in front of the mirror.

She dreaded speaking to David about it. Still, after all that cancer talk at the party, and then lying awake wondering and worrying about herself, she couldn't keep it inside any longer. She had to tell David now.

But it wasn't until five minutes of one that the front door slammed and his voice called her name. He looked less gray and sodden than when he had left that morning. He said he'd been for a walk in the fields and found the perfect place for an out-patient clinic. "You ought to stroll out there sometime, Mary Laine," he said. "You'd love it. Take away every pain you ever had."

She smiled and kissed his cool cheek and asked him if he'd like a glass of sherry before lunch. That would give her a chance to broach the matter on her mind.

But she couldn't. "You are not a child," she kept reminding herself. "What's more, you've been married nearly thirty years. Your body is almost as much David's as it is your own." But that didn't help. Not then or while he was drinking his sherry or at lunch. "You have to discuss things like this at meal time," Mary Laine urged herself, "because that's the only time you see him." But she could not. And as the meal progressed, the subject seemed more and more impossible. So instead, she talked about New York and the Beckwiths and how she wished they already lived in the city so that she could get to know some of the women she'd met in Vermont, so that Lillian could make her debut. And she did "so wish" he would consider Jack Beckwith's offer to take him into the practice. It was a fine practice.

Although he heard Mary Laine out, David Holliday was irritated. He was trying to develop an armor against her talk. He must remember it was an obsession she could not help—a broken record, for which the best reception was deafness.

After lunch they went into the study to have another cup of coffee and a cigarette. It was dark there—partly because of the cloudy October day, partly because of the paneled walls. And though it was smaller and, of course, far less grand, the room reminded Mary Laine of the library at home, where her father had always summoned his children for serious conferences.... She had gone there once, as a very little girl, to be told about the death of her baby brother; again, because she had gone outside the walled garden without asking Celeste's permission; when they decided to send her to boarding school; and for the last time, the night before her marriage to David Holliday. And surprisingly those memories helped. You did not dawdle in the library at home. You went straight to the point.

So looking at the floor, forcing the words out through stiff white lips, Mary Laine began. "I know what you think," she quavered apologetically. "And you're right. I know that. No matter how badly I feel, I say to myself what you always say about it's being more in my mind than my body. But some things are real. You know it yourself, and so does Martha McLeod. Things like the bleeding and the anemia. And all those colds I had last winter."

"Yes, I know." The doctor pulled a letter from his pocket and began to reread it. He would not allow himself to get irritated.

"And if those things are real," she continued, "you can't help wondering if something else is too.... I-I've had this swelling in my breast for some time now. Swelling...lumps...and a little pain. And the way they were talking at the party last night. I wish David, I wish you'd just take a look. Now. You could look, and if it's nothing, well, if you say it's nothing, I'll believe you and not mention it again."

"For God's sake, Mary Laine. Last week it was dizziness; the week before, headaches. I believe you and I'm sorry, but I've told you a million times it's death to indulge yourself." He crumpled the letter, already oblivious to what it said, and threw it across the room to the wastebasket.

"I-I'm not trying to indulge myself," Mary Laine pleaded. "But if I'm afraid. . . ."

"You weren't afraid in Vermont," he reminded her. "Why is it you always get afraid after you've complained about not living in New York? How blind do you think I am?"

"I don't think you're blind, David. I just want you to look." Her lips trembled; tears trickled down her face.

David Holliday was surprised at his own harshness and ashamed. But he was too irritated to retract his words.

"I'm sorry," he said gently, touching her shoulder and looking down into her face. "I'm tired and I was gruff. I'm sorry."

She had stopped crying now. Her plump colorless cheeks were still streaked with wet, but the beginnings of a smile quivered about her lips.

He realized she was trying to speak, but he did not give her a chance. "I'm sorry, my dear," he said, glancing at the clock. "I've got to go; late already. We'll talk about it later. Tonight. We'll work it out tonight." And again before she could speak, he squeezed her hand and started out the door.

(3

Jack Isaacs' wife, Lucie, had called the day before and made an appointment to see Dr. Holliday at quarter of two. But it was 2:25 before the secretary told her to go in. The doctor looked tired and gray-faced behind his desk; worried and irritated. But he grinned as he stood up to shake her hand. "Sorry to keep you waiting, Mrs. Isaacs," he said. And he didn't seem in a bad mood. His voice was kind, and he was very friendly. More than that, he seemed to want to take a long time, seemed as anxious to question her as she was to question him.

Lucie was glad of that. Yet, it made her anxious, too—afraid that his polite talk of the weather and seemingly genuine interest in the children might lull her away from her purpose. And when he did stop and lean back receptively in his chair, it took all her strength to speak the words she had made up her mind she must speak.

"Doctor," she began, eyes looking downward, but face carefully calm, "Doctor, I hope you won't misunderstand what I have to say. I hope you won't just classify me as a martyr and let it go at that. Because it's desperately important to me now that I have the truth—good or bad—from someone."

Holliday did not speak. He sat very still, listening attentively.

"What I want to know is this: Am I the root of Jack's trouble? Dr. Richards doesn't tell me, and certainly, Jack will not. But I have wondered more and more of late, if the whole trouble might not be me?" Her lips trembled as she spoke, but there were no tears.

"What's made you think this?" Holliday asked gently. "Has Jack said something?"

"No. Jack says nothing. But Jack's lying. About what, I don't know. But he *is* lying. Surely, you've seen that."

"Yes. But that isn't so strange. Many of our patients lie. . . . What I want to know is, why do you think Jack's lie concerns you?"

"I don't know that it does. I'm not a doctor; I only know that. . . ." She paused for a moment. Holliday saw her face grow grim, her blue eyes mist over. Still, she didn't cry. "I only know," she continued, "that Jack had no symptoms of this trouble before our marriage. . . . How much it shows, I don't know, but . . . but I am deeply in love with Jack. I can't imagine life without him. Still . . . still, I love him so much that if I am what is making him sick and unhappy and . . . well, I am more than ready to step out of his life."

Holliday did not answer immediately. He watched her tears slip down each cheek. And only then did he speak in a reassuring businesslike tone: "In the first place, Mrs. Isaacs, I can assure you you're mistaken. If anything, your husband loves you even more than you love him. You say you can't imagine life without him. And I'm inclined to think, considering his emotional makeup, that left unguarded, he would refuse to endure life without you."

Holliday watched as the young woman's face grew calm again. "However," he continued, "there *is* something here . . . something you may be able to help us with . . . Jack is Jewish, of course. And you, I believe, are not."

"Yes, sir." Her face was still solemn, but easier in the prospect of a definite discussion.

"Did your family, or his, have any objections to the marriage?"

Lucie's forehead wrinkled. "Yes," she began hesitantly. "I guess you might say my family objected, but. . . ." Thinking back, she remembered she had been a little disappointed by her parents' feelings. Still, they hadn't been strong, not strong enough for anyone to say anything to Jack. After all, he had been very gifted, and almost well-to-do, and very attractive—just the kind of boy Daddy would have wanted for a son-in-law if he hadn't been Jewish.

Besides, the third of five daughters, Lucie had never been a favorite child. Little had been expected of her. And at least one unfortunate match seemed a probability in such a family.

"My parents spoke to me," she continued now, looking into the brown eyes of the big doctor. "Mostly about our children. But . . . No. Daddy actually liked Jack very much. I think today he's his favorite son-in-law."

"Hmm. So your family didn't make much over it—your marrying a Jew. But what about Jack's people? Did you sense any disapproval on their part?"

"No. They're . . . They're both dead now, but they were very warm people—simple and good. I was fond of them. I thought they liked me."

Holliday waited some time before he spoke again. Then he leaned forward on his elbows to look into the young woman's face. "You see, Mrs. Isaacs," he said cautiously, "I think you're wrong to regard yourself as responsible for Jack's trouble. But . . . of course, I don't *know*, but I *am* inclined to think it may have something to do with the fact that he's married a Gentile. Perhaps he may feel guilty, for your sake, because his religion is so discriminated against. Or maybe he feels guilty in himself, because he has abandoned the dogma and rituals in which he was reared."

Her blue eyes looked at him questioningly, but it was nearly a minute before she spoke. "Well, what should I do?"

"Nothing. . . . Only remember that the problem, if indeed I'm right at all, in no way concerns you, but rather just the situation."

"But how can you know? And if you don't know, how can you help him? Every day I come, I am more aware of the lie in his eyes. . . . He was never like that before."

"The lie," Holliday replied gently. "Yes, I see it there, too. But we have reason to think, Mrs. Isaacs. . . ." Holliday felt himself straining for the proper words; he could not be kind enough to this girl. "Well, Jack *is* lying, of course, to you and to us. But, we think, no longer to himself."

Holliday paused again there, distracted by the flickering eyelashes in the girl's grimly composed face, acutely conscious of the contrast with Mary Laine's face at lunch. "It seems to me," he continued, "that Jack's growing steadily. He now seems quite aware of what he's been running away from for so long. It only remains for him to face up to that knowledge."

"B-But you think he can do that?" Lucie's lips trembled again. "You don't think it's beyond him?"

"Mrs. Isaacs, I've told you before, we don't keep hopeless cases. That's still true. And it will be the next time you come."

❪ 4

As Lucie Isaacs went out, George Purdy sauntered into Dr. Holliday's office, apparently unaware of the custom of waiting to be shown in. His thin leathery face was smiling, and his voice vibrated with cheer.

"Afternoon, Doctor," he said. "I know you're busy. But I had to stop an' tell you how happy I am; how thankful I am to you for bringing Gladys around like this."

"Well, George, she's still a way to go yet. I'm glad she's doing so well. But I hope you won't be too disappointed if there are more bad times before the finish."

"Oh, I know, Doctor, I know. Like you told me before, I've gotta be patient. Still, I can't help but be happy now." He set a brown paper sack on the corner of the desk. "Here's some nice Winesaps thought you and the Missus might like. Fresh in from the country this morning."

He left still smiling, walking quickly, lightly as if to music. David Holliday shook his head wearily in the hollow silence that followed. He hoped the little man's happiness wasn't premature. For a moment, too, he felt that he himself was lucky. That no matter how hard it might seem, no matter how empty his life with Mary Laine had become, no matter how poor a substitute pity was for love, it was probably easier to face something tangible like that, something you had to accept and live with but could at least understand.

In the midst of these thoughts Mrs. Weaver interrupted him to say Mr. Jesse Gaitors was calling. Automatically Holliday reached for the telephone, the ready grin spreading over his face. "All right? ... Oh yes, Mr. Gaitors. Good to hear your voice. What can I do for you?"

But as the gentle, though deliberate voice on the other end of the line replied, the doctor's smile faded until it was replaced by a frown. "No, Mr. Gaitors," he said at last. "I'm sorry to disagree with you, but I don't think Mrs. Gaitors is ready for that yet. At present she seems to be doing very well, but I'm afraid two months isn't a sufficient test in her case."

For once, however, the usually compliant Mr. Gaitors would not accept Holliday's opinion as final. His dignified voice sounded urgent over the phone, the voice of a man who was trapped. "But it seems most important to me," he persisted hesitantly, beseechingly, "that she believe I have faith in her. She says she wants to come home."

Holliday realized there was nothing he could say on the telephone that would either pacify or convince the anxious man. His mind searched vainly for an honest, but unrevealing, way to explain the situation. And finally, after a little further discussion, they set up an appointment for 2:15 the next afternoon.

After he had hung up, Holliday sat still there for a long time, staring at his blotter. Chances were he could reason with Jesse Gaitors. But if he could not? The one argument that would certainly bring the man around was one the doctor did not want to use—the Italian boy friend. For a moment he accused himself of letting friendship, or at least personal interest, step in where his medical experience should rule. But then he told himself, and he thought with genuine honesty, that for once the two were reconciled. The only way Carson Gaitors could ever truly find herself was to go through experiences like this Italian fellow and work her own way out.

Telling Jesse Gaitors about the affair meant telling Martha McLeod. And that, in turn, would involve demotion to Hall 3 and at least six months of struggling back to where Carson was now. The thought of either that or the other, more drastic, possibility— of Carson leaving as her husband had requested, and the work of the last three years going to waste—filled Holliday with hopelessness. He was convinced that Carson Gaitors was a good person with great potentials if she only had time to develop them. He admired her, even perhaps felt some affection for her, because of a kind of bond between them, because her strength seemed so much greater than his, her weaknesses so similar; and yet she had been driven to surrender where he had not.

And so Dr. Holliday resolved not to use his strongest weapon. Not unless at the last moment a drastic measure seemed the only salvation. He comforted himself again with the reminder that Jesse Gaitors would surely come around.

About 4:30 the youngest Stoughton boy came with his pretty blond wife. They both looked tired and browbeaten. They'd been to see the old man, and he'd told them once more that they were ingrates, that he hated them and never wanted to see them again.

"It's not so much that I can't bear being told that," the young man said now. "I can always remind myself that he's old and sick and not the man he once was. But I hate to see him so unhappy. If there's something we could do—my brothers and I—anything that would make him happier, we'd like to very much. You're the only person I know he consistently speaks well of...."

All three of them laughed softly.

"...So I thought you might have some idea."

"How would you feel about taking him home with you? Maybe if not you, one of your brothers?"

The young man looked surprised. "You think it would be all right?"

"Well, it would be hard on you, very hard. He probably won't ever be really happy again no matter where he is. But he might feel a little less resentful if he were living with one of you or even in an apartment with a companion."

The couple stayed a little longer, discussing various aspects of the proposed change. When they left, they still looked perplexed, but less harried. They said they'd talk to the others and come back the next week. Holliday felt better, too, when they left. He took one of the firm red apples out of the paper sack George Purdy had brought. His mouth puckered with the acid sweetness, and he mused sadly that it was too bad old trees like the ones he had seen that morning could no longer produce such fruit.

(5

Carson Gaitors smiled at her reflection in the expanse of shining mirror as she patted fresh powder on her face and sleeked her dark hair back into its chignon. She sat down then in one of the green leather chairs to smoke a cigarette and study the silver pink lacquer on her nails.

It was at least an hour before Francie would be there for their luncheon date, probably an hour and a half—depending on how late the band had had to play the night before and whether he had had a hangover when he got up this morning.

It was a dull day at the agency. Three cancellations because of the flu, Mr. Rothstein out of town, and another of Olin's long weekends. She'd had almost nothing to do except answer the phone: "Mr. Rothstein is out of town. I'm sorry, Mr. Vaughan isn't in today. Could someone else help you? Mr. Hurlburt or Miss Willoughby?" She'd looked at all the new issues of the magazines and called the drug store for coffee and doughnuts. Then she had felt she couldn't wait another minute for Francie and came in here to the ladies room just to look at pink walls instead of green.

These walls were the same color as the bedroom walls at home—a little rosier perhaps. They made Carson think of this last weekend, of waking up Sunday in the big, soft bed with Jesse beside her, looking down at her with the grave intentness of a watchdog. She had been startled a little seeing his big, gray eyes and drawn face, but it had pleased her too. Not in the exciting, feverish way Francie's velvet eyes did or the tingling touch of his strong brown fingers. But in a much safer, quieter, perhaps even more satisfying way. She had liked the feeling so much that she had shut her eyes again after the first look just to bask in the warm peace of his attention.

And in that dreamy hush with the morning sunshine playing across her face so that her eyes saw it even though they were closed, it came to her sharply, unclouded by doubt, what was right, what she must do. Francie was more fun, more of a thrill. But also just a game, like poker—something that sooner or later you must either lose at or grow bored with. Holliday was right. For all his drawling geniality, you had to give him credit; he knew what he was talking about. Compromise though it might be, there was a future for her with Jesse.

Sunday was gone now; so was the comfortable bed and the sun flickering against her eyelids. It was soggy cold Tuesday, but her mind had not changed. Sometime before long, perhaps even today, she would have to let Francie know this was as far as she could go. One day, in fact, she would have to say good-by. She crushed her cigarette in the glass ash tray and lit another, trying to plan just how she would give Francie the brush. But that was too hard; the kind of thing you couldn't plan but must just do when the moment arose. Besides, there was no need to rush. "After all," she told herself, laughing bitterly, "if you're going to be pure the rest of your life, you might as well have one last fling before you start."

But there was nothing even close to laughter inside her. Rather uneasiness, fear, an almost panicky sense of helplessness. It was the animal in her—she could no longer run away from that—the animal that wanted Francie. And that animal was wild, ferociously powerful. After three long years of earnest battling, it was still there unsubdued, grinning at her with drooling fangs.

"Yet there *is* the good part of me," Carson tried to comfort herself. "I *do* love, or at least feel fond of Jesse. And I *do* appreciate books and fine music and . . . Oh, God!" She could feel tears crowding, aching in her throat, and it took all her strength to keep them there. Deliberately she pushed Francie's dark face to the back of her mind and strained to find some of her old devil-may-care tranquility. The easiest way to do that was to think of Jesse. She could learn to love him. She could make a life with him—have children perhaps, entertain, go to the theater. Perhaps, confronted by hard realities like that, the animal in her *would* at last lie down. Still, that seemed nearly as far-fetched as Francie's request that she go off with him on his next trip.

The only solution seemed simply not to think; to let the forces inside her fight it out for themselves. At last she dropped her second cigarette butt in the ash tray and went back to her desk.

That was only the beginning.
Somehow she got through lunch with Francie. Fortunately, he

did have a hangover and so was not overly ardent anyway. Afterward he put her in a cab at the restaurant, because his apartment was just up the street and he wanted to go back to bed.

Then the long torturing afternoon. Methodically she performed the same pointless duties as in the morning with the same outward composure. But inside she felt torn apart. When the office closed, and it was time to go back to the hospital, it was all she could do to make herself head for Grand Central Station. She missed the first train as usual, because she dawdled and window-shopped all the way. It seemed so pointless going back tonight, so stupid. Like locking yourself in a closet because you were afraid of the dark.

She thought about Francie and Jesse all the way out on the train. She felt lonely and unsure of herself and hopeless. When she got off at Perthville, she wanted to get right on another train for New York. But because that would have meant a fifty-five-minute wait, she finally persuaded herself to go on to Holly Springs. When she got there, the door was already locked. Sullivan opened it with the announcement that the doctor was making rounds.

"Oh." Entering, Carson glanced to the left, saw Dr. Pierson and Miss Tucker, and braced her automatic smile. "Hello, Dr. Pierson."

"Evening, Mrs. Gaitors. How's the big city today?"

"The same," she said with a little laugh. "Dirty as usual."

They all laughed politely. But for Carson it was better than that. Suddenly she felt easy again, more confident than she'd felt all day. She liked Pierson. Nice shy, intellectual sort of fellow—kid-brother type without the naiveness, with that little hard turn to his mouth that let you know he thought for himself. The kind you could talk to and be friendly with without feeling your brain was being picked.

Seeing him here now made her feel safe and normal. Not like a ravenous animal any more. For a moment she almost felt she should talk to him, ask for a new view of this struggle inside her.

But, classifying that as just one more impulse, she forced herself to turn away, down the corridor to her room. There as she counted her money out on the dresser, the eyes of Jesse's photograph attracted her attention. For some reason, she especially liked those eyes tonight. She decided to call him from the office again tomorrow.

(6

It was fifteen minutes since Mrs. Weaver had gone, and nearly thirty since the last visitor. But David Holliday still sat at his desk, frowning down at the list of new interns coming next week. A Jew, an Irishman, a Kutz from Pennsylvania. About average. Dennis O'Toole—what could be more Irish than that?

Mary Laine's anxious face kept wavering before him. "We'll talk about it later," he had said at noon. "Tonight. We'll work it out tonight." He remembered the relief those words had brought at lunchtime, the simple, sensible solution they had seemed to provide. Now they seemed neither simple nor sensible, but rather a threat, a challenge he had made for himself, which he could not evade. "But if some things are real, you can't help wondering about others," he heard the fearful plea again. Perhaps he'd been too hasty; he really had been gruff. He could've looked.

It was dark outside. He took out his watch. 5:35. He should go home now; he'd put it off long enough. Mary Laine *had* looked pale this morning. He'd told himself it was just the party the night before and his own imagination. But she hadn't stayed at the party late, and she never took more than one drink. If she really was sick, he'd never forgive himself. Not just for today, but for all the other times. And after all, it was quite possible. Breast tumors— even malignant ones—were common in women her age.

He shut the folder of papers and placed it carefully in the middle drawer. But just as he was pulling on his raincoat he noticed a silent figure standing in the doorway. Young Pierson.

"Well, hello," he cried. "Want to see me, Phil?"

"Sir, I did. Saw your light and thought. . . . I didn't realize you were on your way home. I can talk tomorrow just as well."

"No, no. Come on in. Too early to go home anyway."

"All right, if you're sure, sir. I really don't mind waiting. It's a minor thing. Something I thought you might be able to advise me about."

"Come on then. Have a seat." The older man hung his coat up again and shut the office door. "Have a cigarette?" he asked, settling back in his desk chair and motioning to the big leather one beside it.

"Thank you, I have some right here."

They each lit a cigarette. Then Holliday asked, "Well, Phil, what's on your mind?"

"Actually it's not important. Not even about me. It's this friend of mine, fellow I knew in med school. He's a psychiatric resident too—at a place in Connecticut." The young man spoke evenly, precisely, but hurriedly.

Holliday nodded.

"You might think . . . I mean, to hear me talk, you might come to the conclusion that he's not too smart or at least has no knowledge of ethics or therapeutic psychology or . . . but actually he's a bright chap. Just a little emotional, inclined to be overly . . . uh . . . anxious. . . . He spoke to me, you see—asked my advice. I didn't trust my own judgment, so I told him about you. . . . How much faith I have in you and, of course, he's heard about you."

"Ummhmm. Hope I can help. What's his trouble?" It was Pierson, himself, of course, and not just a friend. Holliday knew the young man too well to be fooled by this ruse. In the first place, Pierson was too upset to be discussing any problem but his own. And secondly, sympathetic listener though he might be, he was not venturesome enough to plead another boy's case to his chief.

"Probably he'll sound like a . . . lovelorn adolescent."

"That's all right. I've been lovelorn myself." Holliday chuckled. "Don't know's anybody can help that, but I'd like to try. What is it?"

"He thinks he's in love . . . with a girl, . . . a patient."

Holliday said nothing.

"He can't really know how the girl feels. . . . He's all . . . all 'shook up.' " Pierson laughed nervously. "He knows it would be foolish and unethical to tell her he loves her. He could wait till she's better, . . . she already is a little; he'll treat her as an outpatient. B-But he's afraid that might hinder her therapy, and he doesn't want to do that."

"Ummhmm. I see."

"Or maybe he should never tell her. He doesn't know what to do. He could leave the hospital or ask to be relieved of the case."

Holliday studied the young man's downcast face. He knew that he must know the girl, but he couldn't be sure which one it was. Though the thin face of the O'Hara girl flashed across his mind, that seemed too much like a fairy story. Still, he decided to advise the boy as if it was the Irish girl. "Your friend, ..." he began cautiously, "he must know the girl very well. I mean, if he's been her therapist all along, he must be familiar with her moods, her way of thinking."

"Yes, sir. I guess he is, ... but he's young. He makes mistakes."

"So do I."

"Perhaps, sir. But you've had experience. ..."

Experience, Holliday thought bitterly. Experience, and yet I can't make my own wife happy or even yield to the little things that would make her less unhappy. Still, once more now he must live up to the world's misconception of his strength. "Well, of course, I don't know the girl or your friend," he continued to Pierson. "But from your description, I'd say he was intelligent and sensitive but very shy, almost timid."

"Yes, sir. He is."

"And the girl? A little the same way?"

"Yes, sir. She is. A-At least I gather so."

"What would your friend do if he gave up his position?"

"I don't know. But he did well in school. He could probably get something pretty easily."

"Don't you think that would be silly?"

The young man's face shot up, flushed, then looked down again. "I . . . uh . . . I don't know, sir."

"But suppose she loves him? That'd change everything, wouldn't it? Mean the beginning of happiness for both of them. ... You know, Pierson, I have an eleventh commandment: 'Thou shalt be happy.' " Holliday forced himself to laugh softly. "Man's greatest duty in life is to be happy. He's more useful that way because he makes others happy too."

"Yes, sir."

"Sometimes life demands a compromise. But it should always be for the sake of happiness, not at the expense of it."

"Yes, sir."

"So, you know what I'd tell your friend? I'd tell him to wait till the girl's ready for discharge; then feel her out. Like he's just asking about another of her problems. Could make them both happy."

"Y-You really think so, sir?" There was a faint smile on Pierson's face.

"Course, I could be wrong, but that's what I think."

"Thank you, sir. He'll be glad to hear that." The young man stood up quickly and pushed his chair back. "I'll see him tomorrow, and I'm sure he'll be grateful for your advice. Thank you." He turned toward the door.

"Hope it's some help to him. . . . Don't go yet."

Pierson turned so that he was half facing Holliday again. "I have to, sir. I'm supposed to be on rounds."

"Well, go along then. Sorry though—I'd take you home for supper."

Pierson thanked him again, then limped out and shut the door behind him.

I V

IT WAS nearly 6:30 when David Holliday got home that evening. But to his surprise, Mary Laine appeared much more composed than at lunch. She did not go to the front door to meet him, but waited in the study, where she had been sewing, for him to come to her.

"Hello, darling," he said, kissing her forehead. "Sorry I'm late."

"That's all right, dear. I expect it on visitors day."

"Well, I feel doubly bad, because I had to rush off at noon and leave you upset about something anyone would find disturbing." And he did feel genuinely ashamed. The more he looked at her calm, white face and the way she methodically pulled each stitch to its proper tautness, the more painful his increasing guilt became.

"There's no need to feel bad," she said gently. "I *was* upset and *unreasonable,* and you were in a hurry. . . . After just a few minutes I realized my impatience wasn't at all justified. When weeks have passed, what difference can a few hours or even a day make?" She continued sewing as she talked. Her face appeared not only composed but relaxed, with even the suggestion of a smile around her lips. Apparently she was speaking sincerely.

But that only made Holliday feel worse. He felt the love for her, which he had worried about fading, rise strong in him again. And with it, more and more bitter guilt, not only for this noon, but also for many other times he knew he had hurt her.

"Well, regardless of all that," he said with a futile attempt at professional objectiveness. "We agreed at lunch to attend to the matter tonight. And I want us to ... I think we should go upstairs right now and let me thoroughly examine what's been troubling you."

"Oh, David! Really, I'm not that much of a baby." Her blue eyes had come up from her work now and were looking directly into his. "Supper's ready to go on the table whenever we're ready, and I think you, at least, need to relax over a drink.... I do want you to examine me, but I think it would be silly not to wait till after supper."

It took no more to persuade Holliday. He was tired, and besides, for once, he felt very much like sitting with Mary Laine. But despite the drinks he poured, they were both too distracted to make the conversation really enjoyable. Mary Laine tried conscientiously not to mention New York or the Beckwiths. Every time Holliday did, in an effort to please her, she interrupted quickly with something about Lillian or his work.

Both of them were relieved to have supper finished so that the anticipated examination could be performed. And it turned out not to be the ordeal they had feared. Mary Laine, still composed despite her fear, felt surprisingly natural undressed and lying on the bed. And Holliday, once confronted by the actual task, was able to forget both guilt and irritation in his professional probings.

As he fingered the soft, full mountains of her white breasts, he did find several lumps, usually close together. Relief seeped through his suppressed anxiety. Yes, just as he had expected, only cystic mastitis. But he went on carefully, determined to be completely satisfied when he finished.

And it was then, at the crest of his new peace, that the horror swept in to displace it. On the far side of her left breast there was another lump, similar to the others in appearance except that it was isolated and considerably larger. Fear tightened his body; he strained determinedly to remain calm. But further examination of the swelling only confirmed his dread. It was firmly fixed in the surrounding tissue. And though he asked her specifically, Mary Laine, who had complained of some tenderness in the other lumps, said she felt none at all with this one.

For a moment Holliday could not speak. Then he told Mary Laine she could get up and dress. He had to struggle to keep his face untroubled. Waiting for her downstairs, he berated himself bitterly for not having shown more concern earlier. That lump had an 80 per cent chance of being malignant. Mary Laine should have seen another doctor, but even so, he did not need another opinion to know a biopsy was urgent. Eighty per cent odds for cancer and maybe the same chances of his losing Mary Laine. He picked up the telephone and dialed long distance:

"I want to speak to Dr. Clyde Ross at his home on East Eighty-ninth Street. No, I don't know the number." When there was no answer, they tried his hospital. He wasn't there either, but the operator left word for him to call. Then Holliday told her to keep trying the Ross home every thirty minutes.

Mary Laine, who had entered the room in the midst of all this, now appeared openly terrified. "It's cancer, isn't it?" she asked tearfully.

Added to his own worry, that irritated Holliday. Whereas he had blamed himself earlier, he now turned that anger on her. If she hadn't cried "wolf" so frequently before, he'd have paid more attention this time.

"No, it's not cancer," he said gruffly. Then, catching himself, he added more sympathetically, "No, of course, I can't say that, darling. . . . I don't really know. You know as well as I do, that cancer is always a possibility with lumps such as these. A *possibility*," he continued urgently. "Not a *probability*."

Her tears brimmed over. She looked at him beseechingly. "Wh-what should I do?"

"I'm attending to that right now." He stood up and put both hands on her trembling shoulders. "Sit down, darling. It really is all right."

She did sit down but still looked at him questioningly, fearfully.

"I'll tell you what I'm doing," he said carefully, as if speaking to a child. "As you said, you do have some lumps—most of them, I think, a type common in women your age and presenting no reason for concern. But one—just one, now—I'm uncertain about. So I'm calling Clyde Ross. . . . I'm in hopes he'll say you can come in tomorrow morning for a biopsy. If I weren't a doctor and a friend, he wouldn't—in fact, couldn't—do it that quickly. The haste is really only necessary for one reason—our peace of mind."

"You mean they'll operate tomorrow?"

"They call it a biopsy. . . . Probably you'll be home in a couple of days with little more than a Band-Aid up there. If on the other hand, by any remote chance, it should be malignant, they *would* operate right then."

"But, David, you don't think. . . ."

The telephone rang then.

❨ 2

As they drove into New York the next morning, David Holliday could scarcely keep his eyes on the road. His thoughts, his eyes, his very being seemed magnetized to Mary Laine, bundled up in her mink coat, beside him on the front seat.

Her face was pale above the pink scarf crossed over her throat, and there were dark hollows under her eyes.

"David. . . ." Her eyes still stared straight ahead; her thin lips trembled visibly. "David, a good many women have this trouble, don't they? I mean, Dr. Ross is quite . . . uh . . . quite familiar with this kind of work."

"Oh, yes, my dear. Clyde's a good man."

She was silent again momentarily. Then wistfully, "David, do you know what percentage of these cases turn out to be cancer?"

He tried to speak matter-of-factly. "No, my dear, I don't. But I think it's small, and even malignant tumors can be totally removed."

"You'll tell me, won't you? I want to know."

"Oh, of course. Don't worry about that." For some reason then, he thought of George Purdy's visit the afternoon before. The big paper sack of apples, the weathered colorless overcoat, the leathery face. He'd been sorry for George yesterday, had decided that he himself was lucky to have a wife with just the mundane problems of middle-age. But that no longer seemed true. Yesterday he'd been depressed about the change in his relationship with Mary Laine, had thought his love for her had dissolved into pity. But today he knew he had been terribly wrong. This thing he felt for Mary Laine was much deeper than pity or responsibility or even what he had always thought of as love. If he should lose her, he, too, would be lost, helpless—in no time a doddering old man like poor Dr. Stoughton, only worse, because he'd feel guilty and regretful too about not making Mary Laine happy while he could.

Glancing at the white, strained face again, he was deeply aware of her confused-child fear. He put out a big hand to touch the black-gloved one in her lap. "Don't worry, my dear," he said gently. "It's going to be all right."

(3

The pillows felt cool and fresh behind her back, really luxurious. And the room wasn't just another hospital room, white and austere, sterile with the scent of ether and adhesive tape. There were big leather chairs, a telephone on the desk, little pots of African violets on the glass-topped dresser. Mary Laine was a little afraid inside, but otherwise she felt almost pleased being here—secure—in her proper setting for the first time in months. All the "best people" in the city came to this hospital for treatment.

There was a knock on the door, and David came in. He couldn't stay, he said, because they'd be starting soon. But he'd be downstairs the whole time, just as he'd promised, and he'd see her again afterward. She clung to his hand. The frightened excitement was spinning in her again, and she felt a little doubtful, after all, that this was just another imagined malady. "Don't go yet, David," she pleaded. "Stay with me."

"I can't, my dear. The nurse is outside right now, waiting to give you an injection.... Don't worry. It'll be over quick, and you won't feel a thing." He kissed her and pulled his hand away.

Then he was gone, and the nurse was standing beside her bed. "Mrs. Holliday, I have a needle for you; Dr. Ross will be ready shortly."

After that the nurse helped her to change into one of the white hospital gowns. Then two more nurses brought a narrow table for her to roll onto. They covered her with a sheet, asked if she was comfortable, and an orderly came to roll the table through the corridors, into an elevator, through more corridors to a sterile-smelling white room. There another nurse told her to "try to relax, Mrs. Holliday. Just a few minutes."

It seemed longer than that. But she didn't mind. The frantic fear had eased to a gentle nag by then—probably something to do with the needle. She could even distract herself. She counted the blocks of tile in the ceiling, then worked out a pattern in them. That reminded her that she'd always been counting things. When she was a child, the bouquets on the wallpaper in her room, the buttons on her frocks—"rich man, poor man, beggar man, thief...." When she was a girl, the beaux she could count on for dance bids, and later, the weeks, the days, the hours until her marriage to David. Now the longing, almost pleading calculation of the years that must elapse before David would come to New York.

Her mother's voice came back to her then, "I know, Mary Laine, that you may sometimes worry about the temporary hardships involved in marrying an unestablished doctor. But really that doesn't matter. David is a fine boy, and you love each other."

"But, Mother," she wanted to say, "it isn't temporary. It goes on and on."

Then there was Lillian's voice. "I wish *I* could have a house-party.... I wish *we* had a big house I could ask people to."

"Here we are, my dear," she heard David's pleasant drawl. "And it's all for you—the carpets, the chandeliers, even a gold mono-grammed telephone dialer." He chuckled proudly, and she looked around the room. The most beautiful room she had ever seen. Marble mantlepiece with a gold-leaf mirror above it, a polished grand piano in one corner, small white buttons on the wall to buzz for servants.

"You happy, my dear?"

"Now?" she asked incredulously. "Already?"

"Now."

But the nurse was there then, bending over her. "Yes, Mrs. Holliday," she said crisply, "the doctor's ready."

The subdued fear fluttered to life again.

⟨ 4

It was easier driving back that afternoon. The comparatively empty road, the cool air rushing past his cheek, the flashes of fall color set David Holliday pulsating with a sense of freedom and relief. It had begun at the hospital when Clyde Ross came out, still in his green tunic, to say that the operation was over.

The easiness had faltered considerably later when he was sitting across the desk from Clyde, watching the intentness of his face, listening to the gravity of his voice.

"You did exactly right, Dave. . . . We were lucky."

"It was malignant then?"

"Yes. But small, little larger than the lump itself. . . . Still, of course, we had to remove the whole breast."

And neither Clyde's face nor his voice had changed as Holliday tried to get some hopeful prediction out of him regarding the recurrence of cancer. "Well, David, I think you can answer that as well as I can . . . as well as anybody can. We just don't know. This one was small; we think we got it all. . . . But it was malignant. And you know as well as I do the uncertainty that entails."

Then he and Clyde had kidded about bald spots and pot bellies. And he had decided it was a relief after all just to know that everything was a good deal safer than it might have been.

But now alone he began to think. Suppose next month another lump appeared, or next year, or even two years from now? There would no longer be any doubt. Just a matter of time, time and acceptance.

Cars were passing him on the highway. Realizing suddenly that he was going only twenty-five, he pressed down on the accelerator and passed a rusty '47 Chevvy. It seemed impossible to him that Mary Laine could vanish from his life. She was as much a part of him as his eyes or an arm or the red birthmark on his thigh. He would not be helpless like George Purdy, because he had the money to pay somebody like Mamie to clean and cook and wash his clothes. For a while anyway, there would be Lillian. Maybe he could lose himself in his work. Still, even at best, he knew what would happen. Eventually he would become like old Dr. Stoughton. Very competent, even skilled at his work, but bitter with the world

—a scowling ill-tempered old man, who sat in a corner cursing life for shutting him out.

Perhaps, he thought, we should move to the city earlier than we planned. That's what Mary Laine wants. That's what she thinks will make her happy. But David Holliday knew too well that if and when they did go to New York it would be as much for himself as for Mary Laine. He had thought it out so many times in recent months and come up with many different answers, all pointing to the same thing: New York might make Mary Laine happy, but New York would also be an escape for him—one more time he would have run away. So, the issue did not really concern Mary Laine very much at all, but was simply a question of whether or not David Holliday should stay at Holly Springs. In going to New York would he be running away or taking a giant step out of a rut?

The patients there would probably be less challenging, but he would have more to do with them, less time and energy wasted in administrative duties, more money and less prestige—but more people to remind him of the prestige he did have.

He might become himself in New York; whereas here at Holly Springs he seemed to have barricaded himself behind a smiling nothingness to combat—or just keep peace with—Martha McLeod. And it was really that that worried him most—that he might go away simply because he could no longer cope with an old maid in a white coat.

There was a green Volkswagen in front of him; he skimmed past it. Holly Springs had seemed the perfect answer once. Yet, now that seemed less and less certain. More probably Holly Springs *was* a rut, and he just was not strong enough to change.

The telephone rang as he opened the front door, and he rushed to it, still in his coat, preparing himself for bad news of Mary Laine. "All right?"

It was Martha McLeod, her habitually bored voice almost urgent. "Thank goodness, . . . I've been trying and trying to get you, Dr. Holliday. . . . Hate to bother you when you have so much trouble already, but. . . . How is Mary Laine? Nothing serious, I hope."

"No, she seems to be doing fine. Clyde Ross operated this morning, and she came through very well. I hope. . . ."

"Well, as I said, I hate to call on you," Martha McLeod continued methodically. "But we had rather an upsetting incident here this afternoon."

"Oh?"

"Yes. Mrs. Gaitors' husband came out. He said he had an appointment with you. Mrs. Weaver had no record of it, but she told him about Mary Laine, explaining that in your anxiety you had probably forgotten. He still appeared quite irritated and finally agreed to see me instead."

"Oh Lord, I'm sorry. I did have an appointment with him, Martha."

"Never mind. . . . He said right off that he had come to take his wife home. I told him, of course, that that was impossible—for practical reasons as well as legal and medical ones. First, because Mrs. Gaitors was away today at work in New York. But far more important, because she was not yet emotionally ready for discharge. He seemed quite distraught, but finally settled down to discuss the situation."

"It worked out all right though?" Holliday interrupted wearily.

"No, it did not. Apparently, she has pressured him intensely. He kept asking for facts and saying he could not understand. His only answer to everything I said was, 'But she seems so well. I have to make her believe I trust her.' "

"Well, how did it end?"

"He signed the ten-day notice of withdrawal. That was the only way I could prevent him from going right upstairs this afternoon and taking her belongings."

"But you realize. . . ."

"Yes, that since he is her guardian there is no way to force her to stay in her present condition. Still, there was no alternative. . . . I've seen her, but I didn't talk to her at any length. I thought that you. . . . She'll be transferred back to Hall 3 on C.O., you know, but I hesitate . . . well, I think she'd be more likely to accept that from you than from me."

"Perhaps . . . Martha, I don't think you can do that to her. I grant you, there is considerable risk. But you know her make-up. Martha, I think this is one time you'd damn well better forget the rules."

A lengthy silence at the other end. Then the same hushed voice at the same dead pace. "At any rate, I think it would be best if you could talk to her before we do anything."

"All right, I will. Tonight. Where are you?"

"In my office. I'll be working till late—ten or eleven."

"I'll come by there afterward."

"Thank you."

As he hung up the phone, David Holliday's feelings were a mixture of guilt, anger, and relief. "Lord!" he growled, "Can't even get a day off for your own emergency!" But actually he was glad. This would leave no room for his own thoughts. He felt no great despair at the situation, hoping that as usual his tact could accomplish what Martha McLeod's stringency could not. At the same time, however, he knew that if there was a failure in this case, or even a crisis, it would be largely his fault.

❬ 5

Carson Gaitors was pleased when Mrs. Sullivan came in to say Dr. Holliday was waiting to see her. Everything had been in turmoil when she arrived home from work that afternoon and had grown steadily worse with each minute since.

To begin with, McLeod had been waiting when she came in the door. "Why are you late?" And how could she explain that she was not late, or at least no more than usual because she was late every day?

"Your husband was here this afternoon, Mrs. Gaitors, and I was distressed to discover how you've misled him."

"Misled him? Dr. McLeod, I haven't seen him since the weekend. I don't know what you're talking about."

"You telephoned him this morning."

"Yes. So what? He's my husband."

"He said you were determined to leave Holly Springs—either with or without our approval. He said you had asked him to help you."

"Well? He's my husband."

"Do you think it's fair to use a relationship which you plan to sever?"

"Maybe I don't plan to sever it."

"You mean you've found no new interest? I don't know why, I rather had the impression you were trying to cope with a modified form of your old problem. . . . Mrs. Gaitors, do you think you're really well enough to leave the hospital?"

"I've never regarded myself as sick."

"Well, I think it only fair to tell you that when a family initiates the withdrawal papers, it is our policy to keep the patient under constant observation for the ten-day interim. As you know, there are only two halls on which we are equipped for this—1 and 3."

Damned little pious-faced sadist! Carson wanted to slap the flat, white face until it was streaked with red and the neat, white pigtails in a disheveled mop around it. But one thing she had learned at Holly Springs was the futility of violence. When she spoke, her voice was carefully measured, the words pronounced precisely: "I don't quite understand what this uproar is all about, Dr. McLeod. I realize that I'm under your jurisdiction. But I know, too, that my husband had an appointment with Dr. Holliday this afternoon. Therefore, I think he could answer your questions better than I."

Carson said that calmly through her anger. And just as placidly Martha McLeod stood up and walked away. But after that, until the moment when Sullivan announced Dr. Holliday, those stooped white-coated shoulders disappearing down the corridor taunted Carson with unknown fears. So Jesse had come through with his promise to sign her out. But could that backfire? Could they commit her despite her husband? If so, could they possibly send her to a hell-hole of a state place? Was Dr. McLeod just trying to frighten her with that talk of C.O. and Hall 3 or could she carry out those threats?

And so, it was a great relief to see Holliday. Of course, he'd have to support McLeod; perhaps he had even told the woman something about Francie. But if anyone could help her it was he.

He did not speak as she approached, simply opened the door and motioned for her to precede him. And even after they were seated, he waited a few moments before he spoke. "Well, I understand you want to leave us!"

She laughed bitterly. "Is that such news?"

He smiled faintly in response. How like her to bring laughter into even this tension. But somehow that flash of humor only saddened him more. There were gray circles under his eyes and a weary droop to his mouth which made the smile almost imperceptible. "No. I hope everybody here wants to leave eventually, but I'd rather they waited for our go-ahead."

Carson did not reply. She had made up her mind to let him lead.

"I had an appointment with your husband this afternoon. But my wife became ill very suddenly, and I had to take her to the hospital in New York. So Dr. McLeod saw him instead. She tells me he signed the notice of your withdrawal."

"Yes."

"She seems to think you had pressured him into it. Is that so?"

A ridiculous question. A merely casual remark could pressure Jesse Gaitors. And Carson, with her captivating good nature, could pressure even him, David Holliday, with no effort at all.

"She's got a right to her opinion. Why don't you ask Jesse?"

"I'd rather ask you. . . . Mrs. Gaitors, how *do* you feel about him these days?"

"If you trusted my word as much as you do Dr. McLeod's, I think that would be pretty obvious. I want to go home."

"To him?"

"Yes."

"You've changed your mind then, haven't you? Since the last time we talked."

"Yes."

"Why?"

"Does it matter? Maybe I've just seen the light. That I can never have what I want; so I might as well make do with what I have."

"Or is it because even Jesse can seem new and exciting after a vacation from him? How long do you think you'll feel this way?" If he could only break her down, force her to admit her uncertainty and insecurity to him alone. That would give him something to work with and arm them both with an answer to Martha McLeod's severity.

But Carson would not answer. Partly because she was angry at his insinuation, and partly because she could not find a suitable answer.

"What about your orchestra leader?" Holliday persisted, leaning forward on his knees. "You break off with him?"

She did not answer immediately. Because it seemed incredible that she could say these things and mean them, honestly. Almost weird, how important Francie Francoli was in her life six weeks before and now how little he mattered. "Oh . . . how?" she said at last. "I just don't have time for him these days."

She had not given Francie the shaft; she had never quite dared —sometimes afraid of hurting him, sometimes uncertain of anything that final for herself. She hadn't been out with him though; indeed, she had scarcely spoken to him for weeks. Several times she had made excuses about being busy, and he seemed to understand. He never even asked her any more.

David Holliday was relieved to hear that. Perhaps he had not been too wrong in withholding the actual details from Martha McLeod. But at the same time he wondered if Carson was lying or elaborating on a reasonably happy picture. Then he reminded himself she had never lied to him before. She had not needed to, because he had let her know he was her friend. He had always tried to make it clear that even when they disagreed he was on her side. If he could make her remember that now, the battle might be half won. But Holliday already felt hollow with fatigue, as if his mind had ceased functioning. Never lied, he reminded himself, sadly, but changed her mind twenty-four hours later. "How long have you felt this way?" he asked.

"Over two weeks."

"Do you really think that's long enough to be sure? Wouldn't six or eight weeks longer be more realistic?"

Her face grew red. "Hell, I've waited over three years now!"

"So?"

"So, I want to get out while I still have a trace of sanity."

The doctor said nothing, just stared at her with his great, brown eyes. He wished this didn't matter so much to him; he wished he could think of Carson Gaitors as just one more patient. If he could, what he accomplished would be twice as effective. Yet, hard as he tried, it seemed he could not. Every time he looked at her he saw his own reflection too clearly.

"McLeod said she was going to put me on C.O. till I left."

"I don't think she meant that. It's necessary sometimes, but not when the patient is able to be reasonable."

"Can I go on working?"

"I'm not sure about that. I'll have to talk to Dr. McLeod. . . . It's not you so much as legal restrictions we must consider here."

"Well, you know me when I feel frustrated."

"I know. I'll do what I can. And I'll let you know tonight." He mashed his cigarette in the green glass ash tray and stood up slowly. "Just one thing," he said then, turning his solemn eyes on her again. "I'll do what I can for you, but I wish you'd do something for me, too. I wish you'd consider seriously the move you're about to take.... You know how I feel about you, Mrs. Gaitors. Certainly, with all our talks, it has become obvious that our relationship is almost more that of friends than of doctor and patient. But you must know, too, that I regard this new idea of yours as dangerously premature and, therefore, very wrong. I won't try to influence you; I realize that would be futile. Still, I'd be failing you as a friend if I didn't tell you.... So I'll just ask you to please, please think it out for yourself."

Carson did not answer. Defiantly her eyes battled his. At last the doctor said good night and walked out into the corridor.

❬ 6

Martha McLeod was still in her office a few minutes later, as she had promised. A pile of outgoing mail to be censored was before her on her desk, and every light in the room was burning. "Well, David," she said looking up benevolently as he stopped in the doorway. "Come in and sit down and tell me, how is Mary Laine?"

That inquiry seemed completely irrelevant to him now. Indeed, he felt annoyed that Martha McLeod could be so falsely polite when her mind, too, was on the problem at hand. Her calm, white face was like stone—the patient, unyielding mountain rock of reason.

"I just saw Mrs. Gaitors," he answered noncommittally. "She seemed somewhat uneasy about her conversation with you."

"Oh... Did you get the impression she had high-pressured her husband into this?"

"No, I wouldn't say that. But knowing both of them, don't you think most of the pressure in their relationship comes from her?"

"I suppose so, but I don't think that excuses her entirely this time. Did she tell you what she plans to do?"

"Yes, go back to her husband."

"You believe she was telling the truth?"

"Oh, yes. But she can always change her mind overnight."

"That doesn't leave us much to work with, does it?" She continued solemnly. "With her husband as adamant as he is, the usual commitment process is out. Do you think you'd have any influence with him?"

"No." Holliday sighed heavily. "I'll call him tomorrow. I have to anyway, to apologize for forgetting the appointment. But I gather his mind is pretty firmly set."

"Well, I hope you're wrong.... I'll call and give the order for Hall 3 transfer and constant observation. Miss Tucker...."

"No, Martha, I don't think you can do that."

"What? Why we always keep withdrawals on C.O. till they go."

"This case is different." It seemed to Holliday his head must split with its throbbing. He had known this dispute would arise. Yet, now he felt too tired to cope with it. "Look, Martha," he added brusquely, "it's time you realized the importance of treating each case individually. Rules are all very well; they greatly simplify the work. But they're made to be broken. Every so often we *have* to try a new approach."

Martha McLeod was momentarily stunned by the controlled anger in his tone. Her pale, frozen eyes were glued to his face. She was angry, too, insulted that Holliday should speak to her in this manner. But those words, "new approach," captivated her. She remembered when she had heard him say them for the first time. "Don't mean to sound like an upstart, Dr. Horace. But I can't help wondering and trusting we'll always make progress." Martha had thought he was very brave to say that, almost daring. Apparently the older doctors had thought that, too—even Dr. Horace. No one was surprised a few years later when the old man retired and David Holliday was chosen the new medical director.

She hadn't even minded herself, though there'd been some speculation about her getting the position. She'd thought it was right because he was strong and hardworking and sensible, because he never failed to look ahead. She'd admired his progressiveness greatly then; now, though, she was inclined to regard it more as a drawback than an asset.

"I don't know," she replied to him finally in a tone far less severe than she had originally intended. "I quite agree with you about new methods. But it seems to me that in a hazardous situation such as this one, experience is our greatest strength."

"... Or detriment," Holliday caught her up. "Can't you see, Martha? It's times like these, with no solution in sight, that really demand a gamble."

"Very well." She turned all her attention on him coldly. "I'll go along with whatever you suggest. But I hope you have considered such possibilities as escape and suicide. . . . We'll keep her on Open Hall. I suppose you want her to continue working also?"

"Well, I do think it would be a good idea. Reason is our only hope, you see."

"No, I do not." Martha McLeod's pasty white face was suddenly tinged with pink. "Have you any idea how desperate this young woman is? It seems to me one thing to play with fire and quite another to plant it under dynamite."

The waves of fatigue swept over David Holliday again. He wanted to startle this stale, obstinate woman, show her that she was fifteen years behind the times and that science was discovering substitutes for patience.

"Perhaps you're right," he said at last. "Still, it's our only hope. We can't force her to stay. And in order to appeal to her reason we must appear reasonable ourselves."

"Yes, I agree," she replied more evenly now. "For that reason, I think you're wise to allow her to stay on Open Hall. But at the same time it seems unnecessarily risky to have her going to New York every day. . . . It will only be ten days. She could simply take two weeks sick leave at the office."

And that might be the best solution after all—certainly fair. A compromise which did not fully satisfy him, but which his weariness demanded. "Very well," he said, "let's do it that way. Open Hall, but no work. . . . I'll call the order up to the hall when I get home. I have to call anyway; I promised Mrs. Gaitors."

"Fine." Martha smiled her pussy-cat simper, and the tension was gone. She was just an agreeable old maid and he a man harried by the illness of his wife. They tried to end the session with trivial conversation. "I'm so glad Mary Laine's all right," she purred. "I know you're relieved."

"Yes. You know, Martha, I took a walk a few days ago . . . out through the potato fields. And really, if they ever give us the money, that's the perfect place for an outpatient clinic. Seems to me the need for one is growing by leaps and bounds. Might be the perfect solution for patients like Mrs. Gaitors."

"Yes, an outpatient clinic would be fine," Martha replied vaguely, with a little angry twitch to her mouth. "But there are so many other things we need more—a new O.T., for instance, a bigger auditorium."

And so he took that as his cue to leave. "I'll call about Mrs. Gaitors," he said with careful indifference as he went out the door.

Out in the cold, wet night, however, the despair he had grappled with all day took possession of him. He hated himself for compromising on Mrs. Gaitors. His conscience told him to go back and make a stand. But his throbbing head and, he thought, his more conservative good sense, told him that Martha McLeod might well be right this time. So he continued homeward.

In the end, though, it took two sleeping pills to silence the word, "coward," which kept echoing through his mind. "You *are* in a rut," he told himself. "Yes, and you *are* afraid of her."

(7

Holliday felt much better the next morning. He could not rid himself completely of the dismal thoughts regarding his weakness with Martha McLeod. But everything else seemed so much brighter and the cool sunny day so full of possibilities, that he had little trouble convincing himself this was simply one more challenge to be met.

Even when he called Jesse Gaitors and found him to be not only politely aloof but quite adamant in his decision to seek his wife's release, Holliday did not feel depressed. He had known all along that it was Mrs. Gaitors they must convince and she alone who could influence her husband.

He pushed the case as far back in his mind as possible and turned to the morning's appointments with unusual energy. First, was a conference with the Isaacs boy. He wanted to be sure to see him before his wife came again. Then the Reilly fellow, which he'd keep as short as possible, and old Dr. Stoughton. After that, if he had time before going to New York that afternoon, he'd see Mrs. Webster and the O'Hara girl.

To his surprise and relief he was even looking forward to his visit with Mary Laine. He had called first thing to see how she was and to apologize for not being able to get in this morning. Her voice over the wire had been almost cheerful, a striking contrast to what it had been before.

Holliday knew that in a day or two depression would set in. She would begin to worry about death as well as the deformity of having only one breast. When the time came, he knew he must try to meet that depression with confidence.

But in the meantime, he could not free himself of what seemed to him a far more critical aspect of Mary Laine's illness. Should he or should he not leave Holly Springs? He told himself repeatedly to call Jack Beckwith for some outside encouragement. But he could never quite persuade himself to pick up the telephone.

Jack Isaacs didn't try to hide his animosity toward Dr. Holliday that morning. He set his jaws sourly and stared defiantly into the doctor's face. He let his tall thin body—which he usually kept so carefully erect—slouch in the chair. And when he spoke, he made his voice hushed with a cool, tempered sneer. He smoked one cigarette after another from the pack the doctor had put in front of him. That made him look nervous, he knew. Some of the men had been talking about it just last night. But what the hell? Holliday knew he was nervous. Besides, he might as well get something from the prying jackass.

Lucie had said Holliday would be coming to see him. Her face had been happy, and she'd announced almost giddily that she wasn't going to worry any more. She'd talked to Holliday, and he'd as much as scolded her for even imagining that Jack would not get well. "And you will," she'd said with certainty, and patted his knee. "I'm sure you will. Dr. Holliday ought to know; he's terribly interested in your case."

It made Jack happy to remember the glow on her face and the lightness of her voice. But he didn't place much stock in Holliday; he'd made up his mind he wouldn't do that. If he got well and out of here, it would be because of some new drug or himself. No flabby hayseed doctor would cure him.

"Saw your wife the other day, Jack."

"I know."

"She was a little concerned about your progress."

Jack said nothing.

"I told her I saw no need for discouragement."

Still no response.

"And I don't think there is. I think it's up to you right now. We can help you, but not till you let us."

"I don't understand," Jack snapped, crumpling his cigarette in the ash tray and reaching for another one. "I do everything to cooperate." His voice was quick, hard, furious. But the cigarette trembled in his hand. "He has no right!" he told himself defensively. "No right at all to pry into my mind, to accuse me of failing to do something I'm paying him to do." But Jack knew those were empty struggling excuses. The calm, brown eyes weren't prying into him; they were soaking him up, swallowing him whole to dissect later.

"Sometimes," the big man drawled. "Sometimes, it takes more than cooperation. You've got to be honest. You have to face facts you might never think of otherwise."

He was touching on the Jewish thing again. The hair tingled on the back of Jack's neck. This was proof of how smart the guy was, how much the brown eyes saw. For a long, long time now, ever since his childhood maybe, Jack could recall the teasing humiliation of being a Jew, of parents with foreign accents who went to the synagogue, of not really belonging with the other boys at prep school. Only a vague whisper told him, "This is so; this is not fair; this hurts me." It was so vague he had finally decided it was his imagination and forced himself to ignore it. Until this fat Southerner thought he heard that whisper, too, and wanted to bring it out in the open again to confront him constantly, not to be silenced.

Holliday was right. If it wasn't the problem, it was at least part of it. You didn't have to be Freud to see that. He knew the mortification of his *bar mizvah*, the stinging guilt when he caught himself mentally computing the store's probable net for the year, the shame when he kissed Lucie and felt the hard angle of his nose against her cheek. Yet, even if that was the trouble, the whole trouble, it wasn't the sort of thing you could expose to the world or even discuss with one man. It involved too much—pain, fear, sadness, above all too much humiliation.

"You know, some people have much more to face than you do," Holliday said. "Much more to give up, to accept, to live with, and much less to do it with."

Jack kept his eyes fixed determinedly on the genial face. What Holliday said was right, but that didn't help. Suppose his troubles weren't as heavy as Joe Schmoe's? He still didn't want to carry them. He realized, though, as his own silence infected the doctor, as the whole room began to echo with his embarrassment, that there was no escape.

The horror of baring himself seemed intolerable. But then, so was this. Sitting here and letting those brown eyes strip away his privacy against his will seemed even more degrading. And those eyes would not be discouraged.

"I'd like to help you," the friendly voice drawled again, a little impatiently now. "More than that, I'd like to help your wife. She's a lovely girl. . . . But I can't . . . any more than anybody else can, until you do your part."

Jack wanted to leap to his feet and squash the pudgy pumpkin face. His long hands tightened into hard, white-knuckled fists. But the words that fell from his lips were quiet, calculatedly casual. "I want to do my part."

And he meant that. He hated this man, because he had cornered him where surrender and escape meant equal disgrace. Yet in this defeat—like any other—he felt compelled to take whatever profit he could.

If Holliday wanted to help him, he must accept that help. And what would the consequences be? Humiliation? He already knew humiliation. Guilt? He knew that too, and fear, and pain, and despair. Whereas he might get well, he might be able to go home with Lucie, he might become a man again. That way Holliday would no longer be his condescending conqueror. That way Holliday would be just a tool in his hands. "I want to do my part," he said again.

V

THE TEN DAYS of Mary Laine's hospitalization dragged for Holliday, despite all there was to do. There was the drive in and out of New York every day, little things Mary Laine always took care of for him, extra errands she asked him to run—all in addition to an exceptional work load at Holly Springs.

But none of that helped the time pass. Just a series of boring obstacles to be overcome before a day could end. No matter what he was doing he wished it was something else. Driving in to town, he wanted to be there. Sitting in Mary Laine's rigidly plush hospital room, he longed for the kitchen at home. In bed at night, he was impatient for the morning so that he could go to work.

For years he had imagined the pleasant things he might do if Mary Laine went away for a week. Yet now none of them appealed to him. There was really no chance to play golf, because it was always dark by the time he got home from New York. And though the cold, blustery evenings were perfect for reading, he somehow couldn't keep his mind on any book. So he spent most of his evenings sitting alone in the kitchen, drinking bourbon and trying to make up his mind about either staying at Holly Springs or calling Jack Beckwith for advice.

Worst of all, it was not apprehension about Mary Laine that obsessed him so. Mary Laine's recovery or death now seemed almost a matter of fate, something over which he had no control. Whereas the other problems did depend on him and demanded immediate solution.

The decision of whether or not to go to New York could be postponed, of course, indefinitely. Yet Holliday felt with increasing urgency that he must make up his mind before Mary Laine came home from the hospital. That seemed the only way to settle the issue on its true points; to avoid sentimental confusion; to prevent Mary Laine's happiness from becoming an excuse for his own weakness.

And Carson Gaitors was an even more pressing problem. Legally, only ten days had to elapse between her letter of notice and her withdrawal. An impossibly short interval in any case, Holliday hought. And when the person concerned mattered as much as he had to admit Carson Gaitors did to him, it seemed both desperate and incredibly tragic.

If Mary Laine's illness were fatal, he would lose in the much too near future, the very basis of his everyday existence. But if Carson Gaitors actually did leave Holly Springs in the next ten days, he would lose immediately not only one of the most challenging cases of his career, but also—and far more important—one of the most valuable relationships of his whole lifetime.

After enough thinking about any of this, the doctor found himself utterly confused. His only hope seemed the possibility that as the moments of decision came, he would automatically rise to meet them. In the meantime, he was grateful for anything that kept his life even partially on its normal keel. And when there seemed a lag in the tangible demands on his time and energy, he took pains to invent new ones.

He made it a point to see Mrs. Gaitors every day. The chances of keeping her there until she was really able to cope with the pressures inside herself were almost nil. But Holliday flattered himself that he alone could convert what hope there was to reality.

She was very angry. Chiefly at McLeod and the hospital in general for discontinuing her work pass. Also, at herself for her helplessness in combating them. Much of this resentment, of course, carried over to Holliday. But at the same time, she was grateful to him. She knew that he alone had prevented her from being demoted to Hall 3 and C.O. Realizing this, Holliday took advantage of it. In their conferences he talked of many things completely unrelated to the actual issue. He made an effort to joke in their old badgering way and tried never to offer advice. She did not confide in him; she was too clever for that. But she made it apparent that he was the closest thing to a friend she had at this time.

With each passing day she seemed a little less confident, not of her decision to leave the hospital, but of her hopes for the future. Not of what she would do, but of whether she would be happy in doing it. Holliday tried neither to reassure her nor corroborate her fears. But from time to time he made a statement or posed a question which he hoped would make her think. He never observed any reaction, but he buoyed himself with the idea that it was just carefully concealed. Whatever his talks did accomplish would not show until the end—perhaps even the very day she was to leave.

(2

"Well, Doctor, how do you feel about it?" Holliday asked. "It's really up to you, you know. It's your life."

Jonathan Stoughton did not answer. He glowered at the floor.

"I think your sons would like to take you home . . . or anywhere you'd like. They feel you aren't happy here. . . . They asked me what I thought. But I didn't want to say till I'd talked to you."

The old man looked up into his friend's full face. He struggled for something to say. None of the old lines would do here. They *were* ingrates, selfish sycophants. But if they offered to take him home, he couldn't call them that. It wouldn't sound reasonable. Not even Holliday would accept that. "They don't mean it," he muttered at last. "They only say it to get you on their side."

"I think they do mean it; they acted like they did. Anyway, what shall I say? Supposing they do mean it, what do you want me to do?"

The old man scowled at the floor again. He couldn't just deny all the things he'd said before—that the hospital was a prison and he hated it. He couldn't humble himself that much, even to his friend. "They won't ask you again," he said. "They didn't mean it."

"But if they did? Would you go?"

"Yes, I guess so," Stoughton growled. "But they didn't mean it."

"Where'd you go? If you had your choice, where'd you go?"

No answer.

"To one of your sons? To some place in the city, a hotel or apartment? A place similar to Holly Springs?"

Interest hovered in the old man's eyes. His wide, white forehead puckered. There were pictures in his mind of the places Holliday had mentioned. Some of them memory pictures, some of them painted from his own imagination, but all of them, much more real than the things around him.

He had never been to any of his sons' homes, for instance, but he knew exactly what they looked like. Jonathan had a mansion full of servants and silver, a proper, refined wife, Agnes, and three little girls who'd been taught since birth it was vulgar to have a good time. Donald and his wife Edna who had no children, compensated for it by making their apartment a gathering place for the Bohemian set. Hinton and Julia, who was all heart and no sense, and their squealing babies lived a cramped life scented with mildew and spaghetti sauce.

"A place in the city?" There was only one place in the city for him—the fine, old stone house where he and Nancy had lived when the boys were growing up. "A hotel or apartment" sounded very nice and free and cultivated. But he couldn't quite visualize that. It meant being alone; and he had never in his life been really alone.

Yet, even that sounded more logical than a "place similar to Holly Springs." Why would he ever want to go to another place where they locked you up and took away your eyeglasses and made you eat breakfast at eight? The only difference he could imagine between Holly Springs and a "place similar" to it was the absence of Dr. Holliday, his only friend.

"You spent most of your life in New York, didn't you?" Holliday continued. "Ever practice anywhere else?"

"A few little towns when I was young."

"But you liked New York better?"

"Well, yes."

"The practice, . . . the patients, . . . you found them as interesting in the city?"

"Oh, yes," Stoughton replied readily. "Even more so. You get a reputation in the city and more difficult cases. In small towns it's mostly routine work."

But then, surgery is different, Holliday reminded himself. Besides, why should he be influenced by Dr. Stoughton, the very symbol of what he feared most for himself. Still, he continued, "You didn't find most of your patients were rich and artificial with imaginary ills?"

"No. Only a few. The usual number." The old man laughed. As usual when speaking of his work, he seemed as normal, as alert as anybody. "Yes, I used to like New York," he added with a little quiver in his voice.

"I imagine you miss working hard?"

"Yes, I guess. I guess anybody misses that, . . . especially when they're locked up in a prison like this, when ungrateful children take over their life, when. . . ." His face turned red, the vein in his forehead swelled thick. "But, . . ." his voice faded then. He looked absently at his long thin fingers. "I wish sometimes I hadn't worked so much."

"Think you might be stronger now, . . . still able to work?"

"No." The fragile fingers trembled. "No, I don't want to work. I forget sometimes; I'd make a mistake. . . . I wish I hadn't worked so much, because I'd have had more time with my wife. She's dead now, you know."

"Yes, I know." Holliday loathed the similarity of their cases. For an instant, it seemed not merely possible, but probable that he was beholding himself ten years hence.

"I wish I'd had more time with her, more things to remember."

"But you remember a great deal."

"More things to remember. . . . She's dead now, I told you that. I'm old and I forget. I can't work any more because I forget. Our house, . . . somebody else lives there now. Things change. People die. But memories last."

❰ 3

Eileen O'Hara was startled when Dr. Holliday stopped in the doorway of the dormitory and asked to talk to her. The words she had planned to say to him roared into turbulent confusion inside her head—a doubly disconcerting sensation after the remote apathy she'd felt of late, the pleasant illusion of unconcern. She was so flustered for a moment that she could only gape blankly at the doctor. Then she stood up too quickly, and the thorazine dizziness swept down, causing her to drop her volume of Yeats. She didn't dare stoop to pick it up. In fact, she had to stand there for a minute, holding onto the dresser, before she felt steady enough to follow him to the conference room.

Once there, seated opposite him, she studied the nubbiness of her tweed skirt and prayed that she might have the strength to guard her privacy from Holliday, and, if her impulsive tongue did blurt something about Philip Pierson, that she would be able to pass over it with grace. At the same time, she tried to tell herself there was nothing to be afraid of. Holliday was just a middle-aged

man, a friendly, kind one at that, who offered no threat. Not long
before he had even seemed a source of comfort.

True, because of the thorazine, she probably wasn't quite the
same Eileen O'Hara. There was a buffer of drowsiness, of nebulous
tranquility between her and the world, between her and herself.
But at least she was aware of that. She still had her will and her
conscience, and there was no reason she shouldn't obey them.

She sat up straight and tried to swallow the sleepiness in her
mouth. Incredible that small orange pills taken four times a day
could do all this, reduce her inhibitions to the point that she even
feared her freedom.

"Been meaning to see you for some time. How've you been?"

"Fine, sir. Much better."

"You like Hall 4? ... Most people do, I think. Much more freedom."

"Yes, I like it. It's very nice."

"Dr. Pierson has you on thorazine, hasn't he?"

"Yes."

"Think it helps? Or don't you know yet?"

"Yes, I can tell the difference. ... Dizzy, a little. Terribly sleepy,
... but that doesn't alter the way I feel." She said this last with
determination. She intended it to mean also that her will-power
had not changed either.

"Ummhmm ... Time maybe ... Well, what about the other patients? Any particular friends?"

The old attempt to draw her out. Eileen smiled languidly. "Oh,
they're all very nice," she said. Strange, how far away her voice
sounded. "Yes, I like them. ... Very nice." Suddenly it seemed she
must ask about Philip Pierson. Just one innocent but leading question. The words hammered at her lips, the tears at her eyelids. And
behind them both the hollow fear that her will might not hold.

Interesting to observe the effects of the new drugs, Holliday
mused. Though, what kind of confirmation could Holly Springs
provide? What could anybody prove with fifteen or twenty patients,
except that all people are different. "You feeling better then?" he
continued, "or still a little depressed?"

"Oh, yes, ... well, I guess, ... I guess I don't really know." She
sucked her cheeks in and interlaced her fingers. "I don't think I'm

depressed. I'm not such a bright one, but then, I never was. But, ...I wonder if...."

Holliday cut in again before the silence took over, "How you and Dr. Pierson getting on?" he ventured hopefully. "Think you're making progress?"

And he had his answer before she spoke a word. At first her thin face went gaunt with surprise. Then color flooded her cheeks. But after that she recovered herself. She opened her eyes, and her lips formed words instead of just trembling. "We're doing well enough," she said primly. "I suppose we're making progress."

"Very nice, isn't he? Nice boy."

"Yes, he is.... I like him, but...I-I sometimes wonder if he's the right therapist for me—if I wouldn't do better with a woman. Be-Because of my problem, I mean."

"Dr. Pierson upset you?"

"Well, no, not really. Just that...I guess he reminds me of sad things."

"The two young men and your father?"

"Yes."

"The feelings you have,...you ever think of Dr. Pierson like you thought of the others?"

She did not answer immediately. She blushed again. "Y-Yes."

He waited until the silence became uncomfortable. "You have some feeling of affection?"

So he knew. Eileen felt her face go scarlet. One more gullible patient in love with her therapist. And there was no excuse. Now she wanted to run.

"Well, I don't see that's so bad," Holliday continued softly. " 'Course, I'm no authority. Besides, there's always the other party to consider. But you're a nice girl; Pierson's a fine young man. Seems natural to me."

She cringed and flattened her lips together.

"Might work out, too," he added with a soothing chuckle. "Has before.... Even ethics has to bow out sometimes. Anyway, ethics isn't boss in my rule book. Know what is?"

"What?"

"Happiness. Most important thing in life, being happy. Help others that way, too."

Eileen did not answer, but her face eased a little.

"You've had troubles in the past.... Losing your father. The boy who died, and the other one. Troubles I guess you don't care to repeat, even if you can't forget 'em."

She nodded agreement.

"But, Miss O'Hara, you came here to learn acceptance of those losses, not to barricade yourself from them by shutting out the world. You've got to live now and in the future."

"I know."

"And you'll be a better person—richer and more generous—if you're happy, if you, ... if you dare to love again, if. ..."

"I have to do what I think is right." Her gray eyes focused on him now, fiery steel.

"That's right.... We all do."

"You may think falling in love will solve all my problems, but I don't agree." Her voice strained loud and taut.

"I didn't say that. I said you shouldn't deny love where it already exists."

"Perhaps it doesn't."

"Only you can know that."

❪ 4

The day Carson Gaitors was scheduled to leave Holly Springs was the same day Clyde Ross permitted Mary Laine to come home. This meant that David Holliday would not be on hand for the crucial moment—either to say good-by or to observe the success of his hours of work. So late that morning, just before leaving for New York, he went in to give Martha McLeod some final reminders on the case. "I hate to run out on you again, Martha," he began, "but Mary Laine might be hurt if I weren't there."

"And she'd be right. That's your first duty.... Besides, I'm not anticipating any complications. Just an open and shut case of signing papers. And I certainly hope I'm capable of that!"

"Oh, of course." David Holliday grinned, but a frown shadowed his forehead, and his eyes drifted far away.

Noting this, Martha McLeod wondered what had come over her easy-going colleague. Why was his forehead creased so much of the time now, as if he were nearsighted or perplexed by something?

Why was his voice always booming a little too pleasantly? Why were his eyes shadowed and sad? It's his wife, she thought; there is more to her illness than he said.

"Certainly," Holliday continued. "Martha, I know of nothing you can't cope with as well as I. But, well, if the Gaitors hesitate, or even if they don't, you might suggest that they wait to talk to me. I'll be back by 4:15 at the very latest."

"Yes, I'll do that.... Do you really believe there's a possibility she'll change her mind?"

"No, I have no reason to hope she'll stay." Holliday's frown deepened considerably, then suddenly released itself with a smile. "Except that I'm an optimist! I never say die until I'm dead. So despite all my fruitless talk of the last ten days, I still hope there is something I can say to the Gaitors that will change their minds."

But as he left Martha's office and loped down the hall toward his own, the hope David Holliday had expressed diminished to anxiety and thence to resentment close to despair.... Perhaps if he went upstairs now and explained his situation to Carson Gaitors personally, she would even agree to wait till he got back. He wanted very much to do that. It seemed so simple and so apt to bring results.

He knew he couldn't, of course. It wouldn't be fair to go behind Martha McLeod's back, truly taking the case out of her hands. So he must just go for Mary Laine and hope. Still, it angered him bitterly to think that something of so much importance to him had to be left to the rigid blunderings of Martha McLeod. And, even worse, it distressed him that the victim of those blunderings should be as good and potentially strong a person as Carson Gaitors.

❰ 5

Mary Laine seemed in much better spirits that afternoon. Her despondency about being "deformed for life" had apparently faded into the background. And her other deeper fears, though undoubtedly still there, were well veiled. She was dressed and waiting when Holliday arrived, and while they waited to see Clyde Ross, she talked happily of her various friends among the other patients. She spoke of them in detail, remarking on the specific things about each of them she most enjoyed. But she was careful not to contrast the "culture" she had found here with the lack of it at Holly Springs. In fact, she was careful not to speak of New York and Holly Springs at the same time at all.

She had observed in David lately an increasing preoccupation with their leaving Holly Springs now and coming to New York. He had offered numerous arguments for the city—more money, more of a life together, more direct contact with patients instead of so much uninteresting administrative work. But Mary Laine realized that it was all really because of her. Probably, she knew in her heart, because of the many pleas she had made—thoughtlessly selfish, even sometimes calculated. She knew this, and though she still wanted very much to come to New York, every time he spoke of it now, the words cut her bitterly.

He's afraid I'm going to die, she thought, and he wants to make me happy while he can. But Mary Laine felt confident in herself that there was very little chance of her dying. In fact, now that something tangible had been found wrong with her and removed, she felt less concerned about her health than she had in years. That, in turn, made her feel more selfish.

They had to wait over an hour to see Clyde Ross, so that it was nearly 4:30 before they got away and onto the parkway. And by that time David, who had appeared restless and uneasy while waiting, seemed almost distraught.

"What's the matter, darling?" she asked.

"Nothing. Nothing. . . . Little bit of a crisis at the hospital, and I'm afraid we won't be back in time."

"Why don't you stop and call? What time did they expect you?"

"No. No good to call. . . . I told them I'd be there by 4:15, but maybe they'll wait."

"I hope so."

David reached over and patted her hand. "Don't you worry," he said. "They can manage perfectly well without me. In fact, they're planning to."

But he drove at break-neck speed, and his thoughts were a muddle of anxiety. Mary Laine reminded him he was going too fast several times. With each warning he did slow down, but in no time at all they would be zooming again. Mary Laine did not ask further about the "crisis," because she had learned years before to remain apart from his work. Instead, she tried to divert him. But all she could think of was Lillian and the Beckwiths, New York and her friends at the hospital.

So when Holliday did thrust aside his anxiety about Carson Gaitors, he was only confronted with the dilemma of his own life, which was as depressing, if not as immediate, as the other. He had not kept his promise to himself. He had not been able in the ten-day time limit to come to a decision about New York and Holly Springs. Now, with Mary Laine home, the choice would be even more difficult.

They reached the Holly Springs gate at 4:46, and much to Holliday's relief, Mary Laine suggested he leave her at home with Mamie and go on up to the office.

"You're sure you don't mind?"

"Darling," she laughed softly, "do you think after nearly thirty years, I give something like this a second thought?"

"You're wonderful. . . . I'll try to get back soon."

([6

The office corridor was unexpectedly dark and still. The lights were out in most of the offices; some of the doors were closed and locked, indicating that the occupants would not be back tonight. Noting that his own was one of these, Holliday glanced at his watch. Nearly 5:10. A sickening panic seized him, and he felt dead, helpless, empty—as if he had just seen his best friend hit by a train. But then his optimism fought its way to the top again.

Of course. Probably waiting in Martha McLeod's office. Slowly, hoping, but at the same time leery of his hope, he paced the corridor to Martha's office. And when that, too, was dark, he thought of the supervisor's office.

Miss Tucker was there alone. She was at the desk checking an order book, and did not look up until Holliday spoke.

"Evening, Miss Tucker. You know of any messages for me?"

"Good evening, Dr. Holliday. No, I don't believe so. Mrs. Weaver usually tells me, besides writing them down."

"Oh. . . . Dr. McLeod didn't want me?" No, of course, she hadn't. Her face propped itself before him with the very words she had said that morning: "Just an open and shut case of signing papers.

And I'm certainly capable of that." In that moment David Holliday hated Martha McLeod more than he thought he had ever hated any human being.

"No," Miss Tucker replied, still marking her place with one finger. An impatient muscle twitched in one of her cheeks. "She didn't mention it. She left about fifteen minutes ago, said she wouldn't be back tonight."

"Well, . . . I wonder, did Mrs. Gaitors leave?"

"Yes."

That single word set Holliday's head spinning. He felt sick in the pit of his stomach, weak, guilty, and ashamed—cut off from the whole world.

". . . I thought Dr. McLeod was as good a scapegoat for you as that farmer drawl. . . . Oh, cut it! . . . You oughta know I can take it straight; don't have to be coddled like a damned virgin! . . ." Those words and others like them came back to Holliday now, the old bawdy laughter and the proud shake of her thick, black hair bringing tears to his eyes.

"Did you see her before she left?"

"Yes, they came to get her things from the safe . . . about three o'clock."

"Oh. . . . Do you know by any chance if they waited to see me?"

"Why, no." A frown darkened the sour face; the alert finger slipped from its place. "Were they supposed to?"

"No. I just wondered. I. . . ." I'd better get out of here, he thought. I'd feel like a damned fool if this bitch saw me cry.

"No, they seemed in a great hurry to be off."

"Well, thank you."

"Anything else, Doctor?"

"No. . . . Good night."

If the corridor had been quiet before, it was tomblike now. Holliday paced it to its end with heavy echoing footsteps. It seemed to take the weight of his whole body to open the front door. "Perhaps it'll work out better than we think." But he knew it couldn't. He knew, too, that no matter how well it worked out, he had lost something he could never find again.

❨ 7

When David Holliday looked back on it, that weekend after Mary Laine's return seemed only a misty confusion of half-finished actions and muddled words. He could recall many things he had done, people he had talked to, but they were all disconnected pictures following no order or sequence of time. Everything until that Sunday evening and his conversation with Mary Laine.

The clearest, pleasantest memory was of his walk through the fields late Sunday afternoon. It was damp and cold; he'd worn his raincoat over his suit. The brilliant reds and yellows of two weeks before had faded to water-logged drabness, and the trees were gaunt gray skeletons against the colorless sky. The dark earth was packed cold-hard beneath his feet. The tall weeds no longer whispered dryly in the wind, but sagged heavily, rain sad. Yes, that was the place for the outpatient clinic, the perfect place. Plenty of room for expansion, comparatively level ground, Post Road frontage on the other side. He wondered if he would ever see the clinic. There would be one, of course, but while he was still here?

It was dark when he got home, and Mary Laine was waiting supper. The house was warm and cozy with the mingled mustiness of chicken soup and burning oak. They ate at the kitchen table—soup and salad and toasted crackers. As far as Holliday could remember, they had not talked at all. He'd still been lost, steeped in his brooding silence, and if Mary Laine tried to interrupt, he had not heard. After supper he said he had a headache and went to bed.

In the darkness, though, wrapped in the luxurious comfort of the cool sheets, he could not sleep. The numbness of the past twenty-four hours fell away, and he was wide awake. A myriad of thoughts rushed to his head. First, of course, Carson Gaitors. Why had he failed? Was it his approach or would the same have happened to anyone? Certainly, no one else would have suffered as great a loss as he. . . . How could he help Pierson and the O'Hara girl? What had happened to suck the life from Martha McLeod's face? Why did she run so hard from happiness? . . . And George Purdy? What did the little, gray man really think about the inexplicable demon that had taken possession of his wife?

In the end he put on his bathrobe and went downstairs. Mary Laine was doing the *Times'* puzzle, but she put it aside when he came in.

"No, don't," he said. "I'll help you. We'll do it together."

"All right." She picked up her pencil again. "What's a young coalfish? In four letters?"

"Young what?"

"Coalfish. Four letters beginning with 'P.' "

"How about 'parr'?"

"Oh, yes. That's a kind of salmon, isn't it? One woman in Vermont, . . . her husband did a lot of salmon fishing. I remember her using that word."

"Uh huh. . . . Got another?"

"Yes. . . . This is on the tip of my tongue, but I can't remember to save my life. Capital of Pakistan?"

"Karachi."

"Of course. Isn't that stupid of me? Mrs. Wilkins, . . . that woman at the hospital. Her husband's here with the UN. She. . . ."

"Yes. I think you told me about her." Holliday lit another cigarette and stared at the embers dying in the fireplace. All this he had heard a million times before; he never listened any more.

"They lead a very active social life. If only. . . ." But Mary Laine cut herself off there.

"That means a lot to you, doesn't it?" His voice was low; his eyes did not shift from the glowing coals.

The room was deathly silent for a moment. Then she murmured, "Yes, I guess so."

"You don't want to wait, do you? You want to go right now."

Her eyes studied him in silent surprise. His calm disconcerted her. She had expected an explosion of anger. "David, I don't think that's fair," she said meekly at last. "You know how I feel."

The doctor said nothing.

"But I haven't forgotten our agreement, darling," she rushed on defensively. "And I mean to carry out my part of the bargain." She was silent again then, peering anxiously at his face.

"Then you think it's right?" he asked. "To leave now? To give up Holly Springs and everything here, to go to New York?"

"I didn't say that. . . . I said I meant to do as we planned." Her voice was low and cautious.

"But that's what you want, isn't it?" Holliday persisted calmly, deliberately. "To make our move to the city now?"

"Well, ... yes, ... I guess so, but only if you want it, too. ... I can wait eight years more. Unless for some reason you've changed your mind—some reason other than me—I think we *should* wait."

"I guess I have changed my mind." He spoke confidently. There was no longer any doubt, even in his tone.

"B-But why?" Her eyes became dark. "What about Holly Springs? The outpatient clinic and all the rest?"

"They don't seem to matter any more." His eyes focused on her delicate pink-white face. It seemed thin tonight. The wrinkles over her eyes, the tic in her cheek made her look tired. Fear mounted in him and his mind strained to agree with his heart. It seemed imperative to convince his conscience he was doing right. "In fact, I guess I need to leave Holly Springs. I guess I'm in sort of a rut here." A rut? or trapped? He thought of Martha McLeod's rigid, white competence and felt disgusted by his own weakness.

"Well, David, you know how I feel." Mary Laine looked up at him beseechingly. "But if we go and you ... If you're dissatisfied all the time and pining for Holly Springs, ... why I couldn't be happy. You'd make life miserable for both of us."

"But I do want to go." Holliday stood up and walked over to her chair. "Can't you see? I want to; I *need* to very much, ... for my own selfish reasons. ... And just as important to me anyway. ..." He dropped his hand to touch her shoulder. "I want to go, because I love you and I want to make you happy." He said that softly, but almost too intensely. He needed to convince himself as much as her.

By then she was standing up, too, with her arms around him, her cheek pressed against his coat. "Oh, David, I am happy," she said. "So very, very happy!"

"I'm glad." He felt guilty saying that, as if he were purposely deceiving himself as well as her.

"We'll have a fine house! ... people in often ... and Lillian's friends. ... Oh, let's tell someone. Let's call the Beckwiths; Jack'll be thrilled you're going in with him. ... David, when will we go? Oh, let's call somebody; I want to tell everybody!"

Holliday kissed the top of her head and gently took one of her hands in his. "I'm glad you're happy, darling," he said. "But we must be discreet . . . not speak of it to anyone yet . . . not till we get it all worked out."

"But the Beckwiths?" She looked up at him, questioning, a disappointed child.

"I'll talk to Jack in the morning. I'll work it out this week."

"But, David, . . ." she whimpered. She sat down and looked at her hands. "It takes away all the fun not to tell people."

His round face changed from solemn to stern. "I'm glad you're happy, Mary Laine," he said, "because I am too. Because, for once, it seems we've found the key to real happiness for both of us. But, darling. . . ." He paused there, waiting for her to look up at him again. "Darling, there's much more involved in this than just our own lives. You know that. . . . There's my work and the patients. You wouldn't want to hurt anybody, I know."

She did look up at him then, and he saw that her blue eyes were misted over. "I love you, darling," he said, smoothing her hair back. "We'll be very happy in New York."

VI

THE WORD spread quickly.

"I don't think Holliday'll be here much longer."

"You hear anything about it, Mr. Marx? About this man Holliday retiring?"

"He's too young to retire."

"But that's what they say, Lucie, . . . that he's leaving."

"He won't go, darling. They won't let him; the place couldn't go on without him."

"What do you think, Phil? If it's true, will it be McLeod or Wilson or somebody new?"

"It's just rumor."

"I've heard his wife's very sick. I've heard she's going to die and he wants to take her away on a long trip."

At first it was just curious questions and vague answers scattered at lengthy intervals. Then one patient had definite information that a change was forthcoming; another had been told authoritatively that it was not. Until finally it was the major topic of conversation everywhere. David Holliday knew this, of course. He saw the curious, fearful eyes turned on him more wonderingly than usual. He caught the whispered comments as he loped down a corridor. But he could not imagine how the rumor started. Only one person knew—Mary Laine. And even if she *had* talked, with Elizabeth Wilson away, there was no one at Holly Springs for her to tell.

Less tactful patients asked point blank, "Is it true you're leaving, Dr. Holliday?" He stumbled around at first, searching for a pat answer which would neither lie nor reveal the truth. But by the time Evelyn Barrow got him—rolling her brown eyes, twisting a strand of her long hair—he was ready.

"You needn't worry, Miss Barrow," he boomed with easy laughter. "When I leave Holly Springs, you won't have to ask. They'll set off fireworks."

And he was never caught again. He chuckled that answer to scores of people. Each time with more outward confidence. But also, with increasing guilt and relentless shame which made him wonder if people didn't ask because they somehow sensed that he was no longer capable of authority.

The verbal inquiries gradually petered out. But the questions were still there, all around him. Not just with the patients either. He sensed the expectant silence in the doctors' conferences or when he took his midday meal in the staff dining room. He saw young Pierson's anxious, almost hurt questioning look. He noticed that Ellen Collins never joked with him any more or asked his advice; that Martha McLeod's tone was more proper than usual, her eyes less inclined to be friendly. Even with Lloyd Wilson he felt cut off by an invisible barrier.

He wished that he could tell them. Because then the issue could be out in the open—dishonestly, perhaps, but at least with plausible explanations. No one would suspect he was running away; not even Martha McLeod. They would all believe it was because of Mary Laine; and they would say it was fine and big of him to make the sacrifice. They would cite it as proof of the strength they had always known he possessed.

His greatest comfort during that time was Jack Beckwith. Jack's voice was happy and eager when he telephoned him to say that if they still wanted him, he'd like very much to join the office of Clifton and Beckwith. "Want you?" he shouted. "Damn you, Dave, I'm pretty near desperate. Clifton's leaving January 1, whether I get somebody or not." And he was even more confident the day Holliday went into town to settle the technicalities.

"You think I'm too mercenary, Dave. And maybe I am. But next year this time you'll be wondering how you managed so long living like a pauper. . . . We've been doing so well, we've had to turn people away." That was the nicest thing about Jack—the fact that he did not seem to care why Holliday was moving. As far as he was concerned, his friend was simply doing what was sensible.

But the same enthusiasm in Mary Laine wore heavily on Holliday. She was happy now, excited and gay; planning, planning, planning; apparently undisturbed, or at least, willing to try to overshadow her worries about her health. That pleased David Holliday, of course. But at the same time, he couldn't stand her constant chatter. It made the move seem even more empty. Often, too, it made him feel as if he had had nothing to do with the decision after all, as if he was just being swept along by a tide which he had neither the strength nor the wit to swim against.

Every day he put off going home. But it wasn't easy finding uses for his time. He no longer liked interviewing patients. He felt always that the helping hand he offered was really teasing cruelty; because it would be withdrawn probably before the victim could take hold.

Nor was there any point any longer in taking the bleak walk across the frozen potato fields and fruit orchard. The barrier which he felt with Lloyd Wilson and the other doctors might be invisible, but it was also very real. He *was* cut off, one apart. His own feelings had severed his ties with Holly Springs. So that this barren land, once a symbol of hope, the site of his longed-for outpatient clinic, now only made him feel more depressed, useless, and obsolete.

❰ 2

It occurred to Philip Pierson during his conference with Evie Barrow that afternoon that a change had transpired in him. He could look squarely at her soft, wavy hair now, at her sensual brown eyes, at the olive green sweater stretched over her breasts, without a single quiver of embarrassment.

"Of course," he reminded himself, making another note on his pad. "There's been a tremendous change in her. Hall 4 now instead of Hall 1." Then, scanning his notes, he realized the difference was even greater than that. "Quiet," he had written. "Somewhat depressed. . . . Not mute, but untalkative. Answers politely, but no attempt at conversation." Yes, the contrast was distinct; the opposite arc of the cycle.

Still, there *was* a difference in him, too. No longer the debilitating fear of women. Instead, a protective remoteness, and even, with some patients, a determinedly cool superiority. Now, for instance, with this girl who had once caused him so much anguish, he wasn't even moved by the pity he would have once felt for any person in her position. She *was* pretty. But he knew the hard ugliness, the basic coarseness that lay beneath her present shadow of demure sadness. And even in this phase he dreaded conferences with her, because they took time from things that mattered more.

"What things?" his conscience reproached him. A shiver went down his back, and he felt the pen tremble between his fingers. "What things besides Eileen O'Hara?"

He thought about that further on his way to Atkins for a conference with Eileen. But there seemed no honest pardon for the taunting importance he had allowed her pensive face to take in his life. And in the conference room, he was her captive once more, entranced again by the simple pleasure of being near her.

He tried not to look at her too closely. Partly for her sake, but more, because suddenly his whole body seemed to tingle with anticipation. It was with real fear that he scanned her face for the changes he must note. Still the pale, too-controlled mask of composure, the cautiously shielded eyes. But the tightness was gone from around her mouth—also most of the puffy numb look the medication had caused at first. She was alert and reasonably relaxed and when the gray-green eyes did look up, the laughter was there as well as the sorrow. Yes, moving along. Open Hall now. Soon the end of the thorazine. Brief observation. And then, good-by.

That realization touched off an almost panicky mixture of sadness and longing in Pierson. He strained for control, and in an urgent effort to focus his thoughts on the situation at hand, he launched into the questions commonly asked a patient advanced to a new hall. Increased tension? The other patients? Change in symptoms? Sleeping?

She answered easily, more readily, he thought, than ever before. She was sleeping all right, though naturally not as well as with the full dosage of thorazine. She never had been a sound sleeper. Perhaps a little more anxiety, too, but she thought everybody must feel inadequate in the last step before the outside. She said she didn't know too many of the other patients, but that she'd decided she was naturally an introvert and liked it that way. She'd know when she met someone she wanted for a friend. A bluff, of course. But at least it was a happy one that satisfied her as well as him. And the assurance in her voice, the daring in her eyes showed the will to give life another chance. Healthy signs, but at the same time, ones which renewed Pierson's consternation.

If she could be daring, why couldn't he? If she had the courage to look life in the face again, why shouldn't he risk being hurt just this once? Being afraid to endure pain for something that mattered to him so intensely made him feel more cowardly than ever. He reminded himself how shy he was by nature; also how much more ill at ease he felt here than with Miss Barrow. But that only made his weakness seem more despicable.

"Wait until the girl's ready for discharge," Holliday had advised. "Then feel her out." Yet, how could he ever do that? A wild and alien boldness surged in him—a boldness born of impatience and longing and passion he had not known he was capable of. In spite of himself, the thoughts of her body were upon him again—not only the small, vibrant body itself, but her warmth and tenderness. How could he wait? But then, just as suddenly, just as wildly, his fear swept back. She was almost ready for discharge now. How could he possibly in the short time left, steel himself to the point of baring his heart to her?

And even if he did do that, even if he found she loved him as much as he thought he loved her, how would they battle the prejudice of ethics and convention? Dr. Holliday said it could be done. But after all, Holliday had been at this a long time; he'd made a business of not conforming. Besides, if the talk about Holliday leaving were true, Pierson would be left completely alone to face the consequences.

He studied the fragile, determined face before him; tried to measure its capacity for bearing pain—not just the unthinking, haphazard pain of life, but the bitter undeniable pain of deliberate cruelty. She's seen a lot, he thought. She should be very strong. But suppose she didn't love him? And why should she—someone with a crippled foot and all his inadequacies? Suppose in addition to the condemnation of society he had to face a cool, impassive "no" from her lips?

(3

Eileen had awaited that conference with happy excitement. She'd been thinking a great deal of her last talk with Holliday. With humiliation, of course, but also, surprisingly, with a new sense of strength. She had been weak, sinful, to speak out as she had, but as long as it was past and could not be remedied, she might as well profit from the experience. "Shouldn't deny love where it already exists," the big doctor's words rang repeatedly through her head. Until they no longer sounded weak, but rather sensible, even good.

Eileen could not declare her feelings, but she had decided that she would let them show. She would not hide her love any more, even from herself.

Now, though, as she looked at Phil Pierson, at what seemed restrained boredom on his serious face, it seemed foolish even to consider slackening her defenses. Especially if the rumors (which she had refused to believe) about Holliday retiring were true. What could be more rash than to expose your very soul's sadness at the recommendation of a pleasant-faced old man who went away?

Eileen stole another look at the young doctor's dark face. Fortunately, he was concentrating on his pad, his dark brows knit as if he were pained as well as perplexed; his lips slightly pursed as if locked in determined silence. Why should that make her stomach tighten?

He'd never given her any reason to think his concern for her was anything but professional. He'd been kind, understanding, but never even overly sympathetic. Yet, the sweet-sad yearnings Eileen was straining to control seemed stronger than anything she had ever felt before—even for Kenneth.

Kenneth. . . . Thoughts of him were almost a relief now. Standing beside her before one of the gaudy shop windows. The subway clatter and the honking of the taxis, but above it all the echo of his laughter. The doctors were right; she did remember Kevin and her father, and losing them. But those losses were logical and explainable, tied neatly with the finality of death, whereas Kenneth. . . .

"How do you like Open Hall?" the doctor interrupted. "Any new friends?"

She mentioned Mrs. Purdy. They weren't really friends, just acquaintances. But it filled the silence.

"How are you sleeping? . . . Any new symptoms since we began decreasing the thorazine?" All old questions, ones she could answer with a minimum of thought. Yet, today Eileen felt the need to do more than that, to paint a picture as convincingly bleak as possible. And that was difficult. She did not want to lie, but it seemed insufferable—leaving Holly Springs and saying good-by to this sensitive man.

He's afraid, too, she told herself. He's ashamed of his deformity. Probably he'd like very much to be loved. But then she sneered inwardly. "Everybody isn't a shrinking violet! Least of all, doctors. . . ." Still, it would have helped to know. If only she could think of some real problem. Once there had been her depression and obsessions, then the thorazine with the complications which accompanied its numbing tranquility. But now all that was past. No more excuses. No more depending on someone else. She was in control again. And once more she must accept the responsibilities of life—never again to run away.

Eileen had known from the first that it must be this way. No miraculous fairytale ending; just acceptance of what had seemed unbearable before. But at first there had been no Philip Pierson to complicate matters. Only the torturing memory of Kenneth, the smaller losses of her father and Kevin. She had promised herself she would never let anything like them happen again. Now, in the dimness of the conference room, watching the crooked foot move ceaselessly forward and back, forward and back, she made that same promise once more.

❴ 4

Ben Womble lay flat on his bed, eyes staring blindly ahead. Still, he heard the heavy footsteps plodding down the corridor and knew whose they were even before Dr. Holliday's bulging figure passed the doorway. And though the footsteps soon subsided in the opposite direction, they left Ben thinking of the times Holliday had come to see him.

Long sitting silences. Except for the doctor's questions, his probings to make Ben own up to information gathered from the radio and x-ray records. Ben thought he had done well by those questions; always cleverly protected his privacy. So that the doctor had to go away knowing no more than when he came. Now they said Holliday was going to leave. People hardly talked of anything else nowadays. But Ben didn't think that would make much difference, except that for him it might even be a little safer, because nobody else seemed quite as prying or quite as determined to make him get well.

Of course, Ben knew it was perfectly logical for people to want to get well and for doctors to want to help them. Provided they weren't just Ben Wombles. Jack Isaacs, for instance. Ben, himself, had helped Jack, or tried to. That had been one of the things he refused to talk to Holliday about.

Looking over at the other bed now, where Jack lay with a book propped up on his chest, Ben told himself again that Jack was pretty nice. No matter how guilty Jack was or of what, he just liked him and felt sorry that they had him here for something.

Jack felt the boy's eyes on his face. He wanted to look up from his book and make those eyes the surprised prisoners of his own. That had happened accidentally several times in the ten months they'd lived together. A clear picture of those times was imprinted on Jack's memory—the startled dilation of the blue eyes followed instantly by a downward flutter of the eyelids. But Jack didn't want people probing his mind, and he would not probe theirs. He fixed his eyes sightlessly on the print before him before he even spoke to Ben. "You seen Holliday lately?" he asked.

"No."

Jack didn't look, but he knew Ben was staring glassily through the doorway. The boy did that nearly all the time now. He scarcely talked at all any more—even to answer a question. Just giggled or nodded or went right on staring. To Jack that was not only sad but disturbing. It weakened his faith in both doctors and people in general and, above all, in himself; because he remembered that a few months before—when the kid had just finished his shock treatments—he and Ben had been almost close. At least, as close as Jack cared to be to anyone. Ben had occasionally even opened conversations himself then, and sometimes they had lasted as long as ten minutes. Very different from this weird staring silence punctuated with eery giggling.

"Jim Reilly says Holliday is leaving," Jack tried again. "You heard anything about that, Ben? Your father say anything when he was here?"

But there was no response at all this time. Jack glanced again at the glassy stare and felt his insides quiver. "Yes," he told himself, eyes back on his book, "Holliday must be going. If it weren't true, the staff'd be falling over themselves to deny the rumors." He'd tried to tell Lucie that the day before, but she'd refused to listen. She'd said Holliday would never leave until he was too old to work.

Lucie'd been prettier than usual yesterday, despite the wisps of gray coming in her bangs and the fine lines in her forehead. There was an intangible sadness about her now, a sort of weariness behind her smile that he didn't remember from before. Jack could not bear, in addition to that, to dash all her hopes, by destroying her child-faith in the fat, moon-faced man. Instead, he told himself he was a fool to let that concern him at all. Holliday was retiring? So what? Just one more doctor down the drain.... But Jack couldn't forget that Holliday was *not* the same as all the others.

Miss Gardner came in then with the brown book they used for Visiting Day permissions. Jack didn't look up, but he knew the nurse's eyes were sneering at him over her glasses, bristling with cold sarcasm, dissecting him like a toad.

"What permission do you want for Saturday, Mr. Isaacs?" As usual she was irritated by his indifferent, superior way of partially ignoring her.

Eyes lowered, he replied, "The usual—grounds two to five with my wife."

"I should think one day you'd want more than that," her voice rasped with propriety, "if only for your wife's sake."

"Well, I don't. You asked me and that's my answer—grounds two to five."

The hand holding the brown book fell to her side. The anger inside her became frozen ruthlessness on her face. "You know, Mr. Isaacs," she said, "Holly Springs isn't exactly a pleasure resort. Most people here at least try to overcome their fears."

He didn't answer for a moment. Then coolly out of the echoing silence he said, "I think I get your meaning, Miss Gardner, but I'd suggest you take that up with my doctor." Her words had hit through to him, but there was relief in being able to slap her with the same incombatable retort she so often used with patients.

Still she continued undaunted. "You've been here a long time. . . . I guess you've become accustomed to this kind of life. But it's time you realized we don't keep parasites here forever, Mr. Isaacs. Even the doctors leave eventually. Nothing is permanent," she added smugly. "Not even the administration. You won't always be a privileged character."

Jack knew she was right. He couldn't deny the fact that Holliday had helped him. He couldn't even deny the despair which losing that help created in him. His throat was clouded now, his eyes misted; soon the familiar chain of depression and apartness, claustrophobia and panic. But he fought it back, refusing to let this bitch see she had touched him. "You asked for my request," he snapped. "I've given it, and I see no need to listen to your sermon."

The nurse didn't even ask Ben for his request. She turned to him abruptly after Jack's retort and said, in her gentlest, most professionally nursey tone, "I'll put you down for the same, Mr. Womble —grounds two to five with your parents."

Ben did not answer. He just giggled—to show he was on Jack's side—and went on staring.

Poor kid, Jack thought, he'll probably die, an old man, in a place

like this. The thought made him shiver all over again, and tears
sprang to his eyes.

ℂ 5

Jonathan Stoughton sat by himself that afternoon in the alcove
of the Hall 5 living room. His stiff wooden chair was pulled over
beside one of the windows, and he peered out at the bleak sky of
the winter's first snow storm. He gazed at the white flakes scurrying down to melt into the wet ground, but he scarcely saw. His
mind was lost in the speckled Christmas-card mistiness, in the
coziness of discomforts he need no longer enjoy, in memories too
long past to cause pain.

"Jon! Jon! I can do it! Look, Jon. I can do it!" The little girl's
gaiety rang in his deaf ears—his sister Grace—the first year they'd
let her skate on the pond.

"Don hit me, Daddy! He hit me with a snowball."

"He hit me first." The three snow-frosted little boys—they
fought and screamed one minute, rolled and giggled together the
next, and later in flannel pajamas, gathered around the kitchen
table to warm their insides with Nancy's cocoa.

The drifting flakes reminded him, too, of another winter when
he had sat for days beside a window like this one, looking out at
the same kind of blurry, white sky and then back at the hospital
bed where Nancy lay oblivious to his presence or even to her own
dying. The children hadn't been with him then; they'd all been
far away, busy with their own lives.

They're always too busy, he told himself now. Despite Holliday's talk of their wanting to take him home, it had been two
weeks or more since any of them had come. And they certainly
wouldn't pick today to change that. For a while he'd worried that
they might take him away from Holly Springs. But now he'd decided such worrying was foolish. They'd never do it. And even if
they did, he could simply refuse to go, unless he liked the proposed
set-up enough to swallow all his old complaints.

He was much more concerned now about Holliday's retiring.
It was hard to get away from it. Old Marx talked of nothing else.
He thought the place was going to fold up and he would be out in
the cold. Jonathan Stoughton thought that ridiculous. Still, such

talk caused him great anxiety; he turned his hearing aid off whenever it began. He comforted himself with the reminder that it was probably just a stupid rumor, just people talking to hear themselves talk. But he couldn't forget all the other changes that had come in his life, the relentless tide sweeping serenely past against his will, leaving him alone clinging to an empty shell.

Yes, no matter how it hurt, Holliday probably *was* leaving, and he might as well accept it. He tried to convince himself that he had already done that. But he ached with a deserted sadness. . . . There was no answer for these feelings, no escape except into his anger. Now he muttered to himself that Holliday was nothing but a heartless hippopotamus, a flabby fool who found his pleasure in making friends with people and then abandoning them.

Someone was tugging at his elbow. Turning, he found the orderly smiling at him broadly, mouthing words. He turned up his hearing aid.

"Dr. Stoughton," the young man said. "Veezetors. Like we told you, veezetors! Your son and his wife."

Looking beyond the white uniform, the old man saw Hinton and his wife. Julia, her name was, Julia. They stood there, grinning proudly, all bundled up in outdoor clothes. "Hello, Dad," Hinton said, and the girl came forward to kiss him.

But there was something different too. He scrutinized them to see what it was. Then, suddenly he saw the suitcase. They had brought a big, brown leather suitcase.

Hinton stood half in front of it. This mustn't be too great a shock. Dr. Holliday had said, "Just tell him and do it, without giving him time to get scared or change his mind. . . . But do it easy. Tell him slowly, so's he can feel more as if it's his own decision."

Dr. Stoughton stood up after Julia had kissed him and coldly allowed his son to squeeze his hand.

"Let's go down to your room, Dad," Hinton suggested. "Where we can visit in peace."

"No," the old man grunted. He frowned at the suitcase and sat down again in his chair. "I'm quite comfortable here."

The young couple exchanged anxious glances, then each warily pulled up a chair from another part of the room.

"You know, Dad, it's going to be a regular old-fashioned Thanksgiving with all this snow."

"Yes, and you should see Davie. They've been teaching them about pumpkins and the Pilgrims at school."

Dr. Stoughton listened blankly, letting them talk as they would, freeing his own mind to wander deafly through the fog it was becoming so difficult to clear away.

"Not long till Christmas either. Christmas will be extra special this year," Hinton added brightly, glancing sideways at his wife. "And we hope you're going to be with us this year, Dad."

The old man still didn't speak, but his eyes flickered, as if the insinuation had registered.

"In fact, ..." Hinton went on hesitantly. "In fact, ... well, I guess you saw the suitcase. ... Dad, if you like the idea, we'd like very much for you to go home with us. ... Today, ... in time for Thanksgiving."

A moment of uncomfortable silence, then Julia moved in, her voice determinedly eager. "Oh, Dad, I think it's so wonderful. You can stay with us if you want. Or Hinton's found this charming little apartment in the city and a fine young man to take care of things for you."

"Why?" His eyes stared blindly. His tone was vague. But that word seemed more an accusation than a question.

The young people exchanged worried frowns. "Why what?" Hinton asked.

"Why have you suddenly decided to take me out of the hospital?" Dr. Stoughton's voice was hard now and toneless.

"Why? Because we thought you'd like it," his son soothed. "We want very much for you to be happy, Dad." He reached out to touch one of the fragile tapered hands, but it was withdrawn indignantly before he could. "Dr. Holliday was terrifically pleased with the idea."

"Dr. Holliday has nothing to do with me. I pay my bills here, and he has no right to put me out. Outrageous!" His face grew red, and the vein in his forehead swelled large. His whole body throbbed with fury which momentarily, even he knew was foolish. But it had caught him in its sweep, and he was no longer strong enough to do anything but go along.

"No, Dad," Hinton said gently. "I don't think I made myself clear. This wasn't Holliday's idea. It was ours—Don's and Jon's and mine. We simply asked Holliday's opinion."

"Well, I don't give a hoot for Holliday's opinion!" Dr. Stoughton bellowed back. "Or for yours either! I may be old, but I'm still running my own life. So, please get out! Get out and leave me alone and never come back again!"

"Now, Dad. . . ."

"I said, get out!" The old man stood up and stamped his foot. Then he reached into his pocket to turn off his hearing aid.

The young couple looked at each other uneasily again, then at the suitcase. Julia smiled and reached out her arms in one more attempt to pacify. But Dr. Stoughton only stamped his foot again and turned scarlet. "I'm not listening," he shouted. "I said, get out! I never want to see you again. Never! Never! Never!"

Then he turned abruptly back to his window. "Well, that's it." He put one withered hand flat against the cold glass; then took it away and peered through the clear silhouette it had left. He told himself he was not sorry about sending them away. Even if he never *did* see them again, at least he had preserved his pride, at least he had proved he still had a mind of his own.

Gradually, the angry red faded from his face, his thin lips became expressionless again. But the sad serenity did not return, and anxiety darkened his blue eyes. When the transparent finger prints had clouded over again, he wandered wearily to the middle of the living room.

There, looking down the corridor, he was just in time to see Hinton's tweed coat and the end of the brown suitcase disappear out the door.

❨ 6

Millie Pratt watched her mother's red-nailed fingers flick cigarette ashes into the glass ash tray. "Tom's so delighted with your progress," Mrs. Milliken crooned. "Not just about your moving up here to Hall 4, but about all the growing up the doctors say you've done."

Millie smiled and looked away to the billiard table. She was glad the doctors thought she was growing up. But she knew inside that she was really no different. She had just fooled them, just as all her life she had fooled people into thinking she was a sweet, quiet, intelligent little girl.

"In fact, darling," Mrs. Milliken continued, "Tom said to tell you the first off-grounds permission you get, he's coming to take you out to dinner."

Millie didn't answer. She studied the tweed of her mother's purple suit, and then, the tiny feather hat set breezily atop her soft blond curls. Millie felt uneasy when people said things like that. She didn't want to go home. She tried not to think about it now; she tried instead to concentrate on the suit and the hat.

It occurred to her that probably her mother's appearance *was* more striking here surrounded by the faded gloom of the hospital. But she could remember other times long before when she had walked along Fifth Avenue with a similar suit and hat. That had been before Mother even met Tom, when she was still married to Daddy, and afterward. The eyes coming at them from the opposite direction had focused on her, registered pleasure and approval, and sometimes, something like an invitation. At first Milllie—little girl, clinging to the slender black-gloved hand, scurrying to keep up with the sharp clicking heels—had been proud that so many people thought her mother was pretty. But later that pride had turned to uneasiness, then to fear, and finally to a disgust close to hatred. She had heard strange noises in Mother's bedroom after she was supposed to be asleep. And she had heard the ladies in the other apartments talk. She hadn't fully understood what they said, but she had understood enough to be ashamed.

"I guess what pleases us most about your move," Frances Milliken continued, "is looking forward to having you home for Christmas. Millie, it's going to be lovely this year." She took another cigarette from her black skin case and lit it with the matching lighter.

Millie watched solemnly, but did not speak.

"Oh, darling, won't it be wonderful when you're home again? We'll do so many happy things: we'll buy you all new clothes, and the club's sponsoring dancing lessons for young people the first of the year. We could even have a party if you'd like—a welcome-home party."

Millie's thin face remained expressionless until the party suggestion; then horror raced across it. "A party!" she gasped. "Mother, we couldn't have a party! Who could you ask? What could you tell them?"

"Why, I know some delightful children just your age. Besides your friends at school. And I don't know what you mean about telling them. I see no need to tell them anything."

"But what will they think? What will you say about where I've been?"

"They won't think anything. I'll say just what I've always said."

"What?" The child's voice was angry now.

"That you've been visiting your father in California."

Millie had no answer for that. Even her anger vanished. She felt only terribly alone—lost, numb, abandoned. She almost wanted to cry like Evie Barrow did sometimes lately in the bathroom when she thought she was alone. . . . Or to pray like Mrs. Purdy used to do. Just to have someone—even someone imaginary, like God— anyone she could talk to and know they really cared. There was Dr. Holliday, of course. She tried to reassure herself with that thought. But he was busy and didn't have time to come often. Besides, Evie said he was going to leave. "Mother, do you know if Dr. Holliday's leaving?"

"Why, Millie, what a foolish question!" Mrs. Milliken put her cigarette out and turned to smile disparagingly at her daughter. "Really, darling, he virtually owns Holly Springs. He must make a fortune, and he's too young to retire."

"Oh. . . ." Millie mumbled hesitantly. "I do hope he's not going. . . . And that they won't close Holly Springs. I wouldn't have any place to go."

"Silly, of course, you would. You'd come home."

"But I don't want to. I don't want to go home." Millie looked down quickly at the lap of her gray jumper. Her face was flushed with surprise and embarrassment.

But Mrs. Milliken was not upset. She had known all along that this was probably true. In the beginning she had felt insulted and hurt. But she had gradually relinquished her resentment. In listening to the various doctors at Holly Springs, she had begun to exonerate herself in an easier, more plausible fashion. Things like this just happened. Nobody was to blame. A mistake somewhere not even remembered; a scene misunderstood by a child; an unintended barb nursed secretly into a hideous hurt. The fault was no one's.

Just as she had become accustomed to the vast difference between her present life and the one she had had with Jeffrey, so she would get used to this—that Millie, her own flesh and blood, did not love her. In fact, that really wasn't so hard to take after all, because Millie was a part of Jeffrey—and Jeffrey was past, gone forever.

Still she automatically played her role as solicitous mother. "No, Millie, you know you don't mean that. Of course, you want to come home. You don't want to stay here."

"Yes, I do," Millie thought. "It's true. I really do." Everything was so much easier here, so much kinder. No reason to feel alone, because everyone was alone here and together in their aloneness. "No, I don't want to go home," she said again. Then she added the idea of Dr. Collins' with which she had always disagreed. "I want to go to boarding school."

"Well, we'll see, darling," Frances Milliken replied. "We'll see." But the idea took hold immediately. How much simpler that would be—to just put the child in a school where there were sensible, straight-laced teachers paid to do parents' worrying for them. In that way, the past could be cut off completely and at the same time she would know she was giving Millie an education. The world would see that, too.

After her mother had gone, Millie went back to the dorm and took out the needles and blue wool she was learning to knit with. Evie was in there lying on her bed reading a book. But Evie never talked much any more, and this once Millie was glad. She thrust the needle in and wrapped the yarn cautiously around in the knit two, purl two pattern the lady at O.T. had called ribbing.

As she did, her mind just as correctly began to develop an immunity to all the anxieties about Dr. Holliday and going home. "If worse comes to worse," she told herself deliberately, "if Dr. Holliday really does retire and Collins and McLeod tell Mother I can go home, I can just act real depressed again. Not talk or eat and lie awake at night so the night nurse will write it down. Dr. Holliday would catch on. But the others don't know me that well."

She felt much better then. She wanted to hear something that would make her laugh. "Evie," she said, raising her voice so that the other girl could hear her across the room.

"What?"

"What was that you called my mother?"

"When?" Evie looked up half-heartedly from her book.

"The first time you saw her, when she came to see me on Hall 1."

"Oh. A lady bitch."

"I like that." Millie laughed gleefully. "And, Evie, you know what? You're absolutely right."

VII

THE FAREWELL luncheon for David Holliday was the most elaborate occasion Mary Laine had seen in all her years at Holly Springs. Flowers on every table, place cards, individual ash trays. And a host of waiters, each dressed immaculately in white coat and black trousers. From her seat of honor between David and Lloyd Wilson, Mary Laine tried to count the long white-clothed tables crowding the assembly room. But it was hard to tell where one left off and another began. Then one of the waiters bumped a fruit cup down in front of her.

Beside her, David, too, was looking out over the tables. Looking for friends on the Board of Governors, Mary Laine told herself. But she knew that he was not, that his eyes were empty and distant, seeing nothing. At last she nudged him to remind him of his fruit.

"Oh yes, my dear. Daydreaming again." He took two hearty mouthfuls, but then put his spoon down again to continue gazing. He had been like that so much lately—remote, perplexed, perhaps a little depressed—that Mary Laine had almost come to think of it as natural. She comforted herself that in reality he did and should have a great deal on his mind. This move to New York would be a great change, and regardless of all the reasons he had quoted to her for wanting it, he must also feel sadness for the things to be left behind. A few times Mary Laine had even questioned the sincerity of those reasons. But after repeated reassurance, she had finally decided there was nothing to do but believe.

After the fruit there was roast beef with peas and mashed potatoes, and a basket of hot rolls which Martha McLeod handed to Mary Laine, because Lloyd Wilson had gone off somewhere. As she took the basket, Mary Laine found herself marveling once again at the genteel tranquility which Martha never failed to maintain. Today she looked sweet and old ladyish in her pale blue dress with the purple orchid perched uncomfortably on one shoulder. But even today, at perhaps the biggest moment of her life, her face was as placid as a slab of dough, her voice quiet, fragile as glass.

David took a roll and set the basket down in the middle of the table. "Perk up, darling," he whispered, patting her hand. "I'm just a little nervous. It's not easy being on the spot like this, people expecting you to say something."

"I understand," Mary Laine said. But inside, it was not that simple. Her own determinedly suppressed fear was gradually, hungrily coming to life again. It was not so hard to keep it quiet when David was confident. But now his face looked very tired, almost thin. His eyes were still and dull, like those of a burnt out jack-o-lantern. So that for Mary Laine there no longer seemed any refuge from the weakness of herself.

Determinedly, though, she looked around the room again. It was natural; anyone who had had cancer had reason to be afraid. But she must not let that fear ruin this proudest moment of her life. She had never realized before how much people thought of David. Not just people here at Holly Springs either, but among others, all these members of the Board of Governors who had cared enough to come out here today despite the winter weather.

A waiter bumped her again, this time with a raspberry tart. Lloyd Wilson had come back and was gobbling down his cold roast beef. The speeches would start soon. Waiting, Mary Laine searched out the faces she knew.

Near the end of their table was Elizabeth Tucker, the supervisor David called a "sadistic sour-puss." Her tight-lipped primness certainly made the name seem fitting. Ellen Collins was sitting on the other side of David. She was to be named women's director in place of Martha McLeod, and in honor of the occasion she was all dressed up in an orange silk dress too small for her horsy frame.

Her purple orchid made Mary Laine even more pleased that her own was white.

At that point, one of the old men on the board got up and mumbled something. Then Lloyd Wilson stood up and started a long spiel which finally ended as expected: "Dr. David Holliday is leaving us, retiring after more than twenty-five years of service to Holly Springs." Mary Laine searched the faces for reactions to the already familiar announcement. But for the most part, there was none; even the younger doctors appeared to feel nothing—just a little out of place, a little too conscious of their manners. Only Phil Pierson, whom she knew better than the others, seemed to scowl more intently than usual.

"We are fortunate, though," Lloyd continued, "in having a person in our midst to fill this vacancy as adequately as any human being could. Our new director will be Dr. Martha McLeod." Loud applause followed that, but when Mary Laine looked at Martha, she found her just smiling demurely down at the table cloth. That was the sort of thing David was always criticizing Martha for. The least she could do was look up and smile directly at the people who welcomed her so warmly.

Next Lloyd made the announcement about Ellen Collins. And then it was David's turn. Mary Laine sat very still, tense but proud, as he stood up. At first she felt that his drawling words were scarcely audible. But then a great hush fell over the people, and his voice grew louder. Some of the faces grew sad, but most just remained expressionless, open-mouthed with listening.

At intervals everybody clapped. Each time when they stopped, David went on, and gradually his tone grew more robust, discarding its earlier wistfulness. He said that he didn't believe in long good-byes, in fact, that he never said good-by at all if he could help it. "And," he added, grinning, "I feel terribly sorry for Martha McLeod. Now that you've elected me to the Board of Governors, she won't have a moment's peace!"

Mary Laine smiled broadly at that. But when she looked up, she saw the sadness in his eyes and knew without question that the "pain" he spoke of was not mere courtesy. He looked weary and desolate even while he talked, even while his lips still smiled. And with his "pain," his weariness, came her own fear to push aside and trample down her earlier happy pride.

(2

After the luncheon Phil Pierson decided to go to his room in the staff residence instead of back to the office. His head ached, and he felt dizzy. As he limped down the hill, hands deep in his pockets, his shoulders sagged.

"Hurt puppy," he scoffed at himself. "Whimpering off with your tail between your legs." And looking like that, even feeling like that was ridiculous—because he had known this was going to happen. Holliday had told him outright over a week before. Nearly a month ago, in fact, he'd hinted about "half considering private practice in New York." And even before that, there'd been rumors.

He went up to his room and lay on the bed face down, so that his quivering stomach was braced against the mattress, his burning eyes buried in the pillow. He stayed there for some time, hoping the darkness might bring relief. But instead, it made him more aware of his own weakness. "And it's not just physical," he chided himself. "Clubfoot's nothing. An inconvenience. An inadequacy one must adapt oneself to.... But you've done that all right. You can't excuse yourself with that.... You *are* weak. The very basis of your personality is weak and cowardly and deceitful."

Moisture from his eyes dampened the pillow. "Not because you're being too severe. Just because it's the truth and you're sorry for yourself.... But there's still more truth. And that's the worst of all: You don't *have* to be so weak; you *could* try to change."

Gradually, his eyes became dry again, his thoughts composed themselves in a grim calculation of hope. The weakest thing of all, he realized now, was the childish dependency he had developed for Dr. Holliday. Perhaps, though he feared it, the doctor's leaving would be his salvation. Pierson could not really believe that, but it was a last resort. Clinging to its comfort, he let himself be lulled into gray numbness.

But then, as always, he was seeing Eileen's face—the sad eyes, disappearing sometimes beneath a feathered shadow of lashes, the sculptured-marble contour of her cheeks—and it would not go away.

Finally he got up and sat down in the chair by the window, forcing himself to look out at the winter sunlight. But, though he pushed Eileen's face from his mind, he couldn't get rid of his thoughts—the familiar, shameful daydreams of the time when she would be completely his, of how he would caress her, of how her small, gentle fingers would touch him. And after that, the realization that none of that could ever come true. He was alone now—more alone than at any time he could remember—because he had glimpsed love, longed for it, yet, lacked the courage to reach out and take it.

Love? How could he call it that? What did he know of love? Perhaps he was right to be afraid. Probably this feeling he thought of as love was only a new expression of his own selfish loneliness. If he weren't sexless, if he *was* capable of warm human longing and gratification, surely he would have the courage to express that desire. And if he did not? ... Probably if he asked her, Eileen would even say she didn't love him. Because, seeing in him what he, himself, could only suspect, how could she?

Somehow he must find himself. Because suddenly now, especially without Eileen, both his past and his future seemed empty. He was abandoned with neither happiness nor dedication. All he believed in had been proven false.

Holliday was leaving. Because he wanted to, they said; because he thought he could do more service somewhere else. But Phil Pierson knew—as must anyone who had even the vaguest knowledge of the big doctor's thoughts and feelings—Phil Pierson knew he was going against his will. Holly Springs was the man's life work. He could only be leaving because his wife was sick and he could not oppose her. That seemed weakness enough. But it was even more disillusioning when you remembered: "Man's first duty is to be happy."

Suddenly all his anger and longing, fear and despair focused fully upon Dr. Holliday. That smiling face seemed as empty and mushy as an overripe melon. The easy, once consoling and reassuring, laughter echoed in his ears as hideous mockery. He had blindly placed his faith in this man and now he was leaving him to face failure, loneliness, and despair alone.... "But you didn't have to believe," Pierson's conscience interrupted there. "You could have forced yourself to be strong, to push aside the crutch." Yes, right back where he'd started.

So at last, with the cold shadows of late afternoon, Pierson turned out the light and went downstairs. It had grown cloudy and raw outside; a fine mist was falling. He pulled on his overcoat and hurried out into it; then trudged with determined briskness back up the hill to the office.

(3

David Holliday felt an obligation to talk to all the patients he had come to know, to tell them the news himself, before they heard it from someone else. For days their faces had crowded each other in his mind—Dr. Stoughton, Eileen O'Hara, Jack Isaacs. He remembered the hurt expression he had caught on Phil Pierson's face and felt guilty even for that.

And so, as soon as possible after the luncheon, after escorting Jack Beckwith to his car and going over the mail with Mrs. Weaver, he started his rounds. First, Dr. Stoughton. He felt a particular responsibility toward the old man since the failure of what he had hoped would be a happy solution. But today as he walked along the Hall 5 corridor in search of the old doctor, Holliday made a conscious effort to keep his mind blocked against his surroundings. He moved mechanically, as one deprived of all the senses. Because today his old fear of a similar fate for himself seemed closer than ever before.

He finally found Dr. Stoughton seated alone in an alcove off the living room. At first he refused to see Holliday. "I have nothing to say to you," he said through trembling white lips.

"Well, for once, Doctor," Holliday went on pleasantly, "for once I've got something to tell you."

"If it's about going to my son's, forget it. I pay my bills here, and I intend to stay as long as I feel like it.... I regard your interference as outrageous and highly unethical."

Holliday waited for the redness to fade from the old man's face before he spoke. "I'm sorry you've been offended," he said, "... but actually what I came to talk about today has nothing to do with that."

Dr. Stoughton did not answer immediately. He sat still for a moment with eyes downcast, as if in deep thought. Then looking up again, he replied abruptly, "All right."

By the time they reached the conference room, however, he was much more cordial, or at least receptive. "Few weeks ago, Doctor," Holliday began, "I talked to you about your practice in New York City. Do you remember our. . . ."

"Yes, I worked in New York over thirty years. . . . I was busy, . . . operated at 6 A.M. four days a week, . . . emergencies, too, of course. I. . . ." He stopped suddenly, his face very white. He'd been talking about something, . . . something important; then, all at once, he couldn't remember. The sensation was frightening; it seemed to come more and more frequently lately.

Holliday waited for the old man; he could see he wanted very much to finish. But when he did not, the genial voice continued lightly. "Well, I just wanted you to know I took our conversation to heart." He paused there, but Dr. Stoughton's thin, white face showed no response. "Yes, I took it to heart. . . . In fact, Doctor, I've decided to go into practice in New York myself."

The words did register this time, but it took Stoughton some time to find a reply. At first he just looked dumbfounded—then solemnly composed. "But," he asked, "will you leave . . . this place?" His cracking voice was professionally reserved, but at the end it faltered slightly.

"Yes," Dr. Holliday replied. "That's what I came to tell you, Doctor. I'll be leaving Holly Springs the first of January."

"Oh. . . ." Though otherwise his face reflected no emotion, there were tears in the old man's blue eyes. When he spoke, it was with listless weariness: "Oh, you're going away." Then with only a moment's pause, with no change of facial expression, he added, "My Nancy went away. . . . Maybe I told you. I can't. . . . Yes, my Nancy went away."

"Yes, Doctor, I know." Holliday felt at a loss for words; it seemed best to go on with his original purpose. "I won't be going till after Christmas," he said, "but I wanted to tell you myself. Thought you might be happy with me."

"Indeed, I hope you'll find the city to your liking," Dr. Stoughton answered, some of his old professional reserve creeping back. "I did. . . . We. . . ." And though there were no tears now, Holliday saw a sad loneliness deep in the misted blue eyes. Then, as if bidding a patient good-by back in his own office, Dr. Stoughton stood up and extended his trembling right hand. "Good luck, Doctor," he said. "I shall be wishing you every success."

❲ 4

A few minutes later when he sat opposite young Ben Womble in the Hall 4 conference room, David Holliday wondered if he had deliberately set out to make this afternoon the most depressing one of his life. Every attempt he made at simple, inconsequential conversation failed. No question he asked was answered. The boy just stared straight ahead at Holliday or the wall behind him or the floor. From time to time he giggled; once started humming.

If possible, this saddened David Holliday even more than Dr. Stoughton did. Because he saw that, in effect, this was the same thing, only sixty-five years earlier. And those sixty-five years made a grave and tragic difference. Jonathan Stoughton would stay at Holly Spring, probably until he died, but Ben Womble could not. Holliday made a mental note to call the boy's father for a conference the next day. Here, perhaps, was at least one useful thing he could accomplish in the days left to him. Then, when he had quietly stated his message and still gained no response, he let the boy go. "I'll see you around, Ben," he said. And added, calling after him down the hall, "Ben, would you tell Jack I want to see him?"

To the doctor's surprise, a few minutes later Jack Isaacs did come down the corridor toward him. As usual, he was holding himself almost exaggeratedly erect. But there was a despondent slowness about his stride, and his face appeared grave and tired. He shook hands with Holliday, exchanged greetings and sat down in the upholstered chair opposite the desk.

Then followed an uncomfortable silence during which the doctor, in an effort not to make his announcement too sudden, strained to find the most suitable approach to some of their past discussions. From the shadows under the young man's dark eyes and from the slow, weary way his fingers pulled at each other, Holliday judged he'd been thinking a lot lately—apparently unpleasant thoughts. And he felt it would be extremely unfair for him as retiring doctor to do or say anything to increase that depression.

"How's Lucie?" he asked at last, resorting to the obvious. "Haven't seen her lately. Has the bad weather kept her away?"

"No, sir. She comes on the train . . . every visiting day. She's fine." For once Jack did not struggle to look Holliday in the eye.

There was really no point any longer. The doctor already knew not only that he was trying to hide something, but also what it was he was trying to hide.

Jack knew, also, why Holliday had come this afternoon. To say good-by, or at least make some sort of announcement to that effect. Jack knew all that, and in the face of it, there was something he felt he must say. He studied the floor now in search of the words.

"She's a remarkably strong woman, your Lucie," Holliday continued. "I marvel at today's young wives, anyway, for raising children without servants. . . . But your Lucie, why, she not only does that, but all alone—and commutes out here twice a week besides. Remarkable. . . . She loves you very much, Jack."

"Yes, sir." Jack paused, pressing his lips together in a narrow line. ". . . Dr. Holliday," he began with obvious effort, "you remember that Jewish business we talked about?"

"Yes."

"Well, I've decided you were right. That doesn't bother Lucie. She loves me. Besides, she just never thinks about things like that. . . . B-But, . . . well, there's more to it than that. I've got to live with myself as well as Lucie."

"Yes. . . ." Holliday listened eagerly, but cautiously, his eyes averted.

"My parents were good people, Dr. Holliday—good Jews and good people. . . . They're both dead now."

"Do you feel you've betrayed them?"

"No."

"Do you feel they might think you'd betrayed them?"

"No." Jack felt anger rising inside him, not so much at the doctor as at himself, because he could not say what he must say. "No," he said again, bitterly this time, "I've betrayed myself."

"What do you mean by that?" Holliday asked warily. He had not bargained for this confidence.

Jack did not answer that question. It was the one he needed. It was the one he had been angry with Holliday for not asking. Yet now suddenly he could not face up to it; he could not bring himself to make verbal the confession it demanded. Instead, he just sat there in silence, eyes fixed on the floor.

"Can you tell, . . ." Holliday persisted, "Jack, can you tell me how you've betrayed yourself?"

Still no answer.

After a long silence, the doctor decided to continue with the purpose of his visit. "Actually, Jack," he began, returning abruptly to his usual geniality, "I didn't come here today to pick your brain. ... I came to talk about myself."

"Oh...."

"Yes.... It looks like I've come to a crossroads in my own life, Jack. I've decided to go into practice with a friend of mine in New York City."

"I see," the young voice replied with surprising confidence. "So you'll be leaving Holly Springs."

"Yes. But not right away. Not till the first of the year."

"Oh...." So there it was. And still he could not say what he had told himself he must.

"If you're like most people," Holliday continued, "you may feel this is going to set you back. But I don't think you need to worry, Jack. You're going to get well. You *are* getting well. Because you want to.... That's what counts."

"I hope you're right, sir." Jack's voice remained calm and polite, but inside he seethed. Basically with anger toward himself, but more consciously, offended by Holliday's suggesting he was dependent.

"Actually," the doctor continued, "it doesn't really make much difference who your doctor is. Fight's up to you."

"Yes, sir." Jack calmed down a little at that admission. He reminded himself he had held that to be true for a long time; also that Holliday was just one more doctor who talked big, looked wise, but really was no stronger, no deeper than anybody else.

"Well, I'll be seeing you," the doctor said, standing up.

"All right, sir." Jack stood up too. He allowed Holliday to shake his hand. But he revealed no warmth and kept his face impassive with determined distaste. After the broad back was turned on him, however, he could no longer deny the sorrowful voice inside him that said this had been his last chance and now it was gone.

❨ 5

Millie Pratt was stricken with panic the next day when Dr. Holliday told her he was leaving Holly Springs. At first she merely appeared stunned, shocked into silence. Then her eyes misted, until the tears brimmed over and her lower lip quivered. And still she did not speak. "I knew this," she was thinking. "Long time ago when Evie and Mrs. Purdy started talking about it. For certain that day Mother was here. She said I was wrong, but I knew." But that made the reality now no less frightening.

"I'll miss our talks, Millie," Holliday talked on complacently. "But I won't worry about you. You're on the right track and in good hands. Dr. Collins is a fine woman."

And it was then, without any warning, that the storm broke. Suddenly overwhelmed by the frustrated anger and fear beating inside her, she began screaming at him. "I think you're horrible," she blundered, crying. "Cruel! To let me work up so far and then back out. What'll happen? What'll I do?"

"You're being very childish, Millie." Holliday's face became grimly serious. His drawling voice stern instead of gentle. "After all," he said, "this is only one moment in your whole life.... You flatter me, but I'm not that important. Nobody is."

Still she wept and shouted at him incoherently.

Holliday tried to calm her with the familiar worn-out talk of "adolescence and rejection and self-value." He reminded her of the previously comforting possibility of boarding school instead of home. As a last resort, he told her that in a way she was "very fortunate," that what she was going through would eventually prove a "valuable experience."

But Millie scarcely listened. She kept on crying and begging him not to go. No matter what he said or did, she came back with the same frantic ravings: "What'll happen? What'll I do? They don't understand; they'll make me leave!... What'll I do? Where'll I go?"

Initially troubled, Holliday quickly became irritated, then exasperated. Her childish tantrum both angered him and stirred up his own guilt regarding the move to New York. His only effective defense against that guilt was additional anger. So at last, right in the middle of her cries he stood up and said coolly (cruelly, too, he knew), "Miss Pratt, it seems to me we're getting nowhere.... Perhaps if you think things over quietly, we can talk again to more profit. In the meantime, I have another appointment."

It was a great relief after that to sit down with Eileen O'Hara in the conference room on Atkins Hall. Her meek contentment offered a welcome contrast. He arrived at teatime, and Mrs. Sullivan brought in two cups and a saucer of cookies. When she had gone, Eileen spoke of how she had been drinking tea all her life— since she was just a child and had a cup of milk made warmish by a little of the amber liquid in her father's cup.

A shadow crossed her face when Holliday told her he was leaving Holly Springs, but she didn't seem to take it personally as he had feared she might. She said simply that she was sorry to hear that, that she couldn't imagine Holly Springs without him, and that she was very grateful for all the help he'd given her. Then she wished him "all good fortune in whatever you may venture into."

"How do you feel about yourself, Miss O'Hara?"

"Myself?"

"Yes. The reports are all good. To read them, you're as well adjusted as anybody. But then, I imagine there's a lot inside you doesn't show. How do you feel about leaving Holly Springs, going back out in the world?"

"How do I feel? Oh, like anybody would. Afraid, I guess. But only a little, and just because it's new."

"Have any plans? You and Dr. Pierson worked anything out yet?"

She was silent for a moment. Her eyes leapt to his face, scanned it accusingly, then eased back into guarded serenity. "No, I guess we haven't," she said. "But I'm fairly certain of what I'll do."

"What's that?"

"Oh, I'll go back to St. Timothy's—probably even to surgery. Live in the residence. Take special courses. Become a better nurse. Save my money for a visit home. Same as before."

"And you're satisfied with that?"

"Well, it's not what I'd wish for, I guess—not everything I want of life. But I know that's how it'll be, and my mind knows better than to ask for more. I think I'll be happy enough, too, this time. . . ."

"But you don't speak of marriage or a home or family. Don't you want those things?"

"Oh, . . . Of course, I can't say I don't want them. Everyone must, I suppose." She looked at the floor, but matter-of-factly, not as if to escape. "In fact," she continued slowly, pensively, "I've rather a theory that men and women who never marry eventually become so absorbed in their selfish loneliness that they are as crippled as people physically deformed."

"And still you think you won't marry?"

"I don't know, but I rather think not."

"Isn't that contradictory?"

"No. You see, I'm not truly determined not to marry. It's just that . . . well, . . . I feel I've learned a great deal in my time here. But above all, that life's a compromise—the mid-course between the things you yearn for and the things you fear."

"Sounds rather gloomy to me."

"Oh, no." She smiled sadly. "Just reality. Something I know to be true and can accept because it is. In fact—better than that—because it's not alien to me, I know how to make the most of it and find something very close to satisfaction."

After that, they talked a little more about her future, about the world in general, and how human beings were so often the victims of fate. Holliday wanted to ask again about Pierson, to know whether either of the two had dared to slacken his barriers. But he felt no right to interfere, to revive doubts the girl had managed to subdue. So it was only a short time before he drained his cup and stood up. She smiled as he shook her hand and said she would mention him in her prayers.

Holliday remembered that smile and her voice as he took the outdoor path back to his office. It was gratifying to feel he might have helped the girl. Comforting, too, to know she liked him. Still, he felt depressed. Part of it, he knew, was just feeling sorry for himself, bewailing the empty future he felt too weak to fight. But really, it was bigger than that. Why should any person be forced to accept life on its own meager terms, to be satisfied with half-happiness or less than that?

VIII

"MR. WOMBLE, your father's here to see you."

To Ben, reclining on his bed as usual, no words could have been more shocking. For a moment he even thought he was dreaming. It wasn't visiting day, . . . at least he didn't think so. It wasn't even afternoon yet, because they hadn't had lunch. Besides, his father had come to see him on Christmas, just two days before.

After her terse announcement, Miss Gardner lingered in the doorway, uncertain as to whether she had been understood. It was only after she turned away that Ben sat up on the edge of his bed and rubbed his eyes.

"Hello, Ben. Surprised to see me today?"

It was his father all right. Without looking up, Ben knew the astute, too pleasant voice. He nodded his head in affirmation that he was surprised.

"Where's Jack? All right if I put my things on his bed?"

Ben nodded again and finally raised his eyes to look at his father. He had never realized before how old the man was. His square figure in its neat tweed suit had grown quite heavy and settled-looking. The little hair he had was snow white; the face beneath it yellow in contrast. Surprisingly, too, that face looked almost wizened. The wrinkles stayed in it even when the man grinned as he did now.

"I had to come out this way today to see a fellow about a show, so I just called and asked Dr. Holliday if I couldn't drop in on you a few minutes." After depositing his hat and coat on the vacant bed, Benjamin Womble pulled one of the room's straight chairs closer to his son and sat down.

Ben still had not spoken. He could think of nothing to say. The same as on Christmas Day, when both his mother and his father had come. He'd thanked them for the gifts and, after their insistent prodding, had even opened them. A book, a bathrobe, shirts and some kind of game to play by yourself. But on Christmas, after the gifts, he'd had nothing to say. And today there weren't any gifts.

"Have you read any in the book yet?" his father continued with determined cheerfulness.

Ben shook his head.

"Well, do soon. I'll be interested to hear what you think of it. Toscanini was a curious fellow, ... fascinating. And this is supposed to be *the* biography of him."

The boy nodded again, but his blank expression did not change. For a moment, even as he maintained his bright exterior, Benjamin Womble feared that his tears were going to burst through after all. ... His boy. His pride. His hope. His one and only. The very purpose of his life. It seemed impossible that God could be so cruel! To turn a bright, young, beautiful boy into a living corpse. To cripple a brilliant mind with infantile confusion and make of its owner a helpless parasite. Still, that was what Dr. Holliday had said. And all along Holliday had been the one with the most hope; so that now they must accept his dismal forecast as a more than fair appraisal.

The doctor had written him a letter, requesting that at his earliest convenience he call and make an appointment to see him. And so, he had, for this morning at 10:15. ... He'd been worried about coming, had suspected some bad news of Ben. But even his darkest forebodings had not prepared him for Holliday's words: "As you know, I've always been deeply interested in Ben, even fond of him in a way. ... That's why, much as it hurts me, I wanted to be the one to tell you this.

"We didn't know at first," he had continued in his solemnly measured drawl. "There was no way of telling for sure. And I—an incurable optimist—well, I thought there was every reason to hope. I thought so even last winter and spring. I hoped so last summer; I prayed so this fall. ... But now the evidence is just too obvious to be denied."

Holliday had talked for nearly forty-five minutes after that, but now Benjamin Womble could remember only a few of his words: "progressive deterioration ... possibly incurable ... I will not say hopeless; medicine is making remarkable advances. I won't even tell you not to hope, but I'd be heartless to encourage you in any expectations."

Now as he looked at his son, Womble longed to throw his arms around him and hold him close. Ridiculous, he knew, but somehow he felt that in that way he might be able to give Ben some of the strength he lacked. Just that thought forced him to take a firmer grip on himself, however, and instead of the embrace, he continued his cheerfully empty conversation: "That game, Ben. . . . We brought it to you, because your mother got one for her birthday and has found a surprising amount of pleasure in it. . . . I guess you haven't tried it yet?"

The boy shook his head.

"Well, you ought to soon, . . . some time when you're feeling bored, with nothing to do." He must be careful. It was so hard to remember while talking to that expressionless face that there were thoughts and perhaps strong feelings behind it. Ben must in no way be allowed to sense what Holliday had said. Holly Springs was the right place for now, but in a year or so, if Holliday's fears proved accurate, they would have to look for something else. They were fortunate, at least, in having money, the doctor had told him. Because though it could not buy Ben a new and vital mind, it could assure him of the best care available in his increasing helplessness.

"We won't be able to come Saturday," the father talked on. "A party we have to go to. But your mother told me to tell you she'll be here early Tuesday. And she told me to ask if there's anything you want her to bring."

Ben did not answer, just stared into his father's face. He hoped he would go soon.

"Isn't there something you need, son?"

Ben shook his head.

"Are you sure, Ben? She'd like to bring you something."

Ben shook his head again.

A few minutes more and the father did go. Ben listened as his footsteps padded out of hearing. Then, when he heard the corridor door snap safely to, he himself stood up and went out in the hall. He walked slowly, thinking over his father's visit and hearing again and again the echo of those words from years ago: ". . . Benjy, some day you will be a great man. . . . You must never forget that, Benjy; you must work toward it."

Ben wondered now if his father realized the greatness that was already in him. His face had looked worried today, and he had not knelt down; so probably he didn't see. Of course, the halo was very dim as yet—perhaps not even visible on such a bright day. Besides, this was not the kind of greatness his father had thought about. He had always said "composer."

It would take time, of course, but Ben hoped his father would see before too long. There was just the purity now, and the martyrdom, which might even appear weakness. But later the strength would come, then the whole world would see and know and give praises to the great King Benjamin.

Near the bathroom the corridor branched off into another shorter hall. Ben turned there and walked to the big window at the end of it. Perhaps, he thought, looking out through the gaunt branches of the tall trees, perhaps I can see Father getting in his car. But he could not. There were no cars below; nor even any men. Just the barren, unlandscaped part of the grounds; just the cold sunshine, bright and sterile.... Yes.... Yes, one man. Ben peered closely. A small man, taller than his father, but thinner, and ridiculous!

Ben laughed bitterly, sneeringly. The little man was limping, and he had his overcoat pulled tight around him as if he was trembling with the cold. That seemed so stupid to Ben—weak and foolish and ugly. Why tremble? Why try to walk if you had to limp and tremble? He would never do that.

Disgusted, he decided not to bother with the lunch bell they were ringing. Instead, he went back to his bed for a nap.

(2

Philip Pierson squinted blindly against the cold midday sun. As the wind whistling through the trees blew back the flap of his overcoat, he automatically thrust his hands deeper in the pockets.

Again he had used his lunch hour to walk down here through the potato fields and the twisted fruit trees. And again he did not really know why. It was terribly cold with no big trees or shrubs to break the wind—also a long walk with his bad leg. Yet Pierson found a great satisfaction in these treks, a sense of peace in a world that had come to seem void of both order and goodness. It no longer even bothered him that Holliday had once walked here, too, studying it as a possible site for his prized outpatient clinic. Holliday was going away, and Pierson had made up his mind to forget him.

When the wind cut inside his coat again, he turned back toward the main building. He had a 2:30 appointment with Eileen. And that made him somewhat uneasy—a little happy, a little sad, excited, and afraid. He knew Eileen would be leaving soon. She appeared much better, and most of the staff, including Dr. McLeod, were convinced it was genuine. In fact, if anything, he was the one holding her back. And he knew that despite his practical arguments in staff conference, the real reason was his personal one, simply that he could not bear to see her go.

Pierson trudged up the hill before the wind as quickly as his lame leg would let him. He thought only of the gray-green eyes with their variations of shadow and light. Sooner or later he'd have to let her go. He had hoped once that there might be some solution, some way to a happy ending. But it was too late now. He couldn't even follow Holliday's advice about sounding her out before she left. Not just because Holliday was going, but because he himself was too vulnerable. Because, when you got right down to it, his work was all he had, and it was too much of a risk without someone to back him up.

She was waiting for him inside, sitting beside the mail table working on some yellow knitting. She had been standing at the window before and had seen him limp up to the front door with his coat pulled tight around him. And now as he came down the corridor, her heart was hammering.

Every time she saw him now, Eileen expected to be told she could start the series of weekend passes that would precede her new start in the outside world. The thorazine was over with no "undesirable after effects." She'd been on Atkins Hall three weeks and was probably more stable emotionally than she'd been for years. "Above all," she told herself, "my mind is made up." Still, she did not want to leave. Especially, she did not want to start the weekend passes because they seemed only a way of dragging out the already difficult struggle. She loved him. She had pondered her feelings and weighed them carefully, and there no longer seemed any other possible conclusion. Yes, she knew she loved him. But she knew, too, that here again she could not have what she wanted. She must go away. And this time she couldn't even let her hurt show.

"Hello, Eileen." He scowled and took a firmer grip on his notebook, then cleared his throat and tried a new start. "Miss O'Hara, I presume Mrs. Sullivan informed you of our appointment?"

"Yes, she did." Eileen put aside her knitting and stood up. "I was waiting for you."

"Let's go in the conference room."

The living room seemed unusually large and impressive that afternoon, even more than the ordinary contrast with the small, stark conference rooms on the other halls. They sat there in silence at first, the doctor concentrating diligently on his notebook, Eileen studying the place where her shoe was coming unstitched.

"Of course, Miss O'Hara," Pierson began, again clearing his throat. "Of course, you're much better. In fact, outwardly you seem in quite adequate control of your emotions. This is obvious to all of us on the staff. But I ... I wonder, Miss O'Hara, if sometimes you don't still feel a little hurt, ... perhaps a ... a slight twinge of unreturned affection, a longing to matter to some one person more than ... more than anything else in the world?" His voice spoke each word softly, gently. Toward the end it trembled.

At least, so it seemed to Eileen. And that gave her courage. Or perhaps it was not courage. Perhaps it was just the opposite—the fatal weakness taking over. After a long silence, she glanced up at him, then quickly back at her shoe. She started to speak, then changed her mind, then began again.

"Yes, mostly," she said. "I guess I mostly feel in control. But...."

She hesitated some time, then quickly, as if daring herself every word of the way, she looked him square in the face and said clearly but more softly than before, "But sometimes ... sometimes my love is too big to control. Sometimes I feel I must speak it or explode."

❮ 3

"Did you see Dr. McLeod?" Mrs. Weaver greeted him as he entered his office. "She was in here looking for you a few minutes ago."

"No." Holliday sighed. "Did she say what she wanted?"

"No, sir. But I told her I'd let her know when you came in."

"Don't. I'll go over there."

It was Monday, December 31—officially his last day at Holly Springs. But for David Holliday there was no sense of finality. It was only one more in the endless chain of futilely empty days that must elapse before he could say good-by to this place he had once loved so much and had now come to hate as a constant reminder of his own weakness. Officially his last day, but he had agreed to stay on an extra week to help Martha McLeod with her new duties.

Martha was at her desk when he reached her office. "Good morning," she said pleasantly, looking up at him without a smile.

"Were you looking for me?"

"Oh, yes. But it wasn't at all important. . . . Just something I thought you'd be interested in seeing." She opened her desk drawer and pulled out a newspaper clipping. Pushing it toward him, she said, "This was in yesterday's paper."

She watched curiously as he picked it up, his great fingers fumbling to unfold it, his forehead frowning with his effort to comprehend. Probably she had looked somewhat the same way when Beth Tucker pointed it out to her that morning. There had been almost an air of victory about Tucker as she presented that clipping. She had been the one to discover it, and it was evidence of what happened to people who defied Holly Springs.

"POP LEADER MARRIES" read the cutline under the gray print-grainy picture. "Italian orchestra leader Francie Francoli hugs his wife, Carson, shortly after their marriage in Los Angeles yesterday."

Even Martha McLeod had caught her breath for a moment in reading that. Not because it was a surprise, but rather, because the misfortune she had anticipated had come about so quickly and in such a predictable way. Martha could not feel triumphant. After all, any failure of Holly Springs was in part a failure of her own. But in another sense, this clipping was useful to her. It should prove to David Holliday that her tenets of experience and discipline were well founded, that even in unusual and desperate situations they were better than a stab in the dark.

She watched him now for his reaction. But it was slow in coming. For several minutes the frown on his face did not shift. He seemed to be studying the picture and reading the short item over and over. Then at last he shook his head. "That's her all right," he said. "That face is undeniable. . . . Besides the story." He read from the clipping, " '... former wife of pencil magnate, Jesse Gaitors, and a prominent New York socialite. This is her sixth marriage, Francie's third.' " He shook his head again, more sadly than with disbelief.... The very one he had known about and thought it best not to reveal until the ultimate moment—the ultimate moment that had disintegrated before his eyes.

Certainly, if he had revealed this secret, there would have been a setback of at least six months. The collision of McLeod versus Gaitors would have made that inevitable. Now, of course, such a setback seemed minor compared to the actual outcome. Yet Holliday realized, confronted by the same evidence and the same choices, he'd very probably do the same thing again. Quickly, automatically his thoughts went back to the morning she had made her confession to him. It was not hard to remember that September morning, his first back from vacation. And the image of the young woman seemed equally clear....

She'd begun by tossing her dark mane rebelliously back over her shoulders and laughing affectedly. Her words had come quick and bold, with the joking frankness she always used to speak of serious matters: "An orchestra leader ... very talented ... a little flashy, I guess ... the calypso type ... Italian." And a few minutes later in defense, "I know I shouldn't fall for a Wop, but I did. And how can I help that? How can I help that?"

That memory tightened Holliday's throat into an aching knot. At first, just because of the young woman herself—the vitality, the gallant gaiety she had always shown in the face of fear. But then when the strength of her remembered words hit him full force, he felt weak. His face felt flushed, his eyes burning and blurred. Obviously, she had been asking him for help even then, in the only way she knew how. Probably she had hoped he *would* go to Martha McLeod and that together they would clamp down on her, take the matter out of her hands. Probably she had only told him about it at all because she felt too weak to cope with it herself. And he had not understood. He had failed her miserably.

David Holliday had always complimented himself that he possessed great ability in helping people like Carson Gaitors because he, himself, had many failings and so could meet theirs with the wisdom of firsthand experience. He had felt especially close to Mrs. Gaitors, a closeness much deeper than friendship. Yet now he must accept the fact that, much as she had given him, he had not really helped her at all.

Suddenly, then, Holliday was painfully conscious of being huge and clumsy and useless. The tears blurring his eyes seemed almost certain to overflow. And they must not, Martha was watching, and she must not see that he felt any more than professional interest. "I wonder what the end will be?" he said at last.

"It's difficult to imagine, isn't it?" Martha McLeod sighed in sympathy; her face remained morosely severe.

"Yes. And realistically we can't excuse ourselves. Legally she wasn't under our care, but she should've been. I wish I knew our mistake."

The small white-coated woman sat stiffly erect in her chair. A muscle near her mouth twitched impatiently. "If you'll recall, I was not in favor of keeping her on Open Hall at the time of the crisis."

The pained frown faded from Holliday's face. "I'd do the same thing again," he declared. "That's one thing I'm confident shouldn't have been different. She'd have rebelled violently at a demotion."

"In which case we'd have had no trouble in obtaining a commitment from either her husband or the authorities."

"But think of all that struggle to do over again. It seems to me we should be able to. . . ." He broke off there, because there seemed no point in going on. It was futile to reason with Martha. He felt he was *not* being weak now, that the situation truly *was* impossible.

"Yes, but as it is now, she may as well never have been at Holly Springs," the deadly proper voice reminded him.

Holliday nodded wearily but did not speak. He saw more certainly now that he was right to be going away. He and Martha were an impossible pair. Though her blind rigidity exasperated him, he was probably equally difficult in his own very different way. In this practical test it was not Martha who had failed, but himself. Yet, even now Holliday could not agree with her. "I'll see you, Martha," he said at last. "Thanks for showing me that clipping."

Out in the corridor again his thoughts automatically set forth their defense: "Twenty years behind the times," they groaned. But today that only made an opening for his despair. It seemed almost a fact that dumpy, pasty-faced Martha McLeod was more capable of his responsibilities than he was himself. "She may not be able to look ahead eighty years," he thought. "But she can see what to do now." Yes, a damn good thing he was leaving.

(4

But it was not until the tenth day of January that Mary Laine and David Holliday actually did depart. On January 6, Martha McLeod asked if he could possibly add two days to the week's assistance he had originally agreed to give her. And Holliday, despite the agony those first six days had already been, agreed to stay through the ninth. Agreed, because, weak and guilty as he increasingly felt about leaving Holly Springs, Holliday saw no alternative.

That decision could no longer be altered. He must accept as facts Millie Pratt's panicky abuse and the tragic emptiness in the eyes of the Womble boy's father. Even such small things as Lucie Isaacs' overlooking his invitation to "come in some time before the first of the year."

There were many arguments in favor of his going, of course. Still, even those were powerless at times—when he was admitting a new patient, for instance, as he did frequently during those nine days. It sounded openly hypocritical to say, "No, I'm deeply devoted to Holly Springs, but no longer the director here. Dr. Martha McLeod has just succeeded me in that capacity. I'm retiring to private practice." Who could claim "deep devotion" and still abandon his hospital to the direction of a cold, uncompromising reactionary like Martha? Yet, since that statement seemed the only honorable explanation for his resignation, he used it over and over, each time with more guilt than the time before.

In addition to admissions, Holliday wrote letters, approved order books, accepted telephone calls, and conferred with Martha McLeod about the points for which she felt she needed a clearer understanding. But he also had a good deal of time to sit and think. And that, of course, was the most unpleasant of all his duties. Before January 1 he had carefully avoided thinking. But once his tenure was officially ended, he felt it was important that he have no contact at all with the patients. And at the same time, the barrier between himself and the staff seemed to have grown impregnable. In fact, the only one to whom he really talked was Martha. With the others he did little more than exchange greetings in the hall. There seemed nothing to talk about—even with Ellen Collins or Lloyd Wilson. And he found himself actually avoiding Phil Pierson. He could not bear the hurt accusation in the young doctor's dark eyes. Besides, Pierson automatically reminded him of the O'Hara girl, and that in turn, for some reason he could not clearly identify, increased his sense of failure.

So it was a great relief when Wednesday, January 9, finally crawled to its end. He left early that day, bidding good-by to no one but Martha McLeod. He felt dog tired and beaten. He wanted to go to bed immediately after supper and take off for the city before it was fully light the next day.

But the next morning, it seemed, only began their waiting. The movers, scheduled to start work at 8:30 A.M., didn't even arrive until 11:00. After that, everything not only had to be packed, but loaded on the van before the Hollidays could leave. Mary Laine had to answer questions and approve crating, but Holliday found himself useless to everybody for everything. He took a couple of walks in the cold, gray dampness, but for the most part he just sat in his chair in the study, with a pencil clutched in one hand and a crossword puzzle book and an old medical journal in the other.

Much of the day Mary Laine sat there with him. But for the first time since his decision to leave Holly Springs, she seemed to have nothing to say. In fact, her eyes gazed blindly, and the worry lines around her mouth tightened, as if she were unhappy about leaving. Which, in part, she was. With each piece of furniture she saw carried out to the van, she realized anew that they were leaving the only home she and David had ever known. Her mind was crowded with sentimental memories—their first evening here, the day Lillian was born, David's promotion to director. And those thoughts, or rather, the tender, pensive mood they touched off, were fertile ground for the worries she had about herself. It seemed now that leaving this house and going to the city was as much an end as a beginning. And that, of course, was suggestive of death.

She and David had not talked about her illness much—the operation, its findings, and contingent consequences. He'd told her in the beginning they'd found a very small malignant growth. He'd added that they had not only removed it completely, but also, by removing the whole breast and all the glands in the armpit, had taken the maximum precautions to prevent recurrence. Several times since, he'd reassured her, saying that if she wouldn't take his word for it or even that of the doctors in New York, she should at least be able to discern something from her own feelings and the fact that they had given her no medicine to take. Still, she kept wondering if there weren't more. Something he didn't speak about or even know.

So she was as relieved as Holliday when the movers finally ousted them from the study with its emptied bookshelves. There followed another half hour of waiting for them to finish. The doctor paced the living room, and Mary Laine stood and watched him. The movers left at 5:45, as soon as the van was loaded. But before they even drove off, Mary Laine realized David was already holding her coat for her. "Let's get going," he said. "We'll never have dinner otherwise."

Her throat was tight and aching with sadness. There were tears in her eyes, and when she touched David's hand, she suddenly found herself clinging to it like a frightened child. "I'm sorry, darling," she said, glancing around the empty house. "It just seems so strange that we'll never come here again, that this part of our lives will be cut off completely."

Holliday saw the tears slip out of her eyes and down her cheeks. He felt the fear in her fingers. Still, he himself could only be glad they were finally leaving. For a moment, his eyes, too, wandered in the emptiness around them. But he spoke cheerfully, "Well, you ready to go?"

She did not answer immediately. But when she looked up through her tears, she found in his smiling face the reassurance she needed. "Yes, I guess so," she said. And she smiled back at him despite her trembling lips.

"Come on then. We're late." David Holliday spoke loud and roguishly, as if to jolt himself into happiness. He kissed Mary Laine's cheek and swung his arm about her waist. As they went out into the cold, starless evening, he took her gloved hand in his and squeezed it hard. "You'll see, darling," he said gently. "We're going to be very happy in New York."

BOOK THREE

Down the Hill

I

AS USUAL, that winter Holly Springs settled into a gratifying boredom after the Christmas holidays. No more extra visiting days or special privileges for the staff to supervise. No need for the patients to shield themselves inside and out with forced gaiety. None of the inexorable avalanches of depression which often resulted. Just the dead, uncompromising routine, the unreasoning regulations, the fear and loss of face.

It suddenly turned very cold after the New Year. There was six and three-quarter inches of snow which didn't melt for weeks. A form letter was sent out to all relatives noting the need for "knee stockings, warm sweaters, lined weatherproof jackets, rubbers." Women on the lower halls, where scarves and hats with ties weren't allowed, could be seen walking to O.T. and gym with sweaters wrapped around their heads. Women on the upper halls complained bitterly about the forty-five-minute walks which were compulsory three times a week even in temperatures as low as ten and twelve degrees. But, though she wouldn't yield on that point, Martha McLeod (scornfully referred to as the "Great White Mother") did relent on another. She sent a signed note to each hall on the women's side, reading: "In this abnormally cold weather patients may wear woolen slacks or ski pants on the long walks. However, this privilege must not be extended to the short walks to activities."

The women patients laughed at that last sentence. They said it was typical of her to kill a kindness with such an obvious stipulation. Generally, though, they were relieved about the changes Mc-Leod had enacted, or rather, the fewness of them. The rules were stricter—three weeks on Hall 4 before you got an off-grounds pass, three on Open before you got a weekend. Increased room searches. Coffee at breakfast only. But mostly, things were much easier than they'd anticipated.

On the men's side, however, there were all kinds of gripes. "Like having a WAC run the army," Jim Reilly bitched. "She'll have us all passing inspection before you know it—wearing ties and long-sleeved shirts."

"Yeah," Charlie Watson sneered. "And it gives you a great sense of personal power to have your doc say, 'Well, that sounds good to me, but I'll have to check with Dr. McLeod.' Like asking your grandmother whether to change your socks!"

Martha McLeod was well aware of their talk. She expected it as the natural way of things. And it seemed equally natural that what they said should be critical. She saw it in their faces—staff as well as patients—read it in the letters she censored, heard the bitter words dropped carelessly before she was far enough up a corridor. She was sorry about that, pained a little. But she knew it would pass, like so many other things. And if it didn't? Well, that was the price you paid for advancement.

She was really too busy to worry about what people thought. Though she had turned most of her patients over to other doctors, she still had all the duties that had kept David Holliday busy ten hours a day. And because they were new to her and she took them more seriously, they required even more of her time.

In addition, she had resolved to make several changes. Most of them fell into the simple category of making the hospital's policy and treatment comply with her thinking rather than Holliday's— a tightening up; a stern, realistic hand to deal with problems firmly, with assurance; a cold, calm honesty; none of Holliday's friendly, easygoing bluff—none of his deceptive warmth, which, she felt, not only demanded unnecessary time and energy but also might lead to an unhealthy attachment on the part of the patients. She found an excellent opportunity to practice this resolution in showing the relatives of prospective patients around the hospital. Refusing to elaborate on the bright side of Holly Springs, she always said early in the interview: "It's a long, painful, expensive pull. You might as well make up your mind to that. It will demand great patience from you and complete trust in us. The end result must always be uppermost in your mind. The steps leading there are often illogical and depressing." And all with the same deliberate coldness on her pale face, the same unsympathetic glaze over her blue eyes.

Isabelle Weaver, who had been secretary to Dr. Holliday for nearly twenty years, found the change almost intolerable. Not just that the days were dull now, uneventful and silent, hostile with efficiency, without the drawling voice joking through the open doorway—but also the way visitors fearfully asked her assistance instead of walking casually into the main office. Her feeling for the tight-lipped bustling women was close to hatred. She only stayed because she needed the money.

The first visiting day after Holliday's departure George Purdy brought a box of California pears to the new lady director, not in an attempt to curry favor, but just to be friendly, just to show he made no difference between her and Holliday. But the stone-faced matron didn't even offer him a chair. She just glanced up from the paper she was signing, gave him a sort of fishy half-smile, and said, "Thank you, Mr. Purdy. I do appreciate this, but I make it a policy not to accept gifts. Why don't you take the fruit to the women on your wife's hall? I'm sure they'd get far more pleasure from it than I."

George murmured a disappointed, "Yes, ma'am," and backed out the door. And he never stopped on the main corridor again. He just thanked God Gladys was her old self again and prayed he'd never have reason to talk to Dr. McLeod.

But some people were pleased with the change. Beth Tucker, for instance, felt much happier about her job as nursing supervisor. She knew Dr. McLeod would take every detail of the work seriously, give her all the authority she cared to take, and never do or say anything to offend her sense of propriety. And Evie Barrow, who was still on Hall 4 and still battling depression, felt she had lost nothing in Holliday's departure. It was even easier to meet this grim white-coated strictness than the other's friendly drawling sunshine.

For Eileen O'Hara the difference was negligible. She was on Open Hall and taking weekend passes with her Cousin Dan and his wife Mary. She didn't enjoy those weekends, found them scarcely bearable at times. But they offered a change and a challenge which she felt compelled to meet. Only by enduring those suffocating visits with their monotonous talk of the County Cork and "your poor mother left to her lonesome. . . this devilish arther-itis. . . . Thank the good Lord for your youth, Eileen," could she advance to four-day passes, ten-day passes, and finally the independence which was her dreaded but necessary goal. She missed Dr. Holliday occasionally. He had forced his way too deep into her privacy to forget him completely. But neither he nor Dr. McLeod nor any other symbol of authority held either comfort or doom for Eileen any longer. The future seemed up to her, its direction relentless and inevitable.

And so it went. Renovations were begun to convert the Holliday house into apartments for married interns. A new batch of student nurses came, and those who had been there for three months returned to their home hospitals. A male patient escaped. A new kiln was purchased for Women's O.T. But otherwise it was just the same. Eating, sleeping, therapy, counting, biding the time.

(2

Ben Womble lay on his bed and stared through the doorway. The eerie bird-like humming quavered softly, monotonously from his throat—until a startling hush fell over the room, and Ben realized suddenly that his careful emptiness wasn't complete, his muffled humming almost loud. That frightened him and made him angry, because it happened more and more of late and he knew why.

It was Jack Isaacs' fault. Because he never said anything any more—or made any noise or even turned on his radio—just as he never read books or looked at his pictures or worked on those word puzzles. Sometimes Ben thought Jack did that on purpose, because he saw it made his roommate uneasy or even because he was curious and wanted to pry inside the vacuum Ben had erected around himself.

Ben looked over at Jack now. He was just standing there in the middle of the room, looking—or pretending to look—out the window. "Just let him try!" Ben told himself angrily. "Just let him start meddling in somebody else's privacy. He'll find out one thing anyway—that he's playing with fire." There was really no point in getting angry, though, Ben reminded himself. No matter how hard Jack searched, he couldn't find out any more than was on the surface. He would never know that Ben's purity and increasing strength were born of weakness, or that that weakness had hurt Ben's father deeply because he could not see beyond it. The fact that Jack was prying—if, indeed, he was—was in itself proof of his blindness. Doubtless he didn't even suspect the strength to come to Ben, the strength that could strike him down with vengeance later on. Because, if Jack had faith, he would be able to see the halo around Ben's head, and in that case, would not dare to pry.

Father, poor thing, had no faith. Ben recalled now that he had come to visit several times since Christmas and that each time he had acted dumb and condescending and too cheerful, as if trying to make friends with a dog. That was because he still thought of the weakness and could not see the blessed halo. Finally, the last visit Ben had just asked him outright: "Father, can't you see I've been blessed? . . . Soon you will have to bow and call me King Benjamin." But that had only gotten the poor man all flustered, and then, after a moment, even more devoted to his act of exaggerated friendliness.

Something in the middle of the room distracted Ben again. He looked up to find Jack still frowning out the window, his hands gripping the back of the desk chair. Probably it wasn't fair to think Jack pried. He never had before. Besides, more and more lately, it seemed something must be wrong with him. Perhaps the authorities had got their hands on some more evidence against him. Ben never pondered Jack's trouble deeply, any more than anything else outside himself. Still, there were things that made him wonder. Once, after Jack's pretty wife went home, Ben had thought he heard him crying in a toilet booth. And lately he always knew exactly what Jack was doing—and would do, just because he'd seen him go through the same routine so many times. . . .

Now, for instance, he would stand before the window for a few minutes, then turn and let himself fall heavily on the bed. After that he would turn over to face the wall and shut his eyes. But he wouldn't be asleep, because very soon his gangling figure would jump up again and charge off toward the smoker. Jack hadn't always been that way. Ben could remember vaguely a time long, long before when Jack had seemed easygoing and almost strong, not at all like the person crying in the toilet. Now as he watched him move from the window to his bed, Ben decided he had probably grossly misjudged Jack in thinking he was trying to interfere.

Until the glory came—he must always remember that it would come in time—he must wait and watch. But if in the end, his fears about Jack's interfering proved baseless, he would make it up to him. When the glory came, Jack would be one of the first to know and share it. He and his pretty wife and their children would ascend the golden, cloud-banked staircase directly behind the great King Benjamin. And they would sit on his right hand, the golden lights of their halos mingling just below his, for ever and ever.

"... Praise ye the Lord.

"The Lord's name be praised."

❨ 3

As he stood there, looking out the same damn window of the same damn room, Jack Isaacs wondered just how much longer he could go on this way. He felt so tired of the frozen view from the window, the mustiness, the stark yellow-stained walls, the flap of starched aprons going by in the hall, and the hopelessness of Ben's weird humming. It was more than unpleasant—it was terrifying.

At last he flopped on his bed, hoping to jar the stale thoughts from his mind. He turned on his side, with his back to the room, and shut his eyes. But that no longer worked. Even with his eyes closed, he could smell the sour steaminess of the lunch being cleared away. And he could hear the relentless ticking of the big clock in the living room. For some reason, Ben had stopped humming, but Jack had the distinct impression that the boy's strange blue eyes were staring at him now and taking him apart bit by bit.

He didn't care what Ben saw or didn't see or how he put what he saw together. But just the idea of the boy's eyes fixed on him made Jack uneasy. In the beginning Ben had seemed just a frightened kid whose shyness had overmastered him. But more and more lately he seemed something weird and set apart, something it was bad luck to look at too long. At last Jack gave up trying to compose himself there. He got up from the bed and went to the dresser for his cigarettes. Then he hurried off down the hall to the smoker and its wearisome, but comforting babble of conversation.

Jack no longer made any effort to speak to the men there. It was too much trouble, just as being kind to poor Ben had become too big an ordeal. Still, glancing around now, as he drew on the cigarette the student had lit for him, he decided he didn't really dislike these guys. He just didn't have time for them. He thought of the kids—how rapidly they were changing, so that it hurt him to even look at their pictures—and of Lucie, tears springing to her eyes when she was hurt or angry, wringing courage enough from him to change the whole world.

That's what he had to do—get out and face the world. Stop being a whimpering, cowardly bastard and make something of his life. He had to do that now. Ben's inane humming echoed through his thoughts again—and the vacant look in his ice-sheathed, blue eyes. Poor Ben. His toes tightened up inside his shoes. Yes, he had to escape now. Not for himself or Dr. Richards or the "good name" of Holly Springs or even for the kids. Not for anybody or anything but Lucie. At last he mashed his cigarette in the ash tray and stood up.

"Hey, Jack," somebody said, "how about some pool?"

"No." He didn't look to see who had spoken. "No thanks. Got some letters to write." But he didn't go back to his room immediately. He walked over to one of the windows and stood there gazing out. First, at the barren courtyard below. Then beyond that —over the tops of the trees to what he thought to be the hazy silhouette of city skyscrapers.

❪ 4

Millie Pratt glowered at the pattern in the linoleum floor of the Hall 1 conference room and chewed at the inside of her lips. She wanted very much to talk to Dr. Collins this afternoon, to tell her how afraid she was—not about being put back down here with all the weird people, but about not knowing where to go from here or what to do or who to look to.

Yet much as she wanted to, she could not talk. Because she knew that as soon as she did they'd decide she was better and think about sending her home again. So the struggle must continue—the same struggle Millie had been caught up in for nearly six weeks now. In the stress of Dr. Holliday's departure, and despite all the extra time and help Dr. Collins had tried to give her, she had religiously carried out her decision to act confused and depressed. She had stopped eating and sleeping, stayed off by herself all the time without talking to people, finally even refused to co-operate with the routine of O.T. and gym. And as she'd expected, they'd put her on C.O. and demoted her first to Hall 3 and then to Hall 1.

This was about as far as she could get from the things she was afraid of. But Millie wasn't sure how safe she was even here, how quickly the doctors might about-face and start her on the homeward, independent path again. And not knowing, it seemed safer not to gamble. So this afternoon once more she just sat still, saying nothing—and after a while the doctor went away again.

Back in the day room Millie took her candy box full of cards and letters out from under the C.O. nurse's chair and sat down in a corner to go through its contents. She liked to do that. There were some pictures clipped from magazines and a couple of postcards from some old-lady patients who were home now. But mostly they were notes from people like Evie and Mrs. Purdy and Eileen O'Hara. People who were sorry she'd been moved back. Her mother hadn't written in weeks; Dr. Collins said she'd told her not to. Anyway, she hadn't written.

The first note was from Evie. "... So sorry they moved you back.... I knew you weren't feeling well, but.... You're a wonderful person, Millie. Everybody thinks so. They talk about it all the time. You deserve...." For a moment, the lonely fear shrank away, and Millie felt good and warm and lovable. Those were very nice letters.

"They're nice people, too," she reminded herself. But she

shouldn't have thought of that, because it blew all the other good feelings away. It made her remember that the nice people who'd written these letters were getting well, and that soon they would go away and forget her too. Like Dr. Holliday; yes, just like Dr. Holliday. She remembered how scared of him she'd been, even the last time. Yet, the very thing that scared her—his big brown eyes looking deep, deep into her—had also made her trust him and feel safe.

How like before everything was now. The room and the noise and the people. Somebody—a girl sort of like Evie Barrow used to be—was carrying on about the TV. Down the hall was the same old lady who thought she was a baby and stayed in bed all the time and cried when she was alone or when they tried to change her sheets because she'd wet them. Looking out the window at the sky was a quiet girl, who cried silently sometimes and looked sweet like Grace Hill. Sickening the way everything repeated itself. She wished so much that she could see Dr. Holliday; he could tell her what to do. Millie picked up her letters and went out into the hall, away from the noise.

Of course, that was forbidden; no one on C.O. was allowed outside the day room alone. "Miss Pratt," the student said sternly. "Miss Pratt, come back in here." Millie did not answer or turn back, but she sat down on the floor near the door where the girl could see her. And the student was pretty nice. "All right," she said. "But don't you move from there. If you do, I'll call Miss Falkenburg."

It was better there without the blare of the television and the reminder of the dead-faced, stringy-haired women all around her. Millie read Evie's note again and a pink flowered card Mrs. Purdy had sent. But then Falkenburg came.

Her towering white figure moved briskly down the corridor and stopped directly in front of Millie, looming over her. "Miss Pratt," she barked, "you know you should be in the day room."

Millie did not answer. She pressed her lips together and studied her letters.

At that moment Anita Falkenburg wanted to be gentle, but as usual she somehow could not. "Come on," she said, with the same gruffness. "Go in there and watch TV with the others."

Still no answer, no change of position.

"Look, Miss Pratt, you think you make a pretty sad picture. Poor mistreated child that everybody pities. . . . But you just listen, I'm in charge here, and I'm not sorry for you.

"There are too many others here, people who really deserve to be pitied. I can't waste my time on a kid like you, a kid who can get well and out of here as soon as she'll let herself."

Millie did not move.

"Your whole life's ahead of you," the nurse continued. "Happy as you make it. You could start right now by going back in that room. Otherwise, we can put you in a P.B. where it's easier to watch you."

Millie didn't hear the prolonged-bath threat; she'd stopped listening right after the remark about living her own life. "It's your life," Dr. Holliday had said, "and you're the one must live it." She wished she had listened to him. And she hated herself. Not just because she really was what Miss Falkenburg said, nor for the old instinctive reason that since nobody loved her she must not be lovable—but simply because she had allowed herself to be trapped in this situation, because there was nothing left now but to turn around and go back to what she was afraid of.

Slowly, awkwardly, without even glancing at the nurse, she jumbled her letters back into the box and stood up. She hesitated in the doorway of the day room, barely conscious of the television noise or the conglomeration of bickering, laughing, crying, glass-eyed animals of women. Then she noticed the girl who looked like Grace Hill, the one who cried sometimes with her face to the window.

Millie went over and sat on the floor beside her. "My name's Millie," she said.

The girl didn't answer; she just kept looking out the window, as if something were going on out there, something very interesting. So Millie looked too. But there was nothing to see. It was night now, and the sky had turned black. There was nothing beyond the window glass except the empty blackness and the dim reflection of the lights and faces in the day room.

(5

It was raining hard that afternoon. Icy wind moaned around the buildings, and from time to time sent gusts of water splintering against the window panes.

Eileen O'Hara sat and watched it. There was knitting in her lap and an open book on the window sill beside her, but she only saw the rain. Gazed at it and waited, for what seemed hours. There had always been a myriad of memories that rain like this brought to mind—the smoky dampness of the kitchen at home, the puddled paths from the dormitories to the hospital in London, the bleary loneliness of the lights on Broadway.

But now when she needed those thoughts, they would not come. Only the certainty that Dr. Pierson *would* keep his appointment and that today or next time or the time after he would tell her she could go. That in itself was no cause for anxiety. Eileen had developed a kind of resigned anticipation for returning to the outside world. Only, there still remained in her a stubborn hope for the impossible. And with each conference her control seemed to slip a little, so that already she could not be sure the young doctor had not noticed.

Once in the conference room, however, things looked better. The big, cold room itself seemed changed, less like a shabby unused parlor. The ugly overstuffed chairs, the ornately carved tables, the faded carpet, even the small uncomfortable couch on which she sat, all reminded her of other rooms she had known. The principal's office at school, the head sister's consultation room in training, and again at St. Timothy's. Severe, silent rooms, yet comforting in their austerity, safe with low-voiced discipline. Eileen's fears faded.

Philip Pierson had always liked that room, largely because its door was solid wood instead of paned glass like those on most of the conference rooms. Also, because of its size, the sense of privacy seemed greater. Today, the rainy gloom made it nicer than ever. Though the dull light from the window fell across Eileen's face, Pierson knew his own chair was safely in the shadows.

Her face appeared almost easy this afternoon—a little sad still, but quiet and untroubled, as if, given reason, her downcast eyes might look up. Perhaps if he could say the right thing—something that touched her, but not too specifically—but, of course, he could not. He had looked forward to this conference for days with aching longing. Yet as always, with dread and despair. What could he do? What was there left to say?

"I understand there's a square dance this afternoon," he tried at last. "Do you mind missing it?"

"No." She laughed softly, still looking down. "I can't bear the things. They're so loud, and nobody knows the steps."

"What about ballroom dancing?" A natural question. Yet as he spoke, Pierson felt overwhelmed with futility. Because it was not enough. Nothing was now. Nothing he could do or say would weaken her to where he could honestly suggest to the staff that her release be delayed. And worse, what inane waste of the little time he still had with her. He felt spent and frustrated.

"No," she was answering him. "I don't like dancing here.... But I used to before I came, and I suppose I shall again."

Never with me, though, Pierson thought, resentment mingling with his gloom. He had never danced much, had always said he didn't enjoy it. But suddenly there was nothing he wanted so much as to dance with her. Soon she would be gone. Yet now while she was with him, he could not even speak. Grimly he forced his way back with a question: "You've had two four-day passes already, haven't you? That means just one more before you take ten."

"Yes," she replied and then hesitated. She made herself look at him, into his face. She must show him she wanted to leave, that she wasn't afraid. "Yes, one more four, then two tens. And I shall be very glad when they're all over."

"Oh...." Her eyes, looking up now, seemed unusually bright. Her lips moved precisely. "Why is that?" he asked. "The passes unpleasant? Or are you impatient to leave the hospital?"

"Both I suppose. I am anxious to be on my own again. But also staying with my cousins is no pleasure. They're elderly, you see, and inclined to regard me as a child. Besides, I've never known them well. Truthfully it's an ordeal."

The words sounded bright; the lips speaking them moved with certainty. But her face was tense, and the light in her gray-green eyes had gone out. Pierson felt an answering ache tighten inside himself. "Have you no friends you could visit instead?"

"No." She looked down again. "I have few friends, . . . especially in the United States."

"I didn't realize you had that few. . . . You must have been very lonely."

Eileen took those words for a test, an obstacle she must surmount. She forced herself to look up at him again, and when she spoke, her voice was quiet. "No. I'm not so lonely, I guess. I see as many people as I want. And I know a number; we're just not close."

But before she finished, she realized there had been no challenge. He was sitting forward in his chair, so that his features were visible even in the dimness. His dark eyes looked anxious, and his face more than sympathetic—as if her loneliness hurt him more than it did herself. That surprised Eileen. She had known he was sensitive. Yet she had never thought his capacity for pain went beyond himself.

"My work," she continued determinedly. "Well, you know it's very demanding. A nurse is with people all the time. She must be compassionate, yet keep her distance."

Then suddenly—Eileen could not tell whether the error was his or hers—their eyes were tangling. Both struggled to be free, but it was moments before they were. And in that struggle, Eileen saw something else on his intent face—a look of desperate longing, of loneliness more acute than any she had experienced. Though free again, her eyes forgot to look down. Like the rest of her, they were swept up in a flood of tenderness, a need to reach out to that longing and comfort it.

He was speaking though, in a voice imperative with its gentleness. "Why, Eileen? Why must you be so strong?" He leaned far forward in his chair, speaking with his eyes, with his face as well as his lips. "It's not wrong to cry out when you're hurt." Her eyes never left his face.

At last he moved to the couch, where he could be close to her, where his fingers could touch her fingers, where, too, her gentleness could touch him. There, though swallowed up, hypnotized by the closeness, his voice continued. "If you were steel, Eileen—if you felt no pain. But you aren't—you do. And that's what makes you so wonderful." Her eyes still listened, wide and still. Her trembling lips, though they made no sound, seemed to say what he longed to hear. And when his hand closed around hers, he felt the tense fingers relax.

He was sitting very close to her now. Eileen could feel his breath on her cheek. But she no longer felt afraid or trapped. Rather, free, safe, quiet, almost exultant. It seemed incredible, yet it was true. She knew it was true because she could look in his dark eyes and see not only the longing now but the answer to the longing.

His arm went closer around her. "Soon you'll go away, Eileen. Yes, if that's what you want. . . . Still, I must tell you that I love you. So that I will always know I have said it. So that some day, somewhere—if you need to—you can remember." She was small in his arms, smaller than he had imagined, yet warmer, too, more vibrant. His eyes glanced down at her dark hair, at the lovely feathered shadow her eyelashes made on her cheek. His arms tightened, his lips searched out her lips.

But it was then, suddenly, that Eileen's fear returned to her. She had been so safe and free in his arms, because her love was not forbidden or shameful; because truthfully she was only responding to a love someone felt for her. She had wanted his lips for so long that her own involuntarily strained to meet and surpass their passion. But then she remembered. Even as her own love rushed eagerly out to him, she knew that she was lost, more lost than she had ever feared. She struggled frantically to free herself.

Pierson was stunned. It was brutal—the frozen rigidity where a moment before there had been tingling warmth. He was horrified at himself—alarmed with a new awareness of the door, which, wooden or not, could always be opened. His old hurt burned as her mouth locked primly and her body drew back. His eyes opened abruptly, and for a moment his lips did lose her lips. But he realized at the same time that her hand still clung to his. Her eyes were open, too, and in spite of everything, they *were* saying, "I love you." So instead of letting go, he pressed her to him again, closer even than before. His face touched her face, his lips her lips. And this time he was not only happy but strong; not only strong but victorious.

An instant longer she struggled. But then, quite easily, she was motionless again. The protest in her throat was silent. Slowly her lips unlocked, yielded, and finally warmed to his. Her body, too, wilted from its forbidding denial to sweet clinging softness. She was small in his arms again, her heart beating against his heart.

II

JACK ISAACS DRIFTED along at Holly Springs until the middle of March. Then suddenly he felt he could not stand the place another day. Recklessly he struggled for relief. He avoided Ben like the plague. He participated in every available activity. He spent as little time as possible alone. And when nothing else helped, he forced himself to go off the grounds on visiting days.

Those passes in themselves were almost pleasant. He and Lucie went to quiet, dimly lit restaurants. They walked along out-of-the-way sidewalks. And they talked as they had not been able to talk for more than three years. Once he was actually out, Jack's fear gave way to a sense of daring. Instead of trembling, he found himself relieved and proud, blind with amazement at his own strength. But back at Holly Springs the fact that he had been out only made things worse. The days between visits were slower and more depressing than ever.

Until finally, there no longer seemed any decision to be made. There was no alternative to the thing he wanted and dreaded most—going home with Lucie.

He told Dr. Richards first, but, of course, his only reply was the eternally frustrating promise to "take it up with Dr. McLeod." Agonizing silence followed. Then one rainy afternoon nearly a week later Jack found himself faced with the ordeal of talking to the white-coated woman doctor himself.

He had never talked to McLeod before, but that afternoon as he waited, he already knew he hated her. Not just because she was a part of Holly Springs, or even because she was another un-

imaginative, rule-ridden doctor. Rather because of the rigid primness with which she tyrannized people; because with all her obvious
failings, she could still set herself up as an authority and force
others to accept her calculated coldness as natural.

After a mumbled greeting and her usual indifferent nod, she
led him to the conference room. There she informed him tone-
lessly that she had come for a "clearer explanation of your request
to leave Holly Springs." Jack was well aware that her eyes were
fixed on him; he took great care to meet their gaze. But after a moment he realized with surprise that there was nothing to be afraid
of after all. Those icy blue eyes were alert, yes, but not sensitive;
probing, but not perceptive. They seemed a sharp contrast to
David Holliday's wide, brown eyes which had stripped him naked
with their understanding. That reminder made Jack a little sad.

But he didn't have long to think. Though not omniscient, Mc-
Leod's eyes were insistent. He tried to satisfy them first with the
surface explanation he had originally given himself: "I want to
go.... Really, I *have* to go, because I'm afraid. Because if I don't
do it fast, I'll have time to think and back out. I know that once
I'm out I won't be afraid, but waiting and imagining are agony."

"But you've scarcely even been off the grounds," her cool,
monotonous voice came back at him. "How do you think you can
go for good?"

Martha McLeod studied carefully the thin, dark face before
her. She wanted to be fair and reasonable. That was her real
reason for coming here. At first she had had no doubts, had confidently told young Richards he was out of his mind to waste her
time reporting such a request. No one ever went on extended visit
from a closed hall. But then—probably, in part, because of
Richards' sympathetic account—Martha had found herself less and
less certain that the old rule of "time-proven experience" applied
here. Isaacs, after all, did not want a discharge; only to be committed to his wife's care for as long as he could make it. And
perhaps there was sense in that. Martha could remember cases
similar to Isaacs'. She recalled, too, that a majority of them had
found it necessary to leave the shelter of the hospital in something
like a blind catapult, not from a closed hall, perhaps, but with
just as much visible insecurity.

In addition, whenever Martha thought of Jack Isaacs, she remembered David Holliday talking about him. David's face had always taken on a look of extreme benevolence when he spoke of Isaacs, a look very similar to the one that came when he talked about Phil Pierson. And he had always maintained that if Isaacs ever tried the outside, he would make a go of it. So, hard as it was for Martha to admit, probably her main reason for coming was David Holliday. She wanted to be fair; yes, that did come first. But it would have pleased her to find she had to disagree with David Holliday to do so.

The young man's dark face was strong and handsome. But there were hungry hollows under his eyes and the tightness of anxiety around his mouth. Probably, Martha comforted herself, there would be no problem making a decision. And even if the temporary results were unpleasant, what satisfaction there would be in knowing her own carefully disciplined approach of unsympathetic realism had brought those inner seethings to the surface. She listened intently as slowly, simply he presented his side of the story. Most of the time he looked her in the face. But twice his eyes strayed to the floor, and once—when he spoke of his wife— his composed voice faltered. Both were points for her, Martha knew. But again, in spite of herself, she thought of David Holliday—the genial, blundering kindness in him, the intuitive sensitivity she had always admired. Mary Laine was dying now. Clyde Ross had told her it was only a matter of weeks. And I ought to do something, Martha had admonished herself over and over. But passive silence was the only course of action she could remember.

"It's true," Isaacs continued evenly. "For a long . . . yes, months, years I didn't go off the grounds. But for the last three weeks I've gone out every visiting day. And I like being out. It's just when I'm waiting that I dread it."

Martha McLeod was caught up by the determination and uncompromising reason in his sad voice. Her eyes were captivated by the strained stillness of his thin fingers. But she did not waver. "Isn't this a little rapid after the length of your illness?" she persisted.

And somehow that was the last straw for Jack. It was all he could do to be civil. She was so stubbornly and frigidly blind to his feelings. And more than that, so obviously digging for the things he did not intend to tell her. That an important reason for his request *was* Dr. Holliday's leaving, because he no longer saw any hope for himself at Holly Springs. Or that his real reason for going was Lucie, because he couldn't bear to see her hurt any more.

So, carefully, with hushed calm he put it to her: "Yes, it's rapid. I know it's rapid. But I feel, too, that it's the only—or at least the best and easiest—way for me to get out.... Yes, I know what Dr. Richards said, that getting out won't make me well. But it *will* give me a chance to face what I'm afraid of, instead of just sitting here dreading being afraid of it.... And I haven't asked for a discharge, Dr. McLeod; please remember that. I just want a chance to try."

Those words were no different from all the others he had spoken during their interview. Perhaps a little less loneliness in his voice, a little more hardness. But somehow they came through to the woman doctor as none of the others had. She saw that they were by no means the blind pleadings of a sick mind. On the contrary, they were evidence of realistic and logical anticipation. Perhaps the young man was operating more on courage than inclination. But even so, his plan seemed sensible. For once, Martha McLeod realized, she and David Holliday could not disagree.

They sat in silence for a few minutes after he finished. Then at last the doctor spoke: "Mr. Isaacs, you seem to have thought this matter through very sensibly. In fact, hearing you talk, I am almost inclined to agree with you.... But, of course, I can't do that. What the outcome will be, whatever line of action I take must be determined by Dr. Richards and the rest of the staff. I'll take it up with them tomorrow."

Those slow sterile words offered Jack new hope. But at the same time they made him hate and pity the pudgy little woman more than ever. Either she did not dare make a decision on her own or she did not feel capable of conveying that decision to him. Jack looked away from her cold blue eyes to her fat, white hands folded complacently on the desk. Their inertia seemed characteristic of her very being. Jack knew now that she was not only blind and calloused and insipid, but crucially weak as well. For him there was no longer any solace to be found at Holly Springs.

([2

"Well, Ben, I guess this is it. I'm going home today." Jack stood beside his roommate's bed and looked down into the boy's pale face.

But there was no response. Not even the dead "Oh" Jack had anticipated or a grudging nod. Ben's eyes did focus on him, but otherwise there was no evidence he had even heard.

Jack fidgeted a little closer to the bed. There must be something he could say just this once, now at the end. Something to ease his own horror at least, to make the weirdness less powerful. "I'm going home," he announced again to fill the silence. Then, with a deliberate smile and a hollow chuckle, "Let's see you get on the stick, too, boy. I'm counting on going with you to your dad's next show."

Still no answer. Still the blue eyes staring through him.

"Well, good-by, Ben." Jack extended his right hand and held it there obstinately. "Good-by."

The boy did not move for a moment, though his eyes lowered uneasily. Then he giggled softly and grasped the hand held out to him. "Good-by," he murmured. And after that he turned over to face the wall. He tried to hum, too, because somehow that would have made things better. That or giggling again. But he couldn't do either. Because there was something thickening in his throat, something like tears.

Soon he turned over on his other side, so that even with his eyes still lowered, he could see Jack's reflection in the mirror. "Funny," he thought about the sadness. "Because really I'm glad. Jack's good, and now he'll be free. Free and happy maybe. And when the glory comes, . . . soon, very soon, . . . we'll be to-gether forever." Still his throat would not clear, and a mist had come before his eyes.

Jack had turned back to his dresser. He whisked a comb through his hair and rechecked the drawers for things forgotten. But the silence was killing; the silence and Ben's eyes stealthily following his reflection in the mirror. A few more minutes in that room and he'd lose his nerve completely. Lucie had said she might be delayed downstairs. At last he fumbled in his pocket for cigarettes and hurried out of the room toward the smoker. There were three other men there in addition to the student nurse with the matches. Jack got a light and sat down by the window.

After he signed the papers that morning, McLeod had stood up and droned in her old prim way, "I trust all will go well for you, Mr. Isaacs.... But if it should not, I hope you'll remember your friends at Holly Springs...."

"God, how could I forget," Jack scoffed now at the memory. Besides her and Richards and that damned Gardner nurse, the endless notebook records of permissions, eyeglasses, bowel movements, and medications; O.T., gym, hydro; Ben's inane giggle. He had to get out. It was now or never.

He stood up then, determined not to think. Really, there was no point in thinking anyway. He'd made up his mind, and frightening or not, the decision was a good one.... If only there was somewhere he could walk, some place he could flick his cigarette besides that damned metal ash tray. He was standing in front of the window. April. Clean, fresh, song-happy. Reassuring in a way. If you could make yourself blind to buildings and trees and people, give yourself up to the dazzling blueness of the sky, you could almost believe the world was like that—pure and happy.

Jack felt giddy with a reckless, free but terrifying compulsion to be a part of that blue void. No wall, no window, no bars. Until he suddenly stepped backward, sick, shaking his head wearily, and mashed his cigarette in the ash tray.

"Mr. Isaacs...." One of the students. "Mr. Isaacs, your wife is here."

And there she was, his Lucie, smiling at him from the end of the corridor. She was wearing a tweed suit that made her eyes look very blue. Her short, brown hair was windblown. He hurried to her. He squeezed her hands and kissed her cheek quickly without letting her look into his eyes. "Let's get out of here," he muttered.

"All right," she agreed, but not with the same urgency Jack had recognized in his own voice. She was smiling in the quiet strong way he had known she would.

"You all ready?" And her voice was happy. Her eyes were watchful, but not tired, not even afraid. As he met them with his own, Jack knew things were going to be all right.

They did not talk as they walked down the corridor to get the suitcases from his room. To Jack everything that came to mind seemed too big for conversation. For Lucie there was the reasonless fear that words might shatter this moment.

Ben's bed was empty when they reached the room. "Out with his father, I guess," Jack remarked carelessly. But he was sorry; he had hoped they might say a proper good-by after all.

"How is Ben, Jack? Is he getting better?"

"No. The same, I guess, or worse. You know how strange he's been, Lucie."

"Yes ... I'm sorry. He's so young."

Jack heard her voice tremble, and when he looked, the expected tears were shining in her eyes. And that made him feel warm inside, because it was a part of Lucie he had always loved very much. She scarcely knew Ben. She only saw him when she came here, yet she cared deeply and sincerely about what happened to him.

"Don't mind, darling," he tried to comfort her. "It may take time, but he'll work it out in the end, ... just as I have."

"But he's so young."

"Maybe that's good.... Let's go."

She smiled again then, shaking her head deliberately, as if to get rid of all unhappy thoughts. "Yes, let's hurry. The children are beside themselves with excitement."

Down the stairs, through the main corridor, out into the sunshine they went, Lucie clinging to his arm. Already his fear had faded, and as they walked farther and farther away from the main building, he felt a new strength surge upward in him.

There seemed a trace of frightened sadness in Lucie's face when he smiled at her now. But Jack refused to see it as that. Probably just left over from the moment about Ben, he thought. Or better still, her old dependency on him coming back. He nodded to the few people he knew that they passed. And with each step the happy reminder echoed more loudly through his thoughts: "This is the last time, the last time, last time.... Never, never again."

(3

Around and around they walked. It was a beautiful spring afternoon. Bright with sunshine over there, a cool puddle of shade here. Around and around they walked. Beside the magnolias, past the rough, grassless area where the boys played baseball, past the tennis courts, back behind the big stone building, then up the path again near where he was sitting.

Around and around. So many people. A few he knew, but mostly strangers. For a while Dr. Stoughton wondered, Why so many strangers? But suddenly, out of a fog, he remembered. Visitors day. Yes, of course, visitors. Visitors day, his lips repeated the words. Will someone visit me? He glanced up, across the expanse of lawn to where the stick figures were playing croquet. He couldn't hear any more, but he could imagine the hard click of wood when one of them swung his mallet. "Is someone coming? Is there someone to see me?"

"Oh, yes, of course, Doctor. Many."

"Really? What do they want?"

"They want to hear you talk, sir. Discuss your theories. . . . Perhaps, sir, you'd see Dr. Einstein first. He's old, you know. He's been waiting a long time; he's very tired."

"Yes, let me see Dr. Einstein." How foolish that was. Ridiculous imaginings. Einstein was dead now. He'd read that some time ago. He must stop this. He must not let himself wander so from reality. Old men who did that went senile. He ought to get his hearing aid out and wear it, even if he didn't like what he heard. But where was it? He'd hidden it. But where?

Around and around they walked. Visitors day. Someone to see him? The boys? Hinton, Donald, Jonathan? Perhaps Nancy would bring them in their starched white collars and blue Sunday suits. They'd talk about school and butterflies and the black snakes in the brook. Nancy would wear her straw hat with the roses. Perhaps. . . . But he'd forgotten again. All that was changed. Nobody ever came to see him any more. Everybody was dead. He'd seen that last night on the wall of his room. The crosses—one big one and three little ones—and the lilies. And, of course, Nancy had explained it to him. Not really Nancy either, but Nancy's ghost, young and pretty and in the long white nightdress a ghost wears. He was really a very fortunate old man. Not many people were allowed to talk beyond the darkness to the ones they loved.

"What is it like to die? Is it really crosses and lilies? Is it sleep?"

"Some say it's worms and darkness and rotting into the earth."

"No. It's sleep. Else, why would she wear that white night-dress? . . . Yes, it's sleep in cool, flower-sweet sunshine like today."

He looked around him at the other old men seated on the garden benches. Pitiful looking characters. He felt very sorry for them.

The young, dark man in the white suit—the orderly or whatever he was—came over and sat on the bench beside him and tried to say something. But Jonathan Stoughton couldn't make out the words and finally waved him away impatiently. After that he let his eyes wander off again after the younger men walking with their visitors. He squinted to see if he knew any of them. But he didn't.

Once, many years before, there'd been a tall, fat man who came to see him. Happy Bill, they called him, Happy Bill. Very intelligent man. Doctor or lawyer or something. From Virginia or Alabama or maybe Mississippi. He'd talked with a Southern accent. . . . Happy Bill. Jonathan Stoughton smiled mistily. How nice it would be to talk to him again. What had become of Happy Bill anyway? Perhaps he was dead, too, now. Perhaps he, too, had a cross and some lilies. That made the old doctor laugh outright. He couldn't help it. It caught him like a spasm of coughing. Happy Bill in his white nightdress!

When he stopped laughing, he noticed that all the stoop-shouldered old men were standing up. The young man in the white suit was motioning at him to stand up too. But he didn't. They wanted him to go in now with them, like one more sheep. But he had no intention of doing that. Some day they'd just have to learn he had a mind of his own. And now was as good a time as any for that. Because he was not going in yet. He wasn't ready to go into that musty dungeon. He looked away deliberately, out over the iron fence, at the sidewalk and the paved driveway.

There were a lot of cars there this afternoon. If he'd had on his hearing aid, he could have heard their horns and their motors and their doors slamming. Walking along there, carrying a big suitcase, was a young man he recognized. One of his boys? Hinton,

Jonathan? Donald? No, they never came any more. Tall, dark young man with a sweet-looking girl. Must be his wife. Jewish. Curly hair and long angular nose. Yes, the nice young man who had sat next to him at the metal work. The one who smiled at him sometimes or patted his shoulder but never talked. Going somewhere with that big suitcase. On a trip maybe with his wife.

How happy they must be. Young and together. So much time. So much love. So much sweetness. Never mind. Tonight. Tonight when Nancy came, they would go out too. Yes, and they, too, would have love and sweetness and time.

The young man in the white suit was tugging at his arm. The other old men were tottering together far ahead. The young man wanted him to go too. So he did. To argue or struggle would have been futile. It would have washed away the sweetness, the newness and left the day dark and bitter and rotten with worms.

(4

That afternoon Eileen O'Hara went out early to wait for her taxi. The spring sunshine was too dazzling, the warm air too fragrant to stay indoors. Sitting there on her suitcase, Eileen felt almost as if the day had been created in her honor, solely for her and her daydreams so amazingly coming true.

The only drawback was the people; always so many on visiting days—and lately, it seemed, all looking at her. Just imagination, she had scolded herself at first. Then later she had decided it was because she was getting well and did present a striking contrast among so many sick people. But then why did they stare in the city or on the train? Why did Aunt Mary and Cousin Dan seem to watch so much more closely than they had a few weeks before? Could it be true, that old saying about the face of a woman in love?

She shivered and looked down quickly to avoid the eyes of an elderly woman. It wasn't that she minded people knowing she was in love. But certain people—Dr. McLeod or Tucker or even some busybody underling who felt obliged to inform—the idea was devastating. Not for her so much, but for Phil. Helplessly her eyes turned toward the window of his office, then quickly away again. Perspiration prickled her forehead. She must learn to control herself. It seemed strange, taunting, almost painful when he came on rounds and she could only chorus, "Good evening, Dr. Pierson" with the rest. But at least then with all the others sitting there, there was no alternative.

Inside she would have been safe from this temptation. But truthfully Eileen had almost come to like it now—denying herself and knowing at the same time that it was just a game. Knowing that tomorrow she would see him and that one day she would be able to see him and touch him and speak his name as often as she wanted.

She had had all week to mull over everything—Phil's face, and how she could possibly have not seen the love in his eyes, how she would help him and do for him and make him forget about his foot. She would wear her new cotton frock Sunday . . . tomorrow . . . and she must be on time at the Grand Central information circle.

She looked down the drive for her cab, but then remembered she was early. Sullivan had laughed about that when she signed out. "What's wrong, dearie? Not impatient are you? . . ." Poor Sullivan. So lonely, looking after sick people who really had much more reason to be happy than she did. And that could be me, Eileen reminded herself. Only, . . . it never will be now.

That thought was incredibly reassuring. The details of this weekend were so well arranged now that they could take place of their own accord. She was to stay with Jackie Harper, whose commitment for alcoholism had expired over six months before. She had called Jackie Tuesday and gone by her Village apartment on the way back to Holly Springs. They had never been close, yet they had in common their desire for privacy. And it was probably that that had given Eileen courage to ask Jackie's help.

By the end of the weekend, she knew, Jackie would have found out all about her and Phil. That was disconcerting, but they couldn't go on in secret forever. So Eileen had persuaded herself that if someone had to know, no one could be safer than Jackie.

Besides, today even that seemed surprisingly unimportant compared to tomorrow. Just another Sunday, yet, a very special Sunday. So many of them hadn't worked out. Several times she had had to sit home with Cousin Dan and Aunt Mary, because Phil was on duty. Another week his mother had come. Even their first afternoon in Central Park had been painful and uncertain. Now that uncertainty was gone.

The cab drove up then, and the driver got out to help with her bag. "Afternoon, Miss O'Hara," he said. "Nice weather we're havin'."

III

GEORGE PURDY WAS in the back of the store at the time. He thought he heard the screen door open. But it didn't slam, so he didn't bother to go out. The May afternoon was too hot, the beer he was drinking too good. Besides, the only person ever came in the store without slamming the door was Gladys, and Gladys knew where he was if she wanted him. After a few minutes, though, he got uneasy. He thought he heard footsteps and then some rustling, the clinking of change. Finally he set his beer can and cigarette down on the drink cooler and went up front to look around.

He grinned proudly when he saw the back of the man's light blue coat up by the honeydews. Nobody could accuse him of getting deaf. Then, wiping his hands on his stained canvas apron, he sauntered up to where the customer could see him. "Afternoon, sir," he said. "Anything I can help you with?" The coat was prosperous looking. Might be he could unload some of those cans of rattlesnake meat or truffles in wine. But when the big man turned around, George could only sputter in surprise.

"No thank you," the man began. "I . . . Why you certainly can! George Purdy, I didn't recognize you." David Holliday's solemn face crinkled into a smile. He gripped George Purdy's bony hand.

"Doctor, it sure is great to see you again." The weathered, wiry little man grinned idiotically and wiped first one shirt sleeve and then the other across his forehead. "Like old times," he added, laughing nervously.

Holliday laughed too, a little wearily, and thumped one of the plump melons. "I remember going to market with my mother as a boy. She could tell by the sound whether a melon was ripe." "That's the way to do it." George stepped a little closer. "How's the Missus?"

For a moment there was silence. The doctor's big, brown eyes grew wide, then looked down. "Well, George," he said slowly, evenly, "I guess it's mostly over now. . . . They say a week, . . . or a month, but seems to me the end must be nearer than that."

He looked up again then and realized with shame that the storekeeper's face was perplexed. Perhaps he hadn't even heard about Mary Laine's illness. So once again Holliday gave his endless explanation: "Yes, she's been sick, George. I guess I never told you. . . . Cancer. Started not long before we left here. But we were hopeful then. . . . Now, as I said, it's just a matter of time."

The great, round face that had been sober before seemed a death mask now. The flesh hung pale and flabby over Holliday's shirt collar. His habitually smiling lips were pressed together in a grim curve. And George Purdy, listening to his idol, could only gape in silent horror.

David Holliday himself searched desperately for something else to say. Because after all, he had not come here for this, but rather, to escape it, to talk about melons and Holly Springs and springtime, to watch George cut steaks, to smell the sawdust. And now again all he could think of was the sterile, ether-scented hospital room, the thin fingers clinging helplessly to his. All he could hear was the befuddled, childish voice, saying, "David, I don't think that medicine agrees with me. I feel so foggy."

George Purdy shifted his feet uneasily and once more wiped his hands on his apron. "Goodness, Doctor," he said softly, "I'm sorry to hear that. . . . I pray something will work out yet."

"Thank you, George." Holliday grinned, and as he continued speaking, a little of the old boom returned to his voice. "How's Mrs. Purdy? That's really why I came by."

"Oh, she's doing great, Dr. Holliday." The little man beamed with relief. "I remember what you told me—you know, about not getting too cocky—but so far she's fine, just like before. I worry a little, of course, and I watch her. She's still seeing one o' the doctors up there twice a month. But I keep my fingers crossed, and I think the good Lord hears our prayers."

"Well, I'm glad to hear that, George. I've missed seeing you, and I've been wondering."

"Thanks, Doctor. We miss you. And from what Gladys tells me, there's a lot of people on The Hill misses you too."

"That's nice to hear." Holliday edged toward the door. "Well, George, nice seeing you. I'll be back."

"Oh, don't go yet. Come out back and have a cold drink. Gladys'll be along soon."

"No, I can't, George; I'm sorry. I have to get along to the hospital. . . . Board of Governors meeting." Holliday had the screen door open and was standing half in, half out.

"Gladys is going to feel bad about missing you, Doctor."

"You give her my regards. Tell her I'm glad to hear she's doing so well."

"Doctor, she'll be sad, too, to hear about Mrs. Holliday. . . . We'll be praying for you."

"Thank you, George."

❰ 2

The heavy iron gate at the entrance to Holly Springs was flung open as usual, and the shady pavement, winding out of sight inside, looked temptingly cool. Holliday drove slowly, taking the detour to the left, which cut down around the lower grounds and eventually to the nurses' parking area. He told himself it would be easier to get out at night. But he knew, too, that this would give him a walk through the grounds, and more than that, a chance to be peacefully alone.

He headed first for the old orchards. But there was nothing there now. Only a vast expanse of chopped up earth, an abandoned bulldozer, and a billboard facing in the opposite direction so that he couldn't read what it said. Holliday felt a grinding of injustice inside him at the sight. He knew it was the outpatient clinic. *His* outpatient clinic. But he could no longer be glad to see it. Memories trickled into him of how it had been there before. The gaunt little trees twisted by the wind, the furrowed fields, his overcoat buttoned up against the cold. And he wished with all his heart that none of that had changed. . . . It was several minutes before he could tear his eyes away from the blaze of the sun on the edge of the billboard.

Up ahead there was the sweet shrill laughter of young girls like Lillian. Gradually as he got closer he could catch some of the bright words that went with it. Student nurses in their blue dresses and starched white aprons, tiny organdy caps on their heads, books under their arms. Holliday smiled when he came abreast of them and waved his hand in greeting. But they did not see. They went blindly by, still talking very fast and laughing.

Perhaps if he kept on the lookout, he would see somebody he knew. That seemed very important to him now, though he prayed they wouldn't ask about Mary Laine. Just someone who remembered him and the Holly Springs he remembered. Someone who could help him to feel a few things were still the same.

Off to the right some old men were playing croquet in one of the courtyards, and Holliday wondered if Dr. Stoughton was among them. A sad picture they presented—sad and lonely. He remembered what Mrs. Gaitors had said about nobody leaving Holly Springs but alcoholics and the help. And that made him smile, then, scowl. Mrs. Gaitors had always been a lonely person, too. She must be even lonelier now.

But then he reminded himself that places like Holly Springs were by nature destined for tragedy. Many found hope here, of course. Yet, for all those who were eventually able to go away and forget, there were others, like that Womble boy, who could not. Holliday wondered absently if they'd found a place for the boy yet. Probably not. He wondered, too, if he would ever forget the tears in the poor father's eyes.

A nurse was coming toward him along the path on the other side of the road. Something very familiar about that walk, the bristling stiffness. Then he got close enough to glimpse her face and remembered Gardner, the charge on Hall 4 Men. He had never cared for her much, yet he smiled now and waved. "Afternoon, Miss Gardner." She saw him, too. For an instant he caught her eyes on his face. But she walked straight on without speaking.

Then, for some reason he thought of the day perhaps a year ago when the young woman had tried to run away and he had watched, helpless, from an office window. Now it seemed to him that running away wasn't really so bad. Perhaps, in fact, it was more strong than weak. He wished that Mary Laine could do it—somehow relinquish her pathetic grip on life and run head-long into death. That would have been easier for them both. It might even have made her look gallant.

But, of course, she couldn't do that. Her very soul was timid. She must die as she had done everything else; just as she had left Holly Springs. The memory of that day seemed burned into him now. It marked the beginning of the end. The rain and the cold, the empty house. She had wanted very much to go, yet her eyes had brimmed over with tears. And he had loved her very much; probably more than at any other moment before or since.

"Good afternoon t' you, Dr. Holliday. It's grand t' see you back."

The pleasant, Irish voice startled him. But who did he know that was Irish? A big red-headed woman in white. Her ruddy face grinned broadly, and her eyes were very bright. It seemed to Holli-day a long time since he had encountered such warmth. He strained to wave and smile in return. But by then the woman had already passed.

❡ 3

An hour later, David Holliday was uneasy as he walked down the main corridor of Hall 5 Men. He had gone by Martha Mc-Leod's office to ask permission to see several patients—Jack Isaacs, Millie Pratt and possibly Ben Womble, as well as Dr. Stoughton. But Martha had been out. And though Mrs. Weaver had out-done herself to be hospitable, he still felt a little insubordinate being here.

The musty air reeked with the stale pungent odor of incon-tinence. An odor so well remembered from the past that he had known coming up from the floor below on just what step the stench would strike him. Only it seemed much stronger now. Otherwise the place looked pretty much the same—perhaps a little smaller, a little dingier. No familiar faces, though. In fact, all the faces looked alike—shriveled yellow-white shells, ghastly loose-fleshed Halloween masks. Only the eyes varied: some were sleepy and faraway, others bright and hard with desperate fear. They glared at him suspiciously from the doorways of the rooms, from the chairs and couches lining the corridor.

When he found the hall nurse, she smiled and called him by name. He knew her face and the prim pleasantness she exuded, but the name would not come. She said almost nothing about Dr. Stoughton as she directed him into the living room. Only, "I hope the doctor will feel like talking to you."

It was very quiet. Or rather, the various noises blended together into a humming monotony that seemed like silence. Dr. Stoughton was seated in a small, straight chair beside one of the front windows. Slouching there, immobile, he looked almost like an intricate ivory carving symbolizing death. He appeared completely unaware of his visitor's presence. And at first Holliday, noting the absence of his hearing aid, decided he probably could not hear. But then he realized that the blue eyes were far, far away, beyond the room and the iron grating on the window, beyond even the green world outside. He was smiling, too—grinning in a wide inane way that exposed his toothless gums.

"I have his hearing aid in the office," the nurse said. "Usually he refuses to use it, but perhaps. . . ."

"That'd be very kind if you would."

When she left, he put his hand on the old man's shoulder and leaned down to speak close to his ear. "Dr. Stoughton . . . Dr. Stoughton . . . Dr. . . . ."

At first there was no response. Then suddenly the old man tore his eyes away from the window and looked full-face up at Holliday. He swatted the hand on his shoulder away like a mosquito and began to quarrel automatically: "Away! Go away, you wretched ingrate! I have no need of you or your duty gifts. . . . Away!"

Holliday remembered when those words had been snarled bitter and loud, so that the vein in the forehead stood out thick and blue. The face was yellow white now and almost void of expression. The words were scarcely audible, mumbled from between the vacant gums. And that hurt Holliday much more than having them directed at him. Shortly, though, the anger passed and the thin rubbery lips grinned hideously. Strange soft laughter rippled from the old man's throat. He mumbled something, then laughed and repeated it. His skeleton hand reached out greedily to grasp the sleeve of Holliday's coat. He laughed again, and this time by straining Holliday was able to make out his words. "Happy Bill, . . . Happy Bill." Always followed by gurgling laughter.

When the nurse returned, she seemed amazed to find the old doctor in such a good frame of mind. He even took the hearing aid from her and tried to put it on and adjust it himself. But he wouldn't let either of them help him and finally threw it on the floor in exasperation. Then he turned to the nurse and said with dignity, "I'd like to see my guest in privacy, please."

That was one of the strangest conferences David Holliday had ever experienced. They sat in the customary positions opposite each other in the tiny conference room, and the old man, despite a constant coughing and dropping of ashes, determinedly smoked a cigarette.

Of course, conversation was impossible. Stoughton could hear nothing. However, he was very ready to talk—more than any time Holliday could recall.

"I knew you were coming," he began, still smiling and juggling his cigarette. "Nancy told me. . . . I didn't know, though. I couldn't remember. . . . I thought you had died. So I was looking for you to come in the dark in one of those long nightdresses." He laughed feebly at the thought. "Happy Bill. . . . Happy Bill. . . . A long, long time."

At times he talked rationally. About his three sons and their children; about being lonely; how long it had been since he played a game of chess. He reminded Holliday that his wife, Nancy, was dead. He spoke of the "brutality of these people . . . wrap me in wet sheets . . . a rubber tube up my nose." But always there was the other mixed in—the trips he took, Nancy's visits and the lilies she brought, the forces outside that were working to free him from this prison and get him back to his work at the operating table.

Finally, Holliday stood up and extended his right hand. At first Stoughton ignored it, then declared impatiently that he was not ready for his visitor to go. But when Holliday offered both hands to help him to his feet, he took them gratefully and obeyed. Then, as the doctor steered him gently back up the corridor, the old man began to smile and apologize for rushing him off. "You understand, though, Happy Bill," he explained. "These people have been waiting some time to see me. And I know you're coming back."

Holliday nodded genially. He was glad the old man could not hear, because he couldn't trust his own voice to speak. When he left him, Dr. Stoughton was once more seated beside his window, staring out blindly through the iron grating.

❰ 4

"There's a Dr. Holliday to see you, Miss Pratt." The student was one of the scared new batch who looked at you with determined sternness as if you were a dog and might bite.

"Who?" asked Evie Barrow. Her face glowed with excitement.

"A Dr. Holliday," the student repeated primly.

Still, Millie couldn't believe it. She sat there numbly between Evie and the student and gaped at the other women seated around the smoker. Most of them were relatively new so that the name Holliday did not register. Maggie Evans wasn't, of course, or Heath Webster, and she could see the curious listening looks on their faces.

Evie was in a nerval. She kept hurrying Millie—taking her knitting from her and helping to fish her loafer out from under the couch. "Isn't this fabulous, Millie?" she sang. "I bet he's decided McLeod's wrong in keeping you here. I bet he's going to get you out."

Millie didn't answer. Evie was like this a lot lately—all in a tailspin about things like men and getting out of the hospital and trips to Bermuda. Sometimes, even though they were up on Hall 4 again, Millie wondered if Evie weren't getting worse instead of better. Of course, she'd traveled much more than Evie since their last time here—all the way down to Hall 1 and slowly up again. So probably she had no right to judge. Except that it seemed to her, no one, not even Evie herself, understood the extremes of gaiety and sadness that got hold of Evie and swept her along, whereas Millie knew very well why and how she'd been sent down to Hall 1 and back. She'd been in control of herself the whole time, and the only change was that down there with all the weirdly sick patients, she'd made up her mind there was no point staying here any longer. No matter how long she waited, she'd still have to work her way up to the top again and go home after all.

"Oh, Millie! For God's sake, hurry!" Evie burst out at her again.

"What a time to go into a trance. Think of all the people who would give their eyeteeth to see Holliday."

"You know him, too, Miss Barrow?" the student asked meekly.

"Know him? God, how could I help it? He's head of the hospital. Least, he was before Fish-Face McLeod took over. I think...." But she never finished. She jumped up and hurried off down the hall three steps ahead of Millie.

Millie was irritated by that, but she slowed down when she saw what was going to happen. After all, Evie *was* her friend. Besides, it embarrassed her sometimes the way Evie talked to doctors.

"Why hello, Dr. Holliday," she said now. "I'm sure you couldn't forget me—Evelyn Barrow."

"Oh, no. Afternoon, Miss Barrow." Holliday smiled feebly in an attempt to be both pleasant and aloof. He had recognized her sensual body immediately and was already searching for a suitable brush-off. And it was surprisingly easy. He asked how she was getting on, said she looked well and that he was glad to see her up on Hall 4. Then he beckoned beyond her to Millie Pratt, and by the time she reached him, the Barrow girl had already gone off down the corridor.

It was like stepping out of a furnace into a spring breeze, talking to Millie Pratt after old Dr. Stoughton—a relief to see the whole world wasn't twisted and suffocating, dying and alone, though Holliday never allowed himself to forget that tragedies like Dr. Stoughton were the exception rather than the rule, that every day someone else took a giant step into happiness.

Only an hour before he had been astonished by Mrs. Weaver's news of Jack Isaacs: "Mr. Isaacs is no longer here."

"What? Was he transferred?"

"No. He went home. On trial, I think. His wife took him home."

Wonderful. Magnificent. And yet, a little unreal. Almost too good to be true. Somehow it lacked the tangible vividness of Dr. Stoughton's horror and Millie's promise. Perhaps later, with the details from Martha McLeod, he could draw up a more acceptable picture.

"Glad to see you up here, again," he began with Millie now. "I heard you had a little setback."

Yes, she had.

"You feel like you and Dr. Collins are making headway now?"

Yes, she supposed so. Never more than that. Though it seemed to Holliday her reticence was different from before. Not so much fighting and fear, straining to hide the things she didn't want him to see. Now she seemed more shy than afraid—a kind of shyness that would respond, that wanted to be drawn out. Gradually she began to give more than brief adequate answers. Sometimes her explanations were as much as three or four sentences long, and punctuated with hand motions. She still kept her eyes on the floor most of the time, but twice she surprised the doctor by looking him boldly in the face.

And almost at the end of the conference she amazed him even more. "You know," she said softly, twisting her hands into white-knuckled fists and carefully keeping her eyes on them. "Maybe I shouldn't say this, but. . . . You know, I'm glad you came today, but it's not at all like I thought. A while back—after you went away— I wanted terribly for you to come. I guess I thought you were some kind of God that could make everything all right." She tittered feebly, nervously. "But somehow it's different now. I mean, I guess I'm still afraid, even though I know what I'm going to do about boarding school and everything. Only, . . ." she squeezed her hands even tighter and almost shut her eyes, "well, I guess I just don't think of you as God any more."

❰ 5

Phil Pierson was surprised to see Dr. Holliday in the doctors' dining room that evening. He was late as usual, and it wasn't until Charlie Nichols mentioned him that Pierson even realized the former director was there.

"New York food seems to agree with Holliday," the psychologist commented, laughing softly.

"Yes." Fred Richards laughed too. "I think he's fatter than ever."

Pierson followed their eyes silently to the table by the window, and there, like a misfit in a dream, was Holliday. He did look heavier, but really it was more than that. The excess flesh sagged sickly now, instead of looking prosperous as Pierson remembered. Indeed, the whole man seemed to droop—his head, his shoulders, his oversized hands. His brown eyes were dull, his face vacant and remote. . . . It must be true about Mrs. Holliday.

Pierson glanced at the other faces at the main table. McLeod was on one side of Holliday—Ellen Collins on the other. Also Dr. Wilson and Miss Tucker. They were talking coolly, politely about nothing. He could tell by the smiling way they nodded to each other and by the measured murmur of their voices. Also by the careful concentration they used in cutting their pork chops. He was glad Dr. Holliday did not see him.

"He must've come for the Board of Governors meeting," Fred Richards said.

"Yeah." Charlie Nichols and the two younger interns at the table nodded agreeably. Pierson realized that he alone was still staring. He quickly began to butter a slice of bread.

It seemed ironic, Holliday's turning up today. Today when he was in such a turmoil about talking to McLeod. He always seemed to worry about that lately, but today especially. Because time was running out. Because he'd promised Eileen. "Don't do it for me," she said. "It doesn't matter to me what McLeod thinks. . . . I see no reason you should talk to her at all, except for yourself, to feel right inside yourself."

"No, I will. I should talk to her. Even, as you say, if it's just for myself, to know where I stand. And I'll do it, Eileen. I'll see her tomorrow morning."

But that had been Sunday. Now it was Tuesday evening. And he still hadn't talked to McLeod.

"You on rounds tonight, Phil?"

"What? . . . Oh, no. Friday's my night now."

"Why not take in the show at the Colony with Charlie and me?"

"No, . . . I'd like to, Fred, but. . . ." Pierson absently poured more cream in his coffee. Fred Richards being kind again. "I'd like to, but I'm way behind in my paper work." That excuse sounded weak; he'd been using it for weeks. But it was more true now than ever, because the minute he sat down at his desk his mind strayed a million miles away.

"Can't work all the time, Phil."

"No, but I've got to catch up." He glanced at the main table again. And this time his eyes met Holliday's. The older man was smiling at him—that enigmatic, round-faced pleasantness that had always seemed to mean nothing and everything. And momentarily Pierson felt trapped. He did not want to return that smile; to do so would be both weak and hypocritical. During the last few months he had carefully schooled himself in scorn for this man. But now the man was obviously suffering, and in view of that, scorn seemed shameful.

So at last Pierson did smile back. Then in spite of himself, recalling the big man's advice about Eileen, he longed for another talk like that night. . . . But, of course, it could never be. Holliday had changed, and no matter how strong his pity, no matter how deep his indebtedness, Phil Pierson would not be ruled by them.

"What about the others?" he asked himself. "Do you know them? . . . McLeod? Wilson? Ellen Collins?" The answer was "No," of course. He didn't even know the residents. They respected him, he thought, with the old erroneous belief that still water runs deep. But mostly, they were just sorry for him.

"Excuse us." Richards and Nichols pushed back their chairs. "Wish you'd come, Phil."

When they had gone, his eyes stole back to the main table— really more to see McLeod than Holliday. They were busy with the Brown Betty. Pierson tried once more to fathom McLeod's ice-blue eyes. She hated him, he knew. But he had never understood why. "Who can you trust?" he asked himself, "if she hates you and you don't know about the others?"

Eileen, of course. The answer was simple enough; it came quickly, automatically. But then, so did the doubts: "Does she really love you? . . . Or is that just pity too? How can you be sure?"

Once there *had* been reason to doubt her love. Their first afternoon in the park he'd kissed her, and only part of her had responded. Her breath had come short and hungry, her heart had beat frantically, but her body had gone brittle, struggling against him, and when he looked into her eyes, they had been dark with fear.

"But she *does* love you now," he told himself again. "Of course, she does." And it was true. Both of them had changed a great deal in two months. They had gone beyond the painful stage of exchanging long-guarded secrets. Instead they talked confidently of what they would do together in the future.

On Sunday she had waited for him in Grand Central. When she turned to him, both hands outstretched, her face had been anxious. "You look terribly tired. You've been a long walk from the train."

How long had it been since someone worried about his being tired? Pierson methodically spread the blob of hard sauce over his pudding. "And actually her risk is much greater than yours," he reminded himself again. "Or at least it must seem so to her. . . . Feelings she's offered up before and had trampled down each time. . . . You've only got a job at stake, . . . at most your reputation. . . . But what else is there? . . ."

And suddenly he remembered the brutal truth, that aside from Eileen he had nothing but his career—nothing else in the whole world.

The main table was empty now. At least he'd be spared the embarrassment of speaking to Holliday. . . . Tomorrow. He could not do it tonight because of the board meeting. But tomorrow he would go to McLeod. He would stand there on both feet and announce his intentions concerning Eileen. Announce them calmly and directly and without avoiding those blue eyes.

"Excuse me, Doctor. You finished or did you want something else?" The kitchen maid was gathering up the silver. The dining room was empty. He was sitting there alone, fiddling with a spoon.

❬ 6

There were forty-five minutes between supper and the board meeting—an interval Martha McLeod dreaded, because difficult as it would be for both of them, she and David Holliday must spend it together.

She delayed as long as possible, encouraging Ellen Collins and Lloyd Wilson in their talk of hyacinth bulbs and golf scores, contributing substantially herself to discussion of the outpatient clinic. When the visitor, in the course of his other questions, asked the inevitable one about Mr. Isaacs, she parried it skillfully. "No, he's no longer with us." But her anxiety tripled, because she knew he was not satisfied. Later, he would want the full truth.

When he nodded a beaming greeting across the room to young Pierson, she hoped for a rescue, and even had a second cup of coffee to allow time for it—but nothing happened. Holliday remained where he was, and the younger doctor seemed busy with his supper. At last she rose and suggested that Holliday come to her office.

He agreed genially and only after they had gone some distance down the corridor did he ask, "How's Phil Pierson?"

"Oh, the same, I think. . . . Would you like to go back and talk to him? I won't mind at all."

"No." A frown crossed Holliday's face. "No. I don't think he'd want to. Besides, I've a lot to ask you, Martha." He laughed emptily, and they went on.

Yes, she thought unhappily, I know you have. And probably the very first thing will be the Isaacs boy. It seemed not only tragic, but a little unfair that the two things should have occurred on the same day—Holliday's visit and the news of Jack Isaacs' suicide.

The latter had filled her with an oppressive melancholy. She had not really known the young man, at least, no more than she knew all the others: a case, a name, a problem to be met and solved. She had talked to him only once, the afternoon they had discussed his leaving the hospital. Yet, she had liked him, respected him, wanted to help him—as she had his wife the day he went home. And this morning with the news of his death, tears had come to her eyes for the first time in longer than she could remember.

There had been more than sadness to plague her since that telephone call though, more than a sense of selfish loss and futility. Guilt, that for once could not be rationalized or passed off on meddlesome relatives, because she had been in complete accord with Isaacs' plan, had even been proud to give it her approval. She had made a mistake—a mistake which could never be corrected.

Now Holliday would have to know, would expect an explanation down to the last disheartening detail. And inescapable though she knew that explanation was, Martha McLeod felt compelled to postpone it as long as possible. As they entered the dimly lit office, she attempted an even more difficult subject. She asked about his wife.

"No, Martha," he answered her softly, "since you saw Clyde Ross, I expect you know as much as I do. I guess it's all over now but the waiting."

"I'm sorry, David," Martha forced herself to break the stillness. "You must let me know if I can help." Then after another silence, she asked about the New York practice.

Holliday answered her in detail. It was important to him, too, that the conversation be restricted to superficial channels. Seated in the large leather chair she had offered him, he found himself idly judging the plump, white-haired pigeon of a woman. She seemed sad, tired, more nervous than he remembered. Her voice was the same unyielding monotone, her face the same placid mask —but there was a searching emptiness in her blue eyes. For a moment Holliday was ashamed that he had never taken more notice of that emptiness. It seemed tragically destructive to him now, so that he could almost regard Mary Laine and himself lucky in comparison.

Martha McLeod was straining to quiet her fear of Holliday. After all, she knew, it was completely unwarranted. Really she should pity him. Not only had he grown dangerously obese—puffy around the eyes, paunchy under the chin—but his whole person dragged with the weight of his sorrow, as if some hideous disease had eaten away the vitality inside his blown-up clown face. That was even sadder because he was an able doctor. Yet, obviously, New York was not working out either. He'd thought his Southern charm would carry him through there, too. He'd thought he could discipline himself to the point of making his wife's wishes his own. And instead, he had lost everything.

"By the way," Holliday broke into her thoughts, "what about Jack Isaacs? Mrs. Weaver told me he was home, but no details. . . . Then we were sidetracked at supper. . . . How's he doing?" There was dead silence. He had expected at least a modest Dutch-doll smile and some vague, simpering explanation. Instead, nothing. Only a tightening around the stingy mouth, the colorless mask even flatter, even paler. "I presume it was his idea," he prodded. "But how'd it come about? How long's he been out now?"

For a moment Martha McLeod could say nothing. It seemed almost as if the morning's tears would come back, and it was only with great effort that she repeated the reasonable and—she comforted herself—completely truthful explanation she had given the authorities that morning. Those same words softened a little, technical phrases replaced by more sympathetic ones, had proved quite adequate when she talked to the bewildered young widow this afternoon. Yet they seemed out of place, even meaningless confronted by David Holliday.

At last she resolved to tell him simply and briefly exactly what had happened. No excuses, no sentimentality—just facts. She fixed her eyes defiantly on his face. She had made a tragic mistake. But David Holliday must understand that she knew he would have been guilty of the same error. As she talked, her composure returned. Her voice was once more low and even.

"Unfortunately," she began, "the Isaacs story is now quite different from what Mrs. Weaver told you this afternoon.

"Jack Isaacs is dead. . . . We were notified this morning. He took his own life late last evening. Jumped from the window of his fourteenth-floor apartment."

Holliday's face went from white to red to dead yellow. At first the words could not penetrate his benumbed mind. Then a million questions swarmed in. But he did not ask any of them. He looked at the primly powdered face before him, at the thin lips that closed so precisely on each word, at the heartless, fear-frozen blue eyes. And he knew there was no question Martha McLeod could answer for him.

He hated her. Partly because of the fatal mistake she had made. Partly because of her composure in acknowledging that mistake. But most of all because he should have been the one to make that mistake. And because he knew that if he had, he would never have been strong enough to put it aside and move ahead as she was.

Ten minutes later David Holliday was trudging back down the hospital drive to his car. It was dark now, with only dim street lights here and there and no familiar landmarks to distract him from his thoughts.

Suddenly after his talk with Martha McLeod he had decided he could not face the Board of Governors meeting. He had wondered about it earlier that day, mostly because of the people he would see who were bound to ask about Mary Laine. But his final decision had had nothing to do with that. He had simply realized that the whole thing was a sham, that he no longer gave a damn about Holly Springs and that he could neither contribute to nor gain from a meeting of people who did.

His car was closer than he remembered. In only a few minutes he had left Holly Springs and Perthville behind and was skimming easily, if blindly, along the parkway toward the city. He felt strangely alone and baseless, as if there were nothing around him except empty blackness and even that was not real. The car seemed to be driving itself. At the same time, his head throbbed with weariness and his body ached. Yet, even that did not bother him much. He was beaten. He was something that had been and was no more.

What reason could there really be for life when it belonged to someone as weak and spineless as himself, or when it was laden with tragedies like Carson Gaitors, the Womble boy, Jack Isaacs? He himself was a miserable failure. Yet, it seemed to him now, all men were trapped. No one could do anything but exist and eventually meet his doom, and the only choice at all was whether to be courageous or cowardly.

Right now, tonight, he must go back to the white room and hold that wasted hand and wait.

IV

EILEEN WAS ready when Sullivan waddled in. Her scuffed brown suitcase was closed and waiting by the door. And she was just sitting there on the edge of the bed checking through her pocketbook as a diversion from excitement and anxiety.

So, it was a relief to see the big red-haired woman. At that moment Eileen might even have tried to talk to her. That week since her return on Tuesday had been almost perpetual silence. Partly imposed by her own reluctance to discuss her plans, partly because the other patients sensed this and could find nothing else to discuss.

"Here's your money, Miss O'Hara. I called a cab for four-thirty. Was that right?"

"Thank you." Eileen took the yellow envelope and emptied its contents into her wallet. "Seems strange to be doing this for the last time."

"Oh, you won't be losing any tears over us."

"No." Eileen laughed softly, a nervous echo of the nurse's hearty chuckle. "I'll think of you though. I guess there are people here I'll never forget."

"Yeah. . . . 'Specially old Sullivan." The woman laughed again.

"I'm glad things worked out so well for you. Don't often see that."
She turned abruptly back toward the hall. "Just sing out before
you go, won't you? So's I get it for the book."

"Yes, I will."

After she'd gone, Eileen rechecked her purse, then went to the
dresser to comb her hair and powder her nose. The fearful excitement raced in her again. And her watch said only 3:50—30 or 40
minutes more to wait.

He would come slowly, silently up the stairs and stand in the hall
a minute before he tapped sharply on the door. When he came in,
though, once the door was shut behind him, the propriety would
melt into nothingness.

But suppose he didn't come? suppose the supper was served and
it got dark and she waited and still he didn't come? She must be
strong. But the thought set her trembling, and she knew she had
no strength at all without Phil. . . .

She forced herself to walk to the window and look down on the
people, the cars, the patterns of sunshine and shadow below. She
had worried through this same thing a thousand times and convinced herself about it weeks before. Phil did love her—more than
she had ever hoped anyone could. He would be here today on time,
because, if possible, he was even more conscientious about appointments than she was. Still, the habit, the reasonless fear, moved
through its rut made deeper by not seeing Phil this last week.

That had really been the worst part of this week for her—not
seeing Phil until yesterday. And then so strangely, so stiffly in
the austerity of the conference room. Therapeutically, that conference had been a loss. There could be no therapy. Still they must
go through the motions, maintain a lacquer of propriety over the
real which was actually not improper at all.

"How are you sleeping?"

"Fine, . . . well, as well as you could expect."

"You have no qualms about going ahead with our plans?"

"Oh, Phil! I . . . I . . . Why, of course not. . . . Do you?"

"Oh, no. . . . I just wanted to be sure. McLeod hasn't spoken to
you, has she?"

"No."

"I guess she won't . . . but don't be frightened by anything she
says."

"No, . . . I'm so sorry about that. You won't have too much trouble finding another place, will you?"

"I don't think so. I hope not. . . . I'll come for you Saturday as we planned. In time for a 4:30 cab."

"Yes, . . . my cousins are expecting us. They're much impressed you're a doctor."

They had laughed together softly over that in a futile attempt to be natural. "I wish my mother could be a little that way," Phil had said. "I have plane tickets for Sunday morning. . . . And don't worry. At worst, she'll be charming."

After the conference Eileen had sat in the smoker with the others and felt even more lonely than before. All the other women had stared at her, curious but silent. It would have been easier if there were more like poor tactless Evie Barrow who'd wished her "the best of everything" and then added, "I hope you make out better with Phil than I did. He is so fickle."

Looking back, Eileen could almost laugh. Soon—this very afternoon—she would be gone, never to see Holly Springs or those women again. For a few days they would discuss her openly, eagerly, perhaps not even unkindly. But then, they would be caught up in something else and, in time, forget her.

She thought then that it would be nice to wait the last few minutes outside. Probably it was just this room that made her uneasy. She started toward the suitcase. If she went out, Phil wouldn't have to climb the stairs either. But suddenly she stopped again. Her eyes looked to the darkest corners of the room. Suppose he didn't come after all? if the cab came first? No, it was safer here. She walked back to the window, to the light and the lengthening shadows.

❲ 2

Phil Pierson was out of breath that afternoon as he climbed the hill to the main building. A pain in his side came and went with each breath, and his bad leg was so tired he had to drag it along. Worse still, he knew he was late.

It seemed impossible things could have turned out this badly. He'd planned ahead so meticulously, so that nothing would go wrong at the last minute. He'd said his few good-byes the day be-

fore, then packed the last of his things this morning and gone to
the office to get his mail and leave his keys. And the rest of the
day he'd done nothing but wait—sit by the window, reread his
mother's letter, leaf through old magazines, crack his knuckles, and
wait. Still, at the last everything had fallen to pieces. He dropped
his electric razor and took nearly ten minutes to coax it back into
action. After that, a button came off his shirt. And finally, the
plane tickets were hopelessly lost. Twenty frantic minutes later
he found them exactly where he'd put them, in the inside pocket
of his coat.

The suitcase he carried now wasn't heavy (most of his things
had been shipped earlier), but as he approached the visitors' parking area, he looked for a place to set it down. He needed to
straighten his tie, catch his breath, check the time. People had
been talking, he knew, and they would be watching. He must
appear completely self-assured.

There was a small fir tree just before the parked cars at the top
of the hill, and he stopped beside it gratefully. Still gripping the
suitcase, he looked at his wrist watch. Only four o'clock. Relief
rushed through him, catching in his throat with a spasm of stifled
laughter. He set the suitcase down and tightened the knot of his
tie. Then, glancing around furtively, he pulled out a handkerchief
to wipe the moisture from his face. After that he trudged on
toward the hospital at a much more leisurely pace than before.
For once, he even let his bad foot take the lead. He must look
like any other visitor strolling along. He could feel people watching
him. But he would not see them.

How he wished that he could be there and back already, spinning down this hill in the cab with Eileen. Suddenly it almost
seemed he could not get through the next few minutes. If only he
didn't have to be the one to wait. One thing, at least, had turned
out according to plan. It was important that he be here early. To
spare Eileen the waiting. His own nervousness—if that was what
it was—must be nothing compared to hers.

People on the brink of marriage were expected to be nervous.
But Phil Pierson felt honestly, though with some surprise, that
he was not. Worried a little about his work and making Eileen
happy in herself, but not at all about whether he was doing the
right thing. There was no question about that.

Yet, when he reached the entrance to Atkins Hall, he could not go in. It seemed something physical, a kind of paralysis. Just excitement, of course. He placed his suitcase in a corner of the building and forced himself to open the door, . . . but in the semi-darkness inside, the paralysis seized him again. Suppose she wasn't there? . . .

He could not climb the dark narrow stairway. Nor could he push the door and step out into the daylight again. He just stood still. If she wasn't there, he would simply act as if he hadn't really expected her to be. But that was ridiculous; everybody knew. Self-pity swept over him. He had thrown over everything he had in the world, everything. That seemed hard enough, but then to lose your very reason for the sacrifice. And people laughing at you besides. . . . He could feel tears on his cheeks.

It was then—a trick of the darkness, Pierson realized—that David Holliday's image came before him. Not the Holliday he always remembered, but the man who had come to visit that night—huge and grotesque, weak and cowardly, dying in his bigness. Pierson shuddered involuntarily. Mrs. Holliday had finally died. He hadn't liked her. He hadn't understood how anyone could love her. Probably that had been his first reason for doubting the sincerity of Holliday's wisdom. . . . Yet, in that at least, the big doctor must have been sincere. Her dying had broken him.

That seeped into Pierson, and he couldn't fight it off. The thought that he would be broken, too, now in the same way as Holliday; only at thirty instead of sixty. He finally made himself laugh out loud. "You really are ridiculous now. Downright morbid!"

Because Eileen *would* be there. She always was. She must be there now, waiting for him. Slowly he began to climb the stairs.

"This is disgraceful," McLeod had said when he talked to her. "Not merely for Holly Springs. For the whole psychiatric profession." Still, he hadn't retreated. Pierson was proud of that. Thinking of it now seemed to give him strength. He climbed rapidly to the top of the stairs.

The heavy brown door of Eileen's room appeared taller and uglier than he remembered. It was closed, but he paused only long enough to take a deep breath before knocking sharply twice. After that he waited through an eternity.

Then the door opened. And there she was. "Oh, Phil," she said. "I am so happy."

(3

"I'd like to speak to you a moment, Mrs. Joslin."

"Certainly, Dr. McLeod." The Hall 3 charge nurse stood up quickly from the rack of charts. "Please sit down, Doctor."

Martha McLeod automatically took the chair pulled out for her. Then, glancing at her watch, she settled herself more comfortably. "Would you mind telling the operator where I am?" she said. "You have enough staff just now, don't you? I mean, you have time to talk?"

"Yes, certainly." Margaret Joslin turned to the telephone and spun the dial. "Joslin on 3 Women. Dr. McLeod is here if you want her."

When she turned around again, McLeod had pulled her chair up to the desk and was seated there with a note pad and pencil before her. "This may seem to be treading on Dr. Collins' territory," she began, "but I want to assure you I don't intend that. In all probability, you and I will not talk like this again. But as hospital director, I am trying to set forth some policy changes with each charge nurse personally on the men's side as well as the women's."

Joslin's eyes wandered idly beyond the office window to the sunny day outside. The hospital driveway was in constant motion with visitors day traffic. Only the great brick buildings and the stiff shrubs on either side of the front steps appeared stationary. Those, and after a moment, standing between them, a slight feminine figure in a yellow dress that billowed with the wind.

"Economy-wise, for instance," the doctor's voice droned. "Earlier in the year we tried. . . ."

Determinedly Margaret Joslin shifted her eyes from the yellow skirt back to Dr. McLeod, then down to the green desk blotter. Something familiar about that figure in yellow, something about the shoulders, the downward tilt of the head.

"It seems now," Dr. McLeod talked on, "that these 'thrift measures' have been widely misunderstood. The hospital is under no financial pressure. Probably doing even better than usual. I simply...."

The O'Hara girl, of course. Margaret Joslin's eyes slipped back to the window. Not alone though. Naturally not. Pierson's dark suit just blended into the shrubbery. Surprising she hadn't recognized them right off. Especially with all the talk. The girl *did* look sweet. Yes, sweet and innocent as ever in that yellow dress.

You had to give that kid credit. She was a shrewd one. That cold, rainy night she came in, over a year ago—Joslin frowned absently, completely forgetting Dr. McLeod—Eileen O'Hara had seemed as childish, as selfish, as determinedly miserable as the most infuriating lovelorn suicide. She'd wised up quick enough though. Joslin smiled. She'd made a mistake there, completely misjudged the girl. Actually they had something in common. Sense. Practical good sense. Pierson might not be the he-man catch of the year, but intelligent, even brilliant, according to some. They said Holliday had considered him extremely promising. And anyway, even if none of that were true, he was better than nothing. Better than staying down and out, than settling down to a life of loneliness and feeling sorry for yourself ever after.

It annoyed Martha McLeod the way the nurse kept looking out the window. Perhaps she was listening. She certainly made a good pretense of it if she wasn't, nodding and murmuring, "Yes, ... Yes, Doctor" at appropriate intervals. Still, it was disconcerting to never see those eyes.

"What I mean by economy," the doctor went on, "is not simply a widespread cutting of expenses. Rather a saving along one line to be devoted to the benefit of the patients along others. Your time schedule, for instance...."

The view *is* inviting, McLeod thought. A lovely day. Warm, sunny, clean looking. The driveway sparkling in the sun, the neat NO PARKING signs, the red tulips, the cars moving in and out. A pretty picture, too, the girl in the yellow dress. Visitor waiting for a cab. "Perhaps you could space your staff more economically ... some inconvenience ... Still, the patient's welfare...."

No, that was no visitor. It was Eileen O'Hara. How could she have forgotten? Young Pierson, too. He'd said they'd leave this afternoon, and she'd been wondering about it all day. That seemed so out of character for both of them. So retiring, she hadn't believed they would dare to be seen together here. Yet that was what had surprised McLeod most about her talk with the young doctor: the deliberate, almost obstinate way he had spoken. He had asked neither her opinion nor her permission, had stated simply and bluntly that he and the young nurse planned "to be married early in June."

Then before she could point out the folly of such a decision or even express her disapproval, he had stated in the same low but unwavering voice that he realized, "This may be opposed to some policies and traditions of Holly Springs. And even more, Dr. McLeod, to your own concepts of propriety. I can see, also that it might be a cause for some temporary disturbance among the patients. Therefore, I'm offering my resignation for as early a date as is convenient for you to accept it."

She had told him briefly and in no uncertain terms exactly what she thought—even that she was glad he had saved her the trouble of demanding his resignation. Foolhardy to even hope two such emotionally unstable people might make a go of marriage. Seemed almost looking for tragedy. Certainly a doctor with Pierson's training could see that. And suddenly Martha McLeod felt her own face hot, as if flushed with fever, her eyes blinded by the sun. So foolish, they seemed, so reckless. Yet, what really was there to be lost in that?

Thirty years ago, if she had been a little more reckless, a little less selfish.... Mary Laine was dead now. She had gone to the funeral, and she had seen David Holliday standing gaunt and silent beside the grave. He had appeared surprisingly more stable, more at peace with the world than the last time she had seen him. But the distant sadness so much a part of him now somehow seemed far more tragic than the death that had taken Mary Laine. Thirty years ago when they had walked together through the woods, Martha had probably not been too different from the girl out there this afternoon in her yellow dress.... But instead, she had been very wise and very diligent. And only now in the light of David Holliday's grief could she comprehend the depth of her own loss.

She put her fingers up to clear the sun dazzle from her eyes. And in doing so, she realized uneasily that she had left off in the middle of a sentence. She was just sitting there staring out the window. The nurse beside her was too. For a moment the silence echoed around them. Then their eyes caught each other off guard. The nurse blushed and smiled. A nervous titter escaped her throat. She looked down at the desk blotter.

But Martha McLeod did not allow her face to alter. She fixed her blue eyes on the point where they had tangled with those of the nurse. "As for the matter we were discussing," she continued, ". . . economy. It demands above all else a combination of human kindness and good sense."

(4

The "long walk" started late that afternoon. Something about having to wait for the students to get back from class. And that made Ben Womble feel good, because it meant they couldn't go far; they'd have to be back before doctor's rounds.

Outside they had to wait to be counted again and to let the Open-Hall fellows be added to the list. Jim Reilly was one of them. He came over and stood with Ben beside the bucket of sand for cigarettes. "Hey there, Ben, boy. How are you? Miss me?"

Ben didn't answer.

"Had ten days this time. Bet you didn't even know I was gone."

Yes, Ben wanted to say, it was quiet for a change. But he kept his mouth shut and concentrated on rubbing the loose flap of his shoe sole backwards against the rim of the sand bucket.

"Came back a day early," Reilly went on, undiscouraged. "Got kind of upset. It's not easy, you know, going home again. Awful anxiety and depression. My wife decided I better come back before it got worse. . . . Saw Dr. Richards this morning. He told me the doctors know how hard I'm trying. He said they might try one of these new tranquilizers."

Ben still didn't speak. He kicked the side of the bucket.

Reilly was silent, too, for a moment, as if to catch his breath. Then he asked, "Who's your roommate now? Nice?"

"I'm in the dorm."

"Oh, that's hell. . . . Why don't you get out of here, Ben?"

Ben kicked the bucket again.

"Poor old Isaacs," Reilly added, shaking his head with ostentatious despondency. "At least he tried." He was quiet for a moment after that, watching Ben's face expectantly. At last when it was evident there was to be no response, he said, "Well, so long, Ben. See you around." Then he walked over to a group of other Open-Hall patients.

Ben stood there alone, arms folded across his chest, gazing around indifferently until the gym instructor up front yelled, "Okay." Even then he didn't straighten up or unfold his arms; just dragged along slowly behind the long line of men.

What Reilly had said about Jack Isaacs troubled Ben. In fact, the very name troubled him lately. They said Jack was dead now. They said he'd jumped out of a window. And Ben couldn't quite comprehend that. He'd expected Jack to wait for the glory. As a rule, Ben was careful not to think about Jack, because when he did, an uncomfortable quivering ache swelled up inside him. Jack had been nice; Jack had been good. He'd never talked much or complained or interfered. But he'd never really given in to what he thought was wrong either. Actually as far as Ben was concerned, Jack had been dead since the afternoon he said good-by. But somehow the word "dead" made him feel infinitely more alone.

He need not, of course. That was nonsense. Because when the glory came, dead or alive, Jack would be there beside him. Not just Jack either—hundreds of millions of other people, rejoicing and praising his name, kneeling before him. He wouldn't be alone at all then. . . . If "then" ever came. Time seemed to pass so slowly, and people were so blind. The halo had become quite bright, yet apparently they still did not see. And sometimes it was hard for Ben to keep up his faith.

"Nice day," he deliberately informed himself now. The sun felt good on his back. When he was little, his mother had liked to take him out on afternoons like this. She made the nurse stay at home and she'd dressed him up and the two of them had gone for a walk or to some other lady's house. His mother couldn't come today. Tea party or something.

But the driveway, as they approached it, was full of visitors' cars and people climbing in and out. Ben watched them from the corners of his eyes. He knew they were curious. Outsiders always were. He wondered what they thought of him—if they knew who he was.

In front of the main entrance there was a lady in a yellow dress. A young lady, maybe just a girl. And with her a man in a dark suit, who stood very close, looking at the ground. The man looked like any other man, but Ben thought the lady was pretty. Her face, because it seemed happy, but mostly her dress. They were waiting for a cab, because as he walked by, Ben saw one drive up and stop.

The line of men left the driveway and the road to cut across the golf course to the path that led through the part of the grounds where the doctors lived. Beyond that there were open fields and the place where they were building the new outpatient clinic. Ben remembered walking there in the winter and the summer before. There had been potato fields then and old twisted trees. But they couldn't walk there any more. Too many workmen and bulldozers.

Ben's mother thought the outpatient clinic was a "wonderful advancement." She had said that maybe when it was finished Ben could live at home and just come up certain days for O.T. and tennis or to see the doctor. Ben hadn't said anything, but he hoped she'd forget. He'd be King Benjamin by then. But even if he wasn't, he didn't want to go home.

Through the great raw area they had cleared for the new building you could see the town of Perthville—the stores and movie marquees, cars and even people walking by. That fascinated Ben. He didn't like going to town much. Too loud. Too rushing. It was safe here, nice to watch from a distance. A lot of taxi cabs there today, their lettered sides glistening in the sun. Probably one of them had the girl with the yellow dress in it. Ben wondered where she was going.

A gym guy yelled something about speeding it up, and the student nurse bringing up the rear suggested, "Mr. Womble, perhaps you could walk a little faster." Ben heard her and automatically quickened his pace.

But he did not speak. His eyes still watched the taxi cabs. Pretty color, yellow. Warm, happy. How nice to be a girl in a butter yellow dress, riding in a taxi cab. Lucky to be going some place definite, some place you weren't afraid to go.

Afterwards

DAVID HOLLIDAY had come to like the view from that window. It was still barren, perhaps even ugly in its starkness. The new winter grass was too thin and too green, the raw earth beneath it, too red. The few trees spared by the builders were bare now, with just single dry leaves floating down sadly here and there. And somehow even the Holly Springs landscape and buildings in the background did not look as he remembered them.

Yet, that pleased Holliday. Indeed, it was the newness and the strangeness that had given him the courage to come back here twice a week to help with the outpatient clinic. He found it comforting that people no longer knew him here, nor he them; that Mary Laine's house had been converted to apartments; that Martha McLeod's white coat and stringent discipline had replaced his own ridiculous grin. For, nothing in his own life was the same any more, and he sometimes felt taunted when other things remained unchanged.

In the beginning, of course, immediately after Mary Laine's death, it had been just the opposite. He had felt compelled to salvage all remnants from the past and thus reconstruct a familiar life for himself. But the memories had all turned out to be torn and faded. He found himself searching for something that no longer existed.

Outdoors the sun was dazzling, but even protected by the window glass he could feel the icy wind. "It's going to snow," George Purdy had said when Holliday stopped to buy the apples. "I can feel it in my bones."

He never bought apples from anybody but George nowadays. George always picked them out so carefully and polished them on his apron before he put them in the bag. Besides, as Holliday was leaving, George always grinned and said, "You're looking good, Doctor. Better than your old self. . . ." And David Holliday liked that.

"Even more than the apples," he told himself now, still searching the sunny cold for George's snow. But he was smiling, and he felt easier inside—because what George said was true.

About the Author

Lucy Daniels is the author of the critically and popularly successful novel, *Caleb, My Son*, the story of a Negro family in a Southern
city shortly after the Supreme Court desegregation order. Miss
Daniels was born in North Carolina and attended the George
School in Bucks County, Pennsylvania. She was a reporter on the
Raleigh *Times*, and is presently living in Indianapolis with her
husband and their two young children.